CRITICAL ACCLAIM FOR
MORRIS WEST AND HIS NOVELS

HARLEQUIN

"Morris West has been producing highly readable, entertaining fiction for years, and has managed to combine a reputation for seriousness with popular success."
—*The New Statesman*

"West has a talent, possessed by only the very best, for creating the illusion that his people propel the plot, rather than being puppets of it. . . . Perhaps the way West turns his genre into, if not art, then certainly serious fiction, is by the subtlety with which he covers the bones of the plot, and the consequent impression of inexhaustible space in which his characters may maneuver. They never seem to make the expected move; the plot appears to work against normal reader expectation, but every step treads inescapably toward a patterned denouement."
—*National Review*

"Mr. West is a storyteller who delivers the goods in the glossiest of wrappings."
—*The Guardian*

"The classiest of thrillers."
—*Daily Mirror*

THE TOWER OF BABEL

"There is action on every level of international intrigue. . . . Mr. West has not written . . . merely a story of espionage and intrigue in the Middle East. He has written a novel that makes this time and place come alive."

—*Best Sellers*

"The book will thrill. The suspense and complications of an espionage story are fully there. . . . A fascinating portrayal of two people thrust compulsively against each other."

—*Life*

DAUGHTER OF SILENCE

"Morris West shares with Graham Greene a preoccupation with mystery in its religious as well as its whodunit sense. He, too, probes the riddle of faith with an austerely disciplined literary craft; he, too, stands on the Catholic premise even while viewing the world with almost Puritan acerbity. . . . Mr. West skillfully renders the inquisatorial pomp of Italian trial procedure. . . . An illustration of a telling insight."

—*The New York Times Book Review*

"An effective courtroom spectacle [with] calculated surprises."

—*Newsweek*

"Complex and powerful . . . an unusually exciting book."

—*The Observer* (London)

By Morris West

Vanishing Point *
The Ringmaster *
The Devil's Advocate *
Harlequin *
The Shoes of the Fisherman
The Ambassador
The Tower of Babel
Gallows on the Sand
Kundu
Children of the Sun
The Big Story
The Concubine
The Second Victory
The Naked Country
Scandal in the Assembly (with R. Francis)
The Heretic, a play in three acts
Daughter of Silence
Summer of the Red Wolf
The Salamander
Proteus
The Clowns of God
The World is Made of Glass
Cassidy
Masterclass
McCreary Moves In
Lazarus
The Navigator

*Available from HarperPaperbacks

HARLEQUIN

Morris West

HarperPaperbacks
A Division of HarperCollinsPublishers

HarperPaperbacks
A Division of HarperCollins*Publishers*
10 East 53rd Street, New York, N.Y. 10022-5299

This is a work of fiction. The characters, incidents, and
dialogues are products of the author's imagination and are not to
be construed as real. Any resemblance to actual events or
persons, living or dead, is entirely coincidental.

ISBN 0-06-101081-2

HarperCollins®, ®, and HarperPaperbacks™
are trademarks of HaperCollins*Publishers*, Inc.

Cover illustration by Uldus Klavins

A hardcover edition of this book was published in 1974 byWilliam
Collins Sons & Co. Ltd.

First HarperPaperbacks printing: January 1997

Printed in the United States of America

Visit HarperPaperbacks on the World Wide Web at
http://www.harpercollins.com/paperbacks

10 9 8 7 6 5 4 3 2 1

For Sheila

As if we were villains by necessity;
fools by heavenly compulsion.

—*Shakespeare, King Lear, Act 1, Sc. 2*

1

George Harlequin and I have been friends for twenty years; yet I have to confess he is the one man I have ever truly envied. There was a time when I believe I hated him; and it was only his grace and sanity that cured me.

He is everything that I am not. I am big, burly, awkwardly put together, the despair of tailors. He is slim, elegant, a classic horseman, a tennis-player beautiful to watch. I am literate enough in one language, Harlequin is a polyglot, formidable in half a dozen. More, he wears a quite prodigious learning with the offhand charm of a renaissance courtier. I am an antipodean, eager, impulsive, apt to be harsh or simplistic in my judgments. Harlequin is a European, cool, conciliatory, subtle, patient even with idiots.

He was born to money. His grandfather founded Harlequin et Cie, Merchant Bankers, in Geneva. His father made international alliances and opened branches in Paris, London and New York. Harlequin extended the territory, then inherited the Presidency and the largest block of voting shares. The tradition of the house was sacred to him: the character of the client outweighed his collateral; the risk, once taken, would never be abrogated; the contract was never hedged by legal tricks; a handshake was as binding as a formal document; if the client or his family fell on evil times, the motto of the bank held good: *"Amicus certus in re incerta*: a sure friend in an uncertain business."*

I, on the other hand, began as a huckster, pure and simple. I clawed my way through the metal markets, made money and lost it. In the lean years that followed, I was humbled by the concern which Harlequin lavished on me, incredulous of the sums he gambled on my word alone. When my fortunes were restored, I gave him the money to invest, while I took a long cure for peptic ulcers and learned a few of the arts of contentment.

I married early and made a mess of it. Harlequin played the field until he was thirty-five and then made a runaway match with Juliette Gerard, whom he met on my boat while I was still coaxing her to marry me. We did not meet for three years after that. We remained banker and client, but reticent and constrained, until their son was born and they named him for me, Paul Desmond, and I stood sponsor at his christening. The same day, Harlequin offered me a seat on his board of directors. In a hot flush of sentiment, I accepted, and so became ambassador-at-large for Harlequin et Cie and doting godfather to a blond mite who was too like his mother for comfort.

Let me say it plain. We were friends of the heart, but I was still jealous of Harlequin. He was so much the arbiter of elegance; yet so judicious that even the graybeards of the money-game paid him a rabbinical respect. He was too fortunate, too full of too many graces. I suppose you could say he was too obviously happy. He rode, he sailed, he raced thoroughbreds, he collected pictures and porcelain. He was courted by beautiful women and doted on his wife. Yet he was so fastidious of excellence that lesser folk were daunted by him. In odd bleak moments, I wondered why he bothered with a hurly-burly fellow like me. I felt like a court jester bumbling round the most exquisite of princes.

I do not write this to disprize him—God help me! It must be clear that the jester loved the prince and, for his sins, was still in love with the princess. I want to show you how high Harlequin was, how visible and vulnerable, how unconscious of the peril of being himself. Even I did not see it very clearly. Juliette could only guess at it; and, being all woman, she gave it another name.

". . . I feel so useless, Paul. I can give him nothing except myself in bed and another child when he wants it. There are twenty women who could take my place tomorrow. No matter that George doesn't see it. I do. I am not necessary to him, and one day he will know it . . ."

I am no Iago, though sometimes I have wished to be. I told her the only truth I knew.

"Julie, you're married to a lucky man. Be lucky with him. Everything is a joy to him, and you're the greatest joy of all. Accept that and to hell with afterwards."

Then Harlequin came in, bouncing and bubbling, with a new canvas under his arm and a new client on his books and plans for a weekend in Gstaad, where the snow would be deep and the weather promised fair and sunny for the beautiful people.

Soon after, it was April, and Harlequin and I went to Peking because the Chinese were talking business with Europe, and Harlequin wanted a share of it for himself and his clients. I wondered how he, mandarin of the mandarins, would measure against the spartan standards of the People's Republic. As usual, I underrated him. He was instantly at home and at ease. He was fluent in speech, dexterous in calligraphy. His courtesy was impeccable, his patience unlimited. Within a month, he was on comfortable terms with the senior hierarchy, respected by politicos and technocrats alike. He bought largley in antiquities, and jade and carpets. He discussed projects for the manufacture of antibiotics and synthetic drugs and precision instruments. He made friends among scholars and antiquarians. He saw the color of the subtlest Oriental joke and yet never lost face or humor. It was a flawless performance, and our hosts made no secret of their approval.

Yet, it was not all charm and virtuosity. Harlequin was deeply moved by the experience. The things that depressed me, the immensity of the land, the vastness of the tribal enterprise, woke in him the poet and the dreamer. He would stand rapt for an hour watching the epic figures in the landscape—a solitary boatman homing against the sunset, women on a treadmill watering the paddy fields. Then he would break out into passionate but disjointed commentary.

". . . There is a lunacy in our existence, Paul . . . We live by fantasies and fragments. We've destroyed the tribe and condemned ourselves to the solitude of cities. We scramble for superfluous things and then do bloody battle to defend what we don't need. We peddle money and debase the currency we accumulate. We've turned away from the God of our fathers to haunt the parlors of wizards and mountebanks . . . Sometimes, you know, I'm very afraid. I live in a walled garden, pleasant with lawns and flowers. I wonder, in nightmares, if it is not the valley of the assassins . . ."

After Peking, we went to Hong Kong and Tokyo and thence to Hawaii and Los Angeles, where Harlequin was taken suddenly ill. The physician ordered him immediately into hospital, where X-rays revealed a massive infection of both lungs. At first, they suspected tuberculosis, but when the tests proved negative, they began another series of investigations. Juliette flew in from Geneva and I went back to Europe. Harlequin rallied for a few days and then relapsed. They tested him for Q-fever and psittacosis and other more exotic invasions. Then, one day, Juliette called me with disquieting news. The doctors suspected lymphangitic cancer. They had recommended a biopsy. Harlequin had refused.

"But why, Julie . . . why?"

"He says he resents the idea. He would rather wait on what he calls a verdict by nature. It's his right. I don't want to persuade him."

"Is he depressed?"

"Strangely, no. He's very calm. He says he's come to terms with the experience."

"What about you?"

"I'm dreadfully worried. But he needs me, Paul. I'm glad of that, at least."

"Hold the thought, girl. Give him my love. Tell him the boy is flourishing and we'll still be in business when he comes home . . ."

I could make that promise confidently enough. I could not promise to get rid of the vultures who already were wheeling overhead. Every day some solicitous colleague inquired by telephone or telex for news of Harlequin's health. There were questions about policy changes, hints of merger offers in the event of Harlequin's death or incapacity. I had a sudden spate of invitations—to luncheon, dinner, cocktails and small private conventions in half a dozen. capitals. More than one long-lost friend turned up with a useful tip for the market or a parcel of shares at a bargain price. Most significant of all was the personal intervention of one, Basil Yanko, President of Creative Systems Incorporated. His telex from New York was curt and simple:

"In Geneva tomorrow. Require private conference with you 10:00. Please confirm. Yanko."

Of course I confirmed. Harlequin et Cie had underwritten every issue of Creative Systems Incorporated and its affiliate companies. Our holdings in their stock were a license to print money. A dozen major accounts had come to us on their recommendation. Basil Yanko could ask me to tango on a tightrope and I would oblige him.

Not that I liked him. On the contrary, even his appearance put me off. He was a tall, gangling skeleton of a man, with a mouse-gray complexion, a thin trap mouth and black agate eyes with no humor in them at all. He was arrogant, peremptory and devoid of social graces. On the other hand, he was acknowledged as the most original intellect in computer technology. He had begun as a creator of hardware for Honeywell; then he had set up Creative Systems Incorporated and begun designing programs for major institutions—Government agencies, international corporations, banks, airlines, the police. His companies were active in every European country, in the South Americas, in Australia, Japan and the United Kingdom. His wealth was already a legend. His systems were the filaments that controlled millions of puppet lives. We used them ourselves. Basil Yanko made it clear that the systems were using us. We were scarcely settled at the conference table when he thrust an envelope under my nose.

"Read that. It's George Harlequin's medical report."

I was angry and I let him know it. "This is a private document. How the hell did you get it?"

"Easy. The hospital is a research institute which rents computer time from us."

"That's bloody unethical!"

"Read it anyway. It indicates two possibilities. Harlequin has either lymphangitic cancer or a rare virus infection. If he recovers, he will require a lengthy convalescence and his activity will be drastically reduced for some time."

"So . . . ?"

"If he dies, the natural heirs are his wife and an infant son. The management of Harlequin et Cie will devolve upon existing directors and any new talent they can discover. Good bankers are thin on the ground. Logical consequence, a reduction in share value and profit potential."

"That's your logic, Mr. Yanko."

"I'm prepared to bet on it. If Harlequin dies, I want to buy his holdings. I'll top any offers in the market."

"That's a matter for his executors."

"Of whom you are the principal."

"That's news to me."

"You may take it as true."

"And if Harlequin lives, as I have no doubt he will?"

"The same offer stands. You are requested to convey it to him when he is fit to consider it."

"I'm confident he will refuse."

"As an alternative, I'm prepared to buy the shares of his associates, several of whom are willing to sell."

"Under the Articles of Association, George Harlequin has first option."

"I doubt that. He may be disposed to waive or sell the option."

"I doubt that, very much."

"You are too positive, Mr. Desmond. Let me tell you that contingent behavior in non-psychotic subjects can now be computed with seventy-five percent accuracy."

"And Harlequin is one of your subjects?"

"One of the most important."

"He'll be flattered to know it."

"Don't overrate him, Desmond. Don't underrate me. I usually get what I want."

"Why do you want Harlequin et Cie?"

His trap mouth relaxed into a smile. "Do you know how Harlequin got his name? His great-great-grandfather was a mummer who played Arlecchino in the Commedia dell'Arte. Oh, yes, it's true. I know the family history by heart. There's been quite a transformation in four generations. But that's the traditional role, isn't it? Harlequin transforms the world with a touch of his slapstick . . . and then laughs in his sleeve at its discomfiture. By the way . . ." He fished in his briefcase and brought out a bulky folder. "You pay us to run a security check on your accounting systems. That's the report for the last six months. The computer has thrown up some curious anomalies. You'll find some of them need urgent action. If you want clarification or help, my people are at your disposal." He stood up. The hand he offered me was cold and limp as a dead fish. "Thank you for your time. Please convey my respects to Madame Harlequin, and, to her husband, my hopes for his speedy recovery. Good-day, Mr. Desmond."

When I walked him to the elevator, I felt a faint chill as though a gray goose had walked over my grave. The earliest bankers were priests and money still has a ritual language. So, when you tell a banker that there are anomalies in his accounts, it is as if you point a bone at him or chant a mortal curse over his head. In theory, of course, the computer should insure him against such primitive disaster. The computer is a mighty brain, which can store centuries of knowledge, perform miracles of mathematics in the twinkling of an eye and deliver infallible answers to the most abstruse equations. In fact, it seduces man into blind faith and then betrays him to his own idiocy.

We could not buy the brain. We rented its time.

We hired systems experts to explain our needs to it. We employed programmers to feed it facts and figures. We based momentous decisions on the answers it fed back to us. But, because we were haunted by the fear that the programmers might fall into error, or be suborned into malpractice, we used monitors to police the brain for any hint of error or fraud. So, we believed, as religious men should, that the system was safe and sacred, proof against fools or knaves.

There was only one problem: the brain, and the programmers and the monitors, were all members of the same family—Creative Systems Incorporated; the father of the family was Basil Yanko, who was jealous to take us all under his control. Like it or not, we were locked in a magic circle, drawn by a twentieth-century wizard. The report, which lay still unopened on my desk, was a grimoire full of spells and dangerous mysteries. I had to get my courage up to open it. I needed silence and privacy to study it. I told Suzanne to hold all calls, locked my door and settled down to read. Two hours later, I faced the brutal fact: Harlequin et Cie had been milked of fifteen million dollars. The milkman was identified as George Harlequin himself.

Now, a simple question: like the rabbi who ducked synagogue, played golf on Shabbat and hit a hole-in-one, whom do you tell? The culprit—or the victim—was seven thousand miles away in hospital, waiting for a man in a white coat to say whether he would live or die. I had to cover fifteen million before the auditors came in. If I put all my personal holdings on the line, I was good for five million; which left a shortfall of ten. To whom could I explain the need? Who would hold me safe for so much? There are few heroes in the money-game. Bankers are sensitive as sea anemones. Poke a finger at them and they curl up into jelly-blobs, quivering with outrage and apprehension.

I had to prove the report, true or false. But who was there to trust? Computer people are clubbish too. They marry and give in marriage and meet at the county ball. Besides, computer information is like sex. You can sell it ten times over and you still own it. And who is to know or care, provided you don't peddle it under the nose of a passing policeman? If you don't believe me, I can quote you chapter and verse. One of our clients spent twenty million on off-shore oil exploration only to find that his rivals were drilling on his site before the last figures were printed on the tape.

It was one o'clock. At one-thirty, I was due to lunch and talk at the Club Commerciale de Genève. I knew that if I breathed half a word of doubt or discouragement, it would go round the world before the market opened in New York. I locked the report in my briefcase, freshened myself in Harlequin's bathroom, opened my door and my telephone line and summoned Suzanne. Since I have to explain her, let me be done with it quickly.

Suzanne was Harlequin's secretary. She was forty years old, give or take a twelvemonth, and she had been in love with him from the day she walked into his office fifteen years ago. She was graying a little, but she was still a very comely woman with a good body and a bright mind and a commonsensical attitude to sex and friendship. For a while, we were lovers by default. Then we were friends by choice. I would trust her with my life; but I had no right to trust her with Harlequin's. So I told her only half the truth. It was the measure of her worth that she accepted it without question or resentment.

"Suzy, we're in a jam—a big one."

"Basil Yanko?"

"Yes."

"I hate that man."

"So do I. But I have to treat with him. I have to move fast and far. No one but you must know where I am or whom I see. Clear?"

"Quite clear."

"Telephone Executive Charter and have a plane standing by from three this afternoon. Get me Karl Kruger in Hamburg. Call the Club and tell them I'll be late for drinks and on time for the speech. Then go to my apartment, pack a bag, pick me up after lunch and drive with me to the airport. I want to dictate a cable, to be sent in code, to all branch managers. Someone's bugged our computers. We're fifteen million down the drain."

"Dear God! Does George know about this?"

"No."

"Are you going to tell him?"

"Not until we know the medical verdict."

"Is he involved?"

"Up to his neck. Suzy, you have to trust me."

"I do, Paul. But you have to trust me, too."

"What you don't know helps us all. Leave it at that for the moment."

"Remember one thing, Paul. Harlequin is tougher than you think."

"He'll need to be, Suzy . . . Make the calls like a good girl."

Karl Kruger, president of Kruger & Co. AG, was still at his desk, swilling beer and knackwurst, while his juniors were lunching clients at the Four Seasons. I could imagine him, sixty-five years old, grizzled as a Baltic bear, growling at my intrusion.

"*Also!* In Geneva you play marbles with money! Here, we have to work for it. What the hell do you want?"

"Dinner, bed and a talk tonight."

"No chance. Hilde's in town. You know what that means. She's the only woman I can cope with these days."

"So we talk first and then we both take her to dinner. Please, Karl!"

"You sound worried, Paul. Something wrong?"

"Everything. Harlequin's in hospital in California. I've got a dog's dinner on my plate. I need you, old friend."

"Make it six at my house. And if you keep me late, you'll have to sleep with Hilde. *Wiedersehen!*"

"*Wiedersehen,* Karl. And thanks."

I was on time for lunch. I delivered twenty minutes of optimistic flim-flam which would make half a column in the morning press. At three-fifteen we were airborne and at five minutes to six I was knocking at the door of Kruger's stronghold on the Alster Park.

If you met Karl Kruger, you wouldn't like him. Very few people do. The English will tell you he's an old-line junker who played ball with Hitler, bribed the Americans for a clean bill of health and settled down to renew his fortunes in the *Bundesrepublik*. Perhaps he did; perhaps he didn't; I don't know. What I do know is that Helli Anspacher swears he laid out millions to save her husband from the butchers after the Schellenberg plot, and Chaim Herzl in Tel Aviv says he owes him his life and Jim Brandes hid for three weeks in his house after he was shot down in a raid on Lübeck. It's all old history now, too tangled to unravel. I can only give you Karl Kruger as I know him in this year of the Lord.

He is as broad as he is tall, with a shock of iron-gray hair, big ham fists, a shambling gait and a face mottled with strawberry marks and liver spots. He looks as battered as an old boxer; but his mind is clear and quicker by half than yours or mine. He greeted me like a long-lost brother, threw his arm round my shoulder and shoved me, staggering, to the fireside.

"Loving God! You look pale as a nun! Let's put some fire in your belly. I told Hilde you were coming. She says she'll keep her love till she meets you . . . Scotch, isn't it? . . . You know, Paul, I first saw Hilde when she was making kitsch films for Gregory in Munich. That's twenty years ago now and she's still beautiful. So let's put the business to bed first. What do you want to talk about?"

"Fifteen million dollars."

"What are you selling?"

"Nothing. That's the shortfall in our accounts. We've been milked, Karl."

"Who did it?"

"The record says George Harlequin."

"What do you say?"

"I say it wasn't George."

"Have you asked him?"

"I will, when I know whether he's going to live or die."

"So it's wasn't George. Who then?"

"Someone with access to our computer system."

"Name?"

"I say Basil Yanko."

"Why? He's got money running out of his backside."

"He wants to take us over. He told me that today when he delivered our security report."

"And what do you want from me, Paul?"

"Cover for ten million, on call, to keep us clean until I can tidy the books and make necessary transfers."

"Where's the other five coming from?"

"Me. It's all I've got."

"You're a sentimental fool. You bail Harlequin out; but Yanko still has evidence of defalcation."

"If we're covered, it's harder for him to use it. If he tries, it points to complicity. I may never have to call the funds, Karl. For Christ's sake, we're solid as Gibraltar. But I have to buy time until I get authorities from Harlequin and set up an independent investigation."

"Why me? Why not your own shareholders?"

"Yanko says they're in his pocket. You're the only man I can trust to keep his mouth shut— whether you cover me or not."

"And who's going to do your investigation?"

"That's another problem. I need an international expert, or a well-known security firm. It's a tight market and the moment I go shopping, Yanko has to know."

"And he'll buy your man from under your nose."

"Or worse. People get killed in that game, Karl."

"Who said money had no smell? You're in a bad way, young Paul. Pour yourself another whiskey. I have to think."

Karl Kruger thinking was like a stone-crusher masticating gravel. He paced up and down the vast room, puffing and belching and mumbling to himself. He wrenched open the drapes, planted his vast bulk at the casement and stood a long time staring out at the lights of the old Hanseatic city, rooted so deep in burgher money and Baltic mud that it had survived even the cataclysm of mass bombing and the post-war partition of the Reich. Its people are bankers and traders and shipbuilders and roistering sailormen, jealous of their town and its historic liberties. They are shrewd and stolid, fast friends and stubborn enemies. If Karl Kruger would buttress me I could begin to fight. Without him, I was naked to the storm. He turned back to me at last, grim and questioning.

"I've met Basil Yanko. I think I understand him. He's a genius, all head and no balls; so he plays power games. Your George Harlequin, what is he? A playboy, a buffoon, an amateur? Money is a man's business. This town is proof of it. Your Harlequin loiters through it as though it were a children's game."

"Are you jealous of him, too, Karl?"

"Jealous? God in Heaven! I should be jealous of

a man who needs cover for fifteen million because he can't keep track of his own accounts!"

"Come off it, Karl! You know damn well any system can be corrupted. There's a security man in London who gets clients by proving just that. If you'll indemnify him, he'll undertake to steal you blind in six months and pay the money into a trust account. What you're really asking me is whether Harlequin's worth saving. I say he is. You don't have to wear sackcloth and ashes to prove you're a good banker. You live just as well as Harlequin. You've played a damn sight harder in your time. Will you kill him just because you don't like his lifestyle?"

"That's not the point. Why did Yanko pick him? Why not me? Why not half a dozen others we could both name? He picked Harlequin because there's a weakness in the man as well as in your system. I want to know what it is."

"I'm the wrong man to ask, Karl."

"Why?"

"Because he's a good friend, I'm godfather to his child and I'm in love with his wife."

"God Almighty! So, instead of stealing her, you make yourself a martyr to brotherhood! You're a bigger fool than I thought."

"Now that you know it, what's the answer, Karl?"

"You're covered—on one condition."

"What's that?"

"Whether he's on his last legs or not, Harlequin has to know. And I want first option on his shares and on his rights over other shareholdings. If he won't consent, the deal's off."

"That's rough trading, Karl!"

"This is Hamburg, little brother! Nothing for nothing. And keep your fly buttoned if you don't want to catch the clap."

"I'll put the deal to Harlequin."

"Do that. Now, about your investigator . . . You can't shop in the computer market because Yanko will preempt every move you make. Agreed?"

"Agreed."

"You could go to the police."

"We operate in too many jurisdictions. We'd make a scandal in every one."

"You could use private investigators."

"We'd still need a computer man to check back through the system."

"I think you need more."

"I don't understand."

"Yanko has everything at his disposal . . . money, information, global influence. He conjures power. He can build a lie and sell it overnight to half the world. Once you engage him, you must set out to ruin him before he destroys you. That's why I ask if George Harlequin has the guts for it. If not, he'd better sell out now, while he's still got a market."

"I'll put that to him, too, Karl."

"If he's ready to fight, there's a man in New York who can help. He has several names. His real one is Aaron Bogdanovich. He, too, is a kind of genius; but his greatest merit is that he can't be bought."

"What does he do?"

"He organizes terror."

In one instant, we were two thousand years away from the old mansion on the Alster Park. We were back in the black forest called Hamma, with the bale-fires lit, and the warriors drunk and lusting after the kill. In that visionary moment I saw the true name of our trade, a bloody battle for money and power—with the wolves waiting to eat what the axemen left behind.

Karl Kruger sat down heavily, splashed liquor into a glass and tossed it off at a gulp. Then he fixed me with a sardonic eye and quizzed me. "You think I'm joking, eh?"

"No."

"You want to ask questions?"

"Yes. How do you know Aaron Bogdanovich?"

"I'm agent for his bankers."

"Who employs him?"

"The State of Israel."

"Why would he undertake a private service?"

"He owes me a personal debt. I brought his brother and sister out from Latvia."

"And what could he do for us?"

"Almost anything I think. Terror is a flexible trade. The public sees only its crudest products—the murder of an agent, the hijacking of an airliner. In fact, we all live under a blackmailer's thumb. Speculators debase our currency; the Arabs cut our oil supplies. In these terms, Yanko's report to you is a terrorist act."

"How do I get in touch with your Aaron Bogdanovitch?"

"He runs a flower shop on Third Avenue between 49th and 50th Street. You walk in and present my note. I'd better write it now. Hilde will be here soon and we've got a wild night ahead of us."

I was frayed raw. I was free, white and a long way past the age of consent. If Karl and Hilde wanted a night on the town, I was ready to keep them company. We dined at home because Karl has the best chef in Schleswig-Holstein. Hilde, who is plump, comfortable and chirpy as a spring chicken, played *Wirtin* for both of us. Then Karl, flushed and randy, decided to invade Saint Pauli. I couldn't hold him; Hilde didn't want to. So, between midnight and four in the morning, we scoured the Reeperbahn: private bars, sex shows, lesbian joints, gay clubs and sailors' dives where Karl Kruger played the accordion and danced clogsteps on the sawdust floor. I expected him any moment to keel over with apoplexy. Instead, he closed the show with an actor's flourish. As Hilde was unbuttoning his shirt and I was peeling off his socks, he opened one eye and declaimed:

"You see, young Paul, if you can't fight 'em, you do the other thing. If you can't do either, you lie down and die."

It was a fine ringing sentiment for the end of a boozy evening. I doubted I could make it palatable to George Harlequin, the least combative, the most civil of men.

Thirty-six hours later, I was in Los Angeles, pacing the garden of the Bel Air Hotel with Juliette, sharing her elation at the news that George was reprieved from the death sentence, that he would be out of hospital in a week and, in another month, would be ready for light work.

Juliette was full of their plans. ". . . We've decided to go down to Acapulco. Lola Frank is lending us her villa. There's be a staff to look after us. There's a boat and . . . Oh, Paul, it'll be like a second honeymoon! I can hardly wait to get away. It's been a terrible few weeks. I would jump every time the telephone rang. George was like a stranger, so calm and remote. It was as if he had to conserve every particle of strength against the day of the verdict. He never complained. He was always careful for me; but he was living in his own twilight country. Even when they told him the good news, he was so reserved it was almost uncanny. He smiled and thanked the doctor for his care. When we were alone, he held me very close and wept a little; then he said a strange thing: 'Now I know the name of the angel.' When I asked him what he meant, he said it was something he didn't want to explain . . ."

"When can I visit him?"

"This afternoon. Why don't you go along and surprise him?"

"If you're sure . . ."

"Of course. It'll give me a chance to get my hair done and do some shopping. But you won't let him talk business, will you?"

"Not for too long, I promise."

"He'll be so glad to see you. Oh, Paul! Isn't it a wonderful, wonderful day!"

I thought it was a stinking, hellish day. I understood why, in the old times, bearers of ill-tidings had their throats cut. As I drove downtown to see Harlequin, I felt like cutting my own. I toyed with the idea of holding back the news, but I could not do it. Without Harlequin's consent, I had no power to act.

When I saw him, my heart sank. He was sitting in an armchair, dressed in silk pajamas and dressing gown, but so pale he was almost transparent. When I took his hand, it was dry and creped. Only his smile was the same; luminous, grave, but still with a touch of mischief in it. He did not, as the sick are prone to do, claim attention for himself. He brushed off my inquiries with a shrug.

"It's over, Paul. I'm very lucky. I'm glad for Julie. I want to get out of this place as soon as I can. They tell me it's a slow convalescence. Can you hold the fort a while longer?"

"Of course. But I have to bother you with some business. Do you feel up to it?"

"Sure. Go ahead."

"This is bad news, George."

He grinned and shrugged. "Tell me the worst and I'm still a lucky man."

I told him. He heard me out in silence, eyes closed, head sunk on his chest, hands placid in his lap. When I had finished, he questioned me, calmly.

"How was it done, Paul?"

"It's all in the report. We'll need an expert to check out the details, because a wide variety of transactions is involved; but the method is essentially simple. You bribe a programmer to feed fraudulent instructions into the computer. Unless they are canceled, the computer acts on them from now till doomsday . . . You know how we operate in the market. We buy and sell in block for groups of clients and allocate holdings, proceeds and charges afterwards. Our computer was programmed to make a false charge on transactions and pay the proceeds to a coded account in the Union Bank at Zurich. That account belongs to you."

"I've never had an account with the Union Bank in my life."

"The report states your signature is on the opening documents and on the checks."

"You mean the account's been operated?"

"It's been cleaned out."

"By forgery!"

"We'll have to prove that and identify the forger. We'll also have to find who corrupted the computers for all our branches, and who paid to have it done."

"Why didn't we pick up the discrepancy ourselves?"

"Because we all take the computer for granted. So long as daily transactions tally, we don't question it; and we've got such a wide variety of operations, only the accountants and auditors take any notice of the final figures."

"It's madness, Paul! To have me robbing my own company . . . I don't understand it."

"Somebody wanted to make you a clay pigeon. I think it's Basil Yanko."

"If that's true, we can get rid of him and buy other services."

"The hell we can! Have you forgotten how long it takes to install and train operators for one system? . . . Besides, this is just a warning—the first blackmail note."

"It's still a criminal act."

"If we can prove it. Also we've got to cover the bank for the missing funds. I need your instructions on that. For the moment, Karl Kruger and I are standing surety, but, as I told you, Karl wants his pound of flesh."

"Let him have it, Paul."

"In that case, I'll need power-of-attorney over your assets, at least until you're able to travel and act for yourself. That's a risk, too. You may not want to take it."

"I have to trust someone, Paul. If not you, who else is there?"

"So we fight Basil Yanko."

"I didn't say that."

I gaped at him in disbelief.

He gave me a wan, rueful smile. "Don't look so shocked, Paul. I've just walked to the edge of the world and back. I know how little luggage a man needs. I have to tell you I'm not sure I want to hold Harlequin et Cie. I wouldn't want Basil Yanko to have it; but I wouldn't balk at selling it to Karl Kruger. It's a tidy solution. It takes care of Julie and the boy. It lets me out of the rat race."

"If you sell in these circumstances, you're acting under duress."

"That's one side of the coin."

"Then I'll show you the other. If you back down, the bastards win. Because they win, they try again—and not every victim walks away as lucky as George Harlequin."

Suddenly he was gray and sweating. I felt like a criminal for pressing him so hard. I helped him into bed, bathed his face and waited until the faint color came back into his pinched cheeks. The only words I could find to say were banal and pitiful.

"It was too much. I'm sorry, George. Whatever you decide, we're still friends."

He clamped a thin hand on my wrist and pleaded with me. "I'll tell you a secret, Paul. It's hard to wrestle with the dark angel, because he doesn't want you to fight. All he asks you to do is rest and sleep. It's very tempting just to close your eyes and let go. Don't damn me yet. Give me a little time . . ."

"We don't have too much, George."

"I know."

"Do you want me to tell Julie?"

"Not yet. We've been having a few personal problems lately."

"Would you like me to stay awhile?"

"No, thanks. I'm very tired. Come and see me tomorrow with Julie."

It was still early. I did not care to go back to the hotel with its plastic starlets and graying agents. I wanted to be anonymous, free to talk mundane things: the cost of beefsteak, the hackie's bellyache and how the girls weren't what they used to be. I like low life. It's simpler to live and there are more friends to share it with you. I pulled into a bar on the Strip, dim and almost deserted. I ordered a bourbon, bought a beer for the house and settled down to half an hour of laconic lament with the barman.

We had just sorted out the Middle East and were starting on the scandals of the Administration when the telephone rang.

The barman answered it and then turned to me. "Your name Paul Desmond?"

"That's right."

"New York on the line."

"New York?"

"That's what the man said. You wanna take the call?"

He shoved the receiver at me and I said stupidly: "Hullo."

"Mr. Desmond? This is Basil Yanko. I called to welcome you to the United States."

"How did you know where to find me?"

"We're an efficient organization, Mr. Desmond. Do you have any news for me?"

"Advice, Mr. Yanko. Don't invade my privacy."

He laughed cheerlessly.

"Is there any service we can offer you during your visit?"

"None."

"Well, have a pleasant stay. We'll keep in touch. Au revoir, Mr. Desmond."

I put down the receiver and went back to my bourbon.

The barman eyed me shrewdly. "Bad news?"

"I backed a loser."

"Too bad. You can't win 'em all. Another shot?"

"Thanks."

I nursed it morosely while he told me, at length and in detail, how, the night he got divorced, he pulled a jackpot in Las Vegas and had himself—oh, brother!—the best lay in twenty years with a show-girl out of a job.

His good fortune encouraged me so much I decided to call my friend and client, Francis Xavier Mendoza, who lives in Brentwood. He is Old California—the tar pits, mission bells, the swallows of Capistrano, all this and more. He is a minor miracle:

a Castilian gentleman untainted by the vulgarity of the Coast. He has three sons and a beautiful daughter. He goes to Mass on Sundays and Holy days, grows some of the best wine in the Napa Valley and, in his spare time, labors to translate the poems of Antonio Machado into English. In Californian politics, he is a kind of chameleon, always present, always potent, but never easy to identify.

When I told him I needed to see him, he gave me an old-fashioned welcome.

·"My house is your house. Come now, if not sooner!"

Forty minutes later, relaxed in his garden, I put the question to him. "What can you tell me about Basil Yanko and Creative Systems Incorporated?"

He wrinkled his eagle's beak in distaste. "That one? A brute, but a powerful brute. Half the big enterprises on the Coast use his services and lick his boots when they pay his bill. Me, I wouldn't bathe in the same ocean with him."

"What's wrong with him?"

"Legally, nothing. I have to say that. He gives the best computer service in the country—systems, programs, security, the full card. He's a wonder-boy. But once he's in, you can't get him out. He controls your systems, so he knows every move you make. One sign of weakness, and he's camped in the President's office. He did it to three friends of mine and one enemy, who couldn't have deserved him more. Why do you ask, Paul?"

"We use him, too. We think he's doctored our records."

"*Ay de mi!* That's bad."

"Has he done the same to anyone here?"

"There are rumors, but no proof."

"Could we find proof if we dug for it?"

"In California today? Not a hope. For God's sake! The President is discredited, Congress is afraid, the people are demoralized. I doubt I could name twenty men in this town who haven't been bought by someone. I couldn't name ten who would face a public audit of their affairs."

"That's a sad verdict."

"Sad and sinister. I can find you an assassin sooner than an honest man or a brave one. I know . . ." He threw out his arms in a gesture of despair. ". . . I exaggerate, I always do. I'm like Diogenes scowling from his barrel. But these are our times. When you live on credit, as we Americans do, you can always be squeezed. When you climb the corporation ladder, you're afraid of the man above and the one below. That's Yanko's power. He knows everyone's secrets. What he doesn't know, he can invent, feed into the record and present as gospel whenever he chooses."

"How do you beat him, then?"

"Only one way. You live in his world. You fox him in the shadows—for years maybe—until one day you force him into the light and fight him down. However, if you play that game, you need strong nerves. And when you dine out, you always sit with your face to the door and your back to a solid brick wall . . . I give you good advice. Remember it. I'll check around. If I hear anything useful, I'll let you know."

"You're a Christian gent, Francis."

"No merit of mine. I had a mother—God rest

her—who boxed my ears and taught me manners. Now, let me offer you a sherry. It's my best and I'm very proud of it."

He poured the liquor with pride and made the toast: health, money and love and time to enjoy all three. As I drank to it, I had the eerie feeling that Basil Yanko was looking over my shoulder, grinning like a death's-head at the irony.

Years ago, when I was in Tokyo, peddling iron ore that was still in the ground and spending my commission before I earned it, I made friends with Kiyoshi Kawai, dean of Japanese printmakers. He was an old man then, but brimful of sap and visions. Whenever I felt miserable—which was often—I would go to his studio and sit for hours watching him cut the blocks and mix the colors and scold his apprentices if the definitions were a hair's-breath short of perfection.

When Kiyoshi was low—which was a rare, but cataclysmic event—he would cart me off to a transvestite club in Shinjuku, where the boys were dressed as geisha and the few girls were got up like the seven samurai. They fluttered round the master while he sketched them. They poured him endless cups of sake while he improvised *haiku* and transcribed them in his beautiful brush strokes. I found it an unnerving experience, because after a long session of sake and Kirin beer, it was hard to tell the boys from the girls—and I had to get the old man home before he started signing banknotes and handing them around as souvenirs.

It was on one of these excursions that he gave me his recipe for a good life. When he was sober, I had him inscribe it in *Kanji* characters; and wherever I hang the scroll is home to me. The inscription reads: "Never mix colors when the west wind is blowing and never make love with a fox-faced woman." It's a hard saying to explain at midnight; so I set it down as a prologue to the record of a very bad day.

It began with a series of small disasters. I woke early and went to the pool for a swim, slipped on the wet tiles and wrenched my ankle. Then the smog rolled down and in five minutes I was blear-eyed and sneezing. At eight, Suzanne called from Geneva. I gave her the good news of Harlequin's recovery and she responded with a dispatch from the home front. Our branch managers were unnerved by my cable. They were suddenly worried over their clients' interests and their own necks. Would I please clarify instructions? Since I couldn't clarify the alphabet without Harlequin's authorities in my pocket, I dictated a soothing message telling them their president was alive and well and would soon be holding their hands again. Further instructions would follow in forty-eight hours—at least I hoped they would. To cap it all, Juliette telephoned and begged me to join her for breakfast. She was fretful because baby Paul was down with chicken pox and the damn-fool nurse had celebrated the event in a hundred word telegram written in Switzerdeutsch and mutilated in transit. She had other things on her mind as well; and I was elected Father Confessor.

"Paul, we've been friends a long time. We don't have secrets."

"We do, my girl, because we can't live without 'em. Start again."

"Now you're being mean."

"So I'm bad-tempered and horrible and it's not my day. What's the next item?"

"I'm worried about George."

"George and you, or just George?"

"Just George."

"Yesterday you were talking about a second honeymoon. What's happened to change your mind?"

"He told me last night he was thinking of selling Harlequin et Cie."

"Did he tell you why, or to whom?"

"No . . . I thought you would know."

"Listen, Julie, let's not play games. I love you both dearly; but I'm in business with your husband, and I don't tell tales outside the boardroom."

"So he has talked about it."

"I didn't say that."

"And to hell with you, too, Paul Desmond."

"I'm on my way, lover."

"No, please! Wait! . . . I'm sorry. I'm acting like a bitch. But truly, I am worried. George is changed. You don't understand how much."

"For God's sake! He's had a long siege of illness. He's remote. He's depressed. That's normal. You don't expect him to be dancing fandangos, do you?"

"Why does he want to sell the business?"

"Maybe he wants to take his profit, invest the money and sail round the world. Why not?"

"What would he be without it?"

"A happy man?"

"Or another rich idler."

"In all the years of our friendship, I've never known him idle."

"An amateur then, not committed to anything."

"He's committed to you."

"Is he? I often wonder."

"I wouldn't know, Julie. I'm just an old bachelor with itchy feet."

"Paul, I hate you when you grin and shuffle away from an argument."

"What do you want me to do? You're a grown-up married lady. You know the words and the music. Sing 'em to George."

"I'd be out of tune."

"I don't believe it. You just don't want to make up your mind."

"About what?"

"Whether to cut George Harlequin down to boy-size—or grow up to woman-size yourself."

"Don't you know why?"

"I don't want to know. It's your affair, not mine . . . Harlequin wants us both at the hospital this afternoon. I'll pick you up at three."

I left her sitting over the cold coffee and went out to walk in the garden. I was angry with her, with myself, with Harlequin and the whole dyspeptic world. I needed a marital crisis as much as I needed a third leg. If we couldn't produce a policy within forty-eight hours, we might have a palace revolution on our hands. Worse than all, Harlequin—the man apt to all occasions—seemed to be falling apart. Three people had sensed a weakness in him and set out to exploit it: Basil Yanko, Karl Kruger, his own wife. I was the only one who didn't see it. Was I the one-eyed wonder, king in the country of the blind; or was I dumb Paul, oafish and bedazzled by the splendor of a pinchbeck prince? I had to know, if only to retain my own self-respect.

Then, because I was angry, and because when I'm angry I get bull-headed, I decided to start my own private war. I called the New York office of Creative Systems Incorporated and asked to speak with Basil Yanko. I had to identify myself to four people before he came on the line, bland as butter.

"Mr. Desmond, this is a pleasure. What can I do for you?"

"I'll be in New York the day after tomorrow. I'd like to confer with the man who prepared our report."

"It's not a man, it's a woman. Her name is Hallstrom . . . Valerie Hallstrom."

"I'd still like to meet her. Afterwards, I'd like to talk with you."

"Excellent. Would you care to suggest a time?"

"I've made no reservations yet. Why don't I call you when I arrive?"

"Do that, by all means. Have you conveyed my offer to Mr. Harlequin?"

"Yes. He's considering it. I expect to have his decision later today."

"Good! How is he?"

"Reduced, but recovering."

"I'm glad. Give him my best wishes."

"I'll do that. Until we meet then . . ."

I had no idea what I would say to him on that day or any day, but at least I had put a burr under his tail and I hoped it would keep him scratching for a little while. I went back to my room and called the hotel stenographer. When she arrived, we sat out by the pool and settled down to draft authorities and assignments to be executed by George Harlequin. It was a fiddling stop-and-go business but it kept me busy until noon when I strolled round to the bar for a pre-lunch cocktail.

The barman greeted me by name and pointed to a man seated alone in the window angle. "That gentleman, sir. He came in just a moment ago and was asking for you."

He was young, no more than thirty, dressed in a jersey suit of Italian cut. He stood up as I approached and introduced himself, respectfully. "Mr. Desmond? I'm happy to know you, sir. I'm Alex Duggan, Creative Systems Incorporated. Our New York office asked me to deliver an urgent message. I telephoned your suite. You weren't there. I thought I would try the bar. Won't you sit down?"

I sat. The barman set my drink on the table. I asked, "You say you have a message for me?"

"Yes, sir. It's a telex from our President's office. If there's any reply, we'll be happy to transmit it for you."

The message was an evidentiary document, formal and precise:

"On current consolidated figures and a three-year forward projection, we value Harlequin et Cie at eighty-five dollars per share. This communication constitutes firm cash offer for total stockholding at one hundred dollars per share. You are requested refer immediately to Mr. George Harlequin and inform him we are prepared negotiate generous terms for sale or waiver of his existing options. Other shareholders have been informed . . . Basil Yanko, President, Creative Systems Incorporated."

I shoved the message into my breast pocket and scribbled a reply on the envelope:

"Communication received and acknowledged . . . Paul Desmond."

The young man folded the envelope reverently into his wallet. "I'll send this as soon as I get back to the office."

"May I offer you a drink, Mr. Duggan?"

"No, thank you, sir. I never drink on the job. Company policy, you know."

"How long have you worked for Creative Systems, Mr. Duggan?"

"Three years now."

"What do you do?"

"Client relations."

"And what does that entail?"

"Well, sir, I have an exclusive territory. I visit all our users once a month. I check complaints, suggest improvements, make forward projections for extending our service, which is, of course, designed to grow with the client's business."

"Are you well paid?"

"Very. We have bonus schemes, stock options and all that. It's a fine job with good prospects."

"Do you ever see Mr. Basil Yanko?"

"Not often. But we know he's there—oh, yes, sir! He knows what everyone's doing, right down to the cleaning staff. If you don't shape up, you don't last long in Creative Systems."

"So you have a big turnover of staff?"

"Not too big. Enough to keep us on our toes, I

guess. Still, they do say even our rejects are better than most. They all seem to find jobs easily enough."

"That's interesting. Where do they apply?"

"Well, most senior computer people register with three big agencies in New York, and two here on the Coast."

"And does your company run an employment agency, too?"

"No, sir. We train and recruit only for ourselves and our clients. That's the policy. Mr. Yanko's very firm about it."

"Well, thank you, Mr. Duggan. I won't keep you any longer."

"It's been a great pleasure, sir. And your message will be in New York in half an hour."

He was a pleasant young man, just naive enough to be real. I shook hands with him, walked with him to the door, and went back, pensive and unhappy, to finish my drink. Now the burr was under *my* tail. Yanko knew all about contingent behavior in nonpsychotic subjects—yea, brothers and sisters, he knew! A vague offer makes a man restless, a firm offer makes him greedy—and eighteen percent over the market sends him rushing to signature before Father Christmas goes up the chimney again.

Harlequin might refuse to sell, but it was gospel truth that he couldn't pick up all his options at a hundred dollars a share and still meet a fifteen million shortfall. Karl Kruger might buy at ninety, but he wouldn't go a cent over and I couldn't blame him. Harlequin might try to fight a proxy battle—and then Yanko would play his ace: documentary evidence of fraud and misappropriation. After which, our friends, clients and allies would walk away in droves.

It was a fine cheery bulletin to deliver to a sick-room. Harlequin summed it up with grim humor. "We're caught between the crab's claws. There's only one consolation the price is right."

Juliette challenged him, tight-lipped and angry. "Harlequin et Cie was handed to you on a golden plate—and you'd sell it without a blush because the price is right? I'm ashamed of you, George."

He flushed angrily and then turned to me. "What's your advice, Paul?"

"Reason says sell. Instinct says fight."

"Could we win?"

"We could."

"But we could also get badly mauled. Yes?"

"For God's sake, George!" Juliette struck at him again, cold and contemptuous. "Stop hedging and admit it! You've never had to fight anything in your life. Everything was a gift—your own talent even! Now you're being offered another. Fifteen dollars a share bonus to walk away from the company your grandfather founded and that should, by right, be passed down to your son."

Harlequin stood facing her, rigid as a stone man. I was sad for him and ashamed for us all. Finally, he said curtly:

"Sit down, Julie. You, too, Paul."

We sat down. Harlequin stood, backed against the window, his face in shadow, dominating us. Then he began to talk, slowly, reluctantly, as if each phrase were dragged out of some secret recess inside him.

"It seems I've failed you, Julie. I was not aware

of it. I'm sorry. I know you've had your doubts too,
Paul. But there were reasons. I'll try to explain them.
For a long time now I've been disillusioned with this
trade of ours, where we grow money like cabbages
and peddle it like hucksters in an international market. I look at the funds which flow through our
hands, and I ask myself, more and more often, where
they come from: the transfers from Florida that we
know, but can never admit, are gangster dollars; the
oil money from the sheikdoms, where slaves are still
sold, and men have their hands cut off for stealing a
basket of dates; the fugitive funds from depressed
countries; the loot of dictators and local tyrants. Oh,
I know! When it comes to us, it's all clean, disinfected
and smelling of rosewater—and we live like kings
on the proceeds. I'm not proud of that. I'm less and
less proud every day . . . While I lay here, waiting for
the doctors to come and hand me the death sentence,
I wondered how I would answer for my life at
whatever judgment I might have to face on the other
side . . . Then, when all this happened, it seemed like
a way out: cash the chips, walk away, buy time and
leisure to work out the riddle of this world and my
place in it. On the other hand, I know I'm a good
banker, and that honest men trust the name and the
tradition of Harlequin et Cie. But here's the
dilemma—and you've put it to me, Paul—if I fight
Yanko, I fight in his world, on his terms, with his
weapons. I'm afraid of that; but not for the reasons
you think, Julie. You see, I'd like the fight; I'd like
the risk and the brutality and the naked lawlessness
of that other world. I believe I could be the biggest
pirate of them all and smile as I wiped the blood off

the cutlass. But the root question is whether I could live with myself afterwards. Would I seem more of a man to you, Julie? Could you and I, Paul, still sail together and laugh and drink wine on the afterdeck?" He smiled and made a small, shrugging gesture of self-mockery. "Well, that's the speech for the defense. It's the last one I'll ever make."

Julie stared at him, blank-faced. "But you're still selling out, is that it?"

"No, my love. You're a very persuasive woman. I'm going to fight. It's the only way I'll ever know whether the game is worth the cost of the candle."

It didn't have the high brazen ring of a call to arms. As theme music for a second honeymoon, it sounded less than propitious. Even while we plotted the campaign, it looked more like a conspiracy than a battle of the righteous against the ungodly.

When we drove back to the hotel, the Santa Ana wind was blowing and Juliette sat silent and withdrawn beside me. I longed to hold her in my arms and make her smile again, but she was far away in foxcountry, where ghost women bewail the lovers they have lost or misprized. I spent four hours and a small fortune on telephone calls and then took the midnight plane to New York.

2

In New York I am instantly at home, a shameless capitalist bloated with the spoils of free enterprise. I have an apartment in the East Sixties, a Japanese manservant, one good club, and a miscellany of friends, male and female. For all its follies and frenzies, I love the town. I rejoice in its gaudy bustle, its laconic cynicism and its brusque bad manners. It is a risky place to live in, all too easy to die in; but I am happier here than in any other city in the world.

I am also blissfully private, because I have an unlisted telephone, another man's name-plate on the door and the use of the bank's apartment at the Salvador, where I can entertain bores without having them set foot across my threshold. The arrangement has diplomatic advantages as well. The Salvador is a very public place where business is seen and overheard to be done. So it pays me to have the facility of a double life: to bait one lair and relax in the other.

At eight in the morning, rumpled and drowsy, I checked in at the Salvador. At nine I was in my own apartment. By ten, thanks to the ministrations of Takeshi, I was shaved, bathed, fed and restored to human shape. At ten-thirty, I was strolling down Third Avenue to make contact with Aaron Bogdanovich, who traded in terror and very expensive flowers.

The flower trade was booming. Two girls, armed with shears and wire, were making up table arrangements; an exotic young man was packing a bouquet in a box. An ample madam, wearing gold spectacles and a lemon-yellow smock and a voracious smile, begged to know my pleasure and rattled off a catalog of spring blooms before I had time to draw breath. When I asked to see the proprietor, her smile faded and she was no longer interested in my pleasure but only in my name and business.

The information gave her no visible satisfaction. When I presented Karl Kruger's letter, she handled it as gingerly as gelignite, laid it on a saucer and carried it into the back room. A few moments later she was back with the word that I should cross the Avenue to Ginty's Tavern and wait for a call on the payphone. I bowed myself out, feeling leprous and unloved.

At Ginty's I drank tomato juice and counted the bottles on the shelves until the phone rang and a voice commanded me to walk to Saint Patrick's Cathedral and kneel in the first confessional on the right-hand aisle. By now, I thought the whole routine was a bloody nonsense and I said so. The voice chided me, abruptly:

"For banking, we come to you. In our business, we're the specialists . . . Okay?"

Put it like that, of course okay. It wasn't far to

Saint Patrick's, and a little praying might help—provided I could remember the words. The confessional was dark and sour with old guilts. The grille which separated penitent and confessor was covered with opaque gauze. The voice which spoke through it was an anonymous, soothing murmur:

"You are Paul Desmond?"

"Yes."

"I am Aaron Bogdanovich. I have total recall. You will tell me the service you want. I will tell you whether and on what terms we undertake it. Begin, please."

I told him, in a confessional monotone. It was an interesting exercise because it made me see how vaguely I had defined my own position and how much reason there might be for Harlequin's doubts and hesitations. Aaron Bogdanovich was a good listener and a very skilled inquisitor. He asked uncomfortable questions:

"How would you express your needs in order of importance?"

"To stave off a takeover. To investigate the fraudulent operation and clean up our system. To prove Basil Yanko guilty of criminal conspiracy."

"The first two operations are defensive. The third is aggressive. Why?"

"If we fight a defensive war, we are bound to lose."

"Have you counted the possible cost?"

"In money? No. We accept that it may be expensive."

"Money is not the prime issue."

"What then?"

"Life and death. When you go to the police, when you call in a recognized security firm, you hire a man with a gun, to defend your life and your property. Their delegation is limited. They are answerable at law for what they do. We are not answerable, because we operate outside the law. However, we do have certain moralities and we are not assassins for hire. You can buy those in an open market; the contract rate begins at twenty thousand dollars for one killing."

"We are not hiring assassins."

"But violence may be involved and death is consequential to violence. So you have to decide first and we, afterwards, whether the issue is grave enough to warrant a mortal risk."

"Can we discuss that?"

"Not now. I should like you to define your position to your own satisfaction. Then we can meet again."

"Face to face?"

"Why do you ask that?"

"You mentioned moralities. We need to know those we have in common. I've never yet made a bargain with a man I didn't know. I've never signed an open-ended contract. So, it's a face-to-face meeting or we finish here."

"Agreed."

"I suggest my apartment. You name the time."

"Tonight at eleven-thirty. Do you have documents I can study?"

"Here, in my briefcase."

"Leave it in the booth, unlocked, with your address and telephone number inside. I'll collect it after you've gone. One more thing."

"Yes?"

"I serve a country first. I serve its friends and mine by concession and corollary. I cannot put my work at risk. So you must bind yourself to absolute secrecy."

"Agreed."

"You should also know the penalty for breach."

"Which is?"

"Death, Mr. Desmond—and there's no second warning."

It is wonderful how clearly a man thinks when his own death is in debate. As I walked up Fifth Avenue, through the press of the noonday crowd, I measured my own position against that of my sinister confessor. Aaron Bogdanovich had plausible reason for his trade. One death, a hundred deaths, were ciphers against six millions murdered in the holocausts. No life was more important than the survival of a beleaguered nation . . . But a bank? An anonymous society devoted only to the nurture of money. Did that merit a human sacrifice to preserve its assets? Who chose the victim and by what criterion? And what right had Paul Desmond, safe in the rectitude of possession, to appoint himself judge and jury and deputize the executioner?

As I paused to admire the diamonds in Cartier's window, a blind man, with a placard round his neck, rattled a tin cup under my nose. I had no coins in my pocket, so I fished out a crumpled note. As I stuffed it into the cup, I saw too late that it was a ten-dollar bill. I grudged it so unreasonably that it bought me no absolution at all.

I had a luncheon date at the Salvador with our New York manager, Larry Oliver, who is a Bostonian, with beautiful party manners and a finical respect for tradition. If he could have furnished the office with crouch-back clerks, high desks and quill pens, he would have been the happiest of men. Once, Harlequin posted him to London for six months and he came back shocked and wounded by the decline of morals in English banking. The barbarians of Wall Street made jokes about him, but he had ridden us through the crisis of 1970 with hardly a dent in our portfolios. The simplest inaccuracy was anathema to him. A fraud in our accounts was an unthinkable horror. So I expected a difficult meal; in fact, it was a total disaster.

Oliver toyed, unhappily, with his food while I sketched as much of the situation as he needed to know, and filled in the details pertinent to New York. He left his coffee untasted, stood up, tucked his hands under his coattails and began pacing the floor, for all the world like an attorney lecturing a difficult client.

". . . Paul, I understand—believe me I do understand—the gravity of this situation. But why wasn't I informed before this?"

"For Christ's sake, Larry! We only heard in Geneva four days ago. I cabled you and all the other managers instantly. I've spent two days conferring with George Harlequin and the rest of the time traveling. Be reasonable, man!"

"I am trying to be reasonable, Paul. But my reputation is involved, my family name . . ."

"So far as Harlequin and I are concerned, your reputation has never been in question."

"But once this gets out . . ."

"It mustn't get out, Larry. That's the whole point. The shortfall is covered. I'm here in New York to set up a full investigation."

"But through a private agency."

"Possibly several."

He stopped dead in his tracks and wagged a reproving finger at me. "I'm afraid that doesn't meet the bill, Paul—not by half."

"What do you mean?"

"Unless I misread the law, we are the victims of grand fraud. Right?"

"On the face of it, yes."

"That's a matter for the FBI. Why haven't they been called?"

"Because, though we suspect fraud, we have not yet had time to collate and study all the evidence. Besides, we operate in several jurisdictions. It may be the FBI is not the prime agency involved. However, I have a meeting with Creative Systems at which we'll go through the report together. Then I'll report to Mr. Harlequin and we'll decide whether or no to call in Federal investigators."

"Meantime, all our staff and I, myself, am under a cloud. I find that intolerable."

"Naturally. I can only beg you to be patient. We have to coordinate action with all our other branches."

"I see that, of course; but I wonder how much information has leaked out already."

"None, I hope."

"I'm not so sure of that. I was at a foursome lunch yesterday at the Club. There were some odd questions asked."

"Such as?"

"Whether Harlequin would be fit for active work again."

"He will be, very soon."

"Whether I sensed any weakness in our Geneva operations."

"And you assured them there was none?"

"To the best of my knowledge . . . I never make rash statements."

"I know, Larry. I know. What were the other questions?"

"Whether we were open to a takeover bid and whether one had, in fact, been made. I said no, to both."

"Again to the best of your knowledge."

"Yes . . . Then, I was asked whether I had ever contemplated a change. I said I was very happy with Harlequin et Cie, and especially happy in my relations with our President. We have much in common, as you know—an interest in pictures, a respect for sound precedent and, if I may say so, a good family background."

"I'm glad to hear that, Larry. Harlequin is counting on your support at this time."

"Please assure him he has it. But I should be less than honest if I did not say that any shadow on the bank's reputation or my own, would force me to re-think my position."

"I appreciate that. I know Harlequin will want to see you as soon as he gets to New York. Until he does, I'll be in daily contact. And, Larry . . . ?"

"Yes, Paul?"

"Now is the time for all good men . . . You know?"

"I do, Paul. I do indeed. Thanks for your confidence. Now, I'd better get back and mind the store."

He marched out, head high, cheeks glowing with godliness, a good Boston man, in whom, as old Tom Appleton proclaimed, the east wind was made flesh. The intelligence he had offered me was bleak. The word of our trouble was out. There would be new rumors every day. The tap-room gossips would blow them about the town; and soon, very soon, an offer of a hundred dollars a share would look like manna in the desert. I needed a long, stiff brandy. I decided against it because Valerie Hallstrom was due at three-thirty and I would need all my wits when we sat down to discuss her report.

Valerie Adele Hallstrom—I quote from her visiting-card—was a phenomenon. She was tall and blonde. She had one of those open, healthy Scandinavian faces that the travel agents use to seduce you into a Baltic cruise in midwinter, and a figure that was an incitement to riot. Not that she flaunted it— dear me, no! Her suit was a miracle of discreet tailoring. Her gestures were restrained. Her voice a smooth contralto. She knew her own mind and had all the words to express it. At first, I found her distracting. As we worked, line by line, through the document, I found her a very daunting lady indeed.

"You see, Mr. Desmond, if you choose, as you well may, to institute legal proceedings, this report has to stand up in court. The moment I signed it, my reputation and that of our corporation was on the line."

"So you conclude—and your report states flatly—that the frauds originated inside our own organization."

"We have no doubt of it."

"Read me the procedure as you see it."

"Let's take your head office in Geneva by way of example. The computer installation is located in Zurich. You rent usage time, four hours a day, five days a week. You have two direct lines to central computer and you key in by the use of an exclusive code. Anyone who knows that code can use your lines, or someone else's, to feed information and instruction into the computer or to withdraw information from it."

"That's all clear. But it opens loopholes. Either our operators committed the fraud or someone outside tapped in by using our code word."

"Which they would have to get from inside, right?"

"Possibly . . . Now, as I understand it, once an instruction is fed to the computer, it is stored in the memory bank and executed automatically."

"That's correct."

"And no one knows the instruction exists except the person who fed it to the memory bank."

"Exactly. And that's the basis of all the classic frauds. For example, if you have an overdraft limit of two thousand dollars, you can increase it to two hundred thousand just by adding two zeros to the program. After that, it's in the record and you can operate to the false limit without question—unless and until someone checks back to find the original instruction. Another example. You can order the computer to pay a hundred thousand dollars into your account on a given day and erase the transaction from its memory the day after. You withdraw the money from your account by a check marked 'balance of account' and skip the country. Unless it can be proved that you instructed the computer to commit the fraud, its very hard to prove you're guilty of a crime. You have not stated an amount to which you have no entitlement. The mistake was made by the computer acting and operating for the bank."

"So, Miss Hallstrom, let's see exactly what happened in our Geneva office. Here on page 73 of the report. Someone, reputed to be George Harlequin himself, opened a coded account with the Union Bank. The account was opened by post, using documents signed, or apparently signed, by George Harlequin. The signatures match. Harlequin disclaims all knowledge. Therefore, we conclude the signatures are forgeries. Next, someone using our code word, taps into the computer and orders it to charge one percent on every third transaction and pay the proceeds weekly into the Harlequin account at the Union Bank. Since bank charges are getting more and more complicated, because bankers are getting greedier and greedier, this charge could slip by until audit time. Right?"

"Yes. But at audit time it would have to be justified against an original instruction."

"So, if Harlequin were the originator, he would be immediately open to criminal prosecution."

"Agreed."

"But he's not stupid and he doesn't need money. So what would you conclude, Miss Hallstrom?"

"That it would be improper to me to comment, Mr. Desmond. Our contract with you is to discover anomalies and bad practices. This we have done. It is for you to draw conclusions and institute appropriate action."

"Very good. Very sound. Let me put it another way. We're a man and a woman alone in a hotel suite. There are no witnesses. I hope there are no bugs, unless you're wearing one. Would you be prepared to offer, without prejudice, a private opinion?"

"No, Mr. Desmond, I would not."

"But you have one?"

"Yes. That I am bound to rest only on the report I have signed."

"But this is matter arising out of the report."

"A matter of opinion, not fact. If you feel you have a claim to discuss it with Creative Systems Incorporated, then you should refer to Mr. Yanko, under whose direction I work . . . Now, do you want to discuss what happened in the other branches?"

"No. The transactions vary. The method is much the same. The result is identical. George Harlequin is framed with grand fraud."

"May I ask what action you've taken to prevent continuance?"

"We've annulled all computer instructions so far identified in your report."

"Good."

"And we're setting out to trace the originator of the fraud. Your report states that this has to be someone inside or connected with Harlequin et Cie. I note that you make no mention of people in Creative Systems Incorporated."

"On the contrary, Mr. Desmond. We make specific mention on page 84, para. 3, and I quote: 'All Creative Systems personnel connected with these operations have been screened and rescreened and we are satisfied that none of them is in any way involved in the fraudulent operations.' "

"And you expect us to accept that?"

"In default of contrary evidence, yes."

"Miss Hallstrom, I'd like to pay you a compliment."

"Please do, Mr. Desmond."

"You're a very beautiful woman."

"Thank you."

"I wish you were working for us."

"But I am, Mr. Desmond. Wait till you get the bill. My services come very high."

"Are you ever off-duty?"

"Often."

"How would you like to pay me a compliment and come to dinner one evening—if I promise not to talk business?"

"I think I'd like that."

"Where can I call you?"

"I'll give you my card. Telephone me round seven any evening."

"Thank you."

"By the way, Mr. Yanko asked me to say he'll be at your disposal between ten and midday tomorrow."

"Tell him to expect me at eleven."

"Au revoir, Mr. Desmond. It's been a pleasure to meet you."

"The pleasure was mine, Miss Hallstrom."

The hell it was! I thought she was a gold-plated bitch; but at least I had her address and telephone number and half an invitation into her private life.

It was a small victory, but not necessarily a frivolous one. When you deal with massive corporations, you need friends inside the network. Some companies are more affluent than the nations in which they trade. They straddle frontiers and override local jurisdictions. They bargain with the best brains, they buy the best legal counsel in every country. Their personnel command the care of diplomats and politicians . . . But, if you want a straight answer to a straight question, it may take you two years to get it, and you'll need a library to house the interim correspondence. So dinner with Valerie Hallstrom might be a dead loss. It might, on the other hand, be a key to secrets, because the larger the corporation, the more the loyalties were diluted and the more bitter were the faction fights in the upper echelons.

It was six o'clock. Suddenly, I felt tired, scrubby and old. I walked out of the Salvador, strolled ten blocks back to my own apartment and slept until Takeshi called me at eleven.

At eleven-thirty, punctual as doomsday, Aaron Bogdanovich presented himself. He was a tall man, lean, bronzed and muscular. He looked forty. He could have been fifty. There was no way to tell without a birth certificate. His dress was casual but immaculate. He smiled readily. His handshake was firm. After a swift appraising glance at the apartment, he said:

"I have one man watching the street entrance. There's another outside the door. I'd like to bring him in to test the apartment for bugs. I trust you have no objection?"

"None at all."

His man came in, a youthful ghost who prowled the rooms with a detector, nodded satisfaction and then left without uttering a word.

Bogdanovich relaxed. "Now we can talk."

"A drink?"

"Fruit juice, please."

Takeshi served the drinks and left us.

Aaron Bogdanovich smiled at me over his glass. "Well, Mr. Desmond, what have you decided?"

"We're under siege. We have to fight. We accept that there may be drastic consequences."

"And your principal concurs?"

"He has given me an open brief."

"The charges are as follows. You will make available immediately two hundred and fifty thousand dollars in cash. You will hold a like amount on call in any required currency in any named capital. Total, half a million with a maximum overcall of ten percent."

"Win or lose?"

"That's the deal. It's an act of faith. The other side of the bargain is that we accept all our own risks

and never, in any circumstances, pass them back to
the client. If there's blood on the carpet, we clean it
up ourselves. Can you commit for the required
amount?"

"Yes."

"Lacheim, Mr. Desmond!"

"Good health."

We drank the toast and sealed the bargain. We
sat down to supper and Bogdanovich talked me
through the campaign like a general instructing his
staff officer.

"I've read the document. I agree with your conclusions. The fraud is related to the takeover bid.
Yanko is the probable instigator. To prove it, we
have to work inside his organization and yours."

"Can you do that?"

"We can. However, we have to mount a cover
operation to divert attention from our activities."

"How do we do that?"

"You apply to a regular security organization
for assistance. We suggest you use Lichtman Wells,
who are an international outfit. You will request that
the operation be directed personally by Mr. Saul
Wells. He will accept the assignment."

"Why?"

"Be assured he will accept and will appoint suitable operatives."

"Your operatives, in fact."

"I did not say that. Nor should you ask . . . You
see, Mr. Desmond, it is not at all impossible that you
may, one day, find yourself under pressure to reveal
what you know about this operation. Considering

the sanction we have discussed, better you should have nothing to tell, eh? . . . Are you married?"

"No."

"Do you have any relationships or attachments through which you might be blackmailed? A mistress, perhaps? A child?"

"No. But Harlequin has a wife and a child."

"Then, he, too, should know the risks."

"I'll see that he does."

"I wish to meet him, personally."

"He was discharged from hospital this morning. He intended to fly to Acapulco for a holiday with his wife. In fact, they will come to New York. They will use the bank apartment at the Salvador, where we have arranged medical supervision during his convalescence."

"That's wise. You may both have to travel extensively in the near future."

"Again, please?"

"Your bank is in crisis. You will obviously need to visit all branches. Also we may need, for your own safety and the security of our operations, to keep you both on the move."

"That's a scary thought."

"Yes, it is. But consider, Mr. Desmond. Your company is a rich prize and great corporations have no morals. Accidents are easy to arrange. Executives and diplomats are kidnapped and held to ransom. Torture is now a science. Read any daily newspaper and you will see that I do not exaggerate . . . What you do not read is even more sinister. At this moment, there is a body floating in the East River. It is the body of a gunman who was hired to assassinate an Arab delegate to the United Nations. Tonight, Mr. Desmond, at eight-thirty, as the delegate stepped out of a limousine to attend a dinner party. My people would have been blamed for his death . . . I hope I make myself clear."

"Too clear for comfort."

"Money is power, Mr. Desmond. There is no comfort in either."

"So . . . Harlequin and I may have to travel. What else?"

"Act as normally as you can. Yanko expects you to negotiate with him over the shares. Negotiate. He expects an investigation. You give him one. Your managers and executives remain in ignorance of my activities and carry on normal business. Any information you glean, will be passed on to us."

"How?"

"Here in New York, by telephone, from a public phone booth. I will give you two numbers which you will memorize. You will identify yourself by the name of Weizman. When you leave New York, you will make your travel arrangements through an agency which I will recommend. Your contacts in other cities will be communicated when you pick up the tickets."

"I've got one piece of news now. I talked this afternoon with a woman, Valerie Hallstrom. She works for Yanko and it was she who prepared the report."

"Did she tell you anything useful?"

"On the contrary. She refused to go one step beyond the brief. However, I did ask her for a dinner date. She wasn't unwilling and she gave me her card."

"May I see it, please?"

He scanned it for a moment and then handed it back.

I couldn't resist the question. "Do you really have total recall?"

"I do."

"Should I make a date with this woman?"

"Is she attractive?"

"Very."

"Amenable?"

"I'd like to find out."

"Just let me know any arrangements you make."

"Which raises another question. How do you get in touch with me? I'll be moving about a good deal."

"Wherever you are, Mr. Desmond, I shall know. Our fees are high; but we give service round the clock . . . By the way, how long has your servant been with you?"

"Six years now."

"Obviously you trust him. But what do you know about his background?"

"Almost nothing. He was with a friend of mine for five years. When he left New York, I took over the apartment and Takeshi with it. There's a lot of valuable stuff here. Takeshi keeps the household accounts. So far, no complaints."

"It's a good record; but we'll check him out just the same. Do you have any vices, Mr. Desmond?"

"That's a hard one to answer!"

"I have to know."

"Well, let's put it in the negative. I don't gamble. I like a drink, but I haven't been drunk in twenty years. I don't buy sex. My taste is for women only and I never talk their names in the club."

"Any guilty secrets?"

"An unsuccessful marriage."

"Debts?"

"None."

"Thank you, Mr. Desmond. That's all I need for the moment."

"More juice?"

"No, thank you."

"A question for you, Mr. Bogdanovich."

"Yes?"

"Why have you agreed to take this assignment?"

"What you really mean, Mr. Desmond, is why I wouldn't look for a double fee somewhere else?"

"No. I mean exactly what I asked."

"There are two answers, Mr. Desmond. The first is simple. You were recommended by a good friend, Karl Kruger, and you can afford the service. The second is a little more complicated. I have small faith in the rectitude of human beings. I know that every man has a price and that he will die righteous only if no one offers it. I know that every man has one fear by which he can be destroyed. I have ceased to believe in God because I see a creation founded on a destructive struggle for existence. However, I know that order is necessary if life is to remain halfway tolerable. If a passably just man is invaded by a bully, we are all invaded. The only way to stop a bully is to smack him in the teeth. If you're too small to hit him, you hire me . . ." He gave me that limpid, ready smile and shrugged. "It's a specious argument, of course. You'd be a fool to swallow it whole. But even in our jungle, we need a vestige of reason to justify what we do. Now, let me give you the telephone numbers and the name of our travel agents."

When he had gone. Takeshi summed him up in a single, haunting phrase:

"That man, sir, I think he sleeps in a grave."

The headquarters of Creative Systems Incorporated occupied six floors of glass and aluminum skyscraper on Park Avenue. There were three stories of gleaming hardware, patroled by armed guards, and two tiers of aseptic offices where sober young men circulated among tribes and subtribes of secretaries. The sixth floor was Basil Yanko's private domain, a sacred place paneled in exotic wood, hushed by deep carpets, glowing with costly pictures and artifacts. The anteroom was dominated by a middle-aged duchess and two guards, one of whom conducted visitors through the silent corridors, while the other stood watch and ward against intruders.

When I arrived, it lacked two minutes to eleven. The guard checked my name on a typed list; the duchess announced me on the intercom and begged me to be seated. At eleven, precisely, a red light flashed on the panel; the duchess signaled to the guard, who conducted me to the holy of holies, a long chamber where Basil Yanko sat behind a vast buhl desk, bare of papers. The guard retired; the door closed and I walked across half an acre of carpet to shake the cold hand of the master.

He was brusque as ever, but he favored me with a smile and a brief concern for my well-being. "I trust you are rested, Mr. Desmond."

"Thank you, yes."

"And George Harlequin?"

"He has been discharged from hospital. I expect him in New York today. I'm not happy with the arrangement, but he insisted. He will remain under medical care for a time yet."

"I'm sorry to hear that. Has he reached any decision on my offer?"

"Yes. He asks me to tell you he is prepared to negotiate, as soon as he is well enough to engage in business discussions."

"And when might that be?"

"Soon, I hope. It's a matter for his physician in New York."

"Of course. Meantime, I take it you and I can set the groundwork for the talks?"

"Harlequin has given me a directive on that."

"Which is?"

"He is not prepared to engage in any negotiations while he, himself, is under a cloud. He has ordered me to set up a full investigation of the computer frauds, using an independent outfit."

"Have you chosen one?"

"Lichtman Wells. I have my first conference with them this afternoon."

"They're good people. Their operatives are well-trained."

"So I've been told."

"We stand ready, of course, to assist them in every way."

"Thank you."

"The time element is important to us both."

"We understand that."

"I think we need to be precise about it, Mr. Desmond."

"In what sense?"

"Our offer of a hundred dollars a share is firm as of today's date. However, we do have to set a term to it. The money market is volatile, as you well know. We could not be held indefinitely to a premium offer."

"What terms do you suggest?"

"Thirty days from now."

"Too short, Mr. Yanko. It represents only twenty-two working days. We could not possibly complete an international investigation in that time. We need ninety days, at least."

"The way the market is today? Not a hope."

"Your telex stated that your offer was made— and I quote—'on a three year forward projection'."

"The valuation, not the premium."

"Still, let's not quibble over three months."

"Sixty days. No more."

"I'm outside my brief. I'll have to refer to Harlequin."

"Do that, please. When may I expect to know his answer?"

"That's up to him. However, he is a man susceptible to courtesy."

"Which I sometimes lack. I know, Mr. Desmond. Let's put it this way. If Harlequin chooses to delay his response, I must feel free to reduce my time limit by an equivalent period. Fair?"

"Rough. I'll pass it on."

"You're a rough man yourself, Mr. Desmond. However, I respect that. If ever you felt like a change of pace or scenery, I'd be happy to talk terms with you—generous terms."

So, in the sober, legal fashion of business, the threat was spelled out. If we couldn't be bluffed or bought, we would be squeezed between the mill-stones. The sardonic skill of the predator affronted me. I wanted to spit in his eye. Instead I thanked him for his courtesy and walked out into the more human madness of Park Avenue.

At three in the afternoon, I called on Lichtman Wells. The experience was less than comforting, since security people, like insurance salesmen, make their living from the prospect of disaster. The senior part-ner, a white-haired ex-Colonel of Military Police, read me a horrifying list of cases from his files, none of which would have happened if the victims had used the services of Lichtman Wells. Saul Wells, the junior partner, sat patiently through the performance and, when the contract had been signed, revived me with coffee in his own office. He was a small, sandy ferret of a man who champed incessantly on an unlit cigar and punctuated his talk with winks and ges-tures.

"Don't let the old man worry you, Mr. Desmond. He's the salesman of the outfit, so he has to make the big spiel. From me, you get the action, without the dreck . . . How do we work? Well, on the inside it's straight detection. Our operative goes in the front door—no secrets, no false noses—checks procedures, takes statements, looks for holes and contradictions. Outside? . . . Well, that's different. We poke around, find out who sleeps where, who spends more than he makes, who plays sex games

and who plays the tracks . . . that sort of thing. It's
like a jigsaw, you know? All the pieces have to fit in
the end. If there's a piece missing, it's got to be in
someone's pocket or dropped down a drain. I remember once . . ."

He remembered and remembered, and replayed
each episode like a baggy-pants comedian. But, somehow, I warmed to him and I realized that at the end
of two hours his roustabout method had prized out
of me a whole mass of detail which otherwise I would
never have thought to give him. Finally, he stubbed
out his cigar and announced, cheerfully:

". . . So! You know me and I know you. I think
we'll get along fine. Now, we'll cut the comedy. Put
your managers on notice that we'll be moving in immediately. Languages are no problem. I've even got
a girl who talks Eskimo. One thing though, Mr.
Desmond. From here on in, it's guts football. Anyone leans on you, you call our mutual friend."

So far so good. On the one side we had Yanko,
who knew exactly what he wanted and how he was
going to get it. On the other, we had promises,
promises, and very high charges and a series of jere-
miads about how dangerous it was and how much
we needed protection.

I cut across town toward First Avenue where my
friend, Gully Gordon, runs a quiet singles bar and
plays piano for the customers at cocktail time. Gully
is a Jamaican, the only colored man I know with a
Scots burr. He also does Irish, Creole, Nebraska and
Italian, because he used to be an actor until, as he said
himself, "I got wise, laddie, and found myself a cap-
tive audience."

I was walking briskly along the left-hand side of
the street when I was jostled, violently, and sent staggering against a man standing in a doorway. I went
down on one knee, and, as I tried to get up, I was
chopped hard on the neck. I must have blacked out
because the next thing I remember was standing
against the wall and being dusted down by a shabby-
looking fellow in a torn sweater and blue jeans. In-
stinctively, I patted my breast pocket.

He grinned and shook his head: "No, they didn't
get it."

I asked, shakily, who "they" were.

"Roller-coasters! One to push, one to dip for
your pocketbook. Lucky I was right on your heels.
You okay now?"

"I think so. Thanks! Would you like to join me
for a drink?"

"Some other time. Take care now, Mr.
Desmond."

He left me and melted into the press of the
crowd. I was still dazed and shaken and it did not
even occur to me to ask how he knew my name. I was
held by a single, sickening thought: how simple the
violence was, how swift and sudden, and how little
stir it made in the passing throng.

The second thought shaped itself slowly as I
leaned on the piano and sipped my drink and listened
to Gully's dream-music: I belonged in this half-world
of lone travelers and raw adventurers. No matter
that I had climbed out of it years ago and cushioned
myself against it with money and comfort. I knew it
from the underside: the restless rhythm, the whore-
fragrance, the sour blood-taste, the sidling touch, the

pidgin dialect of the market. Sometimes, desperate and solitary, I went back to it, putting on the past like an old coat, musty but comforting.

My friend, Harlequin, belonged to another world. He was a scholar and a gentleman, bred to all the old decencies of Europe. Sure, he could play my role and twenty others; but he was still the *schauspieler*, the actor, miming his way through the plot, with no other commitment than to entertain himself and his audience. I asked myself how he would perform without a script, without a prompter, when the buttons were off the foils and only the winner went home after the duel scene.

Gully Gordon looked up from his keyboard and said softly, "You're sad tonight, laddie. The bastards are getting to you."

"They're getting to me, Gully."

"You need a good woman."

"I do, at that."

"There's one at the bar."

I looked; and there was Valerie Hallstrom, alone, nursing a drink and chatting to the barman. I turned away before she saw me.

"I've met her, Gully. Tell me more."

"Lonely, I know. Two drinks that last an hour, so she's no lush. Then, she goes home—I think."

"Alone?"

"You know how it is, laddie. This is a singles bar. You come here looking. When you've found what you want, you stay home."

"Has she been looking long?"

"Six months, more or less. But you said you'd met her."

"I do business with her boss. I wondered if tonight were a setup."

"No way. She's a regular."

He fingered a soft cadenza and then began to improvise, crooning the melody and signalling to me over the phrases. "She likes it, laddie. Softly, softly, catchee monkey. Come on, lassie. Come on . . . If you blow this one, Paul, I'll never forgive you . . . And good evening to you Miss Hallstrom! Do you have any requests?"

We were side by side, glasses touching, before she recognized me.

She was surprised but not displeased. "Well, Mr. Desmond! Small world."

Thank God for Gully Gordon. He could pick up a cue with the best of them. "He's an old friend, Miss Hallstrom. Only we don't see enough of him— too busy piling up the shekels."

"It's getting harder, Gully; I'm getting older. Do you come here often, Miss Hallstrom?"

"She's a friend of mine, too," said Gully. "What can I play for you, lassie?"

"You're doing fine, Gully. Just play. Had a big day, Mr. Desmond?"

"Paul . . . And I've had a long, lousy day."

"That makes two of us."

"Mine isn't over yet. Otherwise I'd ask you to dinner."

"There's no contract."

"Care to sign one for tomorrow?"

"If you like."

"Where do I pick you up?"

"My place at seven-thirty."

"Sealed and delivered."

"You know, you're rather nice."

"I know. My twin brother's the bastard. He's off-duty tonight."

It was an old line, but it raised a smile from her and a wink from Gully, and it carried us over to a booth, where we sat nursing our drinks while the music washed round us.

After a while, she said, "Gully's is a very special place for me."

"Me, too. I was here the night he opened. All I owned was a pile of debts and the cash I had in my pocket."

"And?"

"He must have brought me luck. Next day, the market jumped and I made a small killing."

"Maybe you'll be lucky again."

"I am. Look what I found."

"Now you say what's a girl like you doing in a singles bar."

"No, I don't. I say this is a lonely town and it's nice to have a place where you're welcomed and no-body asks who you are or what you do. It's better than being a number in a computer bank."

"A philosopher, yet!"

"No. A middle-aged man with a lot of living behind him."

"I think you've worn pretty well."

"And you, young Valerie, are hardly worn at all."

"That's not what you thought yesterday."

"I'm older today."

"I'm sorry I had to give you a hard time."

"Standard practice?"

"No. Orders. And I get seven-fifty a week with fringe benefits for doing what I'm told."

If it was a bait, I wasn't going to rise to it. If it was an indiscretion, there would be more to follow. I decided it was time to go.

"Look, I hate to leave, Valerie, but I must. My president arrived this afternoon. I have to change and dine with him at eight. Which still leaves me time to walk you home, if you like."

"Thanks, but I'll stay awhile."

"Until tomorrow then."

"I'll look forward to it. Good night, Paul!"

It ended with a smile and a hand's touch. I paid the score and carried a drink to Gully at the piano. He still played lefthand chords as he raised the glass in salute.

"Slainte, laddie! You'll be around for a while, eh?"

"I'll be around, Gully. Look after the lady for me!"

"On my soul's honor, sir! Have a nice evening."

When I arrived at the Salvador for dinner, I found Harlequin and Julie relaxed and cheerful. Harlequin had slept most of the journey. There was color in his cheeks. He was restless and eager for my report, but Julie announced firmly that we would have no business talk at dinner, and that she would leave us private afterwards—provided I sent George to bed before midnight. I thought it was a splendid arrangement. I had no wish to introduce Aaron Bogdanovich over the french cutlets; and there were thorny matters to settle with Harlequin himself. I gave him my report over the coffee.

He heard me out in silence and then questioned me closely. "So we have two parallel investigations; one by Lichtman Wells, which will follow conventional lines, the other by Aaron Bogdanovich, which may involve illegality and violence. Correct?"

"Yes."

"Meantime, we have unhappy staff, who must be kept comfortable and loyal?"

"That's your job, George. It can't be done by proxy."

"And on the outside we have Yanko, who is now pressing for a decision in sixty days?"

"Possibly less. He's expecting a discussion with you as soon as you're fit."

"I'm fit now. I'll call him in a day or two."

"Why not let him sweat awhile?"

"Because he's not sweating, Paul. We are. I don't like that. Now, what's the rest of the strategy?"

"Let's be clear on what we have first. Lichtman Wells are investigating the computer frauds. That's defensive, to clear the bank and clear you. Aaron Bogdanovich is investigating Yanko. That's attack, to tie him and his company to the frauds and discredit him."

"But it's still not enough, is it?"

"No. It represents forty-eight hours' work on my part; but I'm only a delegate, not a principal."

"Another question, then. Yanko wants to buy a bank. Why did he choose ours? Why not Herman

Wolff or Laszlo Horvath, who are both willing sellers?"

"Well, Harlequin et Cie is an older and more conservative institution. We have more branches— London, Paris and Hamburg, New York, Buenos Aires, Rio, Lisbon, Mexico City."

"Good reasons, but still not enough."

"We use his systems; therefore, we're more vulnerable."

"Go on."

"That's the best I can do so far, George."

"Then I'll give you two more. As underwriters, we acquired and we still hold significant blocks of shares in Creative Systems and its international affiliates. Therefore, we represent a dissident voice in the affairs of the corporation."

"I wasn't aware of any dissent."

"Believe me, there is. Although it is not yet formal, it is deep and personal. The biggest projects of Creative Systems, those in which Yanko is most personally interested, are in two related fields: police documentation and what is politely called urban control. In effect, we are talking about the surveillance, documentation, strategic control and manipulation of vast masses of people in every continent of the globe. The instrumentation is already in existence, personnel are already in training, existing systems are being enlarged and improved. They are being used not merely against criminals, but against political dissidents and indeed to determine the daily destinies of ordinary people. They lead inevitably to terror, repression, counter-terror and the torture chambers. The company which devises such systems is in a position of immense power and privilege in every jurisdiction, even under opposing systems and regimes. Now, if such a company can enter the international money market, if it can manipulate currency and credit, then you have an empire straddling all geographical frontiers . . . I've seen this situation developing for a long time. I talked about it last year at a bankers' dinner in London. I tried to distinguish between legitimate use of computer facilities and those which constituted a threat to personal liberty. The speech was, I believe, widely reported. I had it printed and circulated to friends. Not all of them received it kindly. Yanko received a copy, which he never acknowledged. I believe now that it determined his present strategy against me and against the Company."

"I'll admit it's very possible, George. Yanko's a sardonic bastard. It's the kind of joke he'd relish. But I don't see how it changes our present situation."

"It doesn't. It simply tells me what I ought to do."

"Let me point out, George, that we can do nothing without evidence. Evidence that clears you and convicts Yanko."

"I don't agree, Paul. I have to run a business. I have to deal in an open manner with a public situation. I can't have Yanko, you or anyone else dictate a role for me."

"But we've hired Bogdanovich. You agreed that we need him. I think you should confer with him and at least coordinate your moves."

He chewed on that for a moment, then gave me that mischievous, disarming grin. "So the moles burrow under the walls, while Harlequin plays in the public square to distract the populace. That makes sense. Set the meeting as soon as possible."

On my way out, I stepped into the phone booth in the foyer and called Bogdanovich. I don't know why—perhaps because I was tired and disposed to be chatty—but I quoted the phrase about the moles and the comedians. Bogdanovich was mildly amused. He capped it with another.

"Comedians yet! So we all die laughing! We'll meet at ten, by the monkey house in Central Park."

Oddly enough, the meeting of these two disparate characters was a success. For a long moment, in the presence of the chattering apes, they measured each other; then they smiled, shook hands, and walked out into the spring sunshine, with myself half a pace behind and the bodyguards, two unshaven young men, ten paces away on either flank. Harlequin and Bogdanovich walked slowly, as if time had no significance for them. They talked tentatively at first, then fluently, but always respectfully, as if each had need of the other's understanding. Harlequin, the eloquent, was quiet and deprecating; Bogdanovich, the man of violence, had need to justify himself and his trade.

". . . You see, Mr. Harlequin, violence begins when rational argument becomes impossible."

"I know. But there is the other side. I can talk myself blind over the cognac, while you are dying at my gate for want of a cup of water. And between us there stands the traitor steward who will indulge me and let you die to enrich himself. How do we resolve this?"

"I have resolved it by the old formula. An eye for every eye. A life for every life. No question, no pity, no guilt."

"Whereas I want absolution for everything I do. I'll tell you a secret. I take refuge in my name: Harlequin, a buffoon. The buffoon is always forgiven, because even his malice attracts laughter."

"While the public executioner is a man without a name, who lives behind a mask. Could you kill a man, do you think, Harlequin?"

"I could be tempted, yes."

"But the act—the final irrevocable act—the finger squeezing the trigger, the thumb on the blade and the hand striking upwards—yes or no?"

"How can I know before the moment?"

"You can't. Afterwards, yes. Then it is simple: stimulus, response, rationalization, sleep. Assassins, like adulterers, always sleep well; but a crumb in the bed will send them crazy."

"Mr. Bogdanovich, what do you think I should do?"

"Your friend here, Mr. Desmond, tells me you see yourself as a comedian. You entertain the town, while we sap the ramparts."

"That was a conceit. But, yes, there is a truth in it. I have charges, trusts, a role to play. The role attracts the trust. The trust creates it. Basil Yanko is in the same galley. He is a genius. Once recognized, he must justify himself every hour of every day."

"So how do you propose to treat with him, Mr. Harlequin?"

"Negotiate, if I can, to buy time for your investigations. If I can't, I'll defy him and pledge myself to the neck to beat his offer."

"Mr. Harlequin, you know that there are dangers in what we are doing."

"Paul has explained them."

"You have a wife and a child. You understand that you may put them both at risk?"

"My wife accepts it—wants it."

"Why?"

"Because it is a thing she can share wholly with me."

"Was it hard to admit that?"

"You know it was. Is anything hard for you, Mr. Bogdanovich?"

"Oh, yes."

"What?"

"This: to walk in the sunshine and watch the girls; to want them; to know that when I sleep with them, I shall wake up screaming, because I have slept with the dead; to see the children and wish they were mine, and know that I dare not have children, because the monsters will eat them in the end. We shouldn't meet too often, Mr. Harlequin."

"No. I understand that."

"Mr. Desmond will keep us in touch."

"Yes."

"When you treat with Basil Yanko, remember one thing. He doesn't understand clowns. He's afraid of them."

"Why?"

"He has never learned to laugh at himself. He will kill anyone who laughs at him."

"That makes me sorry for him."

"He will kill you for that, too. I'm glad we met, Mr. Harlequin. I regret the price is so high."

"It's only money."

"That's the shame of it, Mr. Harlequin. In our world money is the measure of a man. Good luck!"

"Thank you, friend."

"Thank you. Keep in touch, Mr. Desmond."

Then he was gone, a lean, dark figure, loping across the grass with his minions in attendance. George Harlequin stood watching him in silence until he disappeared behind the knoll; then he turned to me and asked, simply, "Paul, how do we tell Julie?"

"Must we?"

"Yes. I think we must."

I was there when he told her. I didn't want to be; but they both insisted, as though I were a gloss, a dictionary into which they both could dip to interpret themselves one to the other. Juliette asked few questions, made no protest. It was as if she understood, for the first time, the full import of her own aggressive attitudes. Harlequin, on the other hand, was vehement and exalted, as if he had experienced a private revelation.

". . . Julie, it was like talking to a man who had come back from the other side, someone who understood the continuity of things—the terrible repetition of human malice and tragedy. So far, you and I have never had to face it. Now we must. And it's for something useless—a bank, a repository of paper: guilders, francs, dollars. That was what I disprized—the perishable thing. You come without it. You go without it. But I've realized it's a magical thing, too.

Hold it in your hand, and you have a genie at your command. That's what men like Yanko want: the genie who can conjure armies out of dragon's teeth. And we say, no! We are the good conjurers. We will give you wheat-ears instead of swords. Will we? Do we? I cannot swear to it. And yet I cannot sell the lamp and then stand by and watch the janissaries rise out of the dust. Why not, Julie? The janissaries will guard you and me and the baby. Why should we care about the others whom we have never cared about before? Why, Paul?"

I was tired by now. I wanted to end the argument and be gone. "Why should we? I don't know. Why do we? . . . Yes, by God! That I know! Because one day, before the sun's up, the bell rings and the bastards are at the door and they're coming for me, because I've got the wrong nose or the wrong skin, or I'm on the wrong list and nobody will say who put me there. I want friends then. I want brothers and sisters. Put me in hell and I want 'em! . . . It's all yours, children. I've got work to do. See you at the bank after lunch, George. The little boy from Boston wants you to hold his hand."

As I walked through the foyer of the Salvador, I stopped by the telex to check the market figures. Halfway through the quotations was a news item:

Yanko bids for European Bank. Mr. Basil Yanko, President of Creative Systems Incorporated, announced this morning that he had made a cash offer of one hundred dollars per share for the total shareholding of Harlequin et Cie, Swiss-based merchant bankers. The offer, which includes a substantial premium, holds good for sixty days. Mr. Yanko pointed out that the structure of his corporation enabled it to comply with the provisions of Swiss law in respect of local corporations. Mr. George Harlequin, President of Harlequin et Cie, who has just been discharged from hospital after a serious illness, was not available for comment. Other shareholders say they have received the offer but decline to signify reactions at this stage.

I tore off the sheet, folded it and handed it to a bellboy to deliver to George Harlequin. It cost me a dollar for the service; but hell! What was a dollar against all those janissaries springing up at all points of the compass rose? It was twelve-thirty on a fine spring day. I braced myself, chin up, shoulders squared, and strode out to face our colleagues in the club.

In the ten minutes after I arrived, I was offered enough liquor to embalm a pharaoh. For the next twenty, I was besieged by friends, acquaintances and nameless bodies who crawled out of the woodwork. All of them asked the same question: "Are you selling? You mean the premium's genuine? . . . Not to Yanko? . . . For Chrissake, Paul, before you make a single move, why not come to us? . . . Is Harlequin on his feet? . . . It's not the big C, is it? . . . We heard . . ."

They had heard, guessed, dreamed and they would do it again with every new shred of gossip. So, knowing they wouldn't believe it, I told them the simple truth: "Yes, the offer's genuine. Yes, there's a premium. No, we're not accepting and we think it's dirty pool to publish the offer before it's even been discussed between the parties. No, it is not the big C. Harlequin's on his feet and fighting mad. If you don't believe me, invite him to speak at the next members' dinner."

I don't know what made me add that last little rider, but Herbert Bachmann heard it, drew me out of the crowd and commanded me to lunch at his table. Herbert is a formidable old turkey, whose forebears walked the street with their notes of exchange tucked into their top hats. He has driven hard bargains in his time, but I have never known him pull a dirty trick and I would rather have his handshake than a dozen notarized signatures from some of his junior colleagues. His questions were barbed, but his concerns were genuine; and I was ready to be as honest as I could with him.

"This fellow, Basil Yanko, what do you think of him, Paul?"

"He's a genius; he's dangerous and his manners are for the pigsty."

"But maybe his mother sees some good in him, eh? So he's a pig; but Harlequin underwrites him and uses his systems. Why?"

"Because, if he didn't, you and the other boys would steal the account."

"Which makes Harlequin a whore like the rest of us."

"Except he wears it better, Herbert."

"Ach! The high Swiss polish, the passion for accuracy, ticktock like one of their silly cuckoo clocks! So what's this I hear about shortfalls?"

"I don't know. What have you heard, Herbert?"

"You've hired investigators, haven't you?"

"Where did you hear that?"

"Around . . . Don't be angry, Paul. You know the way it goes in this town. Pinch your secretary's tushie and they make it a ten second news flash. So how bad is it?"

"Herbert, is this lunch business or pleasure?"

"For you, Paul, pleasure. For me, business. I live here. I sit on committees to try to keep the trade clean. It's hard enough at the best of time, but after Vesco and Cornfeld, we need Basil Yanko like we need the black death. Come clean with me, Paul. If Harlequin needs help, I'll see that he gets it."

"We need secrecy and discretion, Herbert."

"From me, you have it. You should know that by now."

"Fine! the shortfall is fifteen million."

"It's enough, by God!"

"We can handle it. No problems. The real problem is that we believe our computers were rigged."

"That's obvious—but by whom?"

"The record says by Harlequin himself. We believe it was Yanko."

"Until you can prove it, that's slander, Paul."

"I know. But the day Yanko put the report into my hands, he also announced that he wanted to buy Harlequin et Cie. Now the bid's firm—a hundred dollars a share."

"What are they really worth?"

"Eighty-five . . . ninety, if you're an optimist."

"Not bad. Our actuaries figured them at eighty-three to eighty-seven. Is Harlequin going to accept?"

"No."

"The minority shareholders?"

"Some will sell for the premium. Others will sell because of the rumor that someone's got his hand in the till."

"So, why doesn't Harlequin buy out the minorities?"

"He'd have to hock everything to do it. He can't afford to pay a hundred dollars a share and cover fifteen million shortfall at the same time."

"So you get Yanko on the board."

"Over our dead bodies."

"Even so . . . What's Harlequin doing about it?"

"I'm sorry, Herbert, but that you'll have to ask him yourself."

"I will. Tell him to call me at home tonight. Here's my number."

"Thanks, Herbert."

"Don't thank me. I'm an interested party. When I see all that power, all that knowledge locked up in a machine, I tremble. You can't stage a strike against the computer. You can't put it in the dock. But a man you've never seen can read what you have for dinner and how you make love to your wife. Sometimes, I'm glad I'm an old man and can duck most of the consequences. Let me order a brandy. I'm getting morbid."

It was just after three when I got to the bank. Harlequin was already there pouring charm and unguent on Larry Oliver's bruised spirit. It was a virtuoso performance, full of subtle flatteries and appeals to tradition and the code of gentlemen, and the need to stand fast against the encroachments of the vulgarians. At the end of it, Larry was purring like a kitty-cat with cream all over his whiskers.

Outside in the boardroom, Saul Wells was directing the labors of two junior geniuses, who were checking computer printouts against the security report. He drew me over to the window and told me with mournful admiration:

"It's so simple, it's a shame to take the money. Three coded instructions: first, to make the deductions; second, to pay proceeds into a suspense account; third, to remit every Monday by telex to Zurich. The original instructions were punched into the computer on the first of November last year. We've checked the manager's diary entries. Mr. Oliver was on holiday. He was being relieved by Mr. Standish, who makes no mention of the instructions. However, Mr. Harlequin was in New York on and around that date. That's point one. Point two is that the computer operator resigned in January for reasons of health. We have her name, Ella Deane, her social security number and her last known address in Queens. She'll be checked out immediately. Now, if we could chat with Mr. Harlequin . . . ?"

The chat turned quickly into a rapid fire interrogation, which startled even me. Harlequin, however, submitted with smiling equanimity. He had, indeed, been in New York at the relevant time. He had, indeed, written memoranda and dictated letters on various subjects. These were all on file in a locked cabinet in the strong room. Would he produce them? With pleasure. The file was produced. Together they checked through the documents, Harlequin verifying each one and handing it to Wells, who marked it with his own cipher. All of them dealt with policy matters. None could be identified or even construed as an instruction to computerize a standing order.

Saul Wells then asked Harlequin to write his signature and his initials half a dozen times in quick succession. Even when it was hurriedly done, the script was bold and open, with a defiant little flourish at the tail of the terminal letter.

Wells grunted, unhappily. "Like shooting at the side of a barn. I could forge it myself with five minutes' practice. Watch!"

For five minutes by the clock he scribbled away and then produced a very respectable facsimile. Still he was not content. He asked for Harlequin's check book and signed a check for a thousand dollars. I took it to Larry Oliver and asked him to initial it for encashment. Punctilious as ever, he checked date, figure, the amount in words, the signature. Then he initialled the check and buzzed for the head cashier.

I took the check out of his hand. "I'm sorry, Larry; it was a test. That check's a forgery."

We tried the same ploy on the cashier, with the same result. I couldn't resist a reminder that the reputation of the nicest people got smirched without their knowledge. At least Oliver had the grace to look sheepish. Saul Wells was amused. Harlequin was very unhappy.

"But this sort of thing could happen at any time. How many thousands of my signatures are floating round on letters, checks, credit card vouchers? It's a nightmare!"

"Instructive, though." Saul Wells had become suddenly broody. "The signature is so easy to forge; why didn't they put a memo on file, just to complete the picture?"

"I can answer that." Harlequin was emphatic and assured. "It would be out of character for me to sign such a memorandum. It would override the manager—a thing I never do. Also the fraud was repeated in other branches. There could be no guarantee of my presence, in say, Buenos Aires. Better to have confusion at the source and total certainty where the money was received: at the Union Bank in Zurich."

Saul Wells stuck a new cigar into the corner of his mouth and surrounded himself with a cloud of smoke. "Yeah! I buy that. Makes a better case for the prosecution, too. Which is something we should think about, Mr. Harlequin. So far we've traced about six million going out of New York alone. Every one of your clients has been hit with illegal commissions. Any one of them could file charges here in New York. The charges mightn't stick, but they could sure as hell be embarrassing."

3

It was five-thirty when I got back to my apartment. There were messages on my desk: Miss Hallstrom would like me to meet her at eight instead of seven-thirty; Mr. Francis Xavier Mendoza had telephoned from the Coast; and Mr. Basil Yanko would like me to call him at his office before seven. I decided to get the good news first—if there were any to be had—so I called Mendoza. He was cryptic but encouraging.

"About our mutual acquaintance . . . I told you three friends of mine got burnt. One of them is a very stubborn man. He has spent two years compiling a dossier. I have seen it: fascinating material, although not all of it would be admissible under the rules of evidence. I've persuaded him to make two photostats, lodge one in safe deposit and give me the other. I'll send it to you by safe hand. Another thing: there are people in politics and at the Pentagon who love Yanko; there are others who hate him like poison. I've made a list. That will come in the package. Remember I gave you a warning. When you've read the stuff, you'll understand why. How are things in New York?"

"We're being pressed hard."

"I guessed as much. I've just read the news item. If you need help on the Coast, I'm at your service. Vaya con Dios!"

I hung up, blessing him for the decencies he affirmed in a dog's world. Then I called Basil Yanko. He was, for a few moments at least, almost human.

"Thank you for calling, Mr. Desmond. I was anxious for news of Mr. Harlequin."

"He's done some work today; but he's very tired this evening."

"That's only natural. I had thought of calling him to pay my respects."

"I'd suggest you leave it until mid-morning tomorrow."

"Of course. Madame Harlequin is well?"

"Yes, thank you."

"You read our press announcement?"

"Yes."

"Any comment?"

"None. My principal has taken over the situation."

"Very proper; but you did make some rather improper comments in your Club today."

"What I say in my Club, Mr. Yanko, is no bloody business of yours."

"I quote, Mr. Desmond: 'We're not accepting and we think it's dirty pool to publish the offer before it's been discussed with the parties.' In fact, the offer was discussed with you as a Director of Harlequin et Cie. Your statement could be considered actionable."

"On the hearsay of an informer? I doubt it. But if you like to give me his name, I'll be happy to confront him before the Club Committee. Anything else, Mr. Yanko? I have a dinner engagement."

"One small matter, Mr. Desmond. Harlequin et Cie handle some of our investment funds."

"Very profitable, I believe."

"Indeed, yes. But transactions on those funds have been charged with a fraudulent commission. Our attorneys advise that grounds exist for civil and criminal action."

"Then, no doubt, you will discuss the matter with Mr. Harlequin tomorrow. Good night, Mr. Yanko."

I slammed down the receiver and cursed him to hell and back. Then I was furious with myself. Here was I, veteran of a hundred forays in the market, with scars on my back, and profits in the bank, jerking about like Pavlov's dog when Yanko pushed the shock button. It was the simplest of all the techniques of terror: the ever-present informer, the swift admonition from the great master, the threat of doom round the next corner. Suddenly, I dissolved into laughter, threshing about the apartment like a schoolboy, juggling cushions, yelling for Takeshi to fix me a drink, draw me a bath, lay out my best suit, call the Côte Basque for a table, order a limousine from Colby Cadillac, have roses delivered before eight o'clock to Miss Valerie Hallstrom. It was all wrong, wrong, wrong in a hungry world; but if I saved the money and put it through Yanko's creative computers, would there be one grain the more in an Indian rice bowl? I knew there wouldn't be. I told myself, I didn't care. Yet, rock bottom, under it all, was the conviction that if a man on a telephone could send me cowering to bed, it was time, thank you very much, to toss in the cards and blow my brains out in the first convenient alley.

I was in the middle of shaving when I remembered I had to call Bogdanovich. For a moment, I was tempted to let it slide; then I thought better of it. I dialed the number, introduced myself as Weizman and, a moment later, Bogdanovich was on the line.

"Where are you calling from?"

"My apartment."

"You were told to use a pay phone."

"I know. It's late. I almost forgot to call."

"This time you're lucky. I was just about to contact you. There's a man watching your front door."

"Yours?"

"Mine and another. He's parked on the left side in a green Corvette."

"That's awkward. I'm going out to dinner with the lady we talked about."

"What's the program?"

"I have a limousine calling here at seven-forty-five. I pick her up at eight. We're going to the Côte Basque."

"Reverse the order. Telephone her and say you're detained. Send the limousine to pick her up and deliver her to the Côte Basque. You walk to the St. Regis and go into the King Cole Bar. You'll get a message. After that you can move across to the Côte Basque. Clear?"

"So far. What about going home?"

"Which home are you thinking of?"

"Hers, I hope."

"If there's a problem, we'll get word to you. If not, act normally."

"That's a nice open brief."

"It isn't open at all. That apartment's enemy territory until we've had time to go over every inch of it."

"Two way mirrors and bugs in the cocktail olives, eh?"

"I'm glad you can laugh. Now hear this joke. The man in the green Corvette is Bernie Koonig. He has already killed two men and a woman. Enjoy yourself, Mr. Desmond."

It is a measure of the madness of America that the news frightened me considerably, but caused me no real surprise. When a respected sociologist can write glibly about "acceptable levels of violence," when a television personality can interview a man in a mask who claims to have killed thirty-eight people on contract and with impunity, there are no surprises left, only a pervasion of terror, as if the palisades have been breached and the jungle beasts are roaring through the human enclave. So I did as I was told.

When I left my apartment, I saw that the green Corvette was blocked against the curb by a squad car, and two patrolmen had the driver braced against the hood. I, wise ape, saw nothing, heard nothing. I walked to the St. Regis, sat at the King Cole Bar and waited until a newcomer pushed a bowl of peanuts under my nose and murmured the news that I was free to leave.

When I reached the restaurant, Valerie Hallstrom was already seated, with a cocktail in front of her, chatting to the maître. She gave me a warm smile and a hand's touch of welcome. She thanked me for the flowers; she was gracious about my late arrival. We made small talk over the drinks and the menu. By the time the meal was served, we were comfortable together, I working through my repertoire of travelers' tales, she amused and interested, grateful, she said, for a respite from the conventional invasions of business life.

". . . After a while, Paul, this town closes in on you. It's all so urgent, so impersonal—and, then, so meaningless. I was a country girl. My father still breeds saddle-horses in Virginia. I couldn't wait to get away and make my mark in the big city. Well, I've done it, and now I'd like to go home again. But you can't, can you? Home hasn't changed, but you have. What about you, Paul?"

"Home for me is where I hang my Kanji scroll."

"You haven't told me about that."

I told her. I told her the old legend of the women who changed themselves into foxes, leaving their lovers maimed and desolate. I talked about the print-makers and the potters and the loving handcraftsmen of Japan, and the river-people of Thailand, and the man in Rangoon who taught me to read good rubies from bad, and the haunting beauty of the Arnhem jungles, with the dark people chanting around the campfires.

Then she asked, "And what are you now?"

"A trader, a money-man."

"Not only that."

"No. But if I hadn't traded, I wouldn't have traveled. If I hadn't traveled, I wouldn't have had all the rest."

"And your friend, Harlequin, what's he like?"

"George? Oh, George is quite different. He knows. He has the kind of learning I'd give my arm for—languages, history, pictures . . . When we travel together, he's immediately on the inside. I have to think my way in or let him lead me. Last year, we sailed the Greek Islands. Me, I'm the sailmaster; but the moment we touched land, George was chattering away with the fishermen and the priest and the local antiquary. I envy that."

"But you love him?"

"Like a brother."

"Yet you're sitting here with me."

"So . . . ?"

"I'm the enemy. I work for Basil Yanko."

"All the time?"

"Most of it."

"Even when you go to Gully Gordon's?"

"No . . . not there."

"Now?"

"Not now. Tomorrow, maybe. I don't know."

"Does Yanko know you're dining with me?"

"No. If he found out, I'd lose my job."

"You're joking."

"It's true and I'd never get another one in this industry. Wherever I went, he'd still have a hold on me."

"You're on file in the system?"

"We all are. That's the way Yanko works. That's the way all big industry works. The record follows you around; but you never see it. And while it exists, you're never free."

"That's blackmail, tyranny and enslavement."

"I choose to submit to it."

"What for? Seven-fifty a week and fringe benefits?"

"I'm safe where I am."

"Are you sure? There was a man watching my apartment tonight. I have reason to believe he was employed by Basil Yanko."

The color drained from her face. She dropped her fork with a clatter. For a moment I thought she was going to faint. Then, with a great effort, she recovered herself. "Is that true?"

"Yes."

"Oh, God!"

"Relax, woman! I wasn't followed here, neither were you. That's why I changed the arrangements. You see, we have our own protection, too, day and night. Drink your wine! . . . That's better! Whatever Yanko holds over you, can't be worse than this constant terror."

"Please, I don't want to discuss it."

"All right! Now, we play a little game. I say to you: 'Valerie Hallstrom, tell me your dark secret and I will set you free and protect you.' Then you say to yourself: 'See, he only wants to use you. You are safer with the devil you know.' Then, I try to persuade you. You refuse. And in the morning you go back to the office and tell it all to Uncle Basil, who punishes you a little and then consoles you and sends you back, penitent but happy, to write it all into a confidential report for the brain . . . So, let's not play the game, eh? Let's have coffee and Calvados and I'll drive you home in my shiny limousine and leave you safe and innocent on your doorstep."

"You're a bastard, Paul Desmond."

"No, you've still got it wrong. That's my twin brother."

Once again it raised a small, uncertain smile and we sat awhile holding hands and watching the eddy of waiters around the tables and trying to read the faces of our fellow guests before we dared, again, to read each other's. They brought us the coffee and the Calvados and as we sipped the raw potent liquor, Valerie Hallstrom said:

"Paul, I have to warn you. Basil Yanko's a very dangerous man."

"That I know already."

"And George Harlequin is an obsession with him."

"Why?"

"I think for the same reasons that you admire him. He was born lucky; he's highly civilized; people are drawn to him. Yanko dragged himself up from a Chicago slum. He's a genius, a great genius—but he's ugly and rude. He's like a toad with a gold crown on his head; and he knows it. That's what makes him cruel and perverse. I used to feel sorry for him. For a while I even thought I was in love with him. Romantic, isn't it? . . . And the beautiful princess kissed the ugly toad, and lo! he turned into a beautiful young man."

"Only he didn't?"

"No."

"So, that's why you sit in Gully Gordon's, night after night? And you can't fall in love, because the toad-king is always there laughing, because your life is locked up in his mechanical brain."

"It isn't a joke, Paul."

"Do you hear me laughing?"

"I think we should go now."

If this were a lovers' tale—which, God help me, it is not!—I would recount how we drove to her apartment and she invited me in and we danced to soft music and then made love till sparrow-chirp in the morning, and when I left all Basil Yanko's secrets were in my hands. In fact, it was not like that at all. A block from her apartment, she asked the driver to stop the car. She wanted to walk the rest of the way. I offered to walk with her. She refused with a smile and a single cryptic comment:

"Sometimes God likes to know how his children spend their evenings. Thank you for the dinner. Good night, Paul."

She kissed me lightly on the cheek and got out. I made the driver follow her slowly home, so that she would be safe from muggers and junkies. When the door closed on her, we turned crosstown to Gully Gordon's, where I sat relaxed among my peers, listening to the sad, sweet music, until one in the morning.

Sometime in the small, cold hours, I had a dream. I saw a vast, circular plain, naked under a cold moon. In the center of the plain, small and solitary, was a squatting figure, whether human or animal, I could not tell. I knew only that I felt drawn to it by a deep yearning, and held back from it by a visible menace. Around the outer rim of the circle was a multitude of horsemen, some black against the moon, some ghost-white in its glow. Beside each horseman was a hound, motionless at the point. They were immeasurably distant, yet I could see them plainly, as if they were a hand's stretch away. The horsemen had no faces, only masks, blank as egg-shells. I tried to distinguish the features of the squatting figure, but it was as if my eyeballs were compressed and I could not focus.

Then, the horsemen and the hounds began to move, slowly, at a funeral pace, converging inexorably on the lone figure. The horsemen were silent. The hounds were dumb. There was no sound of harness or hoof-beat. The figure moved, stretched, stood up and revealed itself as a nude woman who turned slowly, gyrating like a manikin on a pedestal, until her face was visible to me. It was Valerie Hallstrom, smiling, seductive, oblivious of danger.

I felt an enormous surge of sexual desire. I called to her, but no cry would come. I reached out to her, but was held back by giant hands. Then the cavalcade broke into a gallop and the hounds loped at their flanks and I felt, rather than heard, the wild halloo and the baying and the ground shaking under the hoofbeats as they charged to trample her down . . .

I was groping through the first rituals of the waking day when Saul Wells called. He was excited and voluble. I could almost see the cigar stuck in his mouth. I could hear him chewing on it. The smell of it was like a ghost-mold in my room.

"What is it, Saul?"

"Ella Deane."

"Who?"

"You know, the dame on the computer. The one who left in January. Reasons of health."

"Oh, yes, Saul. Yes?"

"Very sad. For us very bad. She died."

"When?"

"Two weeks ago. Car accident. Hit-and-run."

"What do the police say?"

"Like always. They're pursuing investigations. Convenient, huh?"

"Like always. Anything else?"

"Confirming cables. Our operators move into your other branches tomorrow."

"Fast work, Saul. Thanks."

"One other thing. Ella Deane died rich."

"How rich?"

"Thirty thousand, give or take."

"Where did she get it—and when?"

"I'm working on that. The impossible takes a day longer. I'll be in touch. Ciao for now!"

A little later, while I was dabbing the breakfast egg from my chin, Aaron Bogdanovich arrived, dressed like a delivery man, with a basket of fresh blooms and a salesman's motto:

"Flowers add fragrance to your life, Mr. Desmond."

"And I didn't think you cared, Mr. Bogdanovich."

"Tell me what happened last night." The question was harsh, as though he hoped to surprise me into some damaging confession.

"Nothing happened. We dined. We talked. She told me she would lose her job if Yanko knew we'd met privately. She told me she'd once been in love with him, but it ended badly. She warned me he was dangerous and was obsessional about George Harlequin. Then she asked me to take her home. She insisted on walking the last block alone. We followed her in the limousine. I went on to Gully Gordon's for a nightcap."

"And how did you get home?"

"In the limousine."

"What time?"

"One-fifteen."

"Can you prove that?"

"Sure. I signed the driver's log. Takeshi was up when I got home. I took a shower, got into my pajamas and he served me a cup of tea before I went to bed. Why all the questions?"

"Valerie Hallstrom is dead. She was killed just after she got home."

"God Almighty!"

"I hope you can look just as shocked when the police give you the news!"

"The police . . . ? I don't understand."

"You and I, Mr. Desmond, were the last people to see her alive . . . Is there any coffee left?"

"Help yourself . . . Look, you'll have to start at the beginning. I'm lost . . ."

He gave me that cold, graveyard smile, helped himself to coffee, cream and sugar, then told me:

"While you two were at dinner, I went to Valerie Hallstrom's place. You've seen it, from the outside. It's an old brownstone with a basement and three floors. She owns it all and everything inside is very expensive. There's a Matisse in the bedroom and an Armodio in the salon. There's Dresden china and lots of what they call, I believe, bijouterie. There's a wardrobe full of furs and high-fashion clothes. She has two telephones—one with an unlisted number. The listed one is bugged. The unlisted one is hidden behind the clothes in the wardrobe, where there is also a wall-safe, which I managed to open. I'll tell you in a moment what I found. Now, that little inspection took me from about eight-thirty to nine-thirty. At nine-thirty, the listed telephone rang. I waited until it had stopped and then left, by way of the basement. I sat in my car on the opposite side of the street and waited. At about ten-thirty, a man, carrying a small briefcase, entered the house. He used a key. He didn't come out. He didn't switch on any lights. I waited until I saw Valerie Hallstrom come home. I saw you pass by in the limousine. I saw the lights go on in the living room and in the bedroom, but I couldn't see inside because the drapes were drawn. About ten minutes later, the man, still carrying the briefcase, came out. He walked westward, across town. I followed him. He flagged a taxi and beat the lights at the next intersection, so I lost him, although I did get the number of the taxi. I stopped at a pay-phone and called Valerie Hallstrom's number. No one answered it. I went back to the house. The lights were still on. I let myself in and found her on the living room floor. She'd been shot in the head . . . The epilogue is very simple. I went back to the pay-phone and tipped the police. They were still working when I drove past this morning, and I'm still wondering what would have happened if you'd gone home with her."

"Who was the man? Did you recognize him?"

"No. But I would know him again."

"What did you find in the safe?"

"Money—about twenty-five thousand dollars. A file of computer printouts. A notebook containing a list of companies and their computer codes. All the branches of Harlequin et Cie are listed, each with its own code. I believe that all the other companies are clients of Creative Systems. I took the book and left the rest of the stuff."

"You what?"

"Bargaining power, Mr. Desmond. We've never had it before. We have it now . . . in very, very safe deposit."

"But none of this makes sense."

"I think we'll find it makes a lot of sense, Mr. Desmond. Suppose Miss Valerie Hallstrom were playing her own private game: milking the computers and selling the results outside. Suppose Yanko found out. What would he do?"

"Have her arrested."

"And brought to trial, with the whole sorry mess displayed in court? That would be a crippling blow to Creative Systems and to Yanko himself. It would take him years to recover. No, Mr. Desmond, there are precedents, too many precedents. Some companies have even bought off offending employees and given them first class references, rather than indict them and face millions of dollars' worth of damage. But I don't think Yanko would do that, do you?"

"No."

"So he gets rid of her the cheap way. The safe is found empty. The police assume that Miss Hallstrom surprised an intruder and was shot. It happens every day to wealthy ladies living alone. And Miss Hallstrom's lifestyle helps the story."

"But we know . . ."

"I know, Mr. Desmond." He said it almost tenderly. "All you have heard is a fairy tale, which you will forget the moment I leave. That was our bargain, remember? Later, when I have found the man who killed Miss Hallstrom, we shall see."

"Do you think you will find him?"

"I'm sure of it, Mr. Desmond. It's a very closed profession but the good practitioners are all known. I'll find him."

He went out smiling; but he left behind a whiff of sulfur and brimstone and half a hint of damnation. Slowly, I found myself forced into the same dilemma as George Harlequin. We were bankers; we washed money clean as cheese cloth; but we, ourselves, could never quite escape the taint that attached to it. Then George Harlequin called, brisk, businesslike and so far out of character that even I could not guess the role he had chosen for the day.

"Paul? I wonder if you'd mind coming to the Salvador, say in about twenty minutes. I'm having lunch with Herbert Bachmann. I need to confer with you. Then Basil Yanko is coming here at three. I'd like you to be present. Meantime, there are some other people who are anxious to talk to you . . . Half an hour? Well, do try to make it sooner if you can. Oh, one other thing. Would you mind taking Juliette to lunch? She's very bored with my company, and I don't blame her. Thanks, Paul. A bientôt."

The people who wished to see me were two very polite young detectives from the New York Police

Department. They explained, in alternate versicles, that they had called the bank, that the bank had referred them to Mr. Harlequin, who had kindly consented to call me and that they hoped, sincerely, not to have put me to too much inconvenience. I assured them they had not. They wondered whether Mr. Harlequin would mind leaving us alone for a while.

Harlequin did mind. He minded very much. He expressed it in the phrases of high diplomacy. I was his longtime friend, a trusted director, an officer of an international bank. We were standing on the property of that bank. We were standing on its dignity, too. Unless I specifically desired his absence, he would stay. It wasn't a long argument, but it gave me time to collect my addled wits and to frame a simple, straightforward account.

"I left my apartment at a quarter to eight and walked to the St. Regis. I had a drink in the King Cole bar. At about eight-fifteen, I crossed to the Côte Basque, where I dined with a lady. We left the restaurant at about eleven-thirty in a Colby limousine. I dropped the lady home. The driver took me to Gully Gordon's bar on First Avenue. I stayed there till one. The driver took me to my apartment. My manservant can confirm my arrival at about one-fifteen. He was making a late supper for himself. I shared it . . . Now, may I know the reason for these inquiries?"

"If you'll be patient with us, Mr. Desmond, please . . . ? You dined with a lady. Her name?"

"Miss Valerie Hallstrom."

"Have you known her long?"

"Three days. Miss Hallstrom works for Creative Systems Incorporated, whose systems we use and to whom we are underwriters, and investment bankers. She had prepared a report on our computer operations. We had met to discuss it. She was helpful and enlightening. I invited her to dinner."

"But you didn't call for her at her house?"

"No. I sent the Colby limousine."

"Any reason for that?"

"It was simpler and I wanted to stretch my legs. I'd been inside all day."

"You say you drove Miss Hallstrom home. Did she invite you inside?"

"On the contrary. She asked to be dropped a block from her house."

"Didn't you think that was unusual?"

"Very. But on the other hand . . ."

"Yes, Mr. Desmond?"

"Miss Hallstrom is a business acquaintance. I have no knowledge of her—er—domestic arrangements. New York is a whimsical city. I find it easiest to accept its whims at face value and ask no questions. I asked the driver to follow Miss Hallstrom home. Once we had seen her safely to the door, we drove on. I'm sure you'll be able to confirm all this with Colby Hire and with the driver of the limousine."

"What are your movements in the next few days, Mr. Desmond?"

"They depend entirely on Mr. Harlequin here."

"Mr. Harlequin?"

"Impossible to be definite at this moment, gentlemen. We are engaged in some highly delicate international negotiations. We may be here for a week. I may have to send Mr. Desmond to Europe or to the

South Americas at a moment's notice. Why do you ask?"

One of the detectives produced a manila envelope, tipped out a sheaf of photographs and handed one to each of us.

Even though I was prepared, I felt a shock of disgust and horror. Valerie Hallstrom lay like a rag doll on the floor of her living room. Her face was a bloody mess.

The detective reached across and took the photograph from my hand. "She was shot, Mr. Desmond. Close range with a low velocity .38 pistol."

"I—I don't understand . . . When? How?"

"We're working on that. Would you mind, Mr. Desmond, if we went to your apartment, talked to your servant, checked your belongings?"

"Anything you want. But surely you don't think . . ."

"Routine, Mr. Desmond. It helps you, too."

"Of course."

"Before you go, gentlemen!" George Harlequin stood up, an iron man, dominating us all. "I am witness to this interview. Mr. Desmond has answered freely all questions put to him. He has offered you, gentlemen, free access to his apartment without a warrant. He has given you facts and the means to check them. Meantime, I have a call on Mr. Desmond's services. I wish him to remain here for business discussions which involve the urgent interests of international clients. So, with deference to the police authority, may I make a suggestion: Mr. Desmond telephones his servant and directs him to admit you to his apartment. He remains here at your disposal if you wish to question him further . . . Well, gentlemen?"

They were the new breed: cautious, educated and rational. After a brief conference, they agreed. I called Takeshi, handed over my keys and promised to wait at the Salvador until they returned.

When Harlequin and I were alone, he asked me a single blunt question. "You left out something, Paul. What was it?"

"There's nothing, George."

He was hurt, but he tried hard not to show it. He said, calmly, "Just remember, you are not required to compromise yourself for me."

"I'm not compromised, George. Let's drop it, eh? You're meeting Yanko this afternoon. How are you going to handle him?"

"I'm refusing the offer."

"Then what?"

"I take up my options to buy the minority shares."

"You can't afford it."

"Herbert Bachmann thinks he can raise the funds for me. We're discussing it over lunch."

"Even if he can, you'll put yourself in debt for ten years and with the cost of money today, it could be longer. Besides, what happens if Yanko raises the offer? He could do it, you know, if he traded shares in Creative Systems instead of cash. There's a limit to what even Bachmann can do in Wall Street without frightening the horses."

"Then, let's see what the limit is, Paul. And how

much time we can buy for our other operations. I think Bogdanovich may surprise us."

"He's made it clear, George. He doesn't want you to stage a confrontation just yet."

Harlequin was nettled. His answer was sharp and definite. "We are paying for information, advice and assistance. I decide how we use it. I refuse to be manipulated."

"No quarrel, George; it's your money. But this isn't Europe, and the American scene is pretty muddled at this moment."

"So, we must be clear, Paul. The risk is mine, the decision is mine."

"Do you need me at this meeting with Yanko?"

"Yes. I've told him you'll be here. I invited him to bring one of his own people if he wished. He said he needed no assistance; but, of course, he understood I was still under medical care."

"Arrogant bastard!"

"That helps, Paul. I can't bend to him now. I'm committed; with everything I am, everything I own. If men like Yanko control the machines, there's no hope for any of us."

"How does Julie feel?"

"We're closer. Though I wonder sometimes whether she wouldn't have been happier married to a simple man . . ."

This was dangerous ground. I didn't want to walk on it. Before I had time to phrase a comment, the telephone rang. George Harlequin signaled me to answer it. Basil Yanko was on the line. "Mr. Harlequin?"

"No, this is Paul Desmond . . ."

"Oh, Mr. Desmond, as you know we were to

have a meeting this afternoon. Unfortunately, I am involved in a rather tragic situation, affecting one of my staff. I wonder if we could defer until tomorrow?"

"Certainly. I'll fix it with Mr. Harlequin. Same time at the Salvador, right?"

"Yes, please . . ." He hesitated a moment and then went on. "Perhaps, under the circumstances, I should tell you that the employee in question is Miss Valerie Hallstrom. She was killed last night."

"I know. I've talked with the police. I've seen the photographs."

"You, Mr. Desmond?" Either he was a superb actor, or he was shocked to the marrow. "I don't understand."

"I dined with Miss Hallstrom last night. Apparently I was the last person to see her alive."

"Did she say anything? Did you see . . . ?"

"Nothing, Mr. Yanko. The police are now in possession of the little information I was able to give them. I'm deeply distressed. I wish there were something I could say or do . . . Until tomorrow then."

"Until tomorrow . . ." His voice trailed off into a vague murmur. "Goodbye, Mr. Desmond."

As I put down the receiver, Harlequin asked mildly, "Was that wise, do you think?"

"It was unavoidable."

"Was he disturbed?"

"I think so. I hope so."

"I think you should call our friend Bogdanovich."

"I'd prefer to wait until the police have finished with my apartment."

Fifty minutes later they were back. They had checked the apartment; they had spoken with the driver of the limousine; they had talked with Gully Gordon. They thanked me for my cooperation. All they needed now was a brief signed statement. I wrote it in longhand on Salvador notepaper, signed it and had George Harlequin witness it. They thanked me for that, too, and hoped they would not have occasion to bother me again.

There was only one small detail. They wondered why I hadn't mentioned my meeting with Valerie Hallstrom in Gully Gordon's bar. I told them half the truth and half a lie. The meeting was accidental and without significance. They saw that, of course. What I had failed to understand was that girls who haunted singles' bars often found strange bedfellows. I agreed it was possible. I hoped they didn't mean me. Of course not; but even the most respectable bachelor is hard put to prove that he has slept all night in his own bed . . .

George Harlequin made a great joke of my discomfiture. He even persuaded the officers that they were off duty and could accept a cocktail before lunch. I was not amused, but I managed a happy bachelor smile and told a scabrous little story of my salad days in Tokyo. To hear us laugh, you would never have guessed that we had all been brought together by a murder.

At one o'clock, Juliette came back, flushed and cheerful from a girl-morning in New York. She had visited her hairdresser, had coffee with a friend, shopped extravagantly and was delighted to be squired to lunch at the Fleur de Lys. Julie in festive mood could still turn heads and mine more easily than most. We strolled down Fifth Avenue, arm in arm. We window shopped at Bergdorf's, at Van Cleef's and Harry Winston's. We played "Do you remember . . ." and "Wouldn't it be wonderful if . . ." We drank large martinis and pondered the menu as if it were our last meal on earth. While we ate, we made plans for a night at the theater and a Sunday drive into the country. We talked of a cocktail party to entertain friends and colleagues, and who among the women might be a good match for me. It was a pretty, pleasant party-game and I was glad to play it, as long as the lady was happy.

She knew nothing about the morning's drama; and it was no brief of mine to enlighten her. George Harlequin wanted to make his own decisions. How much he wanted his wife to know was one of them. Besides, I was tiring in the role of godfather, family friend, old Johnny Do-all. My money was pledged; the police were rummaging through my private life; people were breathing heavily into my telephone; and all I wanted to be was hail-fellow-well-met, and an Irish farewell when the girls were too ugly or the drinks ran out too early. It didn't seem too much to ask, but then, I'd never understood women very well. By the time we reached the crêpes Suzette, Juliette had tired of small talk and wanted to make a confession.

". . . I am happy, Paul—happier than I've been in a long time. George is getting stronger every day. He's enjoying this battle. We're more open with each other. When he's upset now, he rasps. There was a time when he was so smooth and polished, I felt a hurricane wouldn't ruffle him. I like him better this way. I'm easier to live with, too . . ."

Now, what do you say, if you're in my shoes? You're delighted. You knew all along things would work out. Marriage isn't always a rose garden. All that and more. But, of course, it isn't enough. The confession has hardly begun.

". . . Paul, I'll be honest with you . . ."

When a woman tells you she's going to be honest, you should face about and run for the shrubbery, but you don't. You sit, patient and smiling. You pat her hand and make murmurs of sympathy, and listen for the hundredth time to the siren song.

". . . I'm jealous of George. I'm insecure. I love him desperately; but just to be married to a man like him is a constant threat. He knows too much. He sees too clearly. I feel he's measuring me at every moment; and all the time I'm falling short of his needs. This crisis has brought us together; but it could also take him farther away, where I can't follow. If he's beaten, yes, I'm there to pick him up and dust him down and love him. But if he wins, then he's a million miles away once more. Can you understand that?"

It's a silly question. Why else are you there, if not to understand, and never say the unsayable: that Julie Gerard married a heaven-blest man; that she wasn't content but must go on itching and scratching to know how he would fare in hell with the rest of us. But you can't say that in the Fleur de Lys. You can't tell her that if she'd married you, she'd be tamed and happy with a tumbling brood at her skirts, and she wouldn't miss the Cezanne in the drawing room, and the Hieronymus Bosch over the lintel in the banquet hall. So you smile and nod, and wonder what will happen when George Harlequin comes home with blood on his hands and dust in his poet's mouth.

Outside, the air was heavy and thunderous. The New Yorkers were still making their noisy, resentful pilgrimage to Nowhere. Their resentment was written on their closed, cautious faces. Their conviction was as clear as if they carried it on banners: Manhattan was a mess. It couldn't get better. It could only get worse. It was a crazy town—money-hungry, man-hungry, woman-hungry. It snarled at you every minute of every hour and if you didn't snarl back, it would gobble you up, body, soul and breeches. Still, there was a challenge to it. If you could beat this town, you could walk tall as a king anywhere else. But you had to beat it all day and every day. If you couldn't, if you felt yourself weakening or waiting for a smile, you should hang on to your marbles, head back to the open range and stay there.

It was no great exercise in logic to conclude that finally you had to lose. Age crept up on you, and the young braves eager to blood themselves. Money became a mad monster, chewing its own tail, eating itself to extinction. Property was a thing you pledged to get credit to buy more property to pledge against another purchase, to capitalize in the end against the long chance that there might be a small pocket in the winding sheet. We were all damned to the treadmill round: a little waking, a little sleeping, a purging by terror and pity, some loving, much loneliness, and two lustrations a day to make us feel clean even if we weren't. Afterwards, came the season when we wondered whether we were not just killing time until time killed us.

Harlequin's luncheon with Herbert Bachmann had produced very modest hopes. Money could be raised to enable him to meet the shortfall and buy out the minority shareholders; but, even at prime rates, the interest bill would be enormous and the profits of the bank would be cut to the bone for a long period. More grievous would be the probable loss of a large slice of underwriting business, which is always based on the promise that if the issue cannot be sold to the market, the underwriter will pick up the residue himself. There would be other damage, too. Investors tend to fight shy of a banker who has to borrow money in the street to keep himself afloat.

Basil Yanko had calculated to a nicety. The premium was high enough to attract the greedy seller and frighten the prudent buyer. There was not enough smell to make a scandal; there was just enough to send new clients to the shop around the corner. George Harlequin could sell out rich, or fight himself bone-poor to a sterile victory. Harlequin saw it as clearly, defined it more precisely, than I; but he also saw a hope, albeit a slim one, of improving his position.

". . . So far, Paul, we've assumed the worst— that every minority holder will want to sell. We've based all our figures on that assumption. Now, I hold first option to buy; so, I propose to contact each shareholder with my offer and my recommendation not to sell at all, to anyone. I want to have face to face meetings wherever possible so that I don't have to put too much in writing. I'm working on that program now. I'll need your help, of course. I've called Suzanne from Geneva. Between the three of us, we should be able to cover the territory in the time. As soon as I've assembled the lists and classified them, we'll set down a plan of operation."

"But you're still determined to reject Yanko's offer out of hand?"

"Absolutely. I find myself insulted by this man, and by all his tactics. Why are you so dubious, Paul?"

"Because, until the investigation is completed, and Bogdanovich gives us some hard information, we have no cards to play. Yanko repeats his offer. You say, no, no, no; and that's the end of the discussion. It leaves us worse off than we are now. Yanko's malicious. You back him against a wall, he'll jump at you like a fighting rat."

"Paul, you have to trust me."

"So be it, George. I've said my piece. I'll call you in the morning and see you here at three tomorrow."

"What's your program now?"

"I'm going to the Club for a steam bath. Then, I'm going to call Mandy Ducaine, find out where the action is tonight and go there. I'm getting thick-headed, George. I need a break."

"Until tomorrow then. Give Mandy my love."

I was angry when I left him. I felt he had shut me out; that my counsels were of no importance to him any more. I missed the old urbanity, the old subtlety, the comic sense of proportion. Now, he was curt and inflexible, another huckster in a harsh hucksters' town. I wished, fervently, that I could dispense myself from the burdens of friendship and go back to the pleasant, if pointless, routines of bachelor life.

After an hour's workout, I felt less dyspeptic and better disposed toward mankind. I called Mandy, who is a cheerful widow with a heart as big as her fortune and whose only fear is a blank date in her social calendar. She was going to the Opera; but, if I cared to drop by for supper, there would be Harold and Louise and Monty and this new Brazilian coloratura and, oh, a dozen others. I told her I would try to make it; but if I couldn't, love and kisses until next time. Which left me with an open card for dinner and the conviction that I was getting too old for the mating dance of the butterflies; so I went down to the billiard-room and won ten dollars from Jack Winters, who has never done anything harder in his life than prune roses and avoid getting married. He scared me. He always did. I could see myself, ten, fifteen years ahead, the first to come, the last to go, pathetically eager for a rubber of bridge or a gossip round the bar.

As I walked home through the first neon twilight and the last ant-scurry of the city, I was oppressed by a terrible sense of loneliness, a panic fear of violence and disaster. The ground of law on which I had trodden so securely for years, was cracking under my feet like river-ice in a sudden thaw. I was involved in theft, conspiracy and murder. I had made contracts for terror—precisely because I was trapped in an apparatus beyond the reach of law, an apparatus which corrupted the law into impotence and subservience.

The machine said, "Yellow alert"; the great powers began to mobilize for war. The machine spewed out an astronomical calculation; a currency was devalued. Even God would forgive you your sins; but the machine would shame you with them until crack of doom—and that, too, it would produce on time . . . So the great illusion was fostered: that man should claim no responsibility because he could exercise none; that he should be submissive because his fate was already determined and imprinted; and only the machine could control the cosmic currents. What nobody said, because everyone was sedulous to hide it, was that the machines were fed by human mechanics, as evil, as good, as wise, as stupid, as the rest of us—and the machine only multiplied their errors into a mad mathematic, beyond which there was no appeal . . . Unless, of course, you attacked the machine with hatchets and bombs and rockets and a mortal contempt; which was the whole nature of modern terror, the nature of the communal despair it produced.

I caught a glimpse of myself reflected in a shop window. I saw a middle-aged man, grim and hostile, closed against all human contact. I turned away, hurrying and thrusting through the crowds in a vain effort to shake off the doppelganger.

When I arrived home, all the miseries of the day were capped by domestic tribulation. Takeshi was having one of his bad days. Now, I have to explain that Takeshi in good humor is a paragon to be prized above wine, women and emeralds. He cooks better than Escoffier. He can iron a shirt so that it feels like a second skin. He dusts, waxes, polishes, as if he

were custodian of the Imperial treasure. On the other
hand, Takeshi in bad temper is an intolerable nuisance. He shuffles about like a geriatric case. He
scowls like a temple demon. He sniffs and moans and
whimpers in a symphony of dolours. When he deigns
to open his mouth, he is either doltish or contuma-
cious. The only remedy I have yet discovered is to
shunt him out of the house, and let him purge himself with sake, poker, and a visit to the mama-san
who runs a roadhouse for Japanese gentlemen on
West Fifty-eighth.

The moment I stepped inside the door, I recognized the signs. I had him out of the place in five minutes' flat. Half an hour later, bathed, shaved and at
least part-human, I was curled up on the divan, with
a drink at my elbow, listening to Von Karajan con-
duct the Pathétique. The package had arrived from
Francis Xavier Mendoza, but I left it unopened. I
had been trotting long enough at the chariot wheels
of the moguls. I was entitled to a little quiet living on
my own account.

I thumbed through a yachting magazine and in-
dulged myself in fantasies of a long cruise under sail,
Europe to the Caribbean, through the Panama, on to
the Galapagos, across to Papeete, Tonga and the Fiji
Islands. I could do it. I ought to do it instead of scrab-
bling in the muck of the marketplace. I could take a
year off, two if I wanted. Crew was no problem.
There was a wide choice of pleasant company. Jenny
Latham was free and eager . . . Paulette, maybe . . .
But why tie myself down? Why not come new to
every landfall, out of the long swing of the ocean into
the landlocked calm . . . I woke to the insistent

buzzing of the doorbell and stumbled out, resentfully, to answer it.

George Harlequin was standing on the mat, smiling a rueful apology. "I've been strolling for an hour. I took a chance on finding you home. If you hadn't been, I'd have left a note."

"Come in, for God's sake! You don't stroll at night in this town!"

"I know. But I had to think. We quarrelled today, Paul. It shouldn't have happened. I'm sorry."

"Forget it, George. It was a bad time for both of us. Coffee?"

"Yes, please. You didn't go out?"

"Mandy's at the Opera. She suggested supper, but I couldn't face it. Takeshi's got the megrims. Where's Julie?"

"Waiting up for Suzanne. She's coming in on a late flight."

"Have you told Julie what happened?"

"Yes." He gave me that boyish, mischief-grin. "She wondered why you hadn't said anything at lunch. I think she's forgiven you by now."

"I hope so . . . Look, there's a package in the lounge. It's a dossier on Basil Yanko. Mendoza sent it from California. Why don't you open it and glance through it while I make the coffee?"

I bumbled about the kitchen for ten minutes, glad that he had come, troubled that I had not told him of my talk with Bogdanovich. It was not fear that had held me back. It was pique and jealousy, the petty triumph of owning a piece of information that was, for the moment, denied to him. It wasn't easy to explain; but, shamed by the grace of his apology,

I had to do it. He was shocked by the details of Valerie Hallstrom's death, but he refused to let me humble myself.

"No, Paul! I've let you carry too much for too long. You've taken the risks. I've played critic and judge. From now on, we work together. No secrets, no disputes. Agreed?"

"Yes."

"I had some bad news this evening. Larry Oliver came to see me. He's been offered another job. He tendered his resignation."

"When does he want to go?"

"At the end of the month. He has three months' long service leave, which covers the notice period."

"Oh, hell! That hurts us, George."

"I've asked Standish to move up. He's happy, of course."

"He's a lightweight; but he'll have to do."

"One thing bothers me, Paul. At law we stand in a weak position. First, there's a prima facie case against me, as president. By putting in Lichtman Wells, we're buying time for me to answer it: but any client who deems himself aggrieved could file a complaint at any moment, in any jurisdiction where we operate. Oliver knows that and he doesn't want any dirt on his lily-white hands. I can't really blame him. Then we're employing Bogdanovich, who operates outside the legal framework and is in effect an illegal agent of a foreign power. You, Paul, are now in the position of withholding evidence in a murder investigation. As if that weren't enough, Basil Yanko telephoned. He had a problem, he said, a problem of professional ethics . . ."

"Signs and wonders! Professional ethics!"

"That's what he said. He pointed out that Miss Valerie Hallstrom had access to highly classified information related to National Security. He had been forced, therefore, to call in the FBI. Inevitably, they would require and could demand access to any and all records, including those of Harlequin et Cie. He hoped I would not interpret this as a hostile move on his part or as an attempt to exert pressure in our negotiations. The matter was out of his hands . . . Now, you can see why I needed a walk."

I saw more than that: I saw banner headlines and a shuddering market, and whole divisions of clients moving out as if it were the retreat from Mons. And there, in the foreground, was George Harlequin, his coffee cup steady in his hand, placid as a Zen master who has just proposed an insoluble riddle.

I tried, haltingly, to talk my way to an answer. "Let's talk about legalities first. You and I are both foreign nationals. There is no evidence that you have committed any crime in New York. There is evidence that your signature was used to collect the proceeds of crime in Switzerland . . . I have only hearsay evidence of a murder. Nobody knows that I have it except you and Bogdanovich. Nobody knows we've hired Bogdanovich except Saul Wells, who cooperates with him. Even if they did, it would be hard to charge any criminal intent on our part. We are free to hire a garbage collector if we choose, provided we don't conspire with him to commit a felony. The FBI is a different colored animal. They have access to our transactions, legal or otherwise, in this jurisdiction, if they deem national security is involved. Inevitably they'll pay us a visit. What do we tell them?"

"The truth, Paul. We are investigating an international fraud. I am involved, albeit innocently. A one-time employee, Ella Deane, has died in an accident and has left a suspicious amount of money. I believe we can add that we are reluctant to accept the report that absolves Creative Systems by a single statement that their employees have been screened and rescreened."

"Are we wise to open that question?"

"I think so. We make no accusations. We express reasonable doubt. We can go even farther. We can point to the coincidence of Basil Yanko's bid to take us over."

"That tips our hand, George."

"Innocent or guilty, Yanko will be worried. The FBI will be worried, too—because Valerie Hallstrom had access to secrets and died violently."

"Once that can of beans is opened, our activities could be restricted."

"Why, Paul? We're very legal people."

"Bogdanovich has to know, before we say anything."

"I agree. Why not call him now?"

"I have to use a pay-phone."

"It's still early. Why don't you get dressed and take me down to Gully Gordon's? You can phone on the way and, if Bogdanovich is free, we can meet him tonight."

"What about Mendoza's report?"

"I'll take it with me and study it. When I'm not

using it, I'll keep it in safe-deposit. It's not the sort of thing to leave lying around. Especially now . . ."

I couldn't resist a grin and a small pinprick of irony. "You're learning fast, George!"

To my surprise, he took me quite seriously. "No . . . I've always known, Paul. It was my private vanity that I could sidestep the rogues and the tricksters, insulate myself against malice by urbanity, shut out violence by a wall of money and privilege. Out there tonight, walking the streets, I saw that it was an illusion. Evil is real. It stalks you. It lies in ambush. It invades your own house. Sooner or later, you have to face it, grapple with it, hand to hand. For me, that time is now. I'm glad we're friends again . . ."

We had two drinks and half an hour of music at Gully Gordon's. When we left, we were met outside by a chauffeured limousine. Aaron Bogdanovich was in the back seat. We cruised downtown to Washington Square, and then uptown again, slowly, while Bogdanovich absorbed our news and gave us his own briefing.

"I agree with you, Mr. Harlequin. You don't play games with the FBI. You give them all the information they could deduce from your records. I don't think it hurts to voice a certain uneasiness about the operations of Creative Systems. You can take it from me the FBI are uneasy too. But, remember, you're foreigners; you don't understand American attitudes and procedures. That helps when you're dealing with Government agencies . . . The one thing you don't mention is your connection with me. Oh, they know I exist! Administration policy favors Israel. So long as I don't rub their noses in what I do and pass on a good tip from time to time, they leave me alone. But private practice, they won't buy. I don't have much news for you yet. We traced the taxi. The driver admits picking up our passenger. He drove him to the TWA terminal at Kennedy. After that, of course, nothing. He could have taken a TWA flight. He could have doubled back to town or crossed to another terminal. No way to know. However, we're combing the contract market . . . We're working also on Yanko's personal staff—his chauffeur, his housekeeper, the maid and his private secretary. The police are looking into Miss Hallstrom's private life. A friend of mine will pull the file for me at a convenient moment. It all takes time if we're to do it properly. Oh, one thing, Mr. Desmond. The fellow in the green Corvette, who was watching your apartment . . ."

"Bernie Koonig. What about him?"

"My boys picked him up for a little chat. He said he was hired by a friend to follow you and report on your movements."

"Who was the friend?"

"A man called Frank Lemnitz. He's Yanko's chauffeur."

"That's one break, at least. Can we use it?"

"I've thought about that. It's a risk; but maybe it's worth taking. Why not drop the name in Yanko's lap when you meet him?"

"Delighted."

"Let me do it," said George Harlequin eagerly. "It might be a bigger surprise. Don't they say in theater there should be two laughs in every joke?"

"Three," said Aaron Bogdanovich. "But you have to be sure the last one isn't on you."

We were late, but not too late, for supper at the Salvador. Suzanne was there and I swept her into my arms and held her a moment longer than usual, because Harlequin wouldn't and, like me, she needed more loving than she had. Her report from Geneva was not encouraging.

The Union Bank was cautious about its rights and precise about its legal position. The Harlequin account had been opened in proper form; all transactions on it had been formally correct; the monies had been paid out in cash against a verified signature. The bank's responsibility ended there. So long as this position was recognized, they would be happy to assist their honored colleague in any permissible fashion.

The Swiss police were slightly more helpful. They had examined the alleged forgery against a genuine signature. They admired the skill of the forger. They pointed out that cash money was difficult to trace, and could be exported legally from Switzerland. Harlequin's position was clear, if uncomfortable: the losses had been covered; unless and until formal complaint was made by a third party, no charges could be laid against him.

News from the trade was ominous. In good John Calvin's city, labor was sacred; money was its holy fruit; anything that tarnished the sanctity of money was anathema. George Harlequin was not excommunicated yet; he was not quite under formal censure. But already, inside the Swiss Bankers' Association, heads were wagging and the whisperers were busy. No clients had been lost as yet; but the flow of investment money had slackened considerably.

Suzanne told it all in that steady, prosaic style of hers, as if she were counting groceries instead of calamities. Juliette was furious, striking one name after another off her visiting list. Harlequin summed it up in a short valediction:

"One thing is clear. We can't just win and come limping home. We need banners and trumpets and our enemies trampled in the dust. It's too late for good rhetoric. Ten in the morning for a council of war . . . Sleep well, children. Golden dreams!"

It was a pleasant wish; but for me it carried no blessing at all. A moment after I had paid off the taxi outside my apartment, three men converged on me from the shadows. One of them said, "We've got a message for you from Bernie." Another slammed me with a cosh. I tried to fight back, but they were experts at the game. I woke in my own bed with my ribs strapped, a pain in the kidneys, a physician in attendance, and a pair of patrolmen waiting to take a statement.

4

The physician was encouraging. I had a cracked rib, extensive bruises, and a large bump on the skull. The rest of me, he thought, was intact; but if I suffered from nausea, painful breathing or blood in the urine, I should call him immediately. He gave me capsules and his card and a bill for the emergency house call, which, naturally, came rather higher than office consultation. He recommended a couple of days' complete rest and then departed to resume his own.

The patrolmen gave me a brisk resumé of the lost hours. Takeshi, returning from his night on the town, had found me huddled and unconscious in the doorway. He had called the police and the doctor, and, between them, they had cleaned me up and put me to bed. Now, if I felt well enough, could I please fill in some details? I felt as though I had just been run over by a tank, but I tried to oblige them.

They pounced immediately on the name Bernie. Did I know anyone by that name? No. Did Bernie Koonig mean anything then? No. Should it? Well, the previous night, they had braced a man by that name just opposite the apartment. Any connection? None at all. Perhaps I had been mistaken for someone else? Probably. I was a constant visitor to New York but I didn't move in criminal circles, as my dozens of respectable friends could testify. Would I recognize my assailants? I doubted it. Everything happened so fast. Yes, it usually did. Would I like to check my pocket book? I checked it. Nothing missing. Well, they'd file a report. If I remembered anything else, I should phone the desk sergeant at the Precinct. Now, Mr. Desmond, get some sleep; that was quite a *schlamming!*

Takeshi saw them out, fed me whiskey to help the painkillers, put the telephone by my bed, made solicitous noises and left me, like Job on his dunghill, alone with my miseries. I drowsed fitfully till seven in the morning and then struggled out of bed to check the damage. I wasn't a pretty sight. My face was bruised and puffy. The bump on my head was the size of an egg. My knuckles were skinned, and the strapping round my torso made me look like a roll of beef. There was an ache in every muscle; but, at least, I could breathe and there was no nausea and no blood. By the time I had sponged and shaved, I was convinced I would live, but doubtful whether it would be worth the bother. However, after a cup of coffee and a slice of toast, I decided to make the effort. I called Aaron Bogdanovich and told him the sorry saga of a *schmuck* called Paul Desmond. He said he would be with me in twenty minutes and hung up.

He arrived without flowers and offered no sympathy at all. "Hoodlum stuff! My boys worked over

Bernie Koonig. He blamed you and returned the compliment."

"Why blame me?"

"Who else is there? We don't advertise ourselves to gangsters, Mr. Desmond."

"I thought we were paying for protection round the clock."

"You are. My man was cruising behind your taxi. When he saw you dropped at your door, he drove past. It was a bad mistake. He will be disciplined for it. I'm sorry."

"We pay a half-million fee. I get a beating and you're sorry. Great!"

"I suggest you can make a profit on the deal, Mr. Desmond."

"How?"

"We decided yesterday to tell Yanko we knew Koonig and the man who hired him. Now we demonstrate. You're the victim of a felonious assault, which can be traced back to Yanko."

"But I told the police I didn't know Bernie Koonig."

"Yanko doesn't know that. All he knows is that you've withheld the information and that you're prepared to use it as a bargaining point."

"Which could set me up for something worse."

"It could. But you'll let it be known that there's a notarized statement ready to be sent to the police. I'd like to be there when you tell him."

"I think you must piss ice-water, Mr. Bogdanovich."

"Time was when it was blood, Mr. Desmond. That's when you really start worrying. I'd like to know how the meeting goes. Call me late tonight. I've got a busy day."

"The flower business, of course."

"No, Mr. Desmond. This time it's SAM missiles. There are three of them floating around in the hands of Black September terrorists. We know there are two in Europe. We think the other may be here in New York. If we don't find them, a lot of people may be blown out of the sky."

After that, of course, there was nothing to say. I dressed painfully, read the morning papers, and at ten o'clock presented myself at the Salvador, feeling rather like a clown who had missed the circus train. Juliette had already left to spend the day with friends; so I was spared the embarrassment of explaining my condition to her. To Harlequin and Suzanne, I told the whole story and how Bogdanovich had suggested we use it.

Harlequin frowned over it for a while and then agreed, brusquely. "So be it then! Let's see how strong Yanko's nerves are! Now, the morning's program. Sorry, it's three o'clock in Europe. Let's call all the people on your list. I'll talk to each one personally. Paul, you and I will draft a cable to all shareholders, and the letter which will confirm it. Then, let's frame two statements—one for Yanko and one for the financial press. The gist of each is that we refuse the offer, recommend non-acceptance by other shareholders and state reasons. Our attorneys will be here at one-thirty to go over the drafts."

It was slow work and frustrating. The lines to Europe were clogged with traffic. Of the fifteen people on Suzanne's list, only five were available to talk; and of these, three were inclined to sell and two were prepared to hold if Harlequin could show good reasons. This was the nub of the problem: we had reasons a-plenty, but we couldn't display them all without running foul of the libel laws. We could object to American control of a traditional European enterprise. We could debate the wisdom of committing a bank into the hands of a company that devised police and surveillance systems. We could demonstrate the octopus tactics of Yanko. But, without the strongest plea of truth and public benefit, and a whole body of evidence in support, we dared not call his personal character in question. It was the old saw: money makyth man; it makyth him purer than the angels—and if you want to prove him otherwise, you need at least as much money as he has.

We filled a wastebasket with false starts; but, by the time the attorneys arrived, we were sure we had produced a small masterpiece of understatement. The attorneys were horrified. What was pure reason in Geneva, was horrendous defamation in New York. In no wise could they permit us to issue it, or even commit it to correspondence. No, gentlemen, no! They would take the drafts back to the office and reconstruct them.

Harlequin deferred reluctantly, then begged them to pause an instant. "Gentlemen, will you look at Mr. Desmond?"

They looked. They made a small chorus of sympathy. I opened my shirt. The chorus died to a silence.

Harlequin continued. "Mr. Desmond was beaten last night. We can trace this crime back to Basil Yanko."

"How, Mr. Harlequin?"

"His chauffeur hired the man who ordered it done."

"You can prove that?"

"Yes."

"Can you prove that the chauffeur was acting under Yanko's orders?"

"We know it to be true. We cannot prove it at law."

"Then, you have no case, Mr. Harlequin."

"Exactly. The law is impotent. Mr. Desmond has no redress, except against a hireling. So, your advice, gentlemen. How do we get redress and protect Mr. Desmond or myself against further invasion? . . . I know the answer. You cannot compromise yourselves by recommending an illegal recourse. You go further. You urge me to preserve Yanko's reputation lest he sue me for defamation. I do that. He invades us deeper. When the law is impotent, gentlemen, how must justice be done? Think about that, please. And let me have the new documents before six this evening."

They went, dubious and unhappy, shocked by what seemed a pointless little tirade. Suzanne made no secret of her displeasure. "George, what in God's name did you expect them to say? They can't challenge the law. They're its servants. You know that. You've always known it."

His answer was vigorous and urgent. "No! That's not the issue, Suzy. The question has to be answered, because the dilemma is universal. The Palestinian can't go home because there's a kilobutz where his home used to be. The Jew can't surrender because he will be killed in a Syrian cellar. The Viet in the cage cannot speak because they give him urine to drink and quicklime to eat. The hungry in the barrios become outlaws because they cannot find work or feed their children; and their advocates swing on the parrot's perch in a torture chamber. My cause is nothing! Whatever happens, I will live and die rich and not deserve a franc of it. Even so, the law is impotent to defend my simplest right—the right to my own good name. That's the core of the argument. That's the point at which I become brother to the outlaw—outlaw myself, perhaps . . ."

I had never known him so passionate or so unrestrained in utterance. It was as if a spring had burst inside him and he could not hold it back. His challenge was not only to us, his cohorts, but to himself as well. Then he said a strange and disturbing thing:

"I'm looking down the muzzle now. I can see the bullet in the breech. I wonder how I'll feel when I'm the man with his finger on the trigger."

Basil Yanko arrived at twenty-five minutes after three—too late for indulgence, just late enough to suggest a deliberate snub. He apologized, of course, but in so offhanded a fashion that it underlined the insult. He hoped we could conclude with reasonable dispatch as he had an appointment in Pleasantville at six and he wanted to miss the crosstown traffic. His car was in the underground park. He would like his chauffeur called just before the end of the meeting. It was all calculated to set our teeth on edge and get the conference off to a nervous start. I was fuming, but Harlequin was unruffled.

It was only after we had settled ourselves at the table that Yanko made reference to my appearance. "What happened to your face, Mr. Desmond?"

"An accident. I've cracked a rib as well. The doctor tells me I'll live."

"You're insured, I hope."

"Yes, I'm insured."

"Well then, let's get down to business. I take it you've considered my offer, Mr. Harlequin?"

"Yes, Mr. Yanko, I have."

"You'll agree it's a generous one."

"Yes."

"Then I take it you accept?"

"No, Mr. Yanko, I refuse."

"Do you expect me to raise the offer?"

"On the contrary. I hope you'll withdraw it."

For an instant, a shadow of surprise passed over his face, then his thin lips twitched into a smile. "Now, why should I do that, Mr. Harlequin?"

"I think you may find it prudent to do so."

"That's not a threat is it, Mr. Harlequin?"

"It's a counsel, Mr. Yanko. At this point, a friendly one."

Basil Yanko leaned back in his chair, joined his hands fingertip to fingertip and raised them to his pale lips. His eyes filmed over. He seemed sunk in meditation. Then he smiled again and said, softly:

"Mr. Harlequin, I know what you are thinking. I am a gross man, devious and greedy, no fit colleague for a European gentleman like yourself. You will not sell your holdings to me. You think to raise enough money to take up your options and buy out the minority—even if the deal cripples you. If you do that, I have two choices. I raise the offer to a point that makes it impossible for you to bid against it. Or I slap you with suits, criminal and civil, in every jurisdiction where you operate: suits for loss and damages, charges of fraud, malversation, all the words in the book! I don't have to win the cases, Mr. Harlequin. The moment the complaints are on the docket, you are ruined. The bank faces a crisis of confidence. In the end I get it anyway . . . Now, let's be sensible, eh?"

It was the most arrogant display of naked power I had ever experienced. I was shamed, humiliated and angry enough for murder.

George Harlequin seemed quite unmoved. There was no tremor of hand or voice, no hint of passion in his answer. "I'm surprised, Mr. Yanko. It seems I have more respect for you than you have for yourself. You're a man of towering intelligence. I cannot understand how you could engage in so crude a tactic—unless, of course, it is a tactic of desperation."

Basil Yanko laughed. It was not a pleasant sound to hear, but a harsh and brutal mockery. "Desperation, hell! Harlequin, you're half a century out of date! This is business! Mid-seventies, American-style! I'm not a little Swiss gnome playing fiddle-fiddle in the Bankers' Club. I'm offering you a better deal than you'll get in any market in the world. You want to discuss it, fine! I'll listen. Turn it down and I grab for the cookie jar."

"Excuse me a moment." Harlequin stood up and walked to the door. "I need a glass of water."

Yanko turned to me. "For Christ's sake, Mr. Desmond! You're his friend. You know the name of the game. Talk sense to him."

"What with, Mr. Yanko? I own one nominee share. When I retire as director, I had it to the beneficial owner. It's your ball; you play it."

A moment later, Harlequin was back, dabbing at his lips with a handkerchief. He sat down, stretched his legs under the table and took up the thread of the discussion.

". . . Ah, yes! We were at the point where I refuse and you, as you put it, grab for the cookie jar. Before you grab, Mr. Yanko, before you take any precipitate action, let me list some facts for you. Item: I have in my possession a dossier on your life and business activities which has taken two years to prepare. Not all of it does you credit. Some of it makes you a highly undesirable colleague. Item: I am, as you know, a substantial shareholder in Creative Systems Incorporated and its affiliates. I have voting rights and certain rights of legal inquiry into the affairs of your companies. Item: Creative Systems depends as much on public confidence as Harlequin et Cie. It depends much more on political confidence to hold and execute large government contracts. Item: Political confidence would be gravely shaken if it could be shown that senior staff of Creative Systems, or even you yourself, Mr. Yanko, were connected with or engaged in criminal activities. Item: If I believed such evidence existed, it would be my duty as a shareholder, and as a reputable man of affairs, to request an inquiry by government agencies. Item: Such evidence exists, Mr. Yanko, and is at my disposal."

Basil Yanko shrugged and waved his hands in a gesture of contempt. "Then, do your duty, Mr. Harlequin. Use it."

"I fear you don't believe me, Mr. Yanko."

"Frankly, no."

"Then, let me demonstrate one small matter. Your chauffeur is waiting downstairs. My secretary has just called him, as you asked. His name is Frank Lemnitz. Acting on your instruction, he hired a known criminal named Bernie Koonig to keep watch on Mr. Desmond's apartment. He has admitted that to investigators retained by me. It was this same Bernie Koonig who had Mr. Desmond beaten up last night. We have notarized statements to this effect ready to file with the police . . . That's just the peak of the iceberg. There's a lot more of it under the water. You see why I advised prudence, Mr. Yanko?"

Give the devil his due, he took it better than I expected. He even managed a faint, frosty grin of approval. His first words were addressed to me:

"I'm sorry you were hurt, Mr. Desmond. That was none of my doing. I must apologize to you, too, Mr. Harlequin. It seems I sold you much too short."

"That's always dangerous in an uncertain market."

"It won't happen again, I promise. Your advice was to withdraw my offer, yes? Suppose I withdraw the threat and let the offer stand?"

"Then we are in a normal business relationship to which there is no objection in law or common practice."

"And on your side, Mr. Harlequin?"

"I should stipulate that as Creative Systems are

in fact under investigation by the FBI, and so long as our business relationship remains normal, no official action is required from me. The information at my disposal is, shall we say, an insurance policy."

"You wouldn't like to cash it in at surrender value?"

"No."

"I didn't think you would. Well, let's sum it up. I've offered, you've refused. You advise your shareholders to do the same. A pity we've come to a stalemate, but a lot can happen in sixty days . . . Good afternoon, gentlemen."

There was no time for postmortems. The cables to shareholders had to be put on the wire. Letters of confirmation had to be typed and mailed. The lawyers came, with a statement so weak and puling that Harlequin tossed it back with contempt; and we went to press with our own second draft. Julie came home in the midst of the brouhaha and demanded to be informed on the day's events. She also wanted to know why I looked like a battle casualty; which raised, in final and definitive form, the issue of how much she should be told.

Harlequin took the view that she should know everything. I claimed privilege, because I had put my head on the block and Aaron Bogdanovich would chop it off at the fall of a cambric handkerchief. Julie claimed, reasonably enough, that it was hard to sleep with a man if you couldn't talk to him; that if there were risks to share, she had to understand them; that if a secretary could be trusted, why not a wife? I urged the argument that chilled me quicker than any: the more you knew, the more vulnerable you were;

and I had scars to prove we weren't playing a pat-a-cake. To which Julie, with rare restraint, replied that we were a small group of friends standing against a hostile world. If confidence were not shared, the group could not hold together. I capitulated then and Harlequin told her the whole story. She was shocked to see how deeply we were committed, how close we stood to the jungle fringe. She was shamed by her own thoughtlessness, angry that we had left her so long in ignorance. She refused ever again to be protected and cosseted.

Harlequin was happier, then. He could reason openly in family conclave. He could admit his needs, instead of hiding them behind a mask of smile and politeness. Even the look of him was different. His talk was more vivid; his gestures less restrained. He was, in a way, simpler, albeit more singular, like a monk who had suddenly found the key to his own heart.

We dined on spaghetti and wine at Bertolo's. The spaghetti was Juliette's idea. She thought—save the mark!—that it would make easier chewing for me than beefsteak. We called for old and sentimental songs from the accordion player. We held hands and sang. We drank death and damnation to the ungodly, while Harlequin intoned curses in as many tongues as he could remember, lest Basil Yanko slip through unscathed. We were like people in the plague-time, huddled round the fire and the bottle, chanting to chase the evil away from our doorstep. But the evil was there and we all knew it: the infection of violence and terror. The moment we stepped outside the charmed circle, we would fall prey to it again.

As we walked back, arm in arm, to the Salvador, the strains of the day caught up with me and I felt suddenly weak and nauseated. I rested a while in Harlequin's suite, but felt no better. Suzanne announced that she would take me home in a taxi and stay the night in my apartment. I protested, but was firmly overruled. Half an hour later, I was propped up in bed and dosed with sedatives, while Suzanne and Takeshi made tea in the kitchen. It couldn't happen; I knew it wouldn't; but I wondered, drowsily, what it would be like to have a woman round the place every day.

In the morning, much too early, I had a surprise visit from Aaron Bogdanovich. Takeshi ushered him into my room, where he sat, perched on the end of the bed, with a cup of coffee in his hand, and put me to the question. "You didn't call me last night. Why?"

"I was sick. Harlequin's secretary brought me home. She's in the guest room."

"If I ask you to call, you will call. My system depends on orderly reporting. What happened yesterday?"

I told him, verse by verse.

He weighed and approved it. "Good! I wondered how Harlequin would perform. What happens next?"

"We wait on answers from shareholders. We put funds together in New York to buy out the waverers. What's your news?"

"We know who killed Valerie Hallstrom. His

name's Tony Tesoriero and he's in Miami. We'll be talking to him soon."

"How did you find him?"

"Wrong question, Mr. Desmond."

"Sorry. I'm not very bright at this hour."

"Saul Wells passed me the word on Ella Deane. She made three large cash deposits in November, December and January. During this period she was friendly with Frank Lemnitz."

"Time to talk to that gentleman, I should think."

"We tried last night. He didn't go home. He didn't report for work this morning."

"He was probably fired after Yanko's meeting with us."

"In fact, he left for London on the midnight special. Friends of mine will meet him there."

"Unless he goes hedgehopping round Europe."

"His ticket was economy one-way to London. Now, Mr. Desmond, how are your nerves?"

"Frayed. Why?"

"This morning, in your mailbox, you will find a plain manila envelope addressed to you. Inside, you will find Valerie Hallstrom's notebook and a printed slip which says, 'Compliments of Valerie Hallstrom.' You will immediately call Mr. Harlequin and your investigator, Saul Wells. Mr. Wells will call the police on your behalf. You will turn the book over to them. Mr. Harlequin will telephone Mr. Yanko and tell him the news."

"Then, all hell breaks loose. The police and the FBI move in on me."

"Right. And you tell them the truth. You found the book in the mailbox. They will both, inevitably, rehearse your brief association with Miss Hallstrom. During these rehearsals—but not too soon—you will remember the one thing you forgot to tell the police— Miss Hallstrom's fear of Basil Yanko."

"And how do I explain my bad memory?"

"Very simply—a remark like that could cast suspicion on an innocent man. Meantime, we'll be chatting to our friend, Tony Tesoriero, in Miami. Any information we get will be filtered to the FBI. That should keep everybody busy for a while."

"I'd hate ever to fall out with you, Mr. Bogdanovich."

"I'm sure you won't, Mr. Desmond. By the way, this secretary . . ."

"Is an old and dear friend."

"Good! It mightn't do any harm if she saw you opening the mail. Perhaps she could even collect it for you?"

"Takeshi does that."

"Better still. Well, good luck, Mr. Desmond . . . Oh, there's one thing. At our meeting, I would like to pick up a hundred thousand."

"I'll have it. When do I call?"

"This time, I'll call you. I may be out of town for a couple of days . . . Good luck!"

I had consented to madness and I knew it; but in a lunatic world, the mad were safer than the sane. They were accustomed to chaos. They expected monstrosity: bombs in the mailbag, poison in the water, headless children in the street, mass-murder by generals. They knew you were shot in airports, raped in elevators, tortured by professionals who were paid with public money. It was as normal for presidents to lie as for policemen to perjure themselves and telephone companies to sponsor revolutions.

In the context of mass insanity, Aaron Bogdanovich was the most reasonable of men. The cold mathematic by which he worked was the only system viable in a world of conflicting moralities and disreputable laws. If God didn't exist, or absented himself too long, then Aaron Bogdanovich and his ilk were the logical substitutes. Even in hell, you had to keep order; and terror was the most refined instrument to hand. You didn't have to use it too often, only to exhibit it by constant threat and occasional bloody example. The only recourse against it was a greater terror still. In the end, mankind had to surrender, if only to live peacefully in the clear light of a frozen wasteland. It was a nightmare logic; but once the premises were accepted, there was no escape from the conclusion.

Then Suzanne came in to see me, and, for a while at least, the nightmare was dissipated. She was calm and caring. We kissed and held hands and remembered, without regret, the passionate yesterdays.

When I asked, lightly, whether she would like to live them again, she smiled and shook her head. "No, chéri. Our hearts wouldn't be in it and we're not young enough to lie to each other. We both missed the train. We're standing on the station holding hands. That's the way I dreamed of us last night."

"I was glad you were here. Thanks, Suzy."

"For nothing. I was pleased to get away from the hotel. I smile when I see you making lover's quarrels with Juliette. I forget how I must betray myself every time George walks into the room. Under the same roof, it's intolerable . . ."

"You can move in here, if you like."

"Thanks, Paul, but no. If you want company, I'll come any time."

"Bless you, woman! Now get out of here and let me dress. There's a big day ahead of us. I'll tell you about it at breakfast."

Fortunately for our designs, Takeshi was a slave to ritual. When he laid the breakfast table, the toast was wrapped like a wedding gift, the butter was rolled, the juice was packed in crushed ice. The mail and the morning paper were brought after the bacon and eggs, and the second cup of coffee. Takeshi slit the envelopes and retrieved the foreign stamps for his nephew in San Francisco. He collected the household bills and paid them from his domestic account. I took the newspaper and my private letters into the lounge, where Takeshi served the third coffee in a fresh cup. After that, he went about his household chores.

The manila envelope was last in the pile of letters. Takeshi noted instantly that there was no stamp and no postmark. I pretended surprise. I weighed it in my hand, remarked that there was no return address and then handed it back to be opened. I made sure he read the enclosure slip and shared my amazement at receiving a missive from a dead woman. Then I asked him to get George Harlequin on the phone and to wait. I told him:

"George, something very odd has come up. It needs urgent action. Suzy and I will be over in about thirty minutes. No, better we don't discuss it on the phone. I think it's a matter for the police. We need Saul Wells there, too . . ."

Saul Wells talked a hundred words a minute, pacing the floor, puffing smoke, scattering ash and little confetti phrases of advice. "You're two foreign gentlemen. You pay me to know. So, when the fuzz comes, you let me talk . . . All you can tell is that the book dropped into your mailbox like pennies from heaven. Of course, you know what's in it. So do I. I've made photostats of each page. That's normal. I'm a security investigator, registered and licensed. I'm also a businessman looking for new accounts. So I contact the other companies noted in that book— highest level, strictest confidence, and with your permission, Mr. Harlequin. You've been taken. They could be taken, too. They're grateful. They're also scared. The minute I'm out the door, they telephone Basil Yanko. He's worried. Which is what we want him to be . . . Meantime, the fuzz have the book and the FBI get it, too. The fuzz are concerned with murder. The FBI are worried about national security, international fraud and a lot of big companies breathing down their necks. You, Mr. Desmond, get asked two awkward questions. Who could possibly have sent you the book—and why? They'll dress those questions up twenty different ways and keep coming back to them. The answer's still the same: You don't know."

"Then I'm lying."

"Did you see the book delivered?"

"No."

"Can you read minds?"

"No."

"So how are you lying? Don't get to feeling guilty, friend. That's fatal. You haven't killed anyone. You haven't stolen anything. You're a foreign banker who's hired local help and wants to conform strictly to the law . . . Now, Mr. Harlequin. You told Yanko you had a dossier on him. Get it copied now. If the Feds ask for the original, you'll have to turn it over—that's assuming Yanko has told them it exists."

"Would he be foolish enough for that?"

"Not foolish, Mr. Harlequin. Shrewd maybe. He handles sensitive contracts. He's been screened a hundred times. When you work for the government, you don't have to be clean—so long as you make honest confessions when they ask for them. You're shocked? My dear sir, if you hire a man to design a missile system, you buy his talents and bury his sins. So long as you've got them on file, you're both safe. Now, you're going to have some awkward questions, too. For instance, do you suspect Yanko of complicity in the frauds? Do you see any connection between the frauds and the death of Miss Hallstrom?"

"I am worried by the coincidence of his offer to buy me out."

"Good. That's the line. The fact that you've called in the Swiss police helps, too."

"There's one other point, Mr. Wells. I told Yanko my investigation had established a connection between Bernie Koonig and Frank Lemnitz. Mr. Desmond's injuries are still rather evident. The question is bound to come up."

"It's covered, Mr. Harlequin. You have a written contract with Lichtman Wells. Can you produce any contract with another investigator?"

"No."

"So relax."

"I feel, Mr. Wells, as if I were living on another planet."

"No, Mr. Harlequin," said Saul Wells, happily. "It's the same old earth. You just haven't been around enough. Now, take a deep breath. I'm going to call the fuzz. Then we'll take ten before you call Mr. Yanko. I can't wait to see his face when he arrives."

In the event, he was denied the pleasure. Mr. Basil Yanko was not available. He had left last night for Europe. His secretary could not tell us when he might return. The police were grateful, but vague. They listened in silence to Saul Wells' voluble explanations. They asked me to confirm them. They made notes. They examined the envelope, took possession of the notebook, signed a receipt for it, thanked us for our help and departed.

Saul Wells was puzzled and unhappy. ". . . We hand them dynamite and they treat it like a can of baked beans. Yanko's up to his neck in grief and he takes off for Europe. Something smells. I don't like it."

Harlequin refused to be perturbed. "This is theater, Mr. Wells. Silence is more frightening than speech. If we are meant to be dubious and fearful, we must not consent to it. The testimony we have offered so far proves itself at every point. Please, let's be calm."

Then the telephone rang. I answered it.

Karl Kruger was on the line from Hamburg. "Hullo, young Paul! How goes it?"

"We're fighting, Karl. And we're holding."

"There, maybe. Here, you're slipping fast. That's why I called. I've been asked to put together an underwriting group for a municipal bond issue in the Bundesrepublik. Not big, but important, you understand. I put Harlequin's name on the list. They struck it off."

"Any reasons?"

"Who gives reasons? You know the trade, Paul. How's the boy behaving?"

"Beautifully."

"I hear he's taking up options at a hundred a share. That makes him an idiot. Where is he?"

"He's here. Would you like to talk to him?"

"In a minute. There's a meeting in Frankfurt tomorrow. Yanko called it. Some of your shareholders will be there."

"Minority votes—and Harlequin has first option to buy. You have second. What can they do?"

"They can shout stinking fish and foul up the market; that's what. Harlequin should know. He should be there. Tell him that."

"Tell him yourself. I'll put him on the line . . . George, it's Karl Kruger."

He took the receiver from my hand and launched into a long and animated discussion in German, while Saul Wells led me into the anteroom and read me a plaintive lecture.

". . . Hear me, Mr. Desmond! I know this town. I know the police and the FBI and how they work. In the press, we've had half a column, then nothing. What did we get from the fuzz? Thank you for the information, routine questions, sweet damn-all! From now on watch your phones and don't talk in front of the help. I'll have a man in each day to check this apartment and yours for bugs. If you want to be private, walk in the park or go to the bookshop."

"Fine, Saul, we'll take your advice. But hell! We're not criminals!"

"No. But you're now in possession of very potent information. You don't know all the companies listed in that little book. I do. It's my business. At least five of them are high security outfits, working on defense projects. So you can be blood brother to the President; but you'll still get a bug on your phone. You're both aliens; and we're scared of aliens, Mr. Desmond. We'd rather protect a homegrown whore like Yanko than a pair of foreign virgins ... You don't know how easy it is to smear someone. Do you ever handle Iron Curtain trade? Have you ever been to China? Have you ever had any connection with agents of a foreign power? And how will you both print out from Yanko's data bank? It doesn't have to be fact, you know. It's opinion, too; but once it's on the card, it's gospel. Excuse me—but it only takes one word to turn the Virgin Mary into Mary Magdalene. Mr. Harlequin may not understand that; and ..."

"I understand, Mr. Wells." George Harlequin stood flushed and indignant in the doorway. "We are to be cowed into surrender."

"No offense, Mr. Harlequin. You pay me to deliver a true bill. I'm trying to do that."

"I know it, Mr. Wells. I prize it. I'm not angry with you; I'm affronted by this whole sordid affair— this meeting in Frankfurt, this subornation of colleagues. I'll be damned in hell before I play ghost-games with Basil Yanko. How many photostats do we have of Valerie Hallstrom's notebook?"

"You've got one. I've got three."

"Give me one more."

"What are you going to do?"

"Mr. Wells, I am a very reputable Swiss. I am going to pay a call on my Ambassador in Washington. I think we'll all go, Paul. The change will do us good. I have your number, Mr. Wells. I'll let you know where to contact me."

"One small word, Mr. Harlequin. Basil Yanko's got a lot of friends in Washington."

"I know. But we have a list of his enemies."

"Test 'em before you tell 'em the time of day. Washington's got a funny climate. Some people don't weather it very well. I wish you luck!"

He was hardly gone ten minutes when there was a call from the bell-captain: a gentleman wished to speak with Mr. Harlequin. Suzanne went down to meet him and inquire his business. A few minutes later, she presented him in person: Mr. Philip Lyndon of the Federal Bureau of Investigation. He was young, bronzed, beautifully turned out and, at the beginning, his manners were impeccable. He was delighted to find me there as well. It would save time and repetition. First, he would like to establish that this was a confidential discussion, on both sides. It had to do with Creative Systems Incorporated, with whom Harlequin et Cie had connections as underwriters, shareholders, bankers and clients. It was understood that Creative Systems were bidding for control of Harlequin et Cie. Mr. Harlequin was President and major shareholder, right? And Mr. Desmond here . . .

"You're not a Swiss, are you, Mr. Desmond?"

"No. Australian. I have a business visa, so you have my personal details on file."

"Yes, we do. What is your position with Harlequin et Cie?"

"I am a working director."

"He is also my most valued colleague and a longtime friend."

"Thank you, Mr. Harlequin. Now to save time: we are aware of your problems, Mr. Harlequin; that is to say, we have seen the report on your computer operations. We know that you have hired Lichtman Wells to investigate them. They may or may not come under our scrutiny in other connections."

"You may not be aware, Mr. Lyndon, that the Swiss police have been fully informed and are working on the case. The operator who was implicated in New York, Miss Ella Deane, is dead. Our legal advisers tell us that we have no further recourse in this jurisdiction—unless and until other information is forthcoming from our investigators."

"That's useful. Since you appointed them, I take it you were not satisfied with the report from Creative Systems?"

"I did not say that, Mr. Lyndon. The report conformed to the contract, which was to check the security system and point out any anomalies in the working of the program."

"Quite. But fraud was committed in all your branches, and so far you have identified only one operator."

"Investigators are still working in other branches."

"Are you satisfied that Creative Systems was not involved in the fraud?"

"It's difficult to answer that question without creating a false impression. There are two points to be made. First, the report exonerates all employees of Creative Systems, but offers no evidence in support. Second, there is the curious coincidence that a takeover bid was made as soon as the report was presented."

"That could, of course, be a piece of business opportunism not over-ethical, but at the same time not criminal."

"It could."

"I take it that you, Mr. Desmond, have acted in this matter as delegate of Mr. Harlequin?"

"Insofar as I have acted, yes."

"When, for example, you discussed the report with Miss Valerie Hallstrom?"

"Yes."

"And when you met her on two other occasions?"

"No. One meeting was accidental. The other was a social occasion."

"After which she was murdered. On that, of course, we have the police record. Mr. Desmond, did you ask Miss Hallstrom to amplify or comment on the security report?"

"Yes."

"Did she do so?"

"She explained its meaning. I invited her to draw conclusions from it. She refused on the grounds that she had no brief to do so."

"Did you press her?"

"No."

"Did you request or induce her to offer any information about Creative Systems?"

"No."

"Did she suggest that she might be prepared to offer it, under any conditions?"

"No."

"Why did you seek a social meeting with her?"

"I'm a bachelor. She is—was—an attractive woman."

"I think," said Harlequin, mildly, "it might save Mr. Lyndon some time if we inform him what happened this morning."

"Please, Mr. Harlequin."

"Well, this morning, Mr. Desmond found in his mailbox a manila envelope, unstamped, with no return address. The envelope contained a black notebook and a printed slip with the words, 'Compliments of Valerie Hallstrom.' The notebook contains the names of a number of companies, ours among them, and a list of their computer codes. Mr. Desmond called me. We met here with Mr. Wells and together we handed the notebook to the police. We assumed they would pass it on to the FBI. Your questions to Mr. Desmond indicate that, so far, they have not done so."

"Indeed not, Mr. Harlequin." Mr. Philip Lyndon was visibly shaken. "This—this is something quite new to me. You're quite sure about the contents of the book?"

"I am. If you'll excuse me, I'll get you the police receipt and a photostat of the entries. I suggested to

Mr. Wells that he should perhaps communicate with the companies named in case their security, too, has been breached . . ."

"I'm afraid that's very irregular."

"Irregular!" Harlequin stopped dead in his tracks. "How irregular, Mr. Lyndon?"

"Computer codes are confidential information."

"I thought they were, too, Mr. Lyndon. A mistake that cost my bank affairs fifteen million dollars . . . That's the receipt. That's the photostat."

"I'll have to keep this."

"No, Mr. Lyndon. It is my property in law. You ask, politely, whether I will permit you to keep it."

"I beg your pardon. May I keep it?"

"Yes, Mr. Lyndon, you may. But you will, of course, give me a receipt for it."

He leafed through the pages, frowning and making little clucking sounds of distress; then, he turned to me. "Mr. Desmond, can you tell me in detail how the notebook came into your possession?"

He wanted detail; he got it: my morning habits, Takeshi's rituals, his nephew's stamp collection, and for good measure, a repeat performance by Suzanne. Then he asked the big-money question:

"Who sent the book, Mr. Desmond?"

"I don't know."

"Why was it sent to you?"

"I don't know."

"But you must have thought about it."

"What's the time, Mr. Lyndon?"

"Just on midday, why?"

"The notebook came to my breakfast table four hours ago. Since then, I've been round and round the mulberry bush with Mr. Harlequin, with Saul Wells, with the police and now with you. I haven't had much time to think. Please, consider the facts. What could I do with the book? Sell it? Eat it? It's material evidence in a murder case. I couldn't get it out of my hands quick enough."

"You didn't buy it, by any chance?"

"From whom, Mr. Lyndon?"

"Miss Hallstrom, perhaps."

"Was she selling secrets?"

"The possibility is being discussed."

"Why would I buy them?"

"Perhaps to discredit Creative Systems. I read your press statement this morning, gentlemen. You're unwilling sellers, I believe; but the price is obviously very attractive to some shareholders."

"Is that a question or a statement?"

"Just a hypothesis, Mr. Desmond—to stimulate discussion."

"There will be no more discussion." George Harlequin's words were bleak and final. He got up, walked to the telephone, called the hotel operator and asked for a personal call to the Swiss Ambassador in Washington.

Mr. Philip Lyndon was a very good interrogator, but his nerve failed him at the last moment. "Please, Mr. Harlequin! I was out of line. I apologize."

"I'm very sorry, Mr. Lyndon." Harlequin was adamant. "The meeting is closed. You have heard the truth. If you do not recognize it, we cannot help you further. I find your innuendo offensive in the extreme. I have reason to believe it may be inspired. If so, it discredits you as a Government servant . . .

Hullo! Oh, Erich! George Harlequin from New York. A diplomatic matter of some importance. Best we use home-talk." He rattled on for five minutes in Switzerdeutsch and then put down the receiver. "Paul, we're going to Washington. I suggest you call your own Embassy while we're there. Now, Mr. Lyndon, let's be very clear. We are, and will be, happy to give you any facts at our disposal on matters touching your inquiry, which Mr. Yanko informed me has to do with high security matters. On the other hand, we will not submit to hectoring interrogation and we shall protect ourselves against it, if necessary, by diplomatic intervention."

"That is your right, Mr. Harlequin." Mr. Lyndon had recovered his manners and some of his courage. "Off the record, I don't blame you. You used the phrase, 'inspired innuendo.' You wouldn't like to amplify that, would you?"

"I'll define it for you, Mr. Lyndon. It's a form of murder. You stifle a man with cobwebs. Good day, sir."

I had never seen Harlequin so angry. He was white to the gills. His eyes were hard as pebbles. He stormed up and down the room, beating fist into his palm, pouring out a tumble of savage words, while Julie and Suzanne stood, shocked and silent, in the doorway.

" . . . I'm revolted. Karl Kruger tells me I should fly to Frankfurt . . . For what? To plead with men I have enriched . . . prove to them that I am not a villain or an idiot! . . . Now we're to be bullied by bureaucrats and agents, frightened like children by whispers in the dark . . . No! No! No! I will die in a ditch first . . . Julie, get us packed. We're going to Washington. Suzanne, make reservations for us all. We'll take the train. Get accommodation at . . ."

"Hold it a moment, George! I make the reservations. That's the arrangement with Bogdanovich."

"Then do it, Paul. Now! Suzy, get Herbert Bachmann on the phone. When you've done that . . ."

"George, please!" Julie planted herself in front of him and laid restraining hands on his shoulders. "You're the bully now. It doesn't become you, darling. Stop it!"

It was a long moment before he mastered himself and the effort was painful to see. When he spoke at last, his voice was harsh and strained. "If I'm offensive, I'm sorry. You wanted me to fight. I warned you that you mightn't like the man who lives in my skin. I have to live with him now. You have other choices."

Juliette stared at him, pale and stricken; then she burst into tears and ran from the room. Suzanne gave Harlequin a swift, reproachful look and hurried after her. I blazed at him:

"For Christ's sake, George! That was a brutal thing to say."

"Was it? In the end, she'll see it as a kindness. You, too, perhaps, Paul."

"Oh, go to hell!"

The Apex Travel Agency was not at all the sort of place where you would expect to book first class travel to anywhere, let alone luxury suites at Embassy Row. It was a fusty little store in the unredeemed area of Greenwich Village, with thumbtacked posters and dog-eared brochures, and a gypsy-faced receptionist dressed in sackcloth and beads. However, when I gave my name and mentioned that I was in the flower business, the place came suddenly to life. The gypsy looked ten years younger. Her smile was a promise of good fortune. Washington was a mess, but she was sure she could fix something: rail bookings would be delivered to the hotel within the hour; a limousine would meet us when we arrived.

The other arrangements took a little longer to explain. Our contact in Washington would be one Kurt Saperstein, also in the flower business, trading under the name, Bernard's Blooms. He had, it seemed, a big wire trade; so communications were no problem. As soon as we were settled, I should let him know the numbers of our rooms. There might also be a contact in Embassy Row itself; but Kurt would tell me about that in due course. He would be responsible for passing information to Aaron Bogdanovich. There was one small caution: Washington was a sensitive town; agents were thick as dandelions on the grass; security was tight; it paid to be extra careful. I crossed the gypsy's palm with credit cards and rode uptown to my apartment.

Takeshi was glad to see me. He, too, had been visited by Mr. Philip Lyndon, who had questioned him about the mail. He had heard of the assault; he wanted to know about that, too; but what appeared to interest him most of all were the names and descriptions of my recent visitors. He was angry because Takeshi had kept him standing on the mat instead of inviting him inside for a cozy talk.

That, of course, was his big mistake. Takeshi has a vast pride in his American citizenship and a very Japanese sensibility about face and dignity. When his sensibility is outraged, he finds it hard to understand simple English and even harder to speak it intelligibly. To remember names and faces becomes an absolute impossibility. So Mr. Lyndon had departed less happy and not much wiser. Since I was going away, it seemed wise to send Takeshi on a little vacation at company expense. His nephew must be pining for him. Takeshi agreed that he must be. He packed my bag and his own, and we left the apartment together.

The journey to Washington was a somber little pilgrimage. George sat at one end of the car dictating letters to Suzanne. I sat at the other, sipping bourbon and playing gin rummy with Juliette. She was calm, but pale and remote as a moon-woman. She played the game with professional concentration, discouraging any but the most trivial talk. I was glad to be dispensed from any part in what was now, all too clearly, a family crisis. I was still angry with Harlequin. I resented the presumption that made him treat me like some kind of retainer in his enterprises, a relief cavalier to his wife. I had pledged a fortune to help him. I had placed myself at personal risk. It was no part of the bargain that I should play whipping boy as well.

Besides, I was troubled by the sudden crack in his self-control. We were engaged in a complicated and dangerous strategy. We were still only skirmishing; and if his nerve failed him so soon, then we were in grave jeopardy. Even Suzanne, the tolerant, the judicious, was concerned. The smiling, humorous gallant, whom she had loved so long, was now tight-lipped and arrogant, no longer aware of the affection which was lavished on him.

Juliette reached across the table and laid a cool hand on mine: "Your play, Paul."

"I'm sorry. I was miles away."

"Had enough?"

"If you don't mind, yes."

"You look very grim."

"It's not exactly a summer picnic, girl."

"Paul, please don't blame George."

I stared at her, dumbfounded. This was another Julie, grave as a nun, passionless and a stranger.

She talked on quietly. "This is hard to understand; but I want you to try. It's hard for me, too. But today I've had to accept it. We've all, always, taken George at face value. He's so good at everything, we've never asked what made him good; I, least of all. You heard what I told him at the hospital: everything was a gift; he hadn't earned any of it. Well, it isn't true . . . When he does something, it has to be perfect; so perfect that it looks effortless and we forget he's made the effort. Riding, sailing, languages, everything has been the same. I've just begun to remember things. Long before he went to China, he would spend night after night practising the ideograms, chanting the sing-song speech, like an opera-singer doing scales. I've seen him on the lake, single-handed, in a high wind, strapped in a trapeze, doing circuit after circuit, in an over-sailed shell. When you see him at the gallops, you forget he knows the stud book by heart. For too long now, I've taken it all for granted; and, when I've struck at him, I've never seen how deep a wound I made . . . He's doing the same thing now; and it's terrible to see. But he did warn us. He said: 'I could be the greatest pirate of them all and smile when I wiped the blood off the cutlass.' He's practising for that, too. He's pushing us away, because the love we have for him is a handicap. He's hardening himself to be the very thing he was afraid of becoming. He told us the truth. We were just too blind to see it . . ."

It was the longest speech I had ever heard her make, and the saddest to hear. It was a confession of personal failure and a premonition of disaster more terrible by far than the loss of a moneyman's empire. It expressed a loneliness beyond our experience: the solitude of the exorcist who in casting out devils knows that he, himself, may be possessed.

". . . So, you see, Paul, you mustn't let him go. Whatever he says, whatever he does, you must hold him to you. You love him; but you haven't lost him yet. I love him, too; but he's far away from me now, and I don't know if I'll ever get him back. Maybe the baby will help in the end. I don't know. Perhaps even Suzanne . . . No, don't shake your head. I've always known she was in love with him. I've never understood why he didn't see it."

"He was in love with you, Julie. He is still."

"Paul, you don't understand!" She was desperate now. Her hand was a vice on my wrist. "He's rejecting love. He's trying to cut it out of himself; because he's stepped into this new world where there is no love at all, only greed and jealousy and terror. You're another kind of man, Paul, my dear. You wear life like an old suit—spots and all. George can't do that. He's never done it. It's heaven or hell for him, with nothing in between . . . I know you love me, Paul. I'm begging you. Stay with him!"

I was still searching for words to say when the conductor was at our side, announcing our imminent arrival at Union Station.

5

In Washington, I found that the gypsy woman had been kind to me. Harlequin and Juliette were located in a large suite on the fifth floor, where they could entertain a regiment if they wanted. For Suzanne and myself, there were two bedrooms with a shared lounge on the floor below. The geography was important. We were insulated from domestic friction. Suzanne had a place to work. We could be private or companionable, as the mood took us. There were chocolates and fruit from the management and, for me, an exotic arrangement from Bernard's Blooms. The note said, "Welcome to Washington. Greetings from Aaron." I had just finished unpacking, when the telephone rang with another greeting:

"Mr. Desmond? This is Arnold, deputy bell captain. I called to see if you had the flowers and the message."

"Thank you, yes."

"That was all, sir. We do a lot of business with Bernard. We like to keep his clients happy. If you need anything, don't hesitate to call me personally. Have a pleasant stay."

I hoped I would, but I was inclined to doubt it. A moment later, Suzanne came in, flushed and irritable. She was tired from the journey and Harlequin wanted all his correspondence typed and ready for signature before he left for the Embassy at ten in the morning. She didn't mind the work, but why did he have to be so distant about it. He'd never been like this before and it wasn't as if there were any need for it. I sat her down and fed her Scotch and sympathy. Then, casual as be-damned, she told me that Harlequin was preparing to dump on the market all the bank's holdings in Creative Systems and its affiliates. The only considerations holding him back were the interests of his clients and the fact that I, too, held a sizeable parcel of stock.

I was furious—because he hadn't discussed it with me, and because a share-dumping operation is about as moral as murder, and often more brutal. The principle is the same, though you need a lot of money and a lot of nerve to make the killing. If you sell large numbers of shares in a given enterprise, you depress the market value. If you keep selling, you create a panic among other shareholders, who rush to unload. The price goes down to bargain basement level. You buy again, and if your timing's right, and you have the cash to cover the deal, you can end up, if not with control, at least with a sizeable profit and possibly enough votes to get you a seat on the board. Which is fine for you, but can be ruinous for other people less fortunate, who see their life's savings wiped out overnight, or their loan limits slashed at the stroke of a bank manager's pen.

I could understand Harlequin's reasoning. The

bank had very large holdings in Creative Systems. Many of its clients had, too. Some of the clients had given the bank discretion over their investments; so that Harlequin could sell without reference to them. If all that stock were tossed back into the market, there would be a stampede of the Gadarene swine. Basil Yanko, himself, would be millions poorer; and to stop the rot, he would have to buy, and keep buying, until the market stabilized again. Add that to his other troubles—a Federal investigation, a list of suspicious clients, and his political problems in Washington—and you had a neat reversal of his threat to Harlequin: a crisis of confidence on a global scale.

I had seen it done before. I had heard it justified, with the cynicism of whore-mongers, as a normal market operation. I had also seen some of its consequences: a friend who jumped out of a tenth story window, another who lapsed quietly into fugue, and several notable bastards who lived rich as Midas ever after. The fact that Harlequin could even contemplate the tactic filled me with disgust and disillusion. I was ready to storm up to his suite and challenge him, but Suzy held me back.

"Please, Paul! If he knows I've told you, he'll never trust me again. Besides, I'm sure he wouldn't do it without consulting you. I know he talked to Hubert Bachmann and asked him to make some calculation about the effect on the market. He hasn't got them yet and he hasn't issued any instructions to the managers. It's a big operation. He'd love to prepare it."

"If he does it, Suzy, I'm finished. For always! I mean that. I don't know what's got into him."

She gave me a long, searching look and said flatly, "Is it any different from what you're doing, Paul—except you're doing it by proxy through Aaron Bogdanovich? Is it any different from what Basil Yanko is doing—except he's willing to raise the market instead of dropping it?"

"No, Suzy, it is different. Ours is a private fight. Yanko invaded us; we're fighting him with his own weapons. But if George does this, a lot of innocent bystanders get killed."

"If they play the market, they take that risk."

"It's plain piracy. George knows it."

Instantly, she was on fire with righteous wrath. "Why are you Simon Pure, while George is suddenly a monster? I'll tell you why! Because you want him up there, perched on a pedestal, like the protector of the faithful! He makes you feel good, even when you're not. He's something to be proud of and jealous of at the same time. You're like Julie. You don't want to believe he's a man. You want to look out the window and see him standing there, every day the same, sunshine and snow, with the pigeons perched on his head. He's like the bronze horseman on the Capitol. So long as he's there, Rome is safe. But George isn't bronze or marble. He's flesh and bones and hotter blood than you ever give him credit for. If he wants to fight, let him fight! Don't tie his hands. I don't want to see him made a mockery in that brigand's hole you call a market! I don't care whether he's right or wrong. I love him, don't you understand? I love him . . ."

Ay—Ay—Ay! Of all the dumb oxen in the world, I was the dumbest. Of all the lovers in the world, I surely was the blindest. I had held this woman in my arms night after night, month after month, and I had never found the talisman that would open the treasure cave of her loving. Well, I had it now; but for all the good it did me, I might as well toss it in to the Potomac. I poured us another brace of drinks and made the timeworn toast:

"Well, here's to crime! . . . I wonder how far he'll go?"

"How far will you go, Paul?"

"I guess, as far as my nerve will stretch."

"Or your conscience."

"Do you think I have one?"

"A confused one, yes."

"What's that supposed to mean?"

"It gets in the way—between you and George, between you and Julie . . . Now, don't be angry, chéri! You and I had a long time together. It was good; but it wasn't the best and we both know why. We both see what's wrong with that marriage. If it ended, you'd probably get Julie. I wouldn't get George. I'm just a piece of office furniture that he hardly sees any more and I'm too old for the mating game anyway. So I'd rather see him happy than miserable."

"I'd rather see them both happy. Julie talked to me on the train. She knows she's done a lot of silly things. She doesn't know how to undo them. I think you could help."

She gave me the old hard look that the sweetest of them get in the summer of their discontent. She shook her head and said coolly:

"No, Paul! I'm dear good Suzy; but I'm not as good as that. If you want to be Julie's white knight,

I'll clap and cheer and help you saddle your charger.
For the rest—No! No! No! . . . At least I'm an honest
bitch, chéri. Could you bear to take me to dinner?"

At eight in the morning, George Harlequin called
me. He was leaving at nine forty-five to make an
early call on his Ambassador. He would like me to
meet him for lunch. He hoped I was rested. I was.
Had I any news from New York? None; I would be
out and about during the morning; I would report to
him at twelve-thirty. Wasn't it a beautiful morning?
I hadn't seen it yet: but I was glad to know there
would be sunshine in our lives. Until later then . . .
And if that was all he wanted to tell me, to hell with
him!

Next door, Suzanne was tapping out letters with
the steady rhythm of a good Swiss machine. I poked
my head round the door to bid her good morning.
She gave me a vague salute and went on typing. I felt
like the last spear carrier in the pageant, draggle-
tailed and unloved; so I went down to the lobby hoping to make the acquaintance of Arnold, the deputy
bell captain. I found a confusion of departing guests,
all clamoring for bills and baggage service and taxis.
I walked out into the sunshine, took a taxi to the
Tidal Basin, leisurely as any provincial tourist, to
commune with old Thomas Jefferson in his shrine
among the cherry trees.

I will tell you a sentimental secret. This is one
place in America which I truly love. This is one man
in all her turbulent history who moves me to admiration and, all too rarely, to meditation. Scraps and

snippets of his wise and tolerant code sound longer in my memory than the strident voices of my own time. He hated "the morbid rage of debate." "If I could not get to heaven but with a party, I would not go there at all . . . Some men look at constitutions with sanctimonious reverence and deem them, like the ark of the covenant, too sacred to be touched . . ." I suppose that, younger and more open, I had seen in him what I had found—and lost—in George Harlequin: a largeness of mind, wit, humor and a soul hospitable to the whole experience of mankind.

Even so early, there were lovers and families on the lawns and I envied them. I was grateful that the shrine was empty, so that I could brood in the solitude of the past, which is like the solitude of the sea, cleansing and healing. The pity was that the past belonged only to those who lived it—and Jefferson knew that, too: ". . . I knew that age well; I belonged to it and labored with it. It deserved well of its country . . ." I, Paul Desmond, belonged to my age, and profited from it, and deserved well of nobody. I would go from this place to another, where they sold flowers and sent greetings by telegraph, and arranged for men to be shot when they opened the door for the message. Other times, other manners! Tom Jefferson was lucky he had not lived to see them; else he would have lost a great many noble illusions.

Mr. Kurt Saperstein of Bernard's Blooms bore no resemblance at all to Thomas Jefferson of Albemarle County. He was short, round and buttery. He had a bald pate surrounded by a hedge of black hair. He wore a suit of midnight blue and a butterfly tie and thick myopic spectacles. His chubby hand was damp,

his smile was wide as a cut in a watermelon. He
talked in a heavily accented rhythm as if he were in-
toning verse.

"My dear sir . . . ! Welcome, welcome! I do hope
you liked the flowers. One of our best efforts if I may
say so. One of our very best. Arnold called you? Delighted. A good man—very good. Now, sir, may I
suggest a stroll. It's a heavenly day . . ."

The moment he stepped into the street, he
changed completely. He walked briskly, talked quietly, and, in spite of his odd appearance, was inconspicuous as a lizard on a rock. I swear I would have
walked past him without a second glance. His briefing was brisk and laconic:

"Instructions first, Mr. Desmond. No further
contact between you and me. I've seen you. I know
you. Arnold brings me your messages. I say mine
with flowers. Most things you want, we can do: car
hire, reliable escorts, a bodyguard, if you need one.
We've got friends in most places: the Pentagon, National Security, the Embassies. We're good at documents, too; but remember they take time . . . I've got
some news for you. Aaron's traveling; but Tony
Tesoriero's nailed down tight in Miami. He can't spit
without hitting a shadow. The FBI have been talking
to Saul Wells. He's sure they'll be visiting you here.
Also he's made the calls he promised and the cat's
having a field day among the pigeons. He thought
your president might get a few calls from other worried presidents . . . That's all I've got so far. Is there
anything you need right now . . . ?"

"Do you know a good journalist who could leak
a story and forget where he got it?"

"Sure. This town's crawling with pressmen, good and bad. Let me think about it. When would you want to see him?"

"Tonight, if possible; but privately, away from the hotel."

"Leave it with me. Arnold will get word to you."

"I need a man who won't talk around afterwards."

The remark offended him. He took ten strides to recover from it. Then he reproved me, curtly:

"Have you ever been to Yad Vashem, Mr. Desmond?"

"I don't even know what it is."

"It's in Israel. A monument to six million dead. We never want to build another."

"I'm sorry."

"How could you know? How can anyone know who didn't smell the smoke of the holocausts? I must get back now to my beautiful flowers and my dear, dear customers . . . Strange people, Mr. Desmond! The rooftrees of the world are cracking round their heads and they don't hear a sound! . . . Shalom!"

I had still time to kill, so I wandered back to join the small crowd of idlers and tourists at the boundary of the White House, where the President lived, beleaguered, among the ruins of his own reputation and the hopes of a great people. I had no right to sit in judgment on him; I was an outlander, a free-booter from far away; but I could not escape the haunting reflection that this man, too, had sought to build an apparatus of terror. He had enlisted a shabby crew of informers, spies, blackmailers, thieves and perjurers and shielded them under the cope of power, which his own citizens had laid reverently on his shoulders on the day of his inauguration.

In the end, the apparatus had broken down; his minions had deserted him; but the terror was still abroad. If the President flouted the law, what writ could run and what contract would hold? If authority was in discredit, the centurions held the fort and the anarchs were in command in the street. If a man could not live private, and walk safe abroad and die, quiet, in God's good time, then the ruffian was king and his scavengers would lay waste the land with impunity . . . It was nearly noon. The taste of infamy was stale in my mouth. I turned away and walked briskly back to the hotel.

I needed to introduce myself to Arnold; but, as I stopped to collect my key, I was greeted by Mr. Philip Lyndon, late of New York, presently, it seemed, in the charge of a wet nurse, Mr. Milo Frohm, who looked more like a banker than most of our colleagues and talked like the Beloved Physician on a house call. Mr. Frohm hoped I could spare them a little time. I told him I was free until twelve-thirty, when I was bidden to lunch with Mr. Harlequin. Where would I like to chat? The bar? They would prefer somewhere more private. My suite, then? Yes, they would be grateful for that. As we rode up in the elevator, I told them of my morning visit to Thomas Jefferson, to whom I found Mr. Frohm was as dedicated as I was myself. I was delighted to have found a soul brother, who knew all about life, liberty and the pursuit of happiness and the moral foundations of the body politic.

Suzy was still working in the suite, but she agreed

to vacate in favor of the law. I asked her, pointedly, if Harlequin had returned from his meeting with the Ambassador. She rose to the cue and told me, no, he had expected a long conference. And, by the way, there was a note to call my own Embassy. She asked would we prefer coffee or a pre-lunch cocktail. Mr. Frohm and Mr. Lyndon opted for tomato juice. I decided on a bourbon and branch water. Mr. Frohm praised my taste for good southern tipple. Mr. Lyndon smiled and said nothing. After we had toasted each other, Mr. Frohm led for the Republic.

"First, Mr. Desmond, let me say that we do appreciate your frankness in a previous interview with Mr. Lyndon. We regret that the phrasing of certain questions caused unwitting offense to you and to your principal. In our job we deal with so many different people that certain lapses of tact are inevitable. I hope you understand?"

"I do, Mr. Frohm. Neither Mr. Harlequin nor myself has any hard feelings toward Mr. Lyndon; but as foreigners we are sometimes shocked by American methods. However . . . what can I do for you now?"

"More questions, I'm afraid, Mr. Desmond."

"May I ask one first?"

"Of course."

"Did you, Mr. Lyndon, check the answers I gave at our first interview?"

"Yes, Mr. Desmond."

"And you found them accurate?"

This time Mr. Frohm answered for him. "In all particulars, Mr. Desmond. However, there are some gaps in the narrative. We'd like to fill those, if we can.

Let's go back to your dinner with Valerie Hallstrom.
That was a purely social occasion?"

"Yes."

"Could you tell us what you talked about?"

"The usual banalities. I told her my life story. She
didn't tell me hers—except that her father bred saddle horses in Virginia and she wondered whether
seven-fifty a week really paid for the wear and tear
of New York."

"She did mention money, then?"

"Seven fifty a week—oh! and fringe benefits. Her
very words."

"Did you specify the wear and tear part of it?"

"In a way, I suppose she did."

"In what way, Mr. Desmond?"

"Well . . . First, she said that if her employer
knew she was dining with me, she'd lose her job and
never get another."

"Didn't that strike you as strange?"

"Very. I told her it was blackmail, tyranny and
enslavement."

"Why blackmail, Mr. Desmond?"

"She explained that she had once been in love
with her employer and it hadn't gone well. She called
him—let me see—a toad with a gold crown on his
head. She warned me that he could be a dangerous
man."

"Anything else?"

"Only one thing. When she got out of the car to
walk home, she said, 'God sometimes likes to know
how his children spend their evenings.' "

"Those are striking phrases."

"They are, aren't they?"

"Why then did you not record them in your first statement to the police and your second to Mr. Lyndon here?"

"I'll tell you why, Mr. Frohm. The police were investigating a murder. Those phrases were hearsay which, though inadmissible in evidence, might have thrown suspicion on an innocent man. The remark about God suggested that it was Basil Yanko who was waiting in her apartment. I don't like what he does in business, but I have no right to hint that he could be a murderer. You ask why I didn't mention it to Mr. Lyndon. That's easy. His last question—the one which broke us up—implied that we might have bought Valerie Hallstrom's notebook to discredit a business rival . . ."

It took Mr. Frohm a long time to test that one for taste and texture; but, finally, he seemed to accept it. "You make your point, Mr. Desmond. Now, let's talk about the notebook. We accept your account of how it came into your possession. In default of contrary evidence, we must accept that you do not know who sent it or why. However . . ." He paused to let the premonition weigh on me. "However, it is a fact that you—or your investigators, acting on your behalf—are, at this moment, making capital out of it."

"Capital in what sense, Mr. Frohm?"

"Mr. Saul Wells is disseminating its contents to interested parties. Already this morning five major companies have called us to report a breach in their security. I am sure there will be others. In the context of your relations with Creative Systems and with Basil Yanko, does that not suggest an effort to secure tactical advantage?"

"It represents an attempt, gratuitous and unsolicited, to save other reputable businesses from the fate which has befallen us."

"Would it not have been more proper to let Mr. Basil Yanko do that himself—or even to have requested us to do it?"

"We have reservations about the business ethics of Basil Yanko."

"Would you care to specify them?"

"At this time, no."

"The second question then, Mr. Desmond. Why not to us?"

"I am a visitor in your country, Mr. Frohm. I would rather not embarrass you."

"You cannot, Mr. Desmond. Please be as frank as you wish."

"To put it, then, as politely as I can: you are a domestic American agency, concerned with many issues, political and criminal. We are a European organization, whose interests might at certain points conflict with yours. Rather than invoke your aid, we thought it better to stand on our legal right of free communication. That is the view of my principal. It is also mine."

"In other words, you don't trust us, Mr. Desmond."

"On the evidence adduced in your own Committees and Courts, Mr. Frohm, you don't trust one another."

To my surprise, he smiled and nodded a reluctant approval. "I asked for that, didn't I? You're a good witness, Mr. Desmond."

"I've had a lot of practice. The Kempetai worked me over for a month in Singapore."

"I hope you find us more civilized than they were."

"I do."

"Thank you. Now, let's look at another gap in the record: you were assaulted outside your apartment. You told the police that you could not identify the assailants. Is that true?"

"It was true at the time. I have since been informed that they were hired by a man called Bernie Koonig, who, in turn, was hired by one Frank Lemnitz."

"Who informed you, Mr. Desmond?"

"Our investigators. I presume you have already discussed this matter with Mr. Saul Wells."

"We have, yes."

"Then you know as much as I do—possibly more."

"What do you know, Mr. Desmond?"

"By hearsay only, that Frank Lemnitz, who is chauffeur to Mr. Yanko, hired Bernie Koonig to keep me under surveillance; that our investigators remonstrated with Koonig—and that Koonig, in revenge, had me beaten up."

"Did you mention this to Mr. Yanko?"

"It was raised at our conference with him at the Salvador."

"What did he say?"

"That he was sorry I had been hurt and that he had nothing to do with the beating."

"But he did admit to having you watched?"

"Let's say he sidestepped the question."

"Why didn't you press it?"

"I didn't need to. He was informed that I reserved my right to file a complaint against the persons involved."

"But you haven't done that, why?"

"I prefer to reserve my reasons also."

"Mr. Desmond, why did Basil Yanko have you watched?"

"I don't know. In retrospect it would seem that he suspected a possible association with Valerie Hallstrom."

"And why would he suspect that?"

"Mr. Lyndon gave me the idea. He admitted that Valerie Hallstrom might have been peddling material from the data bank. That's true, is it not, Mr. Lyndon?"

Mr. Lyndon was embarrassed, but he faced up like a good cadet. "You could have interpreted my remark in that sense."

Mr. Frohm smiled faintly, then turned to me. "So, by extension, Basil Yanko thought you were a possible buyer."

"He might have."

"But you weren't?"

"I'm on record, Mr. Frohm. No offer was made; none was invited."

"Which brings us to the big hole in the wall, Mr. Desmond. Who sent you the notebook and why? Now, you're on record about that, too. But try this for size. Valerie Hallstrom tells you she's scared of Basil Yanko. She acts as if she knows there's someone waiting for her at her apartment. She gives you the notebook for safekeeping. You know it's hot property. You stage the little comedy of sending it to yourself, so that you can use the information quite legally . . . Well, Mr. Desmond?"

"Only one answer, Mr. Frohm. Nonsense! And talking of holes in the wall, you've missed the biggest one. Who killed Valerie Hallstrom and why?"

"We're working on that. The hole is narrowing. We know that two men entered her apartment on that night. One obviously was the killer. The other was the man who telephoned the police. Perhaps it was he who sent you the notebook . . . If you get any ideas, please let us know."

"I'll do that, Mr. Frohm. Another tomato juice?"

"No, thank you. We must go. You've been very helpful, Mr. Desmond . . . By the way, those are beautiful flowers. Where did you get them?"

"That, Mr. Frohm, is something even you shouldn't ask."

"Like that, eh! Usually it's the man who has to buy 'em. Perhaps women's lib means something after all. Come on, young Lyndon, we're off-duty now. I'll buy you a drink and a hamburger."

If that was a hint, I didn't take it. I closed them out and stood backed against the door jamb, sweating from every pore. Milo Frohm was no novice; he was an old hand at inquisitions, foxy and bright and never out of countenance. I needed no crystal ball to tell me I would be hearing from him again. I wasn't too worried about that. I found him an attractive character. We used the same dictionary and the same textbook of elementary logic. The problem was that the logic didn't work any more. I couldn't say how or why: but I felt in my marrow that our major premise was full of holes and our minor one sunk without trace. Which, of course, was not logic at all but sheer brute instinct.

Harlequin was late for lunch. At twelve forty-five I bought the girls a drink and hunted them off to the grill room. At one-fifteen, Harlequin rang and commanded me to take a taxi and meet him at a trattoria in Foggy Bottom. When I asked him why, he told me he had a yearning for *spaghetti alla carbonara* and *cervelli al burro*—which led me to believe that his own brains must be buttered. At one-forty by the clock, we sat down in a corner nook, in what must have been the dimmest and the least popular bistro in the District of Columbia. The spaghetti was overcooked, the wine was pure vinegar: but it didn't matter. From the moment Harlequin began to talk, all I could taste was dust and ashes.

". . . Before we left New York, I called Herbert Bachmann and asked him to advise me what would happen if we started dumping our stock in Creative Systems. He called me at seven this morning. Every broker in town has a list of buying orders as long as your arm—big orders, Paul—better than ten million on Herbert's count."

I couldn't resist it. I told him, bluntly, what I thought about stock dumping and about him for even considering it. He heard me out in silence, then went on, unruffled:

". . . That backlog of orders is significant. I'll show you why in a moment. This morning I spent three hours at the Embassy. Erich Reiman is an old friend of mine. He was sympathetic, but, at first, not very helpful. It was only when I showed him the photostats of the notebook that his attitude changed—completely, Paul, volte-face! He wanted to know everything . . ."

"I hope to God you didn't tell him!"

"Not quite everything; but more than you'd approve."

"Oh, Christ!"   .

"I traded with him, Paul—I had to—point for point."

"You were trading with my life, George."

"I knew it. Now Erich knows it."

"And like a good diplomat, he'll forget it the moment it suits his purpose. I'm not even a Swiss. I'm an expendable nobody from down under . . . Now, tell me about the thirty pieces of silver."

That thrust, at least, went home. The stem of the wineglass snapped in his fingers and the liquor spilled like blood on the white napery. An instant later, he was hammering me with hard and stringent words:

". . . You will hear me first, Paul, and judge me afterwards! Then, if you want to go, you go. What I heard this morning makes nonsense of all our reasoning. We are pawns in a global game that I, for one, had not begun to understand. It was explained to me this morning by a friend—not as close as you, but still, a friend—and I believe him; because he is paid to know and he sits here, where, of all places in the world, the knowing is possible . . . Waiter!" He snapped his fingers, imperiously, and the waiter came running. "Please clean up this mess and bring me another glass."

I expected the waiter to spit in his eye, and I might have been glad to see it. Instead, he went running for fresh napkins and laid them, one on the other, until the stain was hidden. He brought a new glass and a fresh carafe of wine and poured it more reverently than it deserved. He must have been fresh from the old country, because he bowed and apologized before he withdrew. Harlequin drank the wine at a gulp and dabbed the lees from his lips. He was calmer now; but no less urgent:

"This year we have seen—and most of us do not believe it—the end of a millennium. It ended where it began, in the Mediterranean basin . . . Oh, no! This isn't a political lecture. This is hard fact. The desert princes found that they could stop the world by turning off the oil taps. The outcasts from the Fertile Crescent found that they could terrorize the world with hand guns, and grenades, and plastic explosives. It's true! You know it! Every airport in the world is an armed camp. You need a body search before you can visit your dying mother! . . . the other thing—this fabulous beast they call 'the energy crisis.' What does it mean? It means that if British miners stop working, the nation freezes to death. It means that unless Japan bows in vassalage to the sheikdoms, her industry stops dead and there is horror in the streets of a hundred cities. In Africa and the South Americas, progress, slow and painful as it has been, ceases for a decade or more. Then what? Those who have learned the lessons of terror are ready to spread panic and confusion. Those who have power, will try to put the whirlwind back in the bottle—and that will be another kind of terror. The private armies of security men will become the block-fuehrers and the *forces de frappe* of tomorrow . . . You know what they have named next year in the intelligence calendar? The year of the assassins! So now, Paul, my friend, where do we stand—you and I and Harlequin et Cie, Merchant Bankers?"

I didn't know: so I couldn't tell him. His eloquence had silenced my vulgar tongue. He had stormed down my defenses by sheer passion and conviction. I could do nothing but shrug and say:

"Tell me. I'm listening."

"The price of oil has doubled and tripled. What happens to the money? The desert princes are not fools. They have seen that money is a madman's dream—a nightmare of paper. What will they want when their armories are filled and their military highways built and their airfields stacked with fighters? Industry of their own? Technology of their own? Some, yes. But industry breeds a proletariat and spawns a force of migrant workers, who will quickly learn the techniques of terror. So the princes want insurance—a stake in Europe, a stake in America. Not just stocks and bonds—more paper!—but control! Evidence? The Saudis cut off oil from the Dutch. Now they are negotiating to build a Saudi refinery on Dutch soil. What is being discussed in secret has even wider meanings. The Italians are offering a quarter share of their national oil company in return for guaranteed supplies of crude. You can make all the laws you like to exclude foreign control of domestic enterprise, but laws are paper dragons danced through the streets by venal and invisible men. Which brings us at one stride to Basil Yanko . . . He knows, Paul!

He sees! He has the world locked up in his data banks. He will buy me at a premium and sell me for double to the Arabs, using their money. He will sell part of himself, too. Herbert Bachmann identified some of those buying orders. They come by winding roads from the Middle East. Yanko goes farther. He can balance himself between the assassins and the princes, because there are bids from Libya, too, in every market . . . My friend, Erich, showed me the pattern; the details write themselves. Karl Kruger, for instance. How is he so intimate with the Israelis? Banking is not the half of it; sentiment is a tiny part. Hamburg lives on ships. Ships live on cargo. A depressed Europe means a dying Hamburg. The Israelis are the last output of Europe in the Levant. They make no secret of their intent to meet terror with terror. Why was Aaron Bogdanovich so ready to help us? For friendship? No! Our money funds him. He claims to work for us; but we also are working for him." A ghost of a smile twitched at the corners of his mouth. "It's a sordid world, Paul; the only stable currency is the politic lie. If that makes you feel foolish, remember you're not the only one. I felt a fool, too, because the FBI had been in touch with Erich Reiman, long before I got to him. They wondered how much I knew. He convinced them it was very little; but even he was shocked at how little. Do you know what he said to me? 'George, you're in the wrong theater. This isn't Commedia dell'Arte. It's high drama. You haven't much time to learn the script.' "

"Why go on reading other people's lines? Let's get a new book for ourselves."

"And how do you suggest we do that, Paul?"

"Let the Press write it for us."

It took half an hour of argument to convince him; but in the end he consented. We might be digging our own graves; but, at least, we'd have a very gaudy funeral.

Back at the hotel, I had my first meeting with Arnold, the deputy bell captain. He was tall, melancholy and horse-faced, like a deadpan comic from the silent movies. He had two messages for me. The first was an invitation to cocktails at seven at an address in Arlington. The signature was L. Klein. I didn't know any Klein; Arnold didn't either, but the invitation had been passed through Bernard's Blooms, so it seemed wise to accept it. The second message was a tear sheet from a telex machine. It was date-lined UPI London, Thursday. The text was brief, but informative:

An American tourist, identified as Frank Lemnitz of New York City, was found this morning shot dead in his suite at a fashionable West End hotel. London police are seeking to interview a young woman who accompanied Lemnitz to two well-known gambling clubs and who probably returned with him to the hotel. More follows . . .

This time, at least, Aaron Bogdanovich had told the truth. I tore the message into shreds and flushed it down the toilet. I felt like a solitary school boy making up spy games in the infirmary. Then, Juliette came in. Harlequin was dictating correspondence;

she needed company. Why not? I needed it myself.
She kicked off her shoes and curled up on the settee.
I turned the radio to a program of golden oldies and
settled myself in an armchair, feet up and ready to
relax. The music was easy: no tears, no passion, no
profundities: a walk down memory lane, with only
an occasional tug at the heart strings. Juliette looked
better today, a hint more placid and less perplexed.
I felt older and I must have looked it, because at one
moment she frowned and said:

"You're looking tired, Paul. Is anything wrong?"

No, nothing was wrong. My ribs hurt sometimes.
I still couldn't chew beefsteak; but sure an' all, as my
grandfather used to say, I was fit enough to marry
the Widow McGonigle. I thought George was looking well, too. It was hard to believe that, only a couple of weeks ago . . .

"Paul!"

"What, lover-girl?"

"I think I should go home soon."

"What does George think?"

"He left it to me. I wish he hadn't."

"Advice from Uncle Paul. Stay around for a
while."

"Special reasons?"

"Some. Today's forecast is for very dirty
weather."

"I didn't know. As soon as George came in, he
called Suzanne and started dictating letters. When I
asked what had happened at the Embassy, he said
he'd explain later. I was hurt; but I didn't want to
show it. That's why I came down here."

"You're learning, aren't you, sweetheart?"

"Don't hedge, Paul, please."

"I'm not, I promise. George will tell you the news; but it's a long story and it takes time."

"But he told you."

"Yes . . . And I told him he'd sold me out for Judas-money."

"Oh, Paul, no!"

"It was wrong; but I said it. So don't blame him if he's out of humor—and don't hurry home."

"Paul, there's the baby to think of and . . ."

"The baby's got a lot of living to do yet and a much-traveled godfather to help him do it. Listen, lover! If you're out in the rain and there's no one else to take you home, I'll be there. But if Columbine loves Harlequin, she'd better be dressed and made-up for curtain time. If she's not . . ."

"The understudy takes over, is that it?"

"That's it, Julie; and there are lots of lovely girls just dying for a chance in show business. Now, why don't you go upstairs and order coffee for two and tell George I want to borrow Suzanne for half an hour? He shouldn't monopolize the help; even if he is the President."

She didn't go immediately. She came to me and sat on the arm of my chair and took my face in her hands and kissed me on the forehead; and told me how sweet I was and gentle and kind and the best of all possible friends. Three words more and we would have been playing Tumble-me-Tina on the carpet. I'm no saint—God help me! But that—no thank you, sweetheart! Not unless it were caps over the moon and never come back. I was grateful for the kiss; I thanked her for the compliment; I walked her se-

dately to the door and sent her upstairs. I tried to feel
virtuous; but I couldn't. I felt like a Judas-priest,
prowling and mumbling round the convent gate at
midnight.

It must have been written on my face, because
when Suzanne came down, she stood, hands on hips,
surveying me as if I were some very rare, and very
low, form of life. Then she gave me that soft, slow,
knowing smile of hers and said sweetly:

"It's hard, isn't it, chéri?"

"If you know, don't ask."

"I know, darling. I know. The sooner we all go
home, the better."

"It could be all of sixty days."

"Can you last that long?"

"I doubt it. Can you?"

"No . . . Say something sweet to me, Paul."

"Suzy, darling, why don't we fall in love?"

"I'll try, if you'll try."

"How do we start?"

"You kiss me."

After that, the rules were flexible; and even
though we were both out of practice, it was a pleasant game for a warm afternoon in Washington, D.C.
If you want to smile at two people, with youth a long
way behind, playing love games in Embassy Row,
then enjoy the comedy by all means—and see if you
can play it better when the loneliness catches up with
you.

At seven o'clock, precisely, I was ringing the doorbell
of a modest but rather beautiful old house in Arling-

ton. The door was opened by a big sallow woman, whose horn-rimmed spectacles gave her the look of a hostile owl. I told her my name and that I had an appointment with Mr. Klein. She told me I had it with Mrs. Leah Klein and that she was the lady in question. She led me into a small room, cluttered with books, magazines and disorderly files of clippings. In one corner was a littered desk, in another, a cocktail cabinet. There were two easy chairs, one of which was occupied by a large tortoiseshell cat. There was no broomstick; but Mrs. Leah Klein was something of a witch, broad and billowing, with thick, tar-stained fingers and a deep gravelly voice. Her cocktails turned out to be half a tumbler of bourbon for me and, for herself, red-eye rum cut with Coke. After the first long swallow, she dived straight into business:

"Kurt Saperstein tells me you want to plant a story. Right?"

"Right."

"Fact or rumor?"

"Some fact, some inference. I want it, if possible, to originate from London."

"Why?"

"Situation politics."

"Can you dictate it?"

"In rough, yes."

"That's all I need."

She sat herself down at the typewriter, put paper in the machine, lit a cigarette, stuck it in the corner of her mouth and said:

"No commentary, just the facts. Okay?"

"Okay! . . . UPI London filed today a wire story about one Frank Lemnitz, an American tourist,

found shot dead in a West End hotel. Police are looking for a girl who was seen with him in two gambling
clubs. That's the end of their story. Here's mine.
Frank Lemnitz was chauffeur to Basil Yanko, president of Creative Systems Incorporated. He is known
to have underworld connections, notably with a
hood called Bernie Koonig. Basil Yanko is in Frankfurt attending a conference of international bankers.
Are you with me?"

"I'm ahead of you. Keep talking."

"An employee of Creative Systems, Miss Valerie
Hallstrom, was murdered in her apartment three
days ago. That event is in the news files. The following facts are not: the FBI are investigating leak-
ages from Creative Systems data banks. Several
major U.S. companies are involved. The names of
these companies are as follows . . ."

"Spell 'em, please."

I spelt them out, one by one, including our own.
She pounded the typewriter as if it were a mortal
enemy.

". . . Harlequin et Cie has been defrauded of a lot
of money through misuse of its computer services, all
of which are controlled by Creative Systems and its
affiliates in other countries. The author of the fraud
at the New York end is known. Her name is Ella
Deane. She died in a hit and run accident two weeks
ago. She left a large sum of money, all of it banked
in the last three months of her employment. One of
her boyfriends was Frank Lemnitz. Coincidentally,
Basil Yanko is bidding to buy out Harlequin et Cie.
The offer is public. The major shareholder refuses to
sell. The minor ones are still undecided. Everything

so far is a matter of record. You can check it yourself. What follows is part fact, part inference."

"So what's fact?"

"Every major broker in New York is loaded with buying orders for stock in Creative Systems. Some of the biggest orders are from Middle East clients . . ."

"Oil money!"

"Check! And some of it is Libyan."

"Now, the inference?"

"The Arabs want a stake in banking and industry, in the U.S. and in Europe. That's clear from the public record. They have money and muscle to get it. It's our belief that Basil Yanko is helping them. The project is legal; the means dubious and, in our case, criminal. I've brought you a copy of a dossier we've got on his past. You must have him on your own files as well . . . End of story."

"Now, tell me why you want it planted?"

"We want to ease the pressure on ourselves and increase it on Yanko. We want him totally discredited."

"So do a lot of other people."

"Is this enough to do it?"

"No, but it will surely stir up the ant heap. Can you tell me anything more about Valerie Hallstrom?"

"I can, but I won't. If you want to know why, ask Kurt Saperstein."

She swiveled round to face me. She took a long drag on her cigarette. The ash dropped into her lap and she brushed it away, absently. She asked:

"Are you Jewish?"

"No. I'm a goy of the goyim."

"This, Mr. Desmond, is a very hot story. It could get hotter—for you."

"I know. When will it be printed?"

"Today's Friday. With luck, I'll have it ready for the Sundays in England. They'll spread it. We'll have it back on the wires in time for the Monday editions here. Same in Europe. Then the shit hits the fan. It might be wise if you went away for a long weekend."

"Thanks for the tip. I'll think about it."

"Another drink?"

"No, thanks. I'll finish this and be on my way. Do you mind telling me something?"

"What?"

"You seem to be taking an awful lot on trust. Why?"

She threw back her head and laughed—a great rasping man's laugh, mocking and humorless. "Trust! I wouldn't trust my own sister for the time of day . . . If you hadn't been checked, you wouldn't have got within ten blocks of this place! Before that story's filed, it'll be read by experts. If it doesn't fit the facts, you're finished. If it doesn't fit the policy, it isn't filed."

"Then I take it somewhere else."

"Wherever you take it, you need a good rewrite man and a sympathetic editor. In me, you've got both. Don't push your luck."

"I don't like to be pushed either."

"If you don't like beans, don't open the can . . . Lacheim!"

There was a message in my box at the hotel: Saul Wells had just arrived on the shuttle service from New York and was entertaining himself in the bar.

Perched on the high stool, hunched over his drink, he looked more than ever like a ferret, morose, restless and combative. He brightened when he saw me and we sat together in a shadowy corner, out of earshot of the late drinkers. He peeled the Cellophane from a new cigar, stuck it in the corner of his mouth, lit it, and puffed out the news between the smoke clouds.

"First reports from your branches. Same operation with local variations. Where there's a restriction on the export of local funds, only foreign accounts have been hit. In three cases, Mexico City, for instance, your punch operators resigned at material times, but we haven't yet been able to trace them. In two, they're still employed; which may argue that the fraud was built into the systems. In England, we've been lucky. The operator there was a woman called Beverley Manners. She resigned to get married—big office party, a bonus from the manager. She's alive and well and living on a golfing estate in Surrey. According to the report, she's five months' pregnant."

"Is that relevant, Saul?"

"I guess so. We can't harass a pregnant lady. What's more relevant is that her husband works for Creative Systems, UK Limited."

"That's cozy."

"It gets cosier. The lady and her husband are near neighbors and golfing friends of your London manager—and the fraudulent transactions are justified by a telex instruction from Geneva signed by George Harlequin!"

"Have you checked our telex files in Geneva?"

"We have. No trace. The telex was sent from another terminal."

"Quite a conspiracy."

"If you want to crack it, you may have to call in the British police."

"Not yet. Go as far as you can without them. We can't afford to lose more staff or create more publicity. How did you make out with the FBI?"

"They gave me a rough ride. You?"

"The same."

"Anything new?"

I told him of my talk with Mrs. Leah Klein.

He bit hard on his cigar and stared at me in undisguised amazement. "Oh, brother! You've bought yourself a heavyweight. Round Washington, they call her the grave digger, because she's buried some very big names and written some very stylish obituaries. If she's on your side, you're lucky. If not, it's time to leave town."

"She wants us to leave anyway, Saul."

Instantly, he was alert and deadly serious. "If she said that, Mr. Desmond, you go buy the tickets. When Leah starts firing from the hip, even White House staffers run for cover. She gives only one warning—the last."

"I'll talk to Harlequin about it."

"Suggestion, Mr. Desmond: there are good air services to Mexico City. I've got the file on your branch there. It's an excuse, if you need one."

"I'll use it if I have to. If there's nothing else, let's meet in my suite for breakfast. We can go over the reports together."

"Let's meet in the breakfast room."

"Any reason?"

"The best. Your Miss Suzanne let me take a look

at your rooms. They're as hot as the inside of a reactor. Harlequin's is clean—which is odd."

"Not so odd. It's been occupied most of the day."

Saul grinned and made comic motions with his cigar. "If you've been playing games up there, they're all on tape and the monitors have had some dandy entertainment."

"What monitors, Saul?"

"Two choices, Mr. Desmond—the FBI or Basil Yanko's people."

"Pick a name, Saul."

"For my money, Yanko. Reason: the FBI knew Harlequin was seeing his Ambassador and you were supposed to see yours. So I think they'd play by the book."

"The FBI interviewed me in my room this morning."

"If they come back, as they probably will, tell them about the bugs. There's one inside the phone. There's another under the table beside the settee."

"Why don't we rip the stuff out?"

"It makes you look innocent, Mr. Desmond . . . even if you aren't. What with Aaron Bogdanovich and Leah Klein, you're playing a high-powered game. That's another reason why I'd like to see you take that trip to Mexico."

On which comforting note we parted. Saul to spend a Sabbath night with friends, I to render account of my stewardship to George Harlequin and persuade him that Mexico City had a healthier climate than Washington, D.C. It wasn't easy. He had agreed my script; he was reluctant to have it altered by Leah Klein or anyone else. Besides, he needed to

stay in touch with the market in New York. He might
need more talks with Herbert Bachmann. He would
hate to give Yanko the impression that we were running away. I argued that we had to visit Mexico anyway; so why not over the weekend when business
was closed for two days? We were paying for expert
advice: why not take it? To which Julie added a quiet
suggestion that she could fly down to Acapulco and
visit Lola Frank. That way, if we had to come back
to New York in a hurry, we needn't bother about her.
Finally, Harlequin agreed and I went downstairs
again to make the reservations with Arnold. When I
made my request, a faint flush of life showed on his
long, dour visage and he asked:

"How did you get the word, Mr. Desmond?"

"What word? This is a business trip. We've got
an office in Mexico City."

"Oh!"

"Problems, Arnold?"

"No problems. Coincidence, I guess. I just heard
that a friend of yours was on his way down there and
wanted you to contact him. I've got the number
here." He gave me the card and began leafing
through the flight schedules, talking all the while in
monotone. ". . . I guess you'll want the Camino Real.
Same setup as here, right? I'll call them as soon as I
confirm the flight. Ah, here we are! Braniff leaves at
fifteen-fifteen, sets down at Dallas and San Antone,
gets in at twenty-one thirty. First class and a limousine at the airport? No, I guess your own people will
meet you. How long will you stay? Four, five days?
Let's make it a week. You can always cancel. Mail-
ing address? Your bank, okay? I'll let your friend

know the arrangements. Funny how it should just happen, wasn't it? . . ."

The more I thought about it, the funnier it was— a graveyard humor that set the nerve ends tingling and the hairs prickling on the neck. We were back to what George Harlequin called ghost-games: whispers in the dark, creaks in the wainscot, a whole cabbala of signs and symbols to confuse the novice player. As I walked back to the elevator, a familiar voice summoned me. I swung round to see Mr. Milo Frohm two paces behind me. He held out a hand in greeting; I shook it, absently.

He said, "I was going up to see Mr. Harlequin."

"So was I."

"I hope it's not too late."

"It's late enough. And we're leaving tomorrow for Mexico City."

"That's rather sudden, isn't it?"

"Not really."

The elevator came and we did a little mandarin shuffle to see who would enter first. Mr. Frohm was a very courteous man; he saved the rest of his questions for George Harlequin, who entertained him to coffee and brandy, and answered with his old, disarming frankness.

". . . There's no mystery about it, Mr. Frohm. Mr. Wells has just delivered his report on our branch in Mexico City. We need to talk to the manager and local shareholders. While we're working, my wife will visit friends in Acapulco. Do you have any problems for me?"

"Not problems, Mr. Harlequin; concern, perhaps."

"I'm glad to hear it. After my talk with the Ambassador this morning, I felt that we were, so to speak, in enemy territory. Your State Department is not very happy about us Europeans just now . . . Oh, Julie! This is Mr. Frohm of the Federal Bureau of Investigation. Mr. Frohm, my wife."

"I'm happy to meet you, Madame. I'm sorry to disturb you at this late hour."

"Is there anything wrong, George?" She was wide-eyed with innocence.

"Nothing at all, darling. Join us. Please continue, Mr. Frohm."

"Well, Mr. Harlequin, I take it your Ambassador gave you some political background?"

"He did."

"He referred, no doubt, to certain elements of violence in the situation."

"Yes."

"Mr. Harlequin . . ." He coughed, diffidently, and made a little play of fumbling for the right phrase. "I . . . that is to say, we . . . have certain opinions . . . you might even call them positions, which I am not at liberty to divulge. However, you are not, as you put it, in enemy territory. You may feel, with some justice, that you have a personal enemy in Basil Yanko. We may feel—I cannot state that we do—that his business tactics are rough or even reprehensible; but, until they are proved to be illegal, we cannot intervene. We have two murders and a highly charged political situation at home and abroad. In our society violence is endemic and may become epidemic. You, yourself, could be threatened with it. We have to warn you that we cannot always protect you. It is well that Madame Harlequin understands this, too."

Harlequin sat silent for a moment, looking down at the backs of his long, delicate hands. Then, he said gravely:

"Isn't that rather general, Mr. Frohm? By whom are we threatened?"

"Ask yourself, Mr. Harlequin, who stands to profit most from your death. Then, think of this: if you or your staff identify yourselves with a partisan group, you double your personal risk. You know that Frank Lemnitz was murdered in London?"

"We heard. Who killed him?"

"You did, Mr. Harlequin. You killed him with an untimely word." He frowned and spread his hands in deprecation. "That's what I'm trying to tell you. You're a stranger in town. You don't understand the idiom. You're Swiss. You come from a small, orderly country, where you need a license to cough—though you're so well-mannered that you never use it . . . May I ask if you have provided protection for your child?"

"I have requested police surveillance. I am assured it is adequate."

"I hope so. Forgive me, Mr. Harlequin, but this is America on the last reel of the American Dream, which turns out to be a nightmare in Technicolor. It gives me no pleasure to sit here and apologize for my country—even for myself!—but I'm prepared to do it, to make you see the truth."

"And what is the truth, Mr. Frohm?"

"The laws are inadequate. The forces of law are more inadequate still. Some of them are corrupt; but not all. The corruption is spread as trust declines. I'm begging you to trust me, Mr. Harlequin. You, too, Mr. Desmond."

It was my turn now. I wouldn't let it pass; I couldn't.

"Mr. Frohm?"

"Yes, Mr. Desmond?"

"I believe, because I want to believe, that you're an honest man. Will you answer me two questions?"

"If I can, yes."

"Do you have an order to tap my telephone and bug my room?"

"No, I do not."

"Have you or any of your agents done so?"

"To the best of my knowledge, no."

"Somebody did, Mr. Frohm. Saul Wells checked it early this evening."

"Did he check this room, too?"

"Yes, it's clean."

He shook his head slowly. He looked at me, at George Harlequin, at Julie. He got up, went to the telephone and punched out a call, slowly and savagely:

"Call? . . . Milo Frohm. You know where I am. Get Pete over here with his box of tricks—on the double!"

He sat down. George Harlequin poured whiskey into a tumbler and handed it to him. He sipped it slowly and set down the glass with elaborate care.

"You see the problem, Mr. Frohm?" said Harlequin gently. "You must see it now."

Milo Frohm nodded, up and down, up and down, like one of those old porcelain buddhas that the sailors brought home from Shanghai. "Yes . . .

yes . . . yes. I do see it, Mr. Harlequin. At this moment, I'm not sure what we do about it. One thing is certain, though: when you get to Mexico City, you must all be very, very careful."

Our exit from Washington was less than glorious. Rain was falling out of a low, leaden sky. The weekend exodus had begun and we were just four more sheep to be herded through the disinfectant dip and shipped out as quickly as possible. Our hand luggage was searched; we were marched through a detector gate; we were patted and probed and held in a pen, while security men searched the aircraft for lethal devices. Good sheep that we were, we told each other we approved the care that was being taken to save our lives. We deplored the violence that made the precaution necessary; and we committed ourselves with absolute faith to the care of our anonymous betters and our armed shepherds. My faith had become more fragile with the years; so, as soon as we were airborne, I claimed my ration of cocktails and immersed myself in Mendoza's report on the fabulous career of Basil Yanko.

The first part of it was standard folklore: the son of poor Bohemian migrants, he had sold newspapers and delivered groceries to pay for his education, and had established himself by sheer guts and brains in the new science of computer technology. His career in the giant companies was rapid and unblemished. He was well-paid. He saved his money. His parsimony was the only notable feature of his private life. He had no political affiliations and apparently small need of friendship. He submitted, without complaint, to the disciplines of the corporate society. He asked no favors for himself. He gave no quarter to subordinates. He refused all solicitations to company intrigue. His one recorded declaration was a terse adjudication in an executive's dispute: "We make brains and teach people how to use them. For once, let's use our own!"

He was thirty-two when he left the service of the giants and set out to become one himself. His net worth, at that moment, was a quarter of a million dollars, with which he bought a third share in a small data-processing outfit in New York. In the same year, he married the daughter of his senior partner. The next, his wife went to Nevada and divorced him. She, too, was on record with a slightly hysterical character sketch: "He wasn't cruel. He wasn't kind. He just wasn't there. I married him with stars in my eyes; what I was really seeing was flashing lights and whirling tapes . . . When I reached out to him, all I could touch was baked enamel. He wasn't a man. He was a mechanical monster."

Six months before the divorce, Basil Yanko had founded a shell company called Creative Systems Incorporated. It didn't do anything except exist. Six months after the divorce, his senior partner died from an overdose of barbiturates. There were rumors of scandal: fraud in the accounts; industrial espionage; sales of data to his clients' competitors. The dead man had abdicated his defense. Basil Yanko defended him stoutly enough to establish himself as a fairminded, loyal friend and retain his best clients. Then Creative Systems Incorporated bought the company at a bargain price. Basil Yanko owned it all. He could now offer the sole service of a genius, unbound from servitude to lesser spirits. The giants began to send him business. He expanded, slowly, but with a kind of cold certainty, buying talent, selling ideas, delivering always in excess of his contract.

His mode of life changed, too. He lived more richly, entertained more lavishly, but surrounded himself at the same time with an aura of Faustian mystery. It was an act that invited criticism because it suggested the mountebank; but the act paid off when the mountebank demonstrated beyond all doubt that he was a true wizard. Powerful companies funded his research. High men sought his counsel and he, in turn, endowed them with instruments of power.

He married the daughter of one of them, a thirty-year-old plain-Jane, reputed to be a lover of young girls, but rich enough to afford the eccentricity. She was killed when she pressed the starter of her speedboat on Lake Tahoe and the gas in the bilges exploded. Basil Yanko was in New York when it happened. He flew back to mourn at the graveside, collect the insurance and probate a three-month-old will which made him richer by eight million dollars.

Then, he began to expand, devouring small companies, stripping their assets, retaining their best people, tossing the rest back to his rivals. In the palmy days of the middle sixties, when every petty king was paying a fortune for invisible clothes, Basil Yanko went public and made another fortune. He bought hardware. He invaded Europe, buying stock and real estate, making allies and setting up affiliates. There were malicious rumors that he was selling, too: information in return for capital holdings in European enterprise. Mendoza's report cited several cases, but all were based on defective evidence. In one sinister instance, a European drughouse was accused of stealing secrets; while, three days after the news, a senior analyst from Creative Systems was killed in a car crash in the Dolomites.

In a sense, it was all old hat and déjà vu: a rewrite of the histories of the tobacco barons and the oil emperors and the arms peddlers. You knew it happened. It would cost a fortune and three lifetimes to prove it. If you did, no one would give you a medal—even if you were alive to accept it . . . Which was fine; so long as it happened yesterday to someone else. In fact, it was happening today, to us. The boys in the market knew it; but so long as their own pockets were not hit, they could hardly care less. If we won, they might even be embarrassed. If we lost, they would still dine Basil Yanko at the Bankers' Club, and dismiss us with the catchall epitaph: business is business.

The seat belt light flashed on. The hostess told us we were dropping down into Dallas, where they killed John Kennedy and buried the truth with his assassin and everyone lived happily ever after.

6

When we crossed the Rio Grande, I was asleep and dreaming. I woke to see the peak of Popocatepetl, snow-clad and serene, against a sky full of stars. Below were lesser crags and lakes of darkness, dotted with the tiny lights of villages. Ahead and far away was the loom of Mexico City, a golden glow diffusing itself through the smog, spreading itself high among the starfields. I felt a strange sense of liberation and relief as though I had emerged from a long tunnel into a vast but friendly wilderness. Beside me, Suzanne was glowing with the same sudden wonder and excitement. She held my hand and chatted like a child, full of fantasies and half-remembered histories: the plumed serpent, the golden city in the lake, the people to whom time was a sacred mystery, Cortés, who was welcomed as a god and was too human to know it.

George Harlequin came to share the moment with us. He was obsessed by the small lights in the great valleys: tiny treasure-troves of racial memory that would never be recorded, because those who held them could neither read nor write and their language would die with them. He talked of the strange amnesia that afflicts the human race: how what they gained of wisdom in one age, they cast to the winds in a single generation. Hung between heaven and earth, we saw scraps of visions, held, for a moment, stardust in our hands.

When we hit the ground, the visions dissolved in acrid smog; the stardust turned to earth-dust, gritty on the fingers, dry in the mouth. We shuffled like a chain gang through passport control. We waited like patient peons for baggage and customs. We were caught in a churning sea of men, women, children and assorted livestock. Just as we were about to lapse into screaming despair, the sea parted, and José Luis Miramón de Velasco welcomed us into the land of the Aztecs.

In our records, he showed as thirty-five, unmarried, a graduate of the National Autonomous University and the Harvard School of Business Administration, member of an old *gachupine* family: which meant that his ancestors wore shoes and spoke Castilian, while the rest of the country went barefoot and spoke Nahua and bastard Spanish. It also meant that he was rich in his own right, handsome and proud as Lucifer, and could walk blindfold through the labyrinth of Mexican administration.

His welcome was courtly. He presented us at the hotel with regal pomp. He put himself and his services and his house at our instant command. I saw the women pale with amazement that so much and so beautiful a maleness had managed to stay so long unmarried. I forebore to mention that a rich *gachupine* who ran an investment bank in Mexico

City needed marriage as little as he needed pulque and tamales for dinner.

Before he left, he begged the favor of a private talk with Harlequin and myself. He was affronted by what had happened at the bank; he could not sleep calm until the slur on its reputation was removed. Knowing his quite ferocious pride, I feared we were doomed to a rerun of Larry Oliver in Castilian. On the contrary, his immediate concern was for George Harlequin.

". . . You have been ill, my friend. It is monstrous that you should be involved so soon in this—this *sofisteria!* But that is the way of *Yanqui* business. If you will not sell at their price, they lay siege to you, scare you with lawsuits and spies digging into your private life. Well, here at least, we may manage to hold them off. We are damaged. You must know that first. It is argued that a good banker smells a fraud before it happens. It is also argued that we sold stock in Creative Systems; that we contracted for their services; that, if we have fallen out with them now, it is our mistake, not theirs . . . Tomorrow, you and Madame Harlequin are invited to luncheon with Pedro Galvez and two others of your Mexican shareholders. Galvez is the strongman. Convince him and you are out of the shadows and back in business. He wants investment funds for new mines, new access roads; he would rather get them from Europe or Japan than north of the border. There are overtones here, hard to catch, hard to interpret. Our roots are in Europe and in the old indigene life of this country. Our loyalties are to ourselves. Our enmities go back to the Alamo. Hernán Cortés, himself, is not yet absolved . . . Forgive me, I do not explain myself very well. There is something else, too—embarrassing to say, but necessary . . ." He broke off, begging to be pardoned a moment while he set a difficult speech in order. Finally, he came to it. "George, my friend, I have been a fool!"

"It's a common complaint, José," said Harlequin, with a grin. "We all suffer from it."

"This time, George, it is you who are suffering. The last two days I have been working with your investigators at the bank. It is clear that the operator who coded the false instructions was a girl called Maria Guzman, who left us in January. I told your investigators she had dropped out of circulation and that it might be very difficult to trace her . . . That was a lie."

"I'm sure you had good reason for telling it, José."

"I put that to you for judgment. This Maria was—is—a very attractive woman. For a while I—er—entertained her. Then, when she began to be serious, I dropped her. All this was, oh, September, October, last year. Of course she stayed with us. She was good at her job. She was well-paid. Then, in January, she told me she wanted to leave. She had been offered a better place at Petróleos Mexicanos. I gave her a first class recommendation and let her go. For me, the matter was happily closed. It is not the easiest situation when you meet an old flame every morning—and Maria didn't make it any easier!"

"You're an idiot," said George Harlequin mildly.

"I know it. You can have my head on a dish if you want it."

"I'd rather have the facts, José."

"I have them, George. Before I give them to you, I want a favor; I have no right to ask it, but I do. The girl is guilty, no doubt of it. I beg you not to take her to law. If you had ever seen the inside of a Mexican prison, you would understand why. I will pledge what I own against your losses. But I beg you . . ."

"Are you still in love with her, José?"

"Name of God! No! I think she's a stupid bitch; but I was more stupid than she was."

"Very well! No charges. And the last thing I want is your money, José. Now, what have you got?"

"A confession in Spanish, an English translation, two photographs, all notarized."

"How did you get them?"

"I'd rather you didn't ask, George. I'm not proud of that, either. Just read the document."

George Harlequin read it slowly, then handed it to me. The statement was limpid as a teardrop:

". . . I fell in love with a man who was not in love with me. When he told me our affair was finished, I felt foolish and hurt and angry; but I stayed in my job because I knew it shamed him, though it did not make me feel any better. One day, a young man visited the bank to check the workings of our computer system. His name was Peter Firmin. He said he was in Mexico for a month, visiting clients. He invited me to dinner. After that, we saw each other constantly. I opened my heart to him. We became lovers. He said he wanted to marry me: but, first, he must divorce his wife, and that would cost a great deal of money. I had nothing. I could not help. Then he told me that, if I would feed certain instructions into our computer, money would be paid: ten thousand dollars. He said it would be no crime. I was not stealing anything. When it was found out, it would be a big joke against José Luis, because he would have to answer for it. I agreed: but I would not take the money. I gave it to Peter to use for his divorce. He went away. I never saw him again. I wrote many times, to his Company and to the address he had given me in California. My letters were all returned—addressee unknown. No one questioned the computer instructions; but in January, I decided I must leave. All I have left of Peter Firmin is some photographs which I took of him one Sunday in Chapultapec Park. I affirm and declare that this is a true statement and that I have made it of my own free will in the presence of . . ."

One photograph showed a young man, dressed in summer casuals, posed with a balloon seller. In the other he was squatting on his haunches with a tiny Indian girl offering him a flower. He looked cheerful and uncomplicated, like any prosperous young executive out with his girl on a summer afternoon. I had seen dozens of him in a dozen cities and yet . . . and yet . . .

"Do you recognize him, Paul?"

"I don't think so. But there's something familiar."

"I know him," said José Luis Miramón de Velasco. He gave us an embarrassed smile and a shrug of apology. "I did some detective work of my own. He signed a month's lease on an apartment: one of those they rent, furnished, to tourists and businessmen. To do that, he had to show a passport and supply a business reference. His real name is Alexander Duggan and he works for Creative Systems in Los

Angeles, California . . . I told you the girl was stupid. She could have found that out for herself."

I remembered him then: the naive young man in the bar of the Bel Air Hotel, the ingenuous fellow who thought the sun shone out of Basil Yanko's backside, and the sky rained bonuses and stock-options. I began to babble excitedly but George Harlequin cut me off in mid-sentence.

"It's useful, Paul, very useful; but it's far from conclusive. Let's sleep on it . . . José, I'm grateful. Julie and I will lunch with Galvez tomorrow and we'll meet at the bank on Monday morning. Not a word of this to anyone else. Understand?"

He understood. He was chastened; but he did not forget his dignity. He made a brief, sober speech of thanks and then bowed himself out like a courtier who had just been reprieved from the headsman.

George Harlequin lay back in his chair and sighed wearily: "There, but for the grace of God . . . eh, Paul? He'll wear that folly like a hairshirt for a long time."

"It doesn't matter a damn how he wears it, George. He's given us the first solid evidence against Basil Yanko."

"Correction. We have an unsupported deposition by a disappointed woman."

"Come on, George! Put Alexander Duggan in the dock and examine him on that document, you'll cause a sensation!"

"How do we get him there, Paul?"

"Arrest him on a charge of conspiracy to defraud."

"The conspiracy was committed in Mexico City.

We can't extradite him without proof of crime. We can't get that without charging Maria Guzman, which we've promised not to do. No, Paul. Our friend, José Luis, is a very stylish fellow. He clears himself; he incriminates a girl but makes sure she won't be called to testify; he hands us the name of a man we can't indict. What does that say to you?"

"It says I call Saul Wells and send him a copy of the document and the photographs and set him to work on Alexander Duggan."

"Is that all?"

"It's the best I can think of at midnight, after a long day."

"Then I'll give you something to sleep on, Paul. A man doesn't walk into a bank like a telephone mechanic and say he's come to check the computer system. He telephones for an appointment. He presents himself to the manager. His credentials are checked at source, and from his personal documents . . ."

"So Maria Guzman was lying."

"No. As I read it, José Luis was careless. He took the telephone call from a Mr. Peter Firmin of Creative Systems, made an appointment, and in the best Latin style, didn't check back, and accepted his visitor at face value."

"He could also have been a conspirator himself."

"No, Paul, he's too rich to need it."

"In that case, he's too rich for us, George. Get rid of him."

"Not yet, Paul. Let him keep face. We need it as much as he does at this moment. This is another country. Life isn't all business. Style is important, too!"

He was probably right. I was too tired to argue.

All I could say was that you could buy a hell of a lot of style for fifteen million dollars and that a manager who couldn't keep his hands off the help wasn't my style at all. The which, of course, was blithe hypocrisy, because when I got back to my suite, there was Suzanne dressed to kill, loaded for bear, and waiting for me to show her Mexico City on a Saturday night.

I woke, dead and damned, with my mouth full of hot coals. I was blind, too; which was probably a mercy. I certainly wasn't deaf, because the telephone was a torment in my ears. I found it finally and managed a subhuman croak. The caller was an old denizen of the nether world. "Good morning, Mr. Desmond! This is Aaron."

"Oh . . ."

"I expected you to call me last night."

"We got in late."

"And you played much later. She's an attractive woman."

"I'll tell her."

"I want to see you today."

"Where and when?"

"Do you know the Plaza of the Three Cultures?"

"I'll find it."

"Three o'clock outside the church door."

"I'll be there."

"Alone, Mr. Desmond."

"Just as you say. Do you know a good cure for hangover?"

"The best—don't drink. Especially don't drink tequila. *Hasta luego, amigo!*"

There was no cure for living, except dying; so I was forced to suffer it. I shaved shakily, bathed slowly and dressed painfully, trying to ignore the chattering imps inside my skullcase. When, finally, I made the long journey to the lounge, I found Suzanne, miraculously fresh, dressed for the street, just taking the covers off the breakfast dishes. She made little noises of pity, apologized for keeping me out late and stood over me like a Gorgon while I ate what she was pleased to call a civilized breakfast. Then, just as I felt the first faint stirrings of life, she announced that I needed fresh air and exercise. I protested in vain that the only fresh air was in the hotel, and at seven thousand feet above sea level, even that was too thin for comfort. I managed to delay the ordeal by half an hour while I called Saul Wells and briefed him on Alexander Duggan. I gained ten minutes more for a brief visit to Harlequin and Julie. Then, still protesting, I was hustled out into the Sunday splendor.

The Mexicans will tell you their capital is an infested city—infested with rich people, poor people, monuments, churches, history, disease, animals, children, color, noise, legend, police, ghosts, tourists and a hundred different languages. Try to absorb it all at once and it leaves you dazzled and breathless. Take it slowly, pace by Sunday pace, with a sharing woman on your arm, and the mosaic begins to make sense. The Aztecs are still there, walking the asphalt that hides their old capital of Tenochtitlan. The conquistadores are still there, driving Mercedes and Fiats and living like the lords of creation within a stone's throw of festering slums. The Virgin of Guadeloupe still watches over this most Catholic of cities and the serpent-god still stirs, deep in the folk memory. Turn into a shady courtyard, sit on a stone bench and you will think yourself back in old Seville. Poke your head through a cellar door and you will see a huddle of victims, more hopeless than any who waited to have their hearts cut out on the sacred pyramid. Cock an ear to student talk and you will hear wilder revolution than Dolores the priest cried in the countryside. Sit in the boardrooms of the industrialists and they will tell you there is more wealth under the ground than Montezuma ever dreamed.

Buy a balloon, toss a coin to the mariachis and they will play it all away and make you believe that there never was and never could be a gayer place to spend a Sunday.

Came the moment when even Suzanne surrendered and we sat drinking iced beer at a sidewalk café, watching the passing parade and feeling pleasantly remote from it all.

Suddenly, apropos of nothing at all, Suzanne said, "Paul, I have the feeling that we're being watched."

"Of course we are. We're strangers, palefaces . . ."

"I'm serious, Paul. Don't look now, but there's a man standing by a red car on the other side of the street. I've seen him at least four times in different places this morning."

"What does he look like?"

"Youngish, wearing blue trousers and a white shirt open at the neck . . . There's a van coming.

When it passes him, I'll tell you to turn . . . Now!"

I swiveled in the chair so that I sat facing directly across the street. When the van passed, I saw him leaning against a lamp standard smoking a cigarette. He could have been any Sunday idler, ogling the girls, except that the girls were behind him on the sidewalk. I signaled the waiter, paid the check and the pair of us walked swiftly down the street in the direction of the Paseo de la Reforma. The fellow tossed away his cigarette and hurried across the road toward the café. Fifty yards down the street, we stopped a taxi. He was still behind us. As we drove off, I could see him frantically looking for another cab. Suzanne was shaken.

I tried to dismiss it with guesswork. "Aaron Bogdanovich is in town. I'm seeing him today. That was probably one of his people."

"If it wasn't?"

"Then someone hired a very clumsy spy."

"Paul, what's happened to us? I don't recognize anyone any more—not even myself. We're like characters out of Kafka, living in a world of hints and allusions and nameless terrors. We don't have to submit to it. None of us does—especially George. Why, Paul . . . why?"

It was a hard question to answer in a rattling taxi, tearing at breakneck speed down the Paseo. I waited until we were back in the hotel, feet up and quiet in our small, impermanent haven.

". . . Suzy, I can't tell you I've got the right answer—or any answer at all. The best I can do is reason it with you, as I'm trying to reason it with myself, as George is trying to reason it, too. Ask me whether

Harlequin et Cie or even a half-acre cabbage patch
is worth a man's life, I'll tell you it isn't. Ask me
whether we have the right to be sitting here in the
Camino Real while, out there, twelve kids huddle in
a cellar and their father can't get work to feed them:
of course, we haven't. We're wrong. The system's
wrong and it's crumbling under our feet. It's like this
city, which is floating on a lake of sewage. If the
pumps break down, the streets will be knee deep in
filth . . . So we try to make the unworkable work. We
try to keep terror at bay, while we evolve a better
kind of life for everyone. There are those who say it
can't be done; better to blow the whole mess sky-high
and start from nothing. That's a bigger illusion than
Utopia; because, after the blow up, the looters are
back, and the exploiters and the slavers. That's the
terrible paradox: the meek shall inherit the earth; but
the tyrants and the assassins run it. In a sense, they
are necessary to each other. Action provokes reac-
tion. Once you fight, someone or something dies.
One death creates vendetta. And most people are too
confused to see what is happening under their noses.
Let me tell you something I've never told anyone else.
I was in the war in the Pacific. We were holding a position on the underside of a hill in New Guinea. The
Japanese had been shelling us for three days. The
next day they would overrun us. We were ordered to
pull back with our wounded. We got most of them
out. Two were so badly injured, they couldn't be
moved. They were within hours of death. If we took
them, they would suffer intolerable agony for nothing. If we left them, they would be butchered in the
first assault. They begged to be killed. I killed them—

two friends! Right or wrong, Suzy? I've never really known. There was no one to tell me, then or afterwards. Comes a moment when reason fails and only the heart prompts . . . Sorry, girl, that's the best I can do."

She didn't say anything. She came to me, bent and kissed me on the lips and walked out of the room. I looked at my watch. It was two-thirty: time to freshen myself and go meet a man who had all the answers, because he slept in a grave.

The Plaza of the Three Cultures is aptly named. It lies within the confines of ancient Tlatlelolco, where the final, bloody slaughter of the Aztecs took place. A marble tablet celebrates the event and the irony of its aftermath:

ON THE 13TH OF AUGUST, 1521, TLATLELOLCO . . . FELL TO THE MIGHT OF HERNÁN CORTÉS. THIS WAS NEITHER A TRIUMPH NOR A DEFEAT, BUT THE PAINFUL BIRTH OF A MIXED RACE WHICH IS THE MEXICO OF TODAY.

The Mexico of today is celebrated in block after block of steel and concrete and glass; square, featureless and impersonal. The memory of the Aztecs is enshrined in a great, truncated pyramid of hewn stone. Between them both, higher than the pyramid, lower than the concrete blocks, stands the Church of Santiago, with its mismatched towers and its crenellated walls, that give it a grim fortress look.

When I arrived, the Plaza was quiet. Those who

could afford to eat were still at table. Those who could not were dozing through siesta or flirting drowsily on the lawns of Chapultepec Park waiting for the hour of the bullfight. Aaron Bogdanovich sat, relaxed and saturnine, on the steps of the church, chewing on a stick of sugar cane. I dusted off a place for myself and sat beside him.

He gave me an offhand greeting and plunged straight into business. "I hear you've been busy. Tell me about it."

I recited it for him, day by day, hour by hour. Occasionally, he interrupted me and asked me to repeat a phrase or interpret an atmosphere. Most of the time, he sat, munching the sweet fiber and staring, empty-eyed, at the pyramid below us. When I had finished, he tossed away the cane, spat the pulp into the dust and said, without emphasis:

"I passed Leah Klein's story. It made half a page in the London press this morning. Reactions were lively. New York will run it tomorrow."

"Are you happy about that?"

"It helps you: which is what I'm paid to do."

"How will Yanko react to it?"

"He's already reacted. He's on his way back to New York."

"The FBI warned us to expect trouble in Mexico City."

"They were right."

"How much do they know?"

"About what, Mr. Desmond?"

"Frank Lemnitz, for instance, and Valerie Hallstrom."

"Less than I do; more than you."

"That tells me damn-all."

"Don't be angry, Mr. Desmond. It clouds the judgment. You say you and your friend were followed this morning. Describe the man again."

I described him.

Bogdanovich frowned and shook his head. "New to me. My man didn't recognize him, either."

"I didn't see your man."

"If you had, he wouldn't be working for me. However, I'd better tell you now: your troubles will start the moment Yanko gets back to New York. As from tomorrow, you and Harlequin will have bodyguards—day and night. And I don't want any arguments from either of you. If the women go out, together or alone, they'll be accompanied, too."

"If you say so. What news of Tony Tesoriero?"

"We've got him, here in Mexico. I want you and Harlequin to visit him tomorrow. He should be ready by then."

He might have been making monkey-talk for all I understood of it. I stared at him stupidly.

For the first time he gave me that cold autumn smile: "The contract to kill Valerie Hallstrom was let in Mexico City. A lot of that business is done here. So, through friends, we dropped the word to Tony Tesoriero that there was another contract to be discussed. We gave him his fare and a wad of spending money and picked him up at the airport. Since then we've been resting him at a hacienda in the country."

"Why do you need us?"

"It's a part of the strategy. Also, you owe me money. I'd like to collect a quarter of a million tomorrow, in dollars."

"You did mention a hundred thousand."

"The expenses have been high."

"We'll need twenty-four hours to get the dollars."

"Fine. Let's make it the day after tomorrow. I'll send a limousine to the hotel at nine in the morning. It's a fifty-mile drive. You'll be briefed when you get there."

"I'd like to talk about Alex Duggan. I've put Saul Wells to work on him. I wonder if that's enough."

"Why shouldn't it be?"

"Let's say Saul is a conventional investigator."

"And we have different methods?"

"Something like that."

"Could you describe any that you think might be useful?"

"Well . . . no."

"Good! You see, Mr. Desmond, it takes a long time to train people for our sort of work. Very few subjects are suitable. You were thinking about Frank Lemnitz, weren't you? I told you my people would meet him in London. They met him. The girl the police are looking for was our girl. We're looking for her, too. We think she's dead. When they got back to the hotel after making the rounds of the clubs, someone was waiting in the bedroom. That someone shot Lemnitz and walked our girl out of the hotel at gunpoint."

"Why not kill her, too?"

"The way it was done, it looked better. And our girl might have been induced to talk. Nothing is as simple as it sounds. You buy oil from Libya to fly aeroplanes. The Libyans give passports and asylum to the people who blow them up. We train soldiers

for the Shah of Persia and Japanese fanatics shoot up
Lod airport . . . In Israel, we had Jews spying for the
Syrians. The British won't send us parts for our tanks,
while their own soldiers are killed in Ulster by Arab-
trained guerillas. Basil Yanko plots like a mafia don
and Uncle Sam makes him rich with defense contracts. Don't tell me my business, Mr. Desmond. I'm
still learning it myself! As for Saul Wells, let him do
his job in his own way. I'll call him and tell him what
to do about Alex Duggan—which is just to make
sure he stays alive!" For a fraction of an instant, he
softened, and I saw, or thought I saw, a flash of
humanity in his eyes, as he added the sardonic af-
terthought: "Face it, Mr. Desmond! The war goes
on, even when the guns are silent. You want twenty
per-cent on your money, you don't give it to an orphanage; you invest it with the men who make guns
to keep the orphanage filled. Tuesday morning, nine
o'clock. Cash on the barrel head!"

He left me then, and I stood watching him as he
strode down the concrete ramp and past the Aztec
pyramid to the other side of the Plaza. Moved by a
sudden impulse, I went into the church. It was cool
inside, turbulent with images and baroque ornament,
but calm withal, as though the passion that had
created it had all been spent and only the mystery
remained, still unsolved, for ever insoluble. I could
not pray. There was nothing to praise in the world—
least of all myself. There was nothing to ask for. I had
all that money could buy—and it wasn't enough. If
Aaron Bogdanovich were right, there was no hope—
only a deferment of ultimate disaster. Faith, there
was: some men died for it and some killed for it, too.

Love? . . . Well, yes, there was love: strange, tangled, selfless, noble or perverse; but it was there, the last handhold before the leap into chaos. I kneeled and buried my face in my hands and shut myself into a dream-place with the little love I had left to keep.

In the fall of the afternoon, we all met for drinks in Harlequin's suite. For twenty minutes, Juliette held the floor with her tale of a luncheon with the *hidalgos* of New Spain:

". . . My God, Suzy! Fall into the hands of God, not into the hands of Mexican matrons! How many children did I have, and did I not expect any more? Was my husband faithful, and how in Geneva did one arrange the matter of the mistress? And daughters! I should thank God every day I did not have a daughter. Sons are different, you see. With a good father like Pedro, who understands such things, matters arrange themselves without risk—and the boy is better for it. At the beginning, an older woman is always best! Had I taken a lover yet? With a husband who travels so much, a lover is at least to be considered. *Ay de mi!* These North Americans with their liberation of women! What do they do but enslave themselves to work. My Pedro now! . . . Go on, George! Tell them about our Pedro! . . ."

George Harlequin had his own comedy to play: the hovering domestics, the imperious commands, the punctilio of compliment and deprecation, the slow, circuitous approach to the matter at issue.

". . . Which is more complex than it looks, Paul. Our friend, José Luis, is not in favor with the old families, who've been trying to marry him to their daughters for ten years. They say he gambles, too; which is news to me, and bad news, if it is true. Pedro Galvez is a character straight out of Calderón. He will damn the Pope to hell and kneel on his deathbed for the Sacrament. He despises Yanko for an upstart and a *trampista*. He will despise me more if I cannot cheat better. He hates computers and would willingly dispense with them if only he could find people to write honest accounts. When I told him I was gambling everything to buy up my options, he called me a nineteenth-century romantic—but he drank to it, just the same. When I talked of violence, he shrugged and said if you didn't kill the beast, there would be no meat for supper. His promise is good. He'll hold his shares till the last moment, and see that his colleagues do the same. If we win, he'll put business into our hands. If we don't, he'll have a mass sung for our miserable souls. That's my news, Paul. What's yours?"

"The story's broken in London. Tomorrow it hits America. Basil Yanko's on his way back to New York. As of tomorrow, we all have bodyguards. And on Tuesday, we hand over a quarter of a million dollars in cash money."

"No bodyguards!" Harlequin was emphatic. "I'm a civilized man. I will not travel with a train of bully-boys!"

"Bogdanovich insists on it. I agree with him. Suzanne and I were followed during our walk this morning. At any moment during that time we could have been shot. You owe it to all of us—and you owe it to your own child."

"The police are guarding the baby ... So, we have bodyguards—amen! What next?"

"Keep Tuesday free. You and I have an appointment in the country."

"For what?"

"To meet the man who killed Valerie Hallstrom."

"What does that mean, Paul?"

"I don't know. Bogdanovich wouldn't tell me."

"What are we, for God's sake? Puppets?"

"We're strangers, George." Juliette chided him, firmly. "Strangers in an exotic city. You said that yourself, as we were driving home. And I'd like to remind you, dear husband, all I've seen so far is one very stuffy corner of it!"

"Then, tonight, my love, we shall go dancing. You, Paul? ... Suzanne? That's settled then. Paul, why don't you call José Luis and invite him to join us, with whatever talent he's entertaining at this moment."

José Luis had infinite regrets; but tonight it was just not possible. It was a matter of family and friends of family, a reunion of long standing. Perhaps later— if only for an hour. I told him we would be at the San Angel Inn. He said it was a splendid choice: excellent music, exquisite food. He apologized again and wished us good diversion. I offered a silent prayer that I would still be on my feet to enjoy it.

After that, the women left us and Harlequin held me back for a more private discussion. Galvez had given him a copy of Yanko's letter to the minority shareholders, a document which implied a great deal more than it stated:

. . . The growth of Harlequin et Cie has been limited by and to the aspirations of the founding family; and the succession devolves upon a single infant child. Mr. Harlequin himself has proved an able, even an adventurous president, but he has neglected to train a vice-regent, who could in the event of his death or incapacity take over control. His closest associate is Mr. Paul Desmond, who has amassed a large private fortune by speculative dealing; but who is unlikely to recommend himself as a stable centerpiece on any board of directors . . .

Harlequin et Cie provides a secure foundation for growth. It does not, in its present state, have the impetus to growth, or the access to new investment sources which Creative Systems Incorporated could provide . . .

Its information and retrieval system are outmoded and, as recent experience has shown, are not secure against fraudulent manipulation. In the new company structure, we would immediately update these systems on a favored-nation price-scale and operate them both more securely and more profitably . . .

The reputation of Harlequin et Cie has been damaged by recent fraudulent manipulations by company staff, which are still under investigation. The purchase price is set at a premium in order to repair this damage, restore market confidence and to enable a new management to operate in an atmosphere of trust, harmony and aggressive development . . .

There was more in the same vein; and the public executioner could not have done a cleaner job—no blood, no rancour, just a clean professional killing, with even a touch of mercy to it.

I folded the letter and handed it back to Harlequin. "That explains everything, doesn't it—the rumors, the doubts, the slump in business. All we need now is a bell around our necks."

"Do you think Leah Klein's piece will answer it?"

"We'll know tomorrow, George . . . No, wait! Hand me the phone book!"

"What is it, Paul?"

"Let's see what news bureaus are operating in the city . . . They should have the story on the teletype . . ."

"Will they give it to you?"

"We can but try. Worst comes to worst, we'll toss them a little bait: threats against life of George Harlequin and his entourage. We've got FBI authority for that one . . ."

We tossed the bait and we got the story, delivered by the hand of an eager desk man, who recorded for the world that Mr. George Harlequin, presently in Mexico City, had indeed been warned by the FBI before he left Washington that he could be in physical danger. He had, in fact, hired professional bodyguards: but he declined to comment either on the source of the threats or on their relation to the current news item. The desk man departed. We settled down to study Leah Klein's surgical procedures. For a woman so raw and raucous, she wielded a very precise scalpel:

". . . Police in London are investigating the murder of one Frank Lemnitz, who was found shot dead in his hotel suite last week . . . Frank Lemnitz was a criminal and an associate of criminals. He was convicted of armed assault in Chicago in 1960 and served a two year prison sentence. He was convicted on a charge of assault with a deadly weapon in Miami in 1965. This conviction was set aside after an appeal on procedural grounds. At the time of his death, Frank Lemnitz was employed as chauffeur and bodyguard to Mr. Basil Yanko, president of Creative Systems Incorporated, an international computer organization which handles high security contracts for the U.S. and other governments and for international corporations.

"Two days before the death of Frank Lemnitz, another employee of Mr. Basil Yanko was murdered in New York. This was thirty-year-old Valerie Hallstrom, highly-paid systems analyst and sometime friend of Mr. Yanko, who was shot dead in her own apartment. The circumstances of her death are now under investigation by the New York Police and the FBI.

"A notebook belonging to Miss Hallstrom and containing the secret access codes of clients, was delivered after her death to one of those clients, who immediately turned it over to the police. The companies named in the notebook are deeply concerned about this breach of their security. The U.S. Government is even more concerned because of the sensitive nature of the contracts handled by Creative Systems.

"Inevitably it will be asked whether Basil Yanko's highly profitable business with foreign governments and his involvement with oil politics in the Middle East are entirely appropriate to his role as the custodian of secrets and the designer of systems essential to the defense of the United States . . .

"Mr. Yanko has recently made a spectacular bid to take over the old-established European banking house of Harlequin et Cie. The bid has been firmly rejected by the president, Mr. George Harlequin; but with two unsolved murders in his household, Mr. Yanko still spent time in Frankfurt wooing minority shareholders . . .

"The takeover bid has several puzzling features. Creative Systems supply computer service to Harlequin et Cie. A security report signed by Miss Valerie Hallstrom revealed that the system had been fraudulently corrupted with a resultant loss to Harlequin et Cie of fifteen million dollars. On the day this report was issued, Mr. Basil Yanko made his first offer to buy out the bank. This tactic is interesting to those who have studied the career of this brilliant and original man. Apparently, it interests the FBI as well. Asked by this reporter what they thought about all these coincidences, the FBI spokesman replied quote Well, if things coincide, they may connect; we're looking at all possibilities unquote. The career of Basil Yanko, who is acknowledged as . . ."

The rest of it was a patchwork of standard biography and the spiciest pieces from Mendoza's report.

Harlequin gave a small humorless chuckle.

"If it weren't for all those buying orders, I'd start selling as soon as the big board opened in the morning."

In the first flush of elation, I was inclined to agree with him. On second thought, I wasn't half so sure. "Let's examine the realities, George. This report helps us with our shareholders. What it will do for us in the market is an open question. It's not a scandal yet, remember. It just smells like one. After two years of Watergate, people are pretty cynical. Politicians and businessmen are like actors; they're expected to be competent, not continent. The only real sin is stupidity; and Basil Yanko isn't stupid."

"Not stupid at all," said George Harlequin thoughtfully. "But he doesn't understand clowns . . ."

You come to the San Angel Inn as if you were a pilgrim come to heaven, on foot, by narrow cobbled streets and antique squares full of shadows. When you arrive, you are welcomed into a garden full of water music. You are led through a series of paved patios, trellised with vines and flowering creepers, and conducted with ceremony into the imperial past. Nothing here is new except the food and the people and the mariachi music. The rest is venerable with age: the carved beams, the ironwork, the silver, the pictures, the heavy tables and the great leather chairs made for the breeches of grandees.

The lights are muted, the cavernous chambers swallow up the sound, so that you can eat in quiet and talk as many secrets as you choose. If you want music, the mariachis will play for you. If you want to dance, you follow them out on to the patio, where the most vigilant of dueñas would be hard put to scold the most impulsive of lovers. After the fray and flurry of the city, it is a blissful oasis of courtesy and repose.

Here, for the first time in months, I saw George

Harlequin completely at ease. He knew everyone by name, from the busboy to the master of the music. He held long colloquy with the chef and made private jokes with the barman. At midnight, when the musicians took a break, he borrowed a guitar, played ten minutes of passable *sevillanas* and earned himself a cheer from the crowd and a round of drinks from the house.

Juliette was delighted with it all; and when we danced together, she confessed, ". . . I'd forgotten what it was like, just to laugh like this and be silly together. It's almost as though we'd been split into different parts and couldn't put ourselves together again. I'm almost sorry I'm going to Acapulco . . ."

Suzanne took a more skeptical view. ". . . He's acting, Paul. Every moment of this is calculated. Julie's going away. He wants her happy and contented. It's the same mistake he's always made. He'll assume the risks; she'll enjoy the first fruits. And she won't thank him for it, because he's robbed her of the chance to be his woman. My God! How can intelligent people be so blind?"

At one o'clock, José Luis had still not appeared; so we left to a chorus of thanks and benedictions and walked back, slowly, toward the main road where the limousine was waiting for us. It was a pleasant, drowsy promenade. The little squares were deserted now: the shutters drawn, the lights pale and sparse through the lattices. The alleys were silent. Our footsteps rang on the cobbles; our voices echoed back from the blank walls. Suzanne and I walked in front, arm-in-arm, while Harlequin and Juliette followed a few paces behind.

At the entrance to the last alley, we stopped under a pendant lamp to admire the strange, antique perspective: the iron balconies with their intricate scrollwork and their trailing plants, the lamps swinging from their rusted brackets, the pools of glowing gold on the cobbles, the carved bosses over the archways, all converging at the far end to the pillar of neon light which was the entrance to the highway.

One moment the alley was empty, the next there was a man, black against the light, with a gun at his hip. I yelled and threw myself at the women, trying to drag them to the ground with me. I heard the rattle of automatic fire, the splatter and whine of bullets, a man's curse and a woman's scream, running footsteps, silence. When Harlequin and I scrambled to our feet, the alley was empty; but Suzanne was kneeling beside Julie, who lay groaning on the cobbles with blood all over her dress.

At six in the morning in the Hospital de Jesús Nazareno, the surgeon delivered his verdict:

". . . She took two bullets, Mr. Harlequin: one in the thigh, the other in the lower abdomen. Fortunately, there is no spinal damage, but there's quite a mess inside—the womb, the bowel, the peritoneal tissue. We've done the best we can for the present. If there are no complications, we would hope to tidy the rest of it later. I'm afraid, though, she won't be able to have any more children . . . Danger? Yes, Mr. Harlequin, there is danger. Deep shock, massive trauma and hemorrhage. We'll be watching her closely for

the next few days. You can see her for a few moments
if you like, but she won't recognize you . . ."

He went in alone while Suzanne and I waited in
the corridor with a policeman, a detective and a pair
of reporters. When he came out, he looked like a
stone man, gray, grim and pitiless. When the press
men asked for a statement, he recited it in a monotone.

"You are aware that a bid has been made to take
over my company. You are aware that a man has
been murdered in London and a woman in New
York and that both were connected with Creative
Systems Incorporated. I state now that this attempt
on our lives is related to all those events . . . You may
quote me as saying that I shall not rest until the man
who ordered it—and I beg you to mark the phrase—
the man who ordered it, is brought to justice. No further comment at this time."

The detective seized on the words and worried
them like a terrier. Harlequin cut him off with cold
savagery.

"*Tenente!* We have talked to you for three hours.
We have referred you to the Swiss police and the
Federal Bureau of Investigation. Here you have to
look for a hired assassin. The real culprit is beyond
your reach. I will not name him because I can prove
nothing. Bring the statements to the hotel and we will
sign them. I am obliged for your assistance—but in
God's name, let us be done!"

Back at the hotel, he ordered us to eat breakfast
and meet him for a conference inside an hour. I argued, Suzanne pleaded, that he should get some rest.
He refused. He would not let us rest either until cer-

tain essential things were done. If we needed stimulants to keep us on our feet, he would provide the doctor to administer them. He was like a man possessed by a winter demon, frozen and obdurate, beyond any touch of compassion. When we went back to his room, he was already at work. What he demanded of us, what he had already begun to execute, filled me with horror.

". . . Suzanne, the following cable, urgent, in my personal code to all branches. Quote. My wife critically ill following murder attempt Mexico City stop This attempt related recent activities Creative Systems Incorporated stop You are ordered sell at best all repeat all our holdings and all holdings of our discretionary accounts in Creative Systems and affiliates stop You will continue selling whatever losses involved stop You will advise nondiscretionary clients of our intentions stop Noncompliance for whatever reason or on whatever advice will result instant dismissal. Signed George Harlequin, President."

I could not contain myself. I exploded into protest. "George, that's madness! You can't do it!"

"I've already done it, Paul. I've passed verbal orders to London, Geneva, Paris and New York. I've also told Herbert Bachmann and Karl Kruger, to give them a chance to protect themselves. As for your own holdings, I've told Geneva to sell. I'll cover you, personally, against loss."

"For Christ's sake, you'll ruin yourself!"

"Perhaps . . . At this moment, Paul, I don't care. Understand that! I do not care! Suzanne, another cable to all minority shareholders: the first two sentences identical—'My wife etc. etc. . . .' Then, continue, quote, I urge you most strongly reject Yanko offer or at least defer acceptance until outcome police investigations stop Not possible at this stage rule out criminal activity on part of buyer. Signed George Harlequin."

"George, if that cable gets out—and it has to get out—Yanko can sue you for criminal libel."

"I want him to sue, Paul! So you will call Leah Klein and tell her exactly what's happened, exactly what we're doing. When you've done that, call José Luis. He hasn't heard the news; otherwise he would have called. Tell him to get the dollars we need and to meet me here at midday. Then set a meeting with Aaron Bogdanovich as soon as you can!"

It was like watching a man making ready for *seppuku*, laying out the red mat, setting the shortsword on the table, preparing with ritual deliberation to plunge it into his belly. I was to be the *Kaishaku*, the friend who chopped off his head the moment the knife went home. I would not do it. I made one last, desperate attempt to reason with him:

"George, I beg you to listen to me! I owe you a lot: but you owe me something, too, I'm claiming payment. I want you to hear me out . . ."

"Suzanne, please type up those cables. Oh, you could save us time and make that call to José Luis and another to Pedro Galvez. Tell him what's happened, ask him if he would be kind enough to come now." When she left the room, he launched himself into a swift, tumbling monologue: "Paul, you will say nothing! I know it all. We can argue till Doomsday. I will not change one word, one act of what I propose. You think I am frantic—out of my mind with grief.

I am not. If Julie dies, I am dead myself. I have loved
her in a way even she has never wholly understood.
If she lives, I am like Lazarus come back from the
dead to find that his world was for ever changed,
though not a twig or stone of it was different. At
this moment, I can do nothing for Julie. Nothing!
She does not even know that I love her. The sur-
geons will probe her; the nurses will care for her.
Then, if we are lucky, I can hold her hand and bring
her flowers . . . And all the time Basil Yanko sits in
New York and makes a financial equation out of
it! I will not let him do it. I will not let him believe
a moment longer that he may do it. His best weapon
is secrecy and the fear that secrecy engenders. No
more! I'm taking him out into the open. It reduces my
advantage, yes. It gives me one, too. I can stand up
in the light and he can't. In the market, they'll say I'm
a fool, a clown! Let them! I would be more a fool if
I could not cast off the chains by which they want to
bind me: possession, prestige, all the rest. One thing
more, Paul, one only: a warning for you. If Julie dies,
I will kill Basil Yanko. I will not want you near me
at that time . . ."

After that, I had nowhere to stand and nowhere
to fall, and not a word worth saying. Suzanne came
back with the telegrams. I went back to my own
room to call Leah Klein and Aaron Bogdanovich.

Disaster was meat and drink to Leah Klein. She
regretted—though she had grace enough not to say
it—that we didn't have a corpse. However, the surgical details would do almost as well. The stock
dumping would make good copy, too. A friend of
hers had a few shares and he would be grateful for

the chance to unload before the panic started. She would do what she could to dissuade buyers and put the fear of God into brokers. When I quoted Harlequin's phrase on "criminal activity," she gave that big throaty laugh and said:

"So he's that mad, is he? Tell him he's got company in Washington. Also I've had a visit from a friend of yours, Milo Frohm. He wanted to know where I got my information. Which, of course, I didn't tell him. Keep in touch, Mr. Desmond. You're doing fine. And remember, an exclusive from me gets you more space than the wire boys can give you. So, if the lady dies, let me know first, eh . . ."

Aaron Bogdanovich had the news already. He registered regret but no emotion at all. ". . . I had a man follow you to the restaurant last night. While you were eating, he walked over the route twice. He said it was clean both times. When you left, he followed again. He was close behind you when it happened. He didn't show afterwards because he would have been pulled in for questioning. Frankly I wasn't expecting trouble so soon."

When I told him what Harlequin was doing, he was only mildly interested. His prime concern was the security of his own operation. He refused to change the appointment: the timetable was too important. I was angry and I let him know it. He reminded me, coldly, that I had set the priorities of the contract and that Harlequin had endorsed them. The car would call for us at nine next morning, unless Madame Harlequin died in the meantime. For comfort, he gave me only a terse aphorism:

"I can open doors, Mr. Desmond. I cannot

promise what you will find on the other side. I'm sure
Mr. Harlequin understands that."

Then, or afterwards, it was the nearest thing to
an apology he ever uttered.

When I returned to Harlequin's room, I found
him closeted with a man I had never seen before. He
was taller than I, thick as a tree, with a mane of white
hair and bushy eyebrows and a face the color of old
wood, seamed and scored by the weather. His dress
was old-fashioned but cut by a master tailor. He
wore an emerald pin in his cravat and on his finger
a large seal-ring of Aztec jade. Put him in morion and
breastplate and you could have passed him for a lieu-
tenant to old Cortés himself. Harlequin presented
him as Pedro Galvez. We sat down and Galvez continued his interrupted discourse:

". . . As I was saying: forget the police; forget this
hired gunman. They will find him or they will not—
most probably not. In a city of this size, with so many
migrants, so many workless, half the male population
lives outside the law. When we talked at luncheon
yesterday, I confess I was not confident with you.
You have always seemed to me too soft, too civilized!
I do not say it is wrong, only that here, in the New
World, it is not enough. You do not change a ruffian
into an honest man by giving him a collar and tie. So,
when you tell me that you will fight and how you will
fight, I approve! I back you—here at least, where the
name of Galvez means something. Now, you tell me
what you need. I will tell you what I think you need."

"I want a man brought from Los Angeles to
Mexico City."

"You want him kidnapped?"

"I want him enticed across the border to Tijuana and brought to Mexico City. If necessary, I'm prepared to have him arrested the moment he sets foot on Mexican soil and charged with conspiracy to defraud. I'd prefer, however, to talk to him before the police get him."

"Let me think about it. Everything is possible. What next?"

"Our friend, José Luis. You told me he's been gambling."

"Well . . . that, perhaps, gave the wrong impression. He gambles, yes. He plays the horses and the tables—for high stakes sometimes—but he is not in trouble. His father left him rich. He is still rich. But the way he lives is not appropriate for a man who is trusted with other people's money. He keeps strange company. You know the types we get here—promoters, speculators, easy-money operators. He entertains them like princes. He introduces them where he should not. Sometimes he uses the name of the bank to do it. You are not that sort of man; neither am I. I don't approve. I can recommend three men at least who would do much better for you."

"I need him," said George Harlequin firmly. "I need him loyal and happy until I can confront him with Alex Duggan and get a notarized deposition without duress."

"Why not take him to California and make the confrontation there?"

"Because there we have no recourse against Duggan—and no way of forcing him to tell what he knows."

"It seems to me, my friend," said Pedro Galvez

shrewdly, "you have as many doubts about José Luis as I have."

"Doubts, but no certainties."

"Then let me see if I can find some for you. Meantime, I agree: keep him happy and trusting. As for this Alex Duggan. . . ." His old face creased into a smile of malicious amusement. ". . . There was a *Yanqui* once who cheated me of twenty thousand dollars and went back to Florida to enjoy it. We sent him a hundred grams of heroin through the mail. When he opened it for inspection by customs . . . *he aquí!* There are more ways of cooking a rabbit than stuffing it with red peppers!" He turned to me, genial and faintly patronizing. "You don't say much, Mr. Desmond. All this is fastidious to you, perhaps?"

"Yes, it does bother me, Mr. Galvez."

"Why?"

"Yesterday, José Luis was a gambler. Today he keeps vulgar company. It's a change, if not a contradiction."

"It's an idiom," said George Harlequin, sharply. "I understand it."

"That's the answer then. Forgive me, Mr. Galvez."

"For nothing, Mr. Desmond. Each of us is the victim of his own history." He stood up, smoothing the furrows of his coat and vest, and addressed himself to George Harlequin. "Well then, I shall set to work. I beg you, dear friend, to get some rest. I have telephoned the Cardinal to arrange a novena of masses for your wife's recovery. You know what they say: 'God heals and the doctor takes the fee.' You will hear from me soon . . ."

He was hardly out of the room when José Luis telephoned from the lobby. Harlequin was rocking on his feet, and for that matter, so was I. Suzy came in, pale but composed. She had telephoned the hospital. Julie was still in the recovery room; given the nature of the case, her condition was fairly satisfactory. We agreed that once we had disposed of José Luis, we should all get some sleep.

He came like a penitent, groaning and scourging himself. If only he had been with us last night; if only he had known the malice in this affair; if only . . .

Harlequin was in no mood for lamentations. "You have the money, José?"

"It will be delivered this afternoon from the Central Bank."

"We shall call for it at nine-thirty in the morning. I have kept my promise: the police know nothing of Maria Guzman. However, I must know the rest of it. This man who called himself Peter Firmin, who came to check the computers, did you meet him yourself?"

"No. That week I was ill with the *grippe*. Cristobal Enriques was in charge."

"How did he admit a man with a false name and false documents?"

"The documents were in order. It is in the diary. Cristobal called back to the office of Creative Systems. They confirmed the name, and the number of the document. The photographs matched. We have a copy of the letter of introduction on file."

"Did Cristobal ask for a passport?"

"The security instructions do not specify a passport: only a company card with a photograph and a number, and a letter of introduction."

"Thank you, José. Will you now provide me with two notarized statements, one from yourself, one from Cristobal Enriques, setting out those facts? Will you also inquire from Creative Systems how a man whom they identified as Peter Firmin changed to Alex Duggan back in California?"

I interrupted him at that point. "I suggest, George, we stay far away from Creative Systems."

He hesitated a moment and then agreed. "Paul's right, José. Get me just the two statements."

"With pleasure. They will be ready in the morning. Please, what can I do for you, for your poor wife . . . ?"

"Pray, perhaps."

"Ay! If one could believe in praying!"

"José, tell me honestly, who could have done a thing like this?"

"I do not know, George. For money in the pocket, jewels . . . Yes! When a man is hungry enough or greedy enough, murder is a simple thing. For vengeance, a dishonor to himself or his woman, yes again! But this . . . No, no, no! This is gangster business. I think you have to look outside Mexico. What do the police say?"

"They're looking for a man with a gun."

"A bean in a stewpot! No way to find him."

"Do you have friends who could help?"

For a moment he looked puzzled; then, as understanding dawned, he smiled regretfully. "Ah! My bad companions! I have a taste for vulgar company. If you had lived in my family perhaps you would have it, too. I play with them. I shock my friends with them. Sometimes, because they are clever and bold, I make money with them, too. But they are not gangsters, George, my friend . . . Oh, no! Now you must be honest with me. Would you like me to resign? I can do it today or later, when it suits you."

"That's generous of you, José: but I need you; now more than ever."

"You pay me a compliment. One day I shall return it. How did you go with Pedro Galvez?"

"Better than I expected. We have time to breathe."

"He's a strange one: a good friend, a bad enemy. If you need me, I am at the bank. In the evening, at home." He gave a little wry grin. "This time, alone. I begin to think I am cured of youth. You should rest now. Please!"

The moment he left the room, Suzanne was in command. There would be no more talk, no visitors until six. If there were calls from the hospital, she would take them. She had sedatives from the pharmacy. Harlequin must take one and sleep until he was called. He agreed, wearily, and took himself off to bed. I looked at my watch. It was half an hour after midday. We had, all of us, been awake for thirty hours.

As we rode down to our own floor, Suzanne began to tremble violently. I hurried her into the apartment, sat her down and poured neat spirit into her. She gagged on the first mouthful, then ran to her room and slammed the door. I went to my own room, got into pajamas and dressing gown, poured

myself a stiff drink and then went in to see Suzanne.
I found her lying on the bed, her hair in disarray, her
face drawn and tear-stained. I knew how she felt. The
whole thing was a mess, a cruel, bloody shambles of
lies and brutality and wasted hopes. Julie was beyond
our help; Harlequin had refused it and retreated into
the solitude of fanatic. With all the love in the world,
no one could reach him. There was nothing I could
say to Suzy, but the simple, crooning words one uses
to a child. There was nothing I could do, but gentle
her until the pain and the panic subsided. Then I
went back to my own room and slept, fitfully, until
sundown.

In the evening, Harlequin went alone to visit
Julie. He telephoned to say that she was conscious,
though very weak and in much pain in spite of the
heavy sedation. At the clinic they had offered him a
bed for the night, so that he could remain near her.
He asked me to send pajamas, toilet gear and a
change of linen. In the morning, I should collect the
money from the bank and pick him up at the hospital to keep our appointment with Bogdanovich.
Suzanne would keep vigil until we returned. If Julie's
condition deteriorated, I should keep the appointment alone.

A little later, Saul Wells called from Los Angeles. He had located our friend, Alex Duggan, who
lived in some style in an apartment block on
Olympic, with a pretty wife and one child. There
was a vacant apartment in the block; Saul would
rent it as a base for himself. He would devote himself to keeping Alex Duggan in good health. He had
other news, too. The evening press and the television

services had picked up the story from Mexico City. The morning papers would give it big coverage. Leah Klein's story carried the leadline, "Mergers and Murders." In Washington, there was talk of a Congressional inquiry into the security of data banks. So far Basil Yanko had refused to comment. On Wall Street, the market was down and brokers were cagey. They were waiting to see what happened on Tuesday . . . So far, so good. You could hear the thunder, but it hadn't started to rain yet.

After that, we had the evening to ourselves—and a deep desire to spend it safely. We sat at the bar drinking margaritas and listening to the tourist talk. We dined in a far, quiet corner and talked soberly of George and Juliette and the dubious future that confronted us all.

Suzy summed it up, glumly. "Everything's changed, Paul. None of us will ever be the same again."

"If Julie heals, sweetheart, we'll all get better very quickly."

"If she dies?"

"I'm damned if I'd know how to handle George. Could you?"

"Once upon a time I dreamed I could." The words came slowly, dredged up from a well of sadness. "Now I know it's not possible. I've never seen this dark side of him before. Julie knew it. Perhaps that's what she loved in him, and wanted more than the rest of him . . . Funny, I was always so sure she was the wrong woman for George. Now I know I am; and yet I still love him. Hell, isn't it? When this is

over, I think I'll make a change, before it's too late.
Will you give me a good reference, Paul?"

"I'll give you a job if you'll come with me. A better one than you've got now."

"You're not thinking of leaving, too?"

"There's nothing to leave, sweetheart: one share
and a handsome retainer I don't need. I'm tired of the
trade and the bastards who infest it—including me;
but I can't quit until we've got George over the stile
and into green pastures again . . ."

"If you can get him there."

"Do you trust me, Suzy?"

"You know I do. You've never hurt me, Paul.
You could have, but you didn't. Why do you ask?"

"One day—and if it comes, it'll be soon—I may
ask you to back me against George; not for my sake,
but for his. Will you do it?"

"I would have to know why, first."

"He may try to kill Basil Yanko."

She gave no sign of shock or surprise. She was
silent for a moment, then she said quietly, "That's
what I meant. None of us will ever be the same . . .
Yes, Paul, I'll do whatever you ask. Now, please,
buy me a brandy and let's change the subject."

The rest was nonsense-talk: puffballs and platitudes. We sat late and drank too much and were
stone-cold sober at the end of it. When we went upstairs and I held her for a goodnight kiss, she said,
simply, "Please stay with me, Paul. I couldn't bear to
be alone tonight."

The sadness was that I wanted to be alone; and
that I was too ashamed to tell her. Our loving was
warm; she did not see the ghosts that haunted the

dark corners of the room. Afterwards she fell asleep on my shoulder; I drew the covers over her and we lay close, all night: two lonely people, huddled like babes in a darkling wood.

7

At nine in the morning, punctual as death, the limousine arrived at the hotel. Suzanne and I drove to the bank and collected a canvas satchel with a quarter of a million dollars in it. At nine-thirty, we arrived at the hospital. George Harlequin was waiting for us at the door. His news was neither good nor bad. Julie was holding her own. There was some post-operative infection. The physicians hoped to hold it in check. The surgeon was not dissatisfied. There was a room where Suzanne could rest and read. If Juliette were awake, she could visit for a few moments. We drove out of the hospital compound, fought our way through a snarl of traffic and headed north along the Avenue of the Insurgents.

Our driver was an elderly, taciturn fellow with a dark Indian face. However, he consented to tell us that our destination was ten miles beyond Tula and that, on the way, we should see most interesting antiquities: the feathered serpents of Tenayuca, the Pyramid of Saint Cecilia and the Procession of the Jaguars. Time was when Harlequin would have insisted on scrambling over every inch of it. Now he sat, blind and mute, in the corner of the seat, asking nothing but a speedy journey and the swiftest possible dispatch of our business. I tried to interest him in the scenery. He would have none of it. When I told him of my talk with Saul Wells, he grunted approval and fell silent again. It was only when I asked about Juliette that he showed any animation at all.

". . . She looked so pale and small, like a wax doll. I hardly dared to touch her. They are drip-feeding her, but she complains that her mouth is always dry . . . She asked for you, Paul. I told her you would come when she was stronger. She's worried about the baby, too. I wondered whether we should fly him over with the nurse. The doctor advised against it . . . The staff are very kind. They come every half-hour. I sat with her most of the night. I felt quite helpless; but when she woke she would grasp my hand . . . There was a priest who came. Very young. He wanted to bless her. I told him we were born Calvinists. He said it was only men who kept lists and made distinctions . . . I let him lay hands on her . . . Very primitive, but afterwards, she seemed to be in less pain . . . O Christ! Why is life such a blasphemy!"

I wished I could tell him; but I lacked the wit and the words. His face hardened again and he lapsed into a brooding silence.

After Tula, we climbed northwestward along the flank of a saw-toothed ridge and through a precipitous defile which opened into a large circular plain, the crater of a long-dead volcano. In the center of the plain was a lake, fringed by a reed swamp, from which the land rose to green pastures and terraces of corn and food crops. Against the far lip of the crater was the hacienda, a long, low building of hewn stone, with lawns and flower gardens in front and, at either end, the out buildings and the peasant dwellings and the stables and the pens for sheep and cattle. It looked rich and private and feudal, like an ancient duchy that had survived the revolutions and continued to ignore the democrats.

At the entrance to the house, Aaron Bogdanovich was waiting to meet us. He spoke a few words of salutation to us both and inquired, solicitously, after Julie. Then he led us into a broad chamber, with a tiled floor and a stone fireplace and colorful mats and heavy Spanish colonial furniture. He pointed to a few special pieces of Toltec artifacts and then summoned a manservant to bring us coffee. He explained, vaguely, that the place belonged to friends of diplomatic friends. I noted, as I had done in New York, that he addressed himself to Harlequin with deference and a care to be respected. When the coffee was brought, he stood by the stone mantel and explained the mission of the day.

". . . You are to meet a man who is, in many respects, similar to me. That is to say, he makes a profession of murder. The difference between us is not great. I am better educated. He is an intelligent urchin. I claim to be a patriot. He does not claim to be anything but a mercenary. Now, when you meet him, you will believe he is perfectly lucid. In fact, he is severely disoriented by heavy sedation, by sensory deprivation and suggestive procedures. He cannot yet distinguish between reality and illusion. You, Mr. Harlequin, will confirm the illusion. You have come to hire his services to kill a man in New York. You are prepared to double the asking price, but you must first know his full credentials. I will lead the discussion. You will interpolate questions when I signal. You, Mr. Desmond, will remain silent, unless I invite you to speak. Questions, Mr. Harlequin?"

"Are we to meet him face to face?"

"Yes."

"Isn't that dangerous?"

"You must accept my word that it is not."

"You spoke of sensory deprivation. Does he know what has happened to him?"

"By fragments only . . . Let me explain. We met him at the airport, as friends, and brought him here to await this meeting. He accepted that. He was drugged at the dinner table. When he woke, he was suspended in midair in a cellar, bound and with a black hood over his head. There was no sound, no change of temperature. Whenever he moved, he gyrated in emptiness. Result, swift disorientation. He was sedated again and drip fed. When he woke, he was again suspended in darkness, but this time subjected to cacophonous sounds and high-frequency notes, interspersed with vocables in pattern. Result, deep hallucination. This morning, he woke in his own bedroom, attended by a pretty nurse, who explained that he had been stricken with a virulent local fever. So far, he believes that he has been in delirium, but that, with the aid of stimulants he is fit to meet his clients . . . That, in brief, though not in depth, is the modern refinement of torture. One can be trained to resist it for a very limited period. Tony Tesoriero has never had such training. We believe he is sufficiently prepared for this meeting. If he is not, then I may have to resort to other measures. If you feel squeamish, re-member how he earns his living—a very good living as you will learn. Wait here, please, gentlemen!"

He was gone perhaps ten minutes. George Har-lequin sat, placid and blank-faced, staring at the heaped logs in the fireplace. I walked across to the door and and stood looking out across the fall of the green land to the farther rim of the basin, dark against the pallid noon-day sky.

Behind me, Harlequin said, "There's no need for you to stay, Paul. I have no feeling about this at all."

I had feelings; but I was coward enough to keep them to myself. I had started him on this walk into hell; the least I could do was bear him company and try to walk him out again, still human. That was the real ter-ror of the moment: we were, by mutual consent, after intelligent deliberation, bent upon the fracture and fragmentation of another human being. No matter how debased he was, nor how brutish, he was still a man, born of woman, suckled at the breast, held up one day to the tribe for a promise of its continuity.

When Tony Tesoriero came in, leaning on the arm of his nurse, with Aaron Bogdanovich, his host and patron, he did not look brutish at all. He was somewhere in his mid-thirties, slim and small-boned, with the kind of dark aquiline comeliness one sees often among the Albanesi of Puglia and Sicily. His eyes were dull and puffy; he moved sluggishly and his voice was blurred, as if his tongue were too large for his mouth. His accent was Brooklyn and Little Italy. He sat down heavily. The nurse stationed herself be-hind him. Aaron Bogdanovich stood leaning on the stone ledge above the fireplace, toying with a Toltec figurine in the shape of a jaguar. He might have been the chairman of a charity, discussing arrangements for a Sunday fair:

". . . Tony, these are the gentlemen who want to hire you. Gentlemen, this is Tony Tesoriero. He's been sick the last few days—tick bites. We found punctures on his arms that showed he had been bitten. However, in two or three days, he will be completely recovered. Now to begin, Tony, the money's here . . ."

"How much?"

"Show him, please."

Harlequin opened the canvas sack and spilt bundles of notes on the tiled floor. He said, "Now, Mr. Tesoriero, some questions."

"Call me Tony. Everyone else does. What questions?"

"I want a man killed in New York. Can you do it?"

Tony made a sluggish mime of tolerance and amusement. "You pay. I hit. That's the contract."

"Do you guarantee results?"

"It's my job. So far, I done twenty-three hits—all clean."

"What's the price?"

"It starts at twenty grand and goes up to fifty—plus expenses. Also you pay insurance."

"What does that mean?"

"I get pulled in, you pay the attorneys, and three hundred a week to my girl, while I'm inside—if I stay there."

"How do I know you won't talk?"

"I talk; you get me killed; so, I don't talk. You

got to know that or you don't ask me down here, right?" He faltered over the last words and a puzzled look came into his dull eyes. "That's it . . . That's what I want to know. Who put you on to me?"

Aaron Bogdanovich smiled patiently. "I told you, Tony . . . The Hallstrom job. The woman in New York."

"Oh, yeah . . . yeah. Blonde broad. She was set up from Mexico City . . . What was the guy's name?"

"Basil Yanko."

"No . . . No! Something else . . . Mexican . . . Say, how come you know him and you don't know his name?"

"We do know, Tony." Bogdanovich was gentleness itself. "We just told you. We're trying to find out if you're as bright as you say."

Tony looked puzzled and hostile, like a punch-drunk fighter. "What do you mean, bright? I took the contract. I got thirty grand. I made the hit. Does that make me dumb or something?"

"You've just proved it, Tony. The price on that contract was fifty. I know because Basil Yanko told me. It seems to me you were robbed of twenty . . . Yanko won't be happy about that, either."

"*Porca madonna!* All these years and Tony Tesoriero gets conned! Okay, soon as I get out of here, I got a private settlement to make."

"Not if you want this job, Tony." Bogdanovich was like a schoolmaster with an over-eager pupil. "My friends need a clean hit, no risks and you get sixty grand."

"But to be conned out of twenty! It just ain't right."

"That's why we're asking where it went wrong, Tony." Aaron Bogdanovich explained it patiently. "Fifty grand came down from New York to a guy in Mexico City. We know him. He's a straight dealer. Now, maybe, he passed the contract through someone else and that someone else skimmed it . . . That's what we're trying to establish."

It was painful to watch him trying to pick through the memories and impressions scrambled inside his skull-case. He began to reason, slowly, ticking off the points on his fingers. "Okay, let's start again. A guy in Miami tells me he's got a friend in Mexico City who wants to talk contract—just like you. I come. I meet him. I take the job. I get paid, I don't meet two guys—I meet one. He's old. He looks like a Don, with white hair and a green pinky ring and—oh, yeah! I remember—an emerald stickpin as big as a nut. Now that guy's name was Pedro Galvez, same name as I got in Miami. Is that the one you're talking about?"

"The same one." There was no hint of emotion in Harlequin's tone. "Pedro Galvez."

"Is he a friend of yours?"

"Not any more, Tony . . ."

"So, how do I get my money back?"

"Take my contract," said George Harlequin. "And I'll get it back for you."

"You mean that?"

"Of course. Sixty thousand and expenses and insurance. We'll talk details tomorrow when you're brighter and fresher. Here's the money." He bent and counted out wads of notes and pushed them across the tile floor with his foot. "When I come back tomorrow, I'll have your twenty; but I need a note from you to collect it."

"What sort of note?"

"Oh, something very simple . . . 'To Pedro Galvez. Basil Yanko gave you fifty thousand dollars to pay me for the contract on Valerie Hallstrom. You still owe me twenty. Give it to the man who brings this note. If not, I'll collect it myself . . .' Then, you sign it. How does that sound?"

"Great—just great."

Aaron Bogdanovich helped him out of his chair, led him to the writing desk and stood over him while he copied the message in the slow, laborious hand of a child.

Then Bogdanovich sealed it in an envelope and handed it to George Harlequin. He asked, "Are you satisfied with Tony?"

"Absolutely."

"Nothing else you want to know?"

"Nothing."

"Tony, you should get some rest now. This is a big job and you need to be fresh for tomorrow. Besides, it's time for your next shot, isn't it?"

"Holy cow! I'm like a pincushion already."

"This will be the last one, Tony," said the nurse cheerfully.

"Okay! See you tomorrow then."

He bent and gathered up the wads of notes and stuffed them into the front of his shirt, making crude jokes about how they would improve his figure. Then, chuckling and mumbling, he shuffled out on the arm of the nurse.

Harlequin turned to Aaron Bogdanovich and asked, "What happens to him now?"

"Just what you heard, my friend. He gets his last injection: a bubble of air in a vein. When it reaches his heart, he will die."

I could not restrain an exclamation of horror.

Bogdanovich swung round to challenge me. "You're shocked, Mr. Desmond? You heard him say he had killed twenty-three people. Do you think you could convict him simply on what you have heard in this room? Never! . . . Besides, there is something you don't know. Valerie Hallstrom was my agent. I trained her. I planted her. Tony Tesoriero killed her. A life for a life. That's the rule. You knew it when you started." He turned to George Harlequin. "This Pedro Galvez, what is he?"

"A friend. One of my shareholders."

"How much does he know about your business?"

"Too much. I told him about Alex Duggan."

"Ach! That's bad news."

"My wife is also his victim."

"We can eliminate him, but we lose a link in our chain of evidence. Let me think about this."

"I'd like to send him a gift."

"What sort of gift, Mr. Harlequin?"

"Tony Tesoriero's body. Do you think you could arrange it?"

"I could, but I won't." Bogdanovich was emphatic. "Tell me more about Pedro Galvez . . ."

"Old family, rich from mining, arrogant with power . . ."

"But not mad or stupid?"

"No."

"So why does he make contracts with hit men— and not for himself, but for Basil Yanko?"

"He needs millions of new development funds: risk money and long-term money—both hard to come by and, at today's rates, expensive. I would guess that Yanko promised him oil-funds once our business was disposed of . . ."

"Which still does not explain, Mr. Harlequin, why an old aristocrat like Pedro Galvez would sit in the same room with Tony Tesoriero."

"Oh, that's very easy." Harlequin's face puckered into a grimace of self-mockery. "It would appeal to him, as it did to me. There's something exotic about owning a private executioner . . . It's a kingly privilege." He stirred the pile of banknotes with the toe of his shoe. "A pile of paper buys the death of a man."

"What it can't buy you," said Aaron Bogdanovich, "is the deferment of your own."

George Harlequin digested the thought slowly. There was no sign to tell whether he found it bitter or sweet. He asked:

"If it was Galvez, why would he give his real name?"

Bogdanovich smiled faintly. "You forget, Mr. Harlequin, this is a professional relationship. It involves insurance. You have to know whether there's money to pay on the policy."

"Is there a telephone in the house?" asked George Harlequin. "I'd like to call the hospital."

"Over in the corner. It's a poor line. You may need some patience."

While he was telephoning, Bogdanovich and I went outside and began pacing the patio together.

Bogdanovich said: "Galvez is a bad surprise. He is also a threat to Alex Duggan, who now becomes very important. We have to decide what to do about him."

"I don't think Harlequin's in a fit state to decide anything."

"I disagree, Mr. Desmond. If we're talking about morals, of course he's working in a completely new system of values. If we're talking about his capacity to plan and execute a strategy, I believe that is considerably greater, because it is not limited by moral considerations. Naturally, that troubles you. Your problem, Mr. Desmond, is that you're a confused man, a muddled man, half-believing, half-denying—the eternal compromiser. Your friend, Harlequin, is not like that at all. He grasps life—or death—with both hands. But I understand your doubts. I accept to be damned to futility. Harlequin will damn himself to a purpose. When the purpose is accomplished and he sees the futility . . . what then? That's your question, isn't it?"

"Yes, I suppose it is."

"I have no answer, Mr. Desmond. Nor am I required to have one. Like Tony, I accept the contract, execute it and prepare for the next assignment . . . Ah, Mr. Harlequin? Did you get through?"

George Harlequin was standing in the doorway, his face bloodless, his eyes blank. "Yes, I got through. Julie died fifteen minutes ago. They said it was a coronary embolism."

Aaron Bogdanovich clamped an iron fist on my

arm and muttered, "Get him back to town. I'll call you. I can't handle a mourning husband!"

I will tell you now that I was the one who mourned. At the bedside I wept without shame. I bent and kissed her cold lips and told her goodbye and murmured a requiescat. Harlequin stood, rigid, aloof and tearless, waiting until I was ready to be gone. What passed between them afterwards, whether he raved or wept, I do not know—and for a while I could not care. It was very strange. Hers was the great death. I felt the small death of parting, the pathos of the never-again, the never-enjoyed, the hope for ever unfulfilled. And yet—the dead are happy that they never know it!—I felt relief, too. She could not suffer any more. I was released from a bondage that I had borne too long, a temptation that had pricked more sharply with every passing year. I was free at last—albeit in a cold and barren desert, I was free.

While we waited for Harlequin, Suzy and I sat together, making the empty, reminiscent talk that follows every death. Her tears were long spent and like all women, at every obsequies, she had to think of the housekeeping afterwards.

". . . I hope he'll bury her here. Otherwise it will drag on so long. We'll need an undertaker, Paul. Will you see to that? I've asked the doctor for sedatives. George will need them tonight. You'll stay in his suite, won't you, Paul? I would, willingly; but it wouldn't be proper . . . Perhaps, he'll be prepared to end it now; finish the whole sordid business and go home. It'll be summer soon. You could take him away on your boat . . . I must pack her clothes, too. It would be terrible for him to do it . . . Oh, Paul, I feel so sad for him . . ."

I could not feel sad for him. I hated him. I was tempted to tell him that now he had another body to dump on Galvez's doorstep. And why not? One death was very like another. Flowers would grow as well from the mouth of Tony Tesoriero as from the dead womb of Juliette Gerard. All the time I was hating myself, because I was the brave warrior with the brazen trumpet who summoned the heroes out to fight, and then blew taps over the body of the defeated, frightening the vultures away from his bones.

Suzanne took my right hand and held it between her own. "Paul . . . please! Don't blame yourself. Don't blame George, either. We can only walk the path we see at our own feet. Please, chéri . . . !"

A long time later, George Harlequin came to join us. He was tranquil now, flat and empty as a lake under the moon. He thanked us both—for himself and for Juliette. He had made the first, necessary decisions. "We will bury her here. Paul, will you please make the best arrangements possible? She should have a religious service. We should inform the Swiss Ambassador, and José Luis, and Pedro Galvez and his family, and the employees of the bank. Suzy, please cable all our offices that they will close for one day, and ask the local managers to insert an obituary notice in the press. I have already called her parents. Afterwards . . ."

"Let's leave that, George."

"Just as you say, Paul."

"I'll call a taxi," said Suzanne.

"I'll walk back."

"We'll walk with you."

"No, thank you, Paul. I'd prefer to be alone."

"George, do you really want Galvez at the funeral?"

"Oh, yes! He's a friend. He had the Cardinal say masses for Julie's recovery."

If you have the choice—and the choice gets more restricted in the year of the assassins—do not, I beg you, die violently in a Latin city. The documents required to consign you out of existence are horrendous; and you will wait in limbo until every last one of them is filled. I was forced to abdicate the task of arranging Julie's obit and leave it to José Luis Miramón de Velasco, who accepted it as a sacred duty, and the smallest amends he could make for his delinquencies. The only thing he would need would be Harlequin's signatures. For the rest, he would ensure for Madame a dignified ceremony and a quiet resting place, near to that of his own family . . .

Then the world invaded us once more. There was a stack of cables and a list of telephone calls a yard long. Our local managers were in panic. The market was in shock. The Press wanted comment and clarification. Every one wanted to know whether George Harlequin was a financial genius or whether he was stark, motherless mad. While Suzanne dealt with the cables, I battled with operators and dial codes and time differentials to answer the most important telephone calls. In New York it was late afternoon. In London it was dinnertime. In Europe it was coffee and cognac and the news of the day on color television, while the cost of living went up and the chances of decent survival went down and down. I had just slammed down the receiver for the tenth time when Suzanne came in with a cable: "I think you need me . . . Milo Frohm." I called Aaron Bogdanovich and read it to him. His comment was dry as dead leaves:

"If you need him, you call him. Question is how much you tell him."

"No other comment?"

"I leave for New York tomorrow."

"There's business here, unfinished."

"It will be finished in New York. Call me when you get there."

Which still left Milo Frohm a very open question. My first thought was to defer it until Harlequin was prepared to answer it for himself. My second was to make a call to Washington and see what ground rules Milo Frohm was prepared to play. If they were flexible, we might well cooperate. If he wanted to be the friendly neighborhood policeman, there was no way at all. I had no quarrel with policemen, especially friendly ones; the only problem was that they had to settle for too little: law and order and a quiet sleep at night—which left too many causes in dispute and a whole cesspool of injustice stinking under the sun.

Milo Frohm was delighted to hear from me. I told him I was grateful for his cable, but that it was difficult to talk business on an open line. After what he had been reading in the press, he thought I exaggerated the difficulty. We couldn't have been more open if we'd put it on television. Well-founded rumor said we were about to be sued for our hide and hair.

I told him we expected it—more, we wanted it. Then I told him of Julie's death.

For a long moment there was silence on the line, then he said, "How is Mr. Harlequin taking it?"

"Biblically."

"Old Testament or New?"

"Old . . ."

"And what are your sentiments, Mr. Desmond?"

"I'd like to play by the rules. I'm afraid, if we do, the crows will eat us."

"Suppose we could bend the rules a little . . ."

"It has to be more than suppose . . ."

"So we do bend them."

"Are we on tape now?"

"Since the beginning . . ."

"Here goes then. Valerie Hallstrom was killed by a hit man called Tony Tesoriero, now dead. He was paid by a man called Pedro Galvez, a big name in Mexico City, who is linked with our company and with Basil Yanko. For evidence, we have a paper signed by Tony Tesoriero. No good in court, but good for you. We are assuming, without proof, that Galvez was also responsible for the murder of Madame Harlequin. Next, the frauds in our bank at Mexico City were committed by a woman, Maria Guzman, paid by one Alexander Duggan, who works for Creative Systems in Los Angeles, California. On that we have notarized depositions and identifying photographs, also notarized. Galvez was told we knew Duggan. Saul Wells is watching Duggan now. The address is as follows . . ."

When I had finished, Milo Frohm asked, "Have you told any of this to the Mexican authorities?"

"No."

"Why not?"

"We offered immunity to Maria Guzman. Duggan is beyond jurisdiction and the rest is hearsay from a dead man."

"Thank you, Mr. Desmond. When do you expect to come back to the United States?"

"That depends on Harlequin. Probably soon after the funeral . . ."

"I'd like to know the travel arrangements as soon as they're made. You're dangerous people to be with; we'll need to protect your fellow-travelers."

I thought he was joking. I made a flippant rejoinder. I found he was deadly serious:

"Politics and money make an explosive mixture, Mr. Desmond. Mix 'em with oil and you get a very big bonfire. Please do as I ask."

At least he was honest about it. He could bend the rules, he could not change the fundamental facts of life in this year of doubtful grace: that no fortress was proof against money, that a pound of plastic explosive could blast an aircraft out of the sky, that a few desperate men could hold a nation to ransom. Which took us by swift strides back to the dark ages, to summary justice and the law of the talion and the kingly privilege of the private executioner . . .

As if she read my thoughts, Suzanne came and put her arms around my neck and laid her cheek against mine. "Enough, Paul . . . You need some time for grieving, too."

"Funny! I don't know how to grieve. There's just a blank space, as though someone had taken a picture down from the wall . . . Is George back yet?"

"Yes. He's just come in. I called his room. He's resting. He doesn't want anyone near him yet. I've put a stop on his phone and told them to redirect calls here."

"He's got to crack soon, Suzy."

"No, Paul." She shook her head emphatically. "I remember something my father used to quote to me: 'Der grosste Hass ist still . . . The greatest hatred is silent.' George is a hating man now. He's lost to us, gone far away."

"Relax, lover. People get tired of hating."

"It lasts longer than loving, Paul."

"Would a whiskey help?"

"It might. Oh, chéri! Hang on to me. I'm very frightened."

While I was pouring the drinks, it hit me like a hammer blow. Once, in a distant yesterday, we were afraid of the potent wizard, Basil Yanko; now we were more afraid of George Harlequin, who had succumbed to his spells and who lay in a darkened room with a splinter of ice in his heart. Because I couldn't face the truth, I took refuge in platitudes. We were halfway launched on one of those foolish consoling dialogues about love and mercy, and how, if you understand everything, you can forgive almost anything, when the telephone shrilled and reception announced that Señor Pedro Galvez desired to see Mr. George Harlequin. Suzanne—God bless her sober Swiss manners!—desired him to wait a few moments while I spoke to Harlequin on the bedroom phone. I expected rage or dull despair. Instead I was directed to receive our guest with courtesy, offer him a drink, and beg a few moments' grace while Har-

lequin made himself decent to welcome him. I passed
the message. Suzanne went down to the lobby. I ti-
died the desk and laid out clean glasses and wondered
what the hell you said to a murderer when his victim
was hardly cold. I need not have worried.

George Harlequin was ready and waiting when
Suzanne ushered Pedro Galvez into the room. His
welcome was florid and emotional. "My dear Pedro!
How kind of you to come! It was not necessary; but
I am deeply touched."

"George, my friend, what can I say? What can I
do?"

"Nothing, Pedro! Your presence does enough!
Liquor, coffee? Isn't it strange how we go back to the
old ways . . . We lay out meat and drink for the
mourners. Please, please, sit down . . . Suzanne! Coffee for Señor Galvez!"

Pedro Galvez settled himself in a chair, a rock of
comfort in an ocean of grief. "My dear George! I believed so firmly it could not happen."

"We all believed, Pedro."

"The arrangements? Perhaps I can . . ."

"It's done, thank you. She will be buried here in
your beautiful city. She always loved it."

"George, this is murder. Something must be
done."

"What, Pedro? I cannot go through the streets
crying blood and vengeance. I would rather let her
sleep in peace."

"I understand; but it is not enough."

"Let me bury her first."

"Of course! Of course! But there should be ceremony, George. It is only proper. You have friends

here, and clients. They will want to pay respect. May
I bring them?"

"If they wish to come, yes."

"Will you stay afterwards?"

"Not long, I think. I am claimed in other places.
There are people who depend on me. I am still under
attack. I must go on fighting. Now, even the fight is
something."

"Do you have any idea, George—half a thought
even—who might have done this terrible thing? If
you have, tell me. I promise you on my immortal
soul, I will find him."

"Pedro, I prize what you say; but I know already
who did it."

"Have you told the police?"

"No."

"But you must! It is essential that they know."

"I wanted to tell you first, Pedro."

"Why me?"

"You have friends in authority. You would not
let a thing like this be buried in the files."

"Never."

"Pedro, you must know what it's like. You love
your wife, your son, your daughters . . ."

"I do."

"One day, I shall have to tell my son that his
mother died, shot by an assassin, in Mexico City.
He's a baby now; but one day he will have to know.
Then he will ask me what I did to the man who killed
her. What shall I say, Pedro?"

"As yet, you have done nothing."

"As yet." Harlequin put a hand into his breast

pocket, brought out the envelope containing Tony Tesoriero's letter and handed it to Pedro Galvez. "Read it, my friend, and tell me what I should do about it."

"It is sealed, George."

"A mistake. Open it, please."

Pedro Galvez thrust a thick finger under the flap of the envelope and tore it open. He unfolded the note and read it. There was no twitch of emotion on his weathered face. Carefully he folded the paper, put it back in the envelope and handed it back to George Harlequin. He stood up, tugged down his waistcoat and buttoned his coat. Then, without a tremor, he made his farewells. "Señor Desmond, Señorita, you will excuse me. George, I understand sorrow. I have experienced it myself. I forgive you this very bad joke."

"Before you go!" George Harlequin stood by the door, one hand on the latch, the other raised to stay him. "The joke isn't finished yet. Wherever you go, there will be a man to watch you. Wherever your wife goes, or your son or your daughters, there will be eyes upon them, too. One day, one will be killed. Another day, one more. But never you, Pedro Galvez—never you. You are untouchable. You know I can do it, because you did it yourself and because, I today, assisted at the death of Tony Tesoriero. You know I will do it because you taught me yourself: unless one kills the beast, there is no meat for dinner . . . When next you call Basil Yanko, tell him what I have told you. Adios, amigo!"

Pedro Galvez stood, straight and sturdy as an old oak in a storm-wind. He said, somberly:

"I can offer you a better bargain, George."

"I know you can," said Harlequin. "Sit down and write. Suzanne, telephone the concierge and ask him to find us a notary."

It is a matter of public record that Pedro Galvez died in his bed sometime between midnight and dawn of the following day. It was known, and so stated by his physician, that he had been suffering a long time from acute cardiac symptoms, aggravated by the strains of an active and fruitful life. He was buried, with much greater pomp, in the same cemetery and on the same day as Juliette Harlequin.

Ours was a sad little ceremony, conducted in an alien tongue, by a nervous young pastor from the Lutheran Church—the closest communion we could find in the city of the Virgin of Guadeloupe. There were few mourners, and all of them, except ourselves, were there by duty, uneasy at the service, faintly guilty at committing a woman to a protestant God. The eulogy was mercifully brief: a stale crumb of consolation for those who had loved her, a pallid panegyric for those who had never known her.

Harlequin stood on one side of the grave, with José Luis; Suzanne and I on the other. Harlequin was pale but composed, his eyes hidden behind dark sunglasses. Suzanne wept quietly. As the casket was lowered into the earth, I closed my eyes, trying to hold back the tears. I heard the thud of the first sods on the coffin lid, the shuffle of the mourners as they moved away, the scrape of metal as the gravediggers filled in the hole.

Then, hand in hand with Suzanne, I turned away. Harlequin was already gone. He was standing by the limousine, shaking hands with the mourners, saying his thanks to the pastor. We drove straight from the cemetery to the airport, where a chartered jet was waiting to fly us to Los Angeles. Milo Frohm had made his point. Harlequin had accepted it without question. We were not common folk any more; the death-mark was printed on the palms of our hands.

Throughout the whole journey, Harlequin worked alone, assiduously, covering page after page with handwritten notes. He was totally withdrawn from us now, secretive and laconic. He no longer discussed; he directed. He received information and declined either to comment on it or indicate how he intended to use it. On the day before the funeral, I had charged him with a lack of simple courtesy to me as a colleague and to Suzanne as a devoted servant. He had answered, coolly, that he regretted the discourtesy, but that he could no longer involve us in actions for which he, and he alone, stood responsible. Already I was open to a charge of conspiracy to obstruct justice, of being an accessory to the murder of Tony Tesoriero. He would not expose me further. For the future—so far as I cared to foresee that future—I should confine myself to the normal business transactions of the company.

I argued that I was already a go-between with Aaron Bogdanovich and Saul Wells and Milo Frohm. He ordered that, in future, he would deal personally with Bogdanovich. Saul Wells was overtly employed; Milo Frohm was a Government agent: I would treat with both under his direction . . . Very well! If he

wanted it that way . . . He did. Praise the Lord!
Amen! I began to dream, longingly, of blue water and
white sails bellying as we sailed on a broad reach to
hell-and-gone.

Suzanne found him easier to deal with than I. She
had nothing to argue. She retreated into the formal-
ities of Europe and refused even the longtime privilege of using his Christian name. Harlequin made no
comment on the change, although I noticed that he
became a shade less peremptory and more considerate in her regard. Thrown back on each other's company, we became closer and more private, more
fearful, too, of the cold despair which consumed our
onetime friend.

It was dark when we landed at Los Angeles. On
the tarmac we were met by two officials from Immi-
gration and Customs who checked us into the country with the minimum of ceremony and delivered us
into the hands of Milo Frohm. He drove us in his own
car to the Bel Air hotel and installed us in adjoining
bungalows, which he claimed were secure and free
from electronic devices.

He was grateful that we had decided to cooperate with him. He would be as frank with us as the
peculiar circumstances permitted. If we had no objections, he would join us for supper. He suggested
that it might be politic to delay our meeting with Saul
Wells. Perhaps, while we were freshening up, he
could study the documents we had brought from
Mexico. He frowned first and then grinned when
George Harlequin handed him a set of photostats and
said that he would prefer to keep the originals in his
own possession. He thought it might be wiser if

Suzanne were excused from our discussions. Later, over coffee and sandwiches, he read us a little homily:

". . . At our first meeting, gentlemen, we talked of a conflict of interests: ours as a domestic agency, yours as a foreign corporation. I think we have both come to see that our interests converge, even if they are not and cannot be identical. Fair statement?"

We agreed that it was. Harlequin added a rider that he was less convinced than I. Milo Frohm noted the point and went on:

". . . Our State Department is at odds with the Europeans because they're making separate oil deals with the Arabs. The Israelis are sore with the Europeans because the French and the Norwegians have blown their spy network and their early warning system against terrorists. They're sore with us, too, because they figure we gave away too much in the cease-fire negotiations. It is against this background that you have to see your situation with Basil Yanko. Politically, he's been useful to us. He's given us footholds in Europe. He has succeeded in attracting Arab money and goodwill to this country instead of to Europe. That's high politics and rough trade. It means a certain amount of dirt has to be swept under the rug. We know that. Regrettably, we accept it if it works and we scream blue murder if it doesn't. As a matter of policy, we'd be happy if Yanko could take you over. As a matter of fact, we're hurting like hell because he played too rough, and you played too clever and every day there's another piece of dirty washing on the clothesline. In short, Mr. Harlequin, you have created a first class scandal at a time when we need it like a hole in the head . . ."

"Are you telling me, Mr. Frohm, that you want to bury it?"

"We'd like to; we know we can't. Basil Yanko has two choices: fight you to a finish or cut his own throat. As of today, his stock is down twenty-eight percent. It will go lower yet. He's serving suit on you for upwards of twenty million damages, and punitive payments on top of that. You'll go to court and to your shareholders with these Mexican documents and whatever else you've dug up and haven't told me . . . Then the Administration's got egg all over its face before it's wiped off the Watergate mess. That's something we'd all like to avoid."

"You can," said George Harlequin.

"How?" Milo was eager.

"Give me back my wife."

"I wish I could, Mr. Harlequin. I wish to God I could."

"Alternately, Mr. Frohm, because you cannot do the impossible, arrest Basil Yanko for conspiracy to murder and put him behind bars."

"On Pedro Galvez's confession? No way in the world."

"It's an authentic document."

"The man who wrote it is dead. He was your friend, a shareholder in your company. It could be argued that he conspired with you to offer that confession as a last act of friendship. It could be argued equally well that he made it under threat of duress—which is what I think happened, Mr. Harlequin, though I have neither the means nor the desire to prove it. But you do have a holograph note from Tony Tesoriero, who is dead, too. We're happy to be

rid of him; so we're not really asking who killed him.
However, we've known for some time that Valerie
Hallstrom was an Israeli agent working for a network which we tolerate for our own purposes . . .
Which reminds me, Mr. Desmond. You sent your
manservant on a holiday to San Francisco. We sent
a man to talk to him. He says you're fond of flowers
and that you normally have them delivered from a
shop on Third Avenue . . ." He sighed and threw out
his hands in momentary despair. "As my English colleagues say, it's a right, royal mess. But some way—
and quickly—we've got to clean it up."

"There's one sure way, Mr. Frohm, and you can
use it. There's no doubt at all about the documents
that link Alex Duggan to the frauds in Mexico. You
need only one more—a confession that he acted
under prompting or instruction from Basil Yanko."

"There's a problem there, too, I'm afraid. Alex
Duggan left home on Tuesday morning to visit a
client in San Diego. He didn't arrive. He hasn't been
seen since. His company and his wife have him listed
with Missing Persons."

"Paul! You told me Saul Wells had him under
surveillance . . ."

"He did."

"Then how the devil did this happen?"

"Very simply," said Milo Frohm wearily. "There
was a pileup on the freeway. Saul Wells got stuck in
it. Luck of the game, I'm afraid. Poor Saul! His pride
is dented worse than his fenders!"

I would have been happy there and then to quit—
close the whole business and go home; but Harlequin
was stubborn as a mule on a mountain path.

"Mr. Frohm, you sent us a cable which I quote: 'I think you need me.' So I consented, on your urging and that of Mr. Desmond, to confer with you, and if I deemed your counsel right, to follow it. Now, what do you advise? To forget the murder of my wife? I will not do it. To let Basil Yanko buy me, lock, stock and barrel, and sell me to the oil-sheiks? No! To cease harassing him in the press for fear he will win damages against me? If I cannot prove these documents in court, I will invoke them at the bar of public opinion. I have committed no crime—and my moral guilts are my own business." He slammed his fist on the table. "I will not be put off, Mr. Frohm! If you or your government wants to make a case against Basil Yanko, I will help you to make it. If you want to protect him, I will fight you, too, and die doing it, if I must. Now, for God's sake, state your case—or go!"

"My case begins with a dilemma, Mr. Harlequin. Our government contracts with Yanko because he's a genius and offers the best service in the market. Our Agency believes Basil Yanko to be guilty of conspiracy to defraud, conspiracy to murder, gangsterism on a grand scale. There's a madness in our system that compounds the vices of the man. We can't prove his guilt, because we can't bend all the rules and if we break the law, we defeat our own ends. We want information. If you can supply it, we won't ask where or how you get it. We won't inhibit your access to sources we can't touch. We will not concern ourselves with what you do outside our jurisdiction. If you break the law of the United States, you do it at your own risk. Do I make myself clear?"

"So far, yes."

"There are other risks, too, Mr. Harlequin."

"I'd like to hear them."

"I warned you that it would be dangerous to ally yourself with partisan interests. You chose to ignore that warning and associate yourself with Aaron Bogdanovich, an Israeli agent, and Leah Klein, a well-known, not to say notorious, journalist with Zionist sympathies. You are now listed, with Mr. Desmond, as targets for terrorist attack. Don't open suspicious mail. Don't admit unidentified visitors. Don't walk alone at night."

"One question, Mr. Frohm."

"Yes?"

"How did we get on that list?"

"You were computed, Mr. Harlequin, as Zionist sympathizers. It's the sort of information Mr. Yanko provides at high cost to restricted subscribers. Wonderful what you can do with a data bank, isn't it? You can even program genocide . . . Now, can we cooperate?"

"We can. Let's discuss details . . ."

Half an hour later, when he had gone, George Harlequin read me his own situation report:

". . . Milo Frohm is like you, Paul. He wants a solution; but he wants it safe. He will tolerate crime; but he will not commit it. He will forget, if I will forgive. Yanko victorious is Yanko innocent. He can't give me back my wife; he wants me to give him a sweet, commodious remedy for a public nuisance. He picked holes in embarrassing documents but declines to put them to proof in court. Now what does that say to you?"

"What someone said better, George: he has a prudent versatility."

"To the devil with versatility!"

"Fine!"

"What's your answer then?"

"Nothing, George. You're set on what you want to do. Go do it."

"I want Yanko dead."

"Kill him then. Or let a contract on him. You know how it's done now."

"I'll do it myself, Paul."

I could have murdered him then. I was bigger than he, and heavier, and angrier than I had ever been in my life. I swung him round and pinned him to the wall with my fingers on his throat. I hit him with every curse in the book.

". . . Now, listen, you bastard! I loved Julie just as much as you. I could have made her happier than you. Your son could have been my son—but at least I stood sponsor for him into this lousy world! His mother's dead. Do you want him to have a murderer for a father? Do you? You're spoilt rotten, George! You're not a man! You're a mountebank. Peel off the mask and there's nothing! No face, no heart, just hate and that's less than . . ."

What it was less than, I couldn't remember. There was an interval of darkness and then I woke up in bed with an ice pack on my head and Suzanne chafing my hands, and George Harlequin standing at my feet, like Mephisto come to claim payment on his bill. I had mislaid my voice and, when I found it again, it had shrunk to a whisper. I said:

"Get to hell out of here."

He didn't go; perhaps he hadn't heard me. He came and sat on the edge of the bed. "I'm sorry, Paul. It was a dirty trick; but you could have killed me."

I wished I had and I tried to tell him so; but my voice stuck in my throat like a fishbone, and I coughed and gagged and spat up a small gobbet of blood. Suzanne went pale.

Harlequin shook his head. "He'll survive, Suzy. He's got a fight or two left in him."

"I'm sorry I wasted this one on a bastard like you, George."

He cocked his head on one side and looked at me like a specimen under glass and said with sour humor, "Saul Wells is coming at nine in the morning. You should be on your feet by then. Be gentle with him, Suzy. He's still rather fragile . . ."

Knowing Saul Wells, I expected no long session at the Wailing Wall. He had a whole pocketful of proverbs for all occasions of death and disaster. Madame Harlequin was dead; he was grieved but not permanently scarred. Alex Duggan had disappeared, but he'd show up as soon as he wanted to make dough or make time. Meantime, Saul Wells, super-sleuth was pursuing his relentless inquiries.

". . . So here's the add-ups and the take-aways. Alex Duggan could be dead, sure. I say he's not because Yanko can't afford another corpse in his stable . . . So he's alive and where is he? When I lost him, he was heading south to San Diego, right? Mexico he doesn't want to see again. He's making for cat-

tle country? The hell he is! Our little Alex is a city boy
and he loves home comforts and a little drinkie with
the girls before he goes home to momma—who, I
should tell you, is, herself, a nice piece of homework.
So it's my guess he's holed up somewhere on the
coast with a beach-bunny. However, he's got to sleep,
eat and buy gas and maybe rent himself another car,
because we have the plates of the one he drives . . .
So, we've got photographs and a description and a
list of the credit cards issued to him through the company. All we need now is to get lucky . . ."

"I'd like to talk to his wife," said George
Harlequin.

"You, Mr. Harlequin?"

"Why not? Do you know her telephone number?"

"Everything, Mr. Harlequin, except what she
wears to bed."

"And where her husband is," said George Harlequin dryly. "Let me have the number. I'll call her
now."

"Why don't we just go round to her house?"

"Please, Mr. Wells! I know what I'm doing! . . .
Mrs. Duggan? My name is George Harlequin. You
don't know me, but my company uses the services of
Creative Systems. Your husband did some work for
us in Mexico City. I understand from his office that
he's been missing for a couple of days. I have some
information which may help you . . . If you prefer, I
could pass it to the company or to the police . . . I'm
at the Bel Air. I can send a car to pick you up. You
can? Splendid. Let's say half an hour . . ."

Saul Wells was still dubious. He said so, in blunt
words, "You say you know what you're doing, Mr.

Harlequin. I hope so. If you blow this one, you may lose Alex Duggan permanently."

"I'll risk that, Mr. Wells."

"He's your witness. Do you want me here while you talk to her?"

"Better not, I think. Your job is to find Alex Duggan and find him quickly."

Saul Wells went out chewing unhappily on his cigar. Harlequin leafed through his notebook and punched out a number. After a few moments, I heard him say, "This is George Harlequin calling. I should like to speak to Mr. Basil Yanko . . . Oh, is he? Thank you. I'll call him there."

"George, what the hell are you doing?"

He looked up at me with a humorless grin. "Calling Basil Yanko. He's here on the Coast."

"What are you going to say to him?"

"I'm going to invite him to a meeting."

"I think you're out of your mind."

"When I call, pick up the extension and listen."

As usual, it took a long time to get through to the great man. It was something of a shock to hear, once again, the curt, dry tones, tinged with faint contempt:

"Well, Mr. Harlequin! This is a surprise. Please accept my sympathy on the untimely death of your wife."

"Thank you. I'm at the Bel Air with Mr. Desmond. We arrived last night. I believe it may be appropriate for us to meet at this time."

"On the contrary, Mr. Harlequin. I think it would be most inappropriate—unless it were in the presence of my attorneys."

"I should have no objection to that. If they

wished to serve papers on me—as I believe they do—it might suit them to do so at such a time. However, if you prefer not to meet, there's no harm done."

"May I have time to consider the matter?"

"By all means. I shall be in Los Angeles until tomorrow evening. You can reach me at the hotel at any time. If I'm out, my secretary will be instructed to make the appointment, which I think should be here on neutral territory."

"I should prefer, Mr. Harlequin, that it be in my office."

"The security is better here. My bungalow has been checked by the FBI. They assure me there are no devices of any kind. After Washington, we had to take precautions. I leave it with you then, Mr. Yanko."

"I'll get back to you. Thank you for calling."

It was a sterile little dialogue and I saw no point in it. I also saw grave dangers in a confrontation with attorneys before we were even at law.

Harlequin shrugged off the objection with a sybilline saying: "If we don't expect justice, the lawyers can neither help nor hurt us."

"This is a litigious country, George. Nuisance is a legal weapon. For God's sake, you've got enough trouble. Don't start buying any more."

"I'm not buying it, Paul. I'm creating it . . . Call me when Mrs. Duggan arrives. I'm going to take a stroll round the garden."

It was then that I broached to Suzanne the idea that I should probably retire from my directorship as soon as we reached New York. It was not all vanity

and pique. If he couldn't bury his dead, I certainly
wanted to bury mine and let the daisies grow over the
grave mound. If he wanted to keep his own counsel,
that was his right. I was too old for fisticuffs, too
frayed for wordy battles. Suzanne told me she was
very close to the same decision. She didn't ask to be
loved, but she could not work for the stranger who
lived now in Harlequin's shoes. He would not be left
without help. He had whole staffs at his disposal. Perhaps that was what he needed—a new series of relationships untainted by old memories. We agreed that
I should discuss the matter with him, show him how
we felt, and give him ample time to make other
arrangements. In the end, surgery might be a kinder
treatment than this constant cupping and bleeding.

Mrs. Alexander Duggan looked like all the girls in the
kitchen commercials: tanned, eager, and in love with
the whole, beautiful world, which, for no reason at
all, had suddenly turned topsy-turvy. Even her distress had a wide-eyed wondering quality about it—
like Cinderella after midnight, hoping for the return
of the fairy godmother. Harlequin was gentle to her;
but the documents and the facts and the photographs
were a brutal revelation. She dissolved into tears and
helpless cries of puzzlement and Suzanne had to take
her into the bedroom to calm her. From the moment
she returned, it was an inquisition, cold and pitiless,
with Harlequin well-cast for Torquemada.

"Mrs. Duggan, my wife is dead—murdered. Four
other people concerned in this affair are also dead.

Your husband will be the next victim, unless we find him quickly."

"But I don't know where he is! You must believe that."

"Mrs. Duggan, let me explain something. This fraud was committed in Mexico. Your husband cannot be tried for it here. I will make no charges against him in Mexico, provided I get a statement from him telling who directed him to organize it. Is that clear?"

"Yes."

"Do you believe me?"

"I want to."

"If you don't, I can do nothing. This visit to the client in San Diego, was it routine, or something special?"

"Routine. He has a monthly roster. San Diego was one of his regular calls."

"Fine. He was doing a normal thing. Now, before he left, did anything abnormal happen? Was he upset? Did he draw money from the bank . . . ? Anything at all?"

"No."

"Did he pack extra clothes?"

"He didn't pack at all. It's a day trip. All he took was a swimsuit and a towel. He liked to have a swim on the way back."

"Where did he normally swim?"

"La Jolla. There's a motel there called the Blue Dolphin. It has a pool and a surf-beach. The police checked. He hadn't been there."

"What about money?"

"I asked him for some before he left. He had

about a hundred and fifty dollars. He gave me eighty and kept the rest for himself."

"What about your bank account?"

"Just our normal drawings. But I've told all this to the police."

"What about other women, Mrs. Duggan?"

"Oh, that . . ." She managed a weak, tearful smile. "He didn't have to run away to play. We're very liberated people."

"Would he run away if he was frightened?"

"Yes, he would."

"Was he frightened, Mrs. Duggan?"

"If he was, I didn't notice."

"Have you been through his papers?"

"He never kept any at home. He had a fetish about that. He said home was to play in. If he had to work at home, he resented it."

"What about letters, postcards, bills . . . that sort of thing?"

"We read them, answered them, destroyed them. I keep the bills in a folder in the kitchen."

"What about documents: title deeds, stocks and bonds?"

"We hold those in safe-deposit at the bank."

"Who has access?"

"We both do."

"Who has the key?"

"I have one and Alex kept another on his key-ring."

"Did he have the key-ring with him when he left home?"

"Of course. He wears it on a gold chain I gave him for his birthday."

"Mrs. Duggan, how was Alex doing in business?"

"Wonderfully well. Next month he was due to become Area Superintendent. The promotion had gone through in a memo from Mr. Yanko himself . . ."

"Do you have money problems?"

"None. We live well, but we've got money in the bank and we don't owe anything."

"So—no money worries, no marriage problems, everything going well at the office, but your husband commits a criminal act in Mexico. Why would he do that?"

"Someone must have asked him to do it."

"What does that mean?"

"Well, someone in the company."

"Who?"

"I don't know. That was another of Alex's fetishes. He said business talk at home gave you ulcers and coronaries."

"What happened to the ten thousand dollars he got from Maria Guzman?"

"I never knew he had it."

"Did he begin spending more when he came back from Mexico?"

"No."

"How long since you've opened your safe-deposit, Mrs. Duggan?"

"I? Oh, twelve months or more. If we need anything, Alex usually goes to get it."

"Mrs. Duggan, I have no right to ask this. You have every right to refuse. I wonder if you'd mind opening it with me now?"

"What do you expect to find?"

"I don't know, Mrs. Duggan. I'm guessing, as

you are. But we're both guessing about the same thing: whether your husband is alive or dead."

"I don't know. I suppose it's all right . . ."

"It's your safe-deposit. You have legal access. If you feel you need protection, I can ask an agent of the FBI to accompany us."

"No! That's not necessary. I'll take you down to the bank now."

"Thank you, Mrs. Duggan . . . Suzanne, if Yanko calls, make any time he suggests, provided we meet here. Paul, get hold of Milo Frohm and ask him to meet me for lunch at Verita's on Santa Monica. Tell him it's rather important."

I called Milo Frohm, who was happy to have lunch. Basil Yanko telephoned to say that he would be present at the hotel with his attorneys at six in the evening. It was a sad waste of the cocktail hour, but we had to consent. Then Suzy and I played truant. We lay by the pool. We swam. We drank Bloody Marys and ate club sandwiches and drowsed under the red flowers of the bougainvillea. Before we knew, it was four in the afternoon; and when we hurried in to change, George Harlequin had still not returned. It was five o'clock when he telephoned to say he was back. At five-thirty, Suzy was summoned to prepare for the meeting; to set out pens and papers and order drinks and canapés. At six plus five, shaved, sober and reasonably sane, I presented myself at the conference with Basil Yanko and his attorneys.

They made a curious trio: Basil Yanko, a gray-haired savant in a silk suit. and a mop-haired junior counselor with a thin face and an air of elfin malice. Suzanne sat apart, pencil poised over her notebook, with a manila folder on the floor beside her. George Harlequin, dressed in a silk shirt and slacks, presided like the director of a very exclusive fashion house. Basil Yanko opened the proceedings with a testy demand:

"Well, Mr. Harlequin, what's the order of business?"

"First, Mr. Yanko, do you want to serve papers?"

"At this time, no. We prefer to do it in New York, if that's acceptable."

"Perfectly . . . If I am not there, Mr. Desmond will accept service under his power of attorney. It's still current, isn't it, Paul?"

"Two months to run, George."

"Good. Satisfactory, gentlemen?"

Gray-hair and junior agreed that it was.

George Harlequin asked, hesitantly: "Indemnities for costs? I presume you're putting up, Mr. Yanko?"

"We aren't; but, if necessary, we will, Mr. Harlequin. Now, what is the purpose of this meeting?"

"I presume you'd like a record of it?"

"Yes, please."

"Suzanne will set it down in shorthand and type it before you leave. We can then agree and sign it. Is that acceptable?"

It was acceptable to Basil Yanko; his henchmen agreed perforce.

George Harlequin leaned back in his chair, stretched his legs, built a pyramid with his hands and smiled over the peak of it. "Mr. Yanko, I state before witnesses and I subscribe in writing as follows: you conspired to defraud my company of fifteen million dollars and, in so doing, to discredit me and secure control of my company. You conspired also to murder Frank Lemnitz in London, Valerie Hallstrom in New York and my wife in Mexico City. I propose within the next few days to make these charges public and to urge them against you in court. I understand that if I cannot prove the charges, I shall have committed the grossest of libels and I stand ready to accept all the penalties and damages I may incur. That is the end of my statement. I am happy to hear your comments on or off the record."

"For the record," said Basil Yanko coldly, "I think you're a criminal lunatic."

"Also, for the record." The senior attorney weighed his words carefully. "Would you tell us why you have chosen to make this extraordinary statement at this time and in this manner?"

"I was informed today by the Federal Bureau of Investigation that Mr. Desmond and I may be the targets of terrorist attack as Zionist sympathizers. We are so listed in a document which emanated from Mr. Yanko's data services. My infant son has been placed under police protection in Geneva. I wish Mr. Yanko to know that, should anything happen to us, he will not be immune from the law because I have already filed evidence in support of the charges."

Junior counsel bestirred himself then and said, blandly, "Obviously, the evidence is insufficient, otherwise Mr. Yanko would now be under arrest—as you may soon be, Mr. Harlequin. With deference to my senior colleague, I suggest that, in the light of recent leaks to the Press, what we are seeing here is a rather crude attempt at blackmail and coercion."

"I would agree coercion," said George Harlequin evenly. "I am trying to prevent the murder of Alex Duggan. I met his wife this morning. She was very helpful . . . It would avail nothing to kill him now, Mr. Yanko."

Yanko made a gesture of dismissal. "I say it again. You're out of your sweet mind. Let's go, gentlemen."

"With respect, Mr. Yanko—" the senior attorney hesitated—"why not wait for the statement to be typed and signed? It's not often a man offers us a rope to hang him."

"You wait for it," said Basil Yanko. "I have work to do."

He strode out, leaving two very embarrassed attorneys to face a ten-minute hiatus while Suzanne typed up her shorthand.

Harlequin smiled. "Please, gentlemen, let me offer you a drink. It's a pity your client was in such a hurry. I have a document to show you . . . only to demonstrate that I am not quite the fool I look."

He opened his briefcase and handed each man a photostat of Pedro Galvez's confession.

They read it poker-faced. The senior attorney asked, finally, "May we keep this?"

"I'm afraid not."

Reluctantly they handed back the paper. They were suddenly more eager for the drinks, and singularly anxious for what they called "a quiet exchange of views." They were in deep dilemma and they knew it. They had to insist on the total innocence of their client. They were troubled by the now sinister aspect of Alex Duggan's disappearance, on which they had received a warning before witnesses. They skated in figures of eight round "meditation and amicable settlement of disputes outstanding."

Harlequin let them talk and then asked the unanswerable, "How do you mediate with murder, gentlemen? How do you buy back the dead?"

They left at seven, two very puzzled men, each with a signed typescript and a very confused idea of what to do with it. As soon as they had left, Harlequin asked Suzanne to pack for him. Milo Frohm was calling for him at eight-thirty. They were flying to London together. This was startling news. He explained it with elaborate simplicity:

". . . Frohm was right, Paul. Basil Yanko has built so many fences around himself that every investigation stops short at an intermediary—Galvez, Tony Tesoriero, Alex Duggan and whoever killed Frank Lemnitz in London. That's the way Yanko has always worked. He delegates power and abrogates responsibility when it suits his plans . . . However, Alex Duggan was not concerned with murder, only with his career. He was directed to set up the fraud in Mexico City; but he was wise enough to take out insurance. He left a signed account of the affair in his safe-deposit box, demonstrating that he was working under direction from Creative Systems. It wouldn't help him in law; but it did protect his career with the company. Also in the safe-deposit, he kept a large reserve of cash—probably the money he was paid for the job and that which he got from Maria Guzman. The bank record shows that shortly before his disappearance, he opened the safe-deposit box—obviously to supply himself with untraceable funds. Our guess is that, after Galvez called Yanko, Duggan was advised to go into hiding. He went, knowing that the letter would guarantee his safety. His wife couldn't surrender it because she didn't know it existed. She can't now because we've got it. There's a guard on Mrs. Duggan and her child, and Yanko's had a warning which you've just heard. Saul Wells is still looking for Duggan. Milo Frohm and I are going to London to pick up the man who stands between Duggan and Yanko. If he'll talk, our case is made."

"The case for fraud, not murder. Which means you've just put your name to the libel of the century. I agree with Yanko. You're out of your sweet mind. Who is this fellow in London, anyway?"

"The one who's married to Beverley Manners, our former computer girl. She's expecting a baby—remember?—and he plays golf in Surrey with our London manager."

"Let's hope he hasn't decided to take a holiday before you get there."

"He can't. Frohm has been in touch with Scotland Yard; they've brought him in for questioning on the murder of Frank Lemnitz. That'll keep him occupied until we get there."

"What do you want us to do?"

"Go to New York. Take two or three days on the way, if you want. Stay there until I return."

"Nothing else?"

"Nothing else, Paul. Enjoy yourself. Give Suzanne a holiday. Nothing will change until I get back. Better you're not embroiled in gossip."

8

It was easy to dispense us from friendship and duty. It was not possible to purge out the memory of recent events and the nagging fear of imminent disaster. It was an insult to wave a slapstick and say, "Lo! The world is transformed. Go disport yourselves among the gilly-flowers!" What were we to do? Eat, drink, do the galleries, take in the shows, ride a tourist bus to see the homes of the stars?

We had seen the underside of the carpet, with all the muck of the world clinging to the knotted threads. Now we were bidden to admire the beauty of the pattern, kneel on it to pray, lie on it to make love. I was so furious with George Harlequin I could hardly bear to wave him out of the driveway. Suzanne was pensive about him and sad; which made me angrier still and spoilt a perfectly good dinner for both of us. At the end of it, she was resolved that she didn't want to set foot in New York. She would be happier to fly back to Geneva, tidy her desk, resign and spend the summer barefoot in Sardinia.

Then, as we sat, morose and unhappy over the coffee, I thought of Francis Xavier Mendoza, and, before the small grace was taken away, I called him. He had read the press reports. The whole affair was a putrid mess. As always, his heart and his house were open. In the morning, he was flying up to the vineyards. Why shouldn't we come and spend a day and a night on the estate and drink good wine and talk simplicities? I called blessings on his head and said we would be delighted. Suzanne was as happy as if she had been invited to the morgue. My friends were mine. Her life was her own affair. The rest of the evening she would prefer to spend alone. She wasn't raucous about it; she was polite and determined. She gave me a perfunctory kiss on the forehead and left me to join the other male rejects in the bar.

Somewhere around midnight, Saul Wells came looking for me. He said he was worn down to the knees, and he looked it. He hoisted himself on to a bar stool, ordered a large vodka on ice, and downed half of it in a single swallow. Then he told me the news. He had found Alex Duggan.

"Where, for God's sake?"

"Would you believe, in hospital; a ritzy private clinic in San Diego."

"What's the matter with him?"

"Nothing."

"I don't understand."

"He admitted himself; said he wanted a complete medical checkup and a couple of weeks' rest and sedation after a long and exhausting sales trip. He's sitting up in a private room, surrounded by paperbacks and admiring nurses."

"How the hell did you find out?"

"Routine and a little luck. Normally we call only

hospitals that treat casualties. Then I remembered a case last year where a guy went underground for six months by moving from clinic to clinic. They've got the beds if you've got the money. They'll give you primary, secondary and tertiary screenings, high colonics, special diets, tests for sterility—anything you can pay for. I know one lady novelist who puts herself into hospital to write her books. She says it's great; no housekeeping, no servant problems, she can wear all her pretties, and when her boyfriend comes to see her, they hang out the 'no visitors' sign. Anyway, to cut it short, I started calling—and found him on the fourth try."

"Did you talk to him?"

"No. I want instructions on that. Your Mr. Harlequin put a flea in my ear this morning. From now I go by the book. I've got three operators watching the place round the clock . . . I hope you realize what all this is costing you?"

When I told him what had happened during his absence, he gave a low whistle of pure joy. "Hell! That boy's hot as chilli sauce and he doesn't know it. Now, let's read the book. We can't pick him up. That's kidnapping. If he leaves, we can follow him; and we may lose him again. Only one thing to do: call the FBI, find out who's pinch-hitting for Milo Frohm and hand the case over to him. Order me another vodka and I'll make the call now. Oh, brother! If Duggan slips away this time, I'll put myself into a psycho ward!"

He came back rubbing his hands and grinning all over his sharp little face. "Great—great—great! Number one priority. They've taken full responsibil-

ity. They're sending word to Frohm in flight. Their
agents will take over from our operators as soon as
San Diego can whistle in the troops . . . So now, Mr.
Desmond, you and I can do a little steady drinking."

"What about Duggan's wife?"

"What about her?"

"Shouldn't someone tell her?"

"Someone should. I guess in the end someone
will—but not us. No, sir! What she doesn't know,
can't hurt her and it can't hurt us . . . Tell you
what, though: in California, I'm out of a job; in Mexico, I'm closed out . . ."

"But you've still got answers to find on Ella
Deane in New York."

"That's a cold trail, Mr. Desmond. With Lemnitz
dead, I doubt we'll ever pick it up again."

"Have you thought about Bernie Koonig?"

"What gives you that idea?"

"My ribs still hurt. They say Lemnitz-Koonig,
Koonig-Lemnitz. What have you got to lose, except
our money?"

"Like you say, what have I got to lose? Maybe
we're on a winning streak now, eh? Drink up, Mr.
Desmond, you're one behind."

It was late when I got to bed, and early in the
morning when Suzanne crawled in beside me to tell
me the sun was just up and the birds were singing and
there was nothing she would like better than a day
among the wine makers—well, almost nothing . . .

Francis Xavier Mendoza took one look at me and de-
clared me unfit for human company. He wondered

how any woman in her right mind could bear to be seen with such a genetic mistake, on whose visage were etched all the evils of the world. I needed sun, clean air and a very broad and general absolution before he would let me within a mile of his precious vintages. Suzanne, he would welcome with red carpets and hibiscus flowers. Me . . . Ay! if he didn't cherish a faint hope for my salvation, he would consign me, unregenerate, to outer darkness.

It was good to be with him. He coaxed the goodness out of you, as he coaxed the flavor of the soil and the bouquet out of the wine, with love and a long patience. The vines were in full leaf and the first tiny grapes were fattening slowly as he walked us along the terraces and through the caves, and the gleaming, aseptic laboratories, talking all the while of the ritual that led finally to the sacramental moment when the raw must became a fine wine.

He recited their names like a litany: Cabernet and Chardonnay and Chenin Blanc, Sauvignon and Semillon and Zinfandel, which Colonel Agoston Haraszthy brought from Hungary in 1857 and which is still unique to California. He talked to Robert Louis Stevenson, who drank Souverain and Schamsberg and made a eulogy about them to shame the snobs of Europe. For a reproof to me, he quoted Tom Jefferson: "No nation is drunken where wine is cheap: and none sober where the dearness of wine substitutes ardent spirits for the common beverage." He raised a laugh from Suzanne when he recited the toast of old Matthias Claudius: "Wer liebt nicht Weiben, Wein und Gesang . . . Who loves not women, wine and song, remains a fool his whole life long."

Before the day was half-spent, he had her charmed out of her mind, and me out of the depression that had enveloped me too long, like a foul fog. After lunch, leaving Suzanne to drowse on the patio, he walked me up and down a cloister of trees, at the end of which was a joyful little sculpture of the Poverello talking to a pair of doves perched on his outstretched hand. I told Mendoza all that had happened in New York and in Mexico. None of it shocked him; all of it saddened him.

". . . Paul, my friend, we are like peasants living in a battle zone. There is death all around us. We are hardened to it. We do not even ignore it; we make it now our staple entertainment . . . We think the Romans were brutes because they staged death games in the arena. Now we simulate them for our children on television and in the films . . . Millions of people line up to see a child masturbate herself with a crucifix . . . A large company has people murdered? Of course it does . . . I believe everything you tell me. I am only surprised there has not been more violence . . ."

"There well may be. George Harlequin has sworn to kill Basil Yanko."

"And that, after all the rest, surprises you, Paul. It should not . . . Murder, like the plague, is epidemic. The legal restraint is weaker than it ever was. How can it be otherwise? After each revolution of the left or the right, the assassins make the laws, and the torturers enforce them. Only the moral restraint still holds—the sacredness of life, the sacredness of a man. Abrogate that, abandon it in despair, as Harlequin has done, murder is the natural recourse . . . But you must not let it happen, Paul."

"I can't stop it. He's isolated himself from me. I won't be party to it, so I'm leaving him. So is Suzanne."

Francis Xavier Mendoza stopped dead in his tracks. He put his hands on my shoulders and swung me round to face him. He was grim as old Moses shattering the tablets. "Paul, I hardly know this man. He is your friend, not mine. But I swear to you that if you leave him now, if you do not stand with him to the last moment and try to prevent this terrible thing, you will never set foot in my house again . . . Never! You have a duty! You have a love! If he were dying of hunger, would you refuse him a crust? Now he is in despair. Will you turn away and let him go raving into this final madness? You can't! You will not!"

"What do I do, Francis? What do I say?"

"Anything, everything, nothing! But be there! Don't let him thrust you away. Swallow every insult. Stay with him. If it ever happened to me—and I know that it could, because I am a passionate man, and my grandfather killed men in these hills—I would hope for some friend to hold me back from that terrible final act." He took my arm and began pacing with me again. ". . . Tell me about Suzanne. I like her very much."

"There's not much to tell. We were lovers once. We've always been friends. Now, because of all this mess, we're lovers again. How long it will last, I don't know."

"Why shouldn't it last?"

"It's late in the day, Francis, old friend."

"All the more reason to be careful of the good

things. Falling in love—that's for children. But loving, that's like the best wine . . . to decant slowly and
hold gently, and savor and sip. You don't grow a
great vintage. You create it . . . I see the way she
looks at you. I see how you lean to her. You could
make a good marriage."

"I made a botch of the first one. I couldn't face
another failure."

"Why should it be a failure? You've both had
time to learn. Whatever the old theologians taught,
you don't make a sacrament by saying the words.
You make it by commitment and by loving. You're
my friend. I hate to see you lonely in the rich years.
Think about it . . . Don't think about Harlequin.
That's settled, eh?"

"If you say so, amigo."

"Good! Now, let's say good-day to the Poverello
and I'll pour you a wine that would charm him down
from his pedestal, if only I could persuade him to try
it."

In the evening, when the desert chill crept along
the land, we dined by candlelight, looking out at the
dark face of the valley and the black peaks and the
full moon climbing above them. We listened to
Segovia and Casals and afterwards Mendoza read us
some of his translations. It was a night of quiet en-
chantment and Suzanne spoke the thought that was
in both our minds.

"What a pity George isn't here. He would have
enjoyed it so much."

"He is here," said Mendoza gravely. "He is in
your hearts and in mine now. What we are doing is
an act of love. Nobody is shut out from it. Before you

go from here, Suzanne, I shall give you a wine that I prize very much. There are only six bottles of it left. You shall have one; but you will not drink it until the three of you are together to share it. Paul has promised me he will stay with Harlequin. I think you should stay, too. And when this plague has passed, I think you and Paul should marry."

"I know you care," said Suzanne gently. "But why so much for strangers like me, like George?"

"I will tell you," said Francis Xavier Mendoza. "I am the most fortunate of men. God made the vine. I make the wine. You drink it and it is changed into you. It's a beautiful truth. When I contemplate it in all its meaning I am so happy I could weep . . . This is the communion that keeps us sane and human. Reject it and we are solitary and beset. Spill the wine of life and we are for ever accursed like Cain in the wilderness . . . I am becoming talkative. Enough! Sleep well, my friends. I should not approve, but I do. I hope you will love happily under my roof . . ."

The next day we were in another world. At San Francisco airport there was a bomb scare and all flights were delayed an hour. We were searched and penned and required to identify our luggage before it was stacked in the hold. There was an air of tension and hostility; voices were raised as harried officials tried to cope with passengers whose nerves were stretched to breaking point.

When, finally, we were airborne, Suzanne buried herself in a fashion magazine while I tried to catch up with the news. None of it was good: crisis in England, with a coal strike and a General Election; the Japanese trading terrorists for the lives of their embassy staff in Kuwait; the Italians with tanks around the Quirinal and the Vietnamese trying to claim an oil barony on the Paracel Islands, which nobody had ever heard of until the Chinese blew a gunboat out of the water. The President was five steps closer to impeachment. The stockmarket was down. Creative Systems was thirty percent below peak. There was no mention at all of our affairs. The threat of a massive libel suit had made the editors cautious. Besides, with such a glut of disasters, the public was jaded and needed new stimulus every day. Now there was a new game in San Francisco. You said good morning to a stranger, shot him through the heart, and walked away, whistling.

I was leafing through the financial pages to see how much poorer I was when I caught sight of a paragraph. Mr. Karl Kruger of Kruger and Co. AG was in New York staying at the Regency. I showed the paragraph to Suzanne, who agreed we should invite him to dinner. She was fond of the old bear, and she could tolerate Hilde, too—unless, of course, Karl had decided to sample the talent in New York. I hoped he wouldn't go roistering down Broadway and get into the same trouble as his celebrated compatriot.

Takeshi was home and in good humor, though faintly cast down by the fact that he had talked too much in San Francisco. However, once assured that his face and my legal status were undamaged, he became almost animated and hovered over our supper like a guardian spirit.

Suzanne stretched herself, luxuriously, on the divan, gave me that soft, slow smile and said, "You couldn't really give it up, could you?"

"Give what up?"

"All this and freedom, too!"

"Is that a proposal?"

"No, chéri, it's an academic question."

"Do you want to debate it?"

"Not tonight. I'm too comfortable."

"Would you answer one for me?"

"If it's not too hard."

"Will you marry me, Suzy?"

The smile vanished. She lay very still looking far beyond me into the shadows. Then she said, "There's never been a price, Paul."

"I know."

"Ever since I was a girl, I've been in love with George Harlequin."

"I know that, too."

"So you wouldn't get a very good bargain."

"Did I ask for one?"

"No . . . But, why, Paul? Why me? Why now? I'm here. I'm glad to be here. You don't have any rivals—though I wish you had . . . No, please, stay where you are! I'll melt in your arms and say 'yes' and be sorry in the morning . . . Tell me why, Paul?"

"Twenty reasons, Suzy. Only one good one: there's nothing and no one in the world I love as much as you . . . It may not be enough. How can I tell? I've lived too long and learnt too little. Anyway, as they say in the market, it's a firm offer."

"And don't they usually add: take it or leave it?"

"They do; I don't. When this is over, Suzy love,

I'm out of the market with the back of my hand and a sailor's farewell. There's no hurry. Think about it."

"I have thought about it, Paul. I've thought about it alone and lying in your arms and happy to be there. I know only one thing: I'm too fond of you to offer you a divided heart. I want to wait until this is over—not to win George, because I never will, but to be sure I'm cured of him, cured of my girl-dreams and ready to be a whole woman to a whole man . . . You're a bigger man than you know, Paul. I'd like you to be very proud of the woman you marry. Please, leave it a little longer." She smiled, a little too brightly, and held out her arms. "Who knows, you may be tired of me long before."

Well, it wasn't the moon, but at least I had the sixpence in my pocket. I was learning to be grateful for small mercies—and perhaps, I was as relieved as she to defer the last commitment. This way there were no ghosts to contend with, only a man driven by a dark demon, cold, loveless and implacable.

In the morning, we went shopping for flowers on Third Avenue. This time we were not unwelcome, and we bought fresh blooms, and a garden in a bowl to be delivered in the apartment. We did not see Aaron Bogdanovich. He had taken the morning off. Sometimes—the madam smiled over her gold spectacles—sometimes he liked to sit in the garden at the Museum of Modern Art and admire the sculpture and, you know, just think. If we didn't find him there, she'd give him the message anyway.

He wasn't there, so we wandered through the galleries and then crossed Fifth Avenue to Buccellati's, where, for my taste, you can still buy the best goldsmith's work in the world—loving handcraft like the old masters used to make up the Ponte Vecchio and in their Aladdin caves on the Lung' Arno. An hour later, I bowed to Suzanne's protests and left empty-handed; but with a ring and a pendant and bracelet held safely to my order in the vault.

As we walked out the door, Aaron Bogdanovich fell into step beside us and said, "Suite 67 at the St. Regis. You're expected for lunch. Your host is Mrs. Larkin. Telephone from the lobby."

A moment later, he had faded into the crowd. We walked past the entrance, down as far as Madison, and then turned back and walked into the St. Regis. When I called number 67, a woman's voice answered:

"Mrs. Larkin's suite."

"Mr. Weizman and friend. We're invited to lunch."

"Please, come on up."

We were met at the door by a gray-haired matron, who ushered us into a drawing room, where Aaron Bogdanovich sat, alert and unsmiling, in an armchair. As I introduced Suzanne, he cut me off:

"I know who she is. Mrs. Larkin will take her to lunch in the restaurant." He gave her a ghost of a grin. "Don't be offended, Mademoiselle. It's necessary. Besides, this lunch is on me. Enjoy it. Mr. Desmond will meet you downstairs when we have finished."

Our own lunch was coffee and sandwiches and the talk was strictly business.

"Question, Mr. Desmond. How much did you tell Milo Frohm about me?"

"Nothing. He told me."

"What exactly?"

"I bought flowers on Third Avenue."

"How did he know that?"

"He sent a man to San Francisco to talk to Takeshi."

"Anything else?"

"That we—Harlequin and I—had allied ourselves with an Israeli agent and with Leah Klein. That he knew Valerie Hallstrom was an Israeli agent. That Harlequin and I were terrorist targets."

"And what did you say?"

"Neither yea nor nay. Nothing."

"And he accepted that?"

"It was the deal. His agency wants to bring down Yanko. If we would pass our facts to him, he wouldn't ask how or where we got them. He's on his way to London now with George Harlequin. The FBI have picked up Alex Duggan in San Diego."

"Yes, I know."

"You knew the rest of it, too."

"I wanted to hear it from you. With luck, you'll nail Basil Yanko for conspiracy."

"To defraud, not to murder."

"Don't be greedy, Mr. Desmond."

"I'm not greedy. George Harlequin wants to kill him."

"For that he needs to stay alive himself. You are both marked. We don't know which one they'll hit first."

"Who is 'they'?"

"A formidable combination, Mr. Desmond: the Popular Front for the Liberation of Palestine and the

Red Army of Japan. The first one you know. The second may not be quite so familiar. It is called Rengo Sekigun. They killed twenty-seven people at Lod Airport, if you remember. They hijacked an airliner from Tokyo to North Korea. They tortured and killed twelve of their own dissidents in Japan. They are totally dedicated to nihilism and violence . . . You have a Japanese servant, Mr. Desmond . . ."

"Takeshi? Now, please . . . !"

"I told you we would check him out. We did. So did the FBI, who were not really interested where you bought flowers. Takeshi has a nephew, who has recently returned from Japan, where he had contacts with known members of the Rengo Sekigun . . . Does that suggest anything to you, Mr. Desmond?"

"Run for the trees?"

"You now have a woman living with you. Someone quite close to you and George Harlequin."

"Hell! Wait a moment! Give me the logic."

"Very well. Yanko is in relations with the oil sheiks and with Libya. Libya finances terror. You attack Yanko. You are within an ace of bringing him down. You suddenly show up on a target list for terrorist attack. The logic holds, Mr. Desmond—believe me."

"So what do we do about it?"

"Pour yourself some more coffee. This may take a little time . . . Terror is a form of social surgery in which a variety of techniques are used. In this case, there are two to be considered: you will be murdered to create fear and panic or you will be held to ransom. Now, I don't think you will be murdered outright. You are not Jews and therefore not very useful for propaganda. You are, however, rich and prominent—very suitable subjects for a ransom attempt: your lives against a lot of money and the release of political detainees, in this or other countries. If the ransom is not paid, naturally you get killed."

"Naturally."

"Now . . . What do we do about it? Let me be clear. I'm in the game and I'm good at it—very good. There is no system in the world that cannot be beaten by a group of determined men and women, who don't care whether they live or die. I can give you shadows round the clock. You have them now. I can lock you in isolation. I can give you a pistol and a pocket-pen full of lethal gas. I can train you in judo and karate. It helps; but I still wouldn't write an insurance policy on your life. I am a better risk than you are because I have no codes to bind me. I am trained to kill and survive. My reactions are totally different. Even so, I am never safe. Your best protection is to recognize the risk, accept it calmly and take certain simple precautions . . . If you are kidnapped, don't resist, stay calm, and wait for the negotiations to work themselves out. Don't try to escape. That's suicide . . . I have no doubt Milo Frohm has given much the same instruction to George Harlequin."

"What about Suzanne?"

"One question only, Mr. Desmond. If she were a kidnap victim would you or Mr. Harlequin pay ransom for her?"

"Of course."

"That's your answer. She runs the same risks as you. Explain them. Let her make her own choice. She may feel more comfortable in Geneva or in Elba, for that matter. She won't be any safer."

"Let's talk about Takeshi."

"Nothing to talk about. He's a good servant. Live with him. It's the nephew who bothers us. We're still watching that situation." He gave me that frigid, humorless grin. "We have another quarter of a million on call from you. We're doing our best to earn it . . . By the way, have you thought what Yanko will do while you're setting him up for indictment with Alex Duggan and his London accomplice?"

"I've thought about it. Hard to see what he can do except dispose of the witnesses; which leaves a lot more bodies lying around—and we'll still have the documents."

"What would you do in his shoes?"

"Well, let me think. First, I'd liquidate as many assets as I could in the shortest possible time. I'd plant them safely in a Swiss bank. Then I'd find myself a nice, offshore haven with no extradition treaty, invest some cash with local authorities and thumb my nose at Uncle Sam . . . We've had some very well-known names work the same racket in the last few years."

"Not bad. But somehow I can't see Basil Yanko as a border-hopping fugitive. It's not his style. Besides, the law's a chancy animal and he knows better than most how to ride it. My guess is he'll try to buy himself out of trouble."

"Whom can he buy?"

"If George Harlequin dropped charges, the Administration and the market would be happy to bury the whole affair. Yanko knows too many secrets."

"Christ! He must know Harlequin wants him dead—whatever the consequences to himself."

"He must think he can deal. He knows Harlequin's extended to the limit. He also knows you've got dangerous documents. That's why he's asked Karl Kruger to come to New York. To mediate a settlement."

"He's nuts!"

"No! He's computed the odds and found them in his favor. If anything happens to you, or to Harlequin, or to that nice woman of yours, the bargaining gets better still . . . In that sense, Harlequin's right. If you don't want to deal, the only alternative is to kill Basil Yanko. Think about it, Mr. Desmond. Talk to Karl Kruger. Talk to Harlequin, too, if he gets back safely . . ."

Karl Kruger was giving a party. It was a large party, an important party. It would begin at seven and go on until ten or eleven. After we had drunk the company under the table, we could talk in his room. Yes, of course, I should bring Suzanne. What kind of a party did I think it was? No, Hilde wouldn't be there: she wasn't built for this kind of thing. He had someone new for us to meet—English this time, very chic, just divorced from a noble lord who was very rich, but couldn't pay his marital debts. He went on, boom-boom-boom, for five minutes until he had battered me into submission. Then, he growled, in his bearish fashion:

"It is not enough to be right, Paul. In the market, you have to be popular—which Harlequin et Cie is not at this moment. So put on your best party clothes and smile, eh! . . . Oh, and if Basil Yanko is there, don't spit in his eye. For my sake, please! And don't close your mind to anything until we've talked . . ."

It sounded ominous; but, as my old grandfather advised me: if you have to eat crow, make sure it's cooked in a good wine sauce. So I phoned Buccellati to deliver the jewelry, ordered Suzanne under pain of banishment to buy herself the best dress she could find to match it, and took myself off to the barber. The treatment cost me twenty dollars and was guaranteed, they told me, to make me look ten years younger. They were lying—which was no surprise; but they did make me feel more fit for the company of my peers, and a little less like a third-rate conspirator, with the axe poised above his neck. I ordered a Colby limousine to pick us up at seven and then called George Harlequin in London. It was midnight and he was just getting ready for bed. I gave him a cautious resumé of my talk with Bogdanovich and told him about Karl Kruger's party.

To my surprise, he said, "Keep all the options open, Paul. We may need them."

"Trouble, George?"

"Yes. Our boy is a very clever customer. We've confronted him with the documents; but he's got good counsel and he won't admit anything. We've got nothing to tie him to the frauds in London—except his wife, who is covered by a forged memorandum. Alex Duggan's statement connects him only with a conspiracy in California to commit a fraud in Mexico—and there is, of course, no complaint from the Mexican police. The London police are co-operative and they're examining the situation with Milo Frohm. Our lawyers in London advise that we may have a long job getting an extradition order . . . The FBI have arrested Alex Duggan and he's being held in custody at his own request. He may find even that is a dubious protection. It's all very awkward. We've got so much and yet the technicalities may beat us, so far as Yanko is concerned. I'm conferring again tomorrow with Frohm, the lawyers and the police; the day after, I'm flying to Geneva to see the baby and meet the police and the banking commissioners. I'll call you from there. Love to Suzanne. Au revoir!"

It was discouraging news—another illustration of the fragility of law and the power of those who had money enough and knowledge enough to manipulate it to their own ends. Five people were dead. There were documents that tied Basil Yanko to every death, but they fell short of legal proof. So Yanko would go to the party at the Regency and men would shake his hand, and women would fawn on him and he would walk away, despising them all.

On the other hand, there was a grain of comfort. If George Harlequin would settle and abdicate his threat, we could all go back to peaceful living again . . . perhaps. There were other threats now, and, as we walked into the street and stepped into the limousine, I found myself pointing and sniffing like a fox sensing danger, searching for it on the wind.

When we arrived, the party was in full swing and Karl Kruger dominated it like an ancient chieftain. His welcome was warm and vociferous. He took one look at Suzanne, then let out a roar of approval and swept her round the company like a new battle-prize. I found myself a drink and began a slow, cautious circuit of the assembly. I found Herbert Bachmann first and he gave me a warm handshake and a word of honest sympathy.

". . . Poor George. I was so shocked. Tell him he was remembered. You must have had a bad time yourself."

"Bad enough, Herbert."

"Now it's worse, not better. Dumping that stock has hurt a lot of people. Money's like gardenias—you mustn't bruise the petals. So far, we've held our group together. The funds will be there when George needs them. Tell me . . ." He drew me away to the fringe of the crowd. "This newspaper talk about murder. How true is it?"

"All true, Herbert. We've got documents . . ."

"Then what is Yanko doing on this guest list?"

"Not enough documents yet, Herbert."

"So it gets dirtier."

"It could. Kruger is here to mediate—at Yanko's request. That's very private."

"Thanks for telling me. It would be a good thing—not the best—but necessary."

"Is Yanko here yet?"

"I haven't seen him. Oh, Paul, when he comes, take it easy, eh?"

"Sure . . . I'll talk to you later."

Not all the greetings were as warm as that one; and some were as frigid as the martinis that prompted them.

". . . For Chrissake, Paul! You could have given us a tip, even a whisper . . . Look, buddy, a private war's fine; but this one! . . . Do you know how much we dropped on Wednesday? . . . The financial pages, okay . . . that's our forum, right? But the crime columns, that's Mafia stuff . . . Frankly, old man, we're very fond of George, and we don't much like Yanko, but . . ."

Somehow I managed to sidle through it, ride over it, waddle round it, until Suzanne came to rescue me with soft words and a compliment for everyone. Then, just when the talk was at its loudest, and the liquor was flowing most freely, Basil Yanko arrived. He came without ceremony, alone. He shook hands with Karl Kruger, talked a few moments and then slid into the crowd, inconspicuous as a cat. Slowly, Suzanne and I worked our way through the crowd toward him and came upon him, finally, talking in low tones to Herbert Bachmann.

Herbert saw us first and beckoned us over. "Mr. Yanko, I think you know these nice people."

"I do indeed . . . Mademoiselle, Mr. Desmond." He bowed but did not offer his hand. "Mr. Harlequin is not here?"

It was Suzanne who answered, prim as dimity. "No. He's in London, Mr. Yanko." She laid a hand on Herbert's arm. "Do you think you could find me a fresh drink, Mr. Bachmann?"

"With pleasure. Excuse us, gentlemen."

We excused him.

Basil Yanko raised his glass. "A handsome woman, Mr. Desmond. My compliments."

"*De nada,* Mr. Yanko—as they say in Mexico."

"A lively party."

"Karl's a very good host."

"A shrewd banker, too."

"Yes."

"Mr. Desmond, a word in season. In business you win something and you hope to lose a little less. At this moment, we are all losing too much. It is time we turned losses into profit."

"Profit's always a good word."

"I'd be grateful if you'd pass it to George Harlequin."

"I'll do that."

"Another good word is compromise."

"I'll tell him that, too."

"Life is infinitely various. One can replace everything except oneself."

"Everything except oneself . . . I like that."

"Sometimes personalities clash, ambitions, too. A mediator is useful. I respect Karl Kruger."

"We respect him, also."

"Then let's leave it at that, eh? . . . Excuse me, Mr. Desmond."

Graceless as ever, he walked away.

Suzanne came back with Herbert Bachmann. Herbert gave me a long, searching look and said, "I hope you were polite to him, Paul?"

"Above and beyond the call of duty. Someone should give me a medal."

"I'll give you a kiss instead," said Suzanne. "Now, can I tell you something? I think we've had enough of this party."

"But Karl said . . ."

"I've changed the arrangements. You're meeting him here at eleven in the morning. Let's go, chéri."

"She's the wisest of us all," said Herbert Bach-mann. "Do as she says."

Karl Kruger, at eleven in the morning, was red-eyed, sore-headed and autocratic. He belched and grunted and marched up and down the room barking at me like the Iron Chancellor.

". . . Realities, Paul! That's what we talk about—realities! In the war, I lost a wife in the bombing and a son on the Russian front. Now, I do business with the people who killed them. Reality! If we don't com-promise and cooperate the world ends in one big firework display. Put every murderer on the scaffold, there is not rope enough in the world to hang them. Reality again! Harlequin has to see this. You must help him to see it . . ."

"Karl! His wife's not cold in her grave!"

"So he can't reason and he won't. But you can!"

"I can reason till I'm blue in the face. It doesn't change things."

"Then you act."

"You've lost me, Karl."

"Listen, *dummkopf!* For God's sake, listen! . . . If you, Paul Desmond, could take control of this sit-uation now, what would you do? Take your time; think about it! You heard the voices at that party last night. They don't give a damn about morals—only money. There was a lot of power there . . . You talked to Yanko. He's bruised and you can bruise him more; but you can't break him—and he's ready for a settlement. Now, what would you settle for, if you could?"

"If I could . . . Point one. He withdraws his take-over bid. Point two. He makes good the fifteen million and all the expenses arising out of it. Point three. He pays the cost of installing a new computer system and training operators—and he doesn't get the contract. Point four. We drop charges against his staff and bury the documents we have—on and not before completion date. That's minimum. Give me time and I could dream up a few more embellishments."

"Now, you begin to make sense, my friend."

"It makes nonsense without Harlequin's consent."

"Not so! You have power of attorney still current. Yanko knows that. I know it. You tell me Harlequin wants to keep options open. This is the best way to do it. Close them and we have a bloody shambles—which will get bloodier for everyone."

"Karl, I know it! Give me an argument that will convince a man whose wife has been murdered."

"You told me you loved her, too."

"I did . . ."

"Now what? A Mexican sculptor's carving the gravestone and you're in bed with Suzanne—who's the best choice you've made in your life. I'm not mocking. I'm glad. Harlequin will come to it. Better soon than late. Well, what do you say?"

"You're an old *schelm,* Karl . . . but I'll try it."

"Good! At last we hear some sanity. I'll call you as soon as I've sounded Yanko on the terms . . . Loving God! I've got a head like a pumpkin!"

At three in the afternoon, he telephoned me. Yanko was ready to talk. He had invited me to dinner at his house. I was prepared to talk, too, but I saw no reason to eat bread and salt with the bastard.

Karl Kruger growled, angrily, "If you mine coal, you get dust in your lunch box! What the hell does it matter? By the way, it's black tie."

At which moment, Suzanne took the phone from my hand and said, calmly, "He'll be there, Karl. I'll see to it." When she set down the receiver, she turned to me. "Paul, chéri, if you don't go, and things turn out badly, you'll never forgive yourself . . . Please?"

So, at eight of the clock, with my pride in my pocket and my temper damped down to a few smouldering coals, I went to dinner with Basil Yanko.

I don't know quite what I expected to find: profusion, certainly, an air of the grandiose that characterized his office, gadgery perhaps, certainly too much of everything. I confess I had the surprise of my life. The apartment was beautiful, but sparsely beautiful, with a kind of mathematical perfection that was at once austere and restful. Basil Yanko was not a collector. He chose things and placed them to speak for themselves; but a catalog would say nothing except that there was money on the walls and no sign of blood. I could not understand how a man so restless and so sinister had managed to achieve an atmosphere of such serenity.

A Negro maid admitted me. A Filipino butler served me a drink and left me. Then a few moments later, Basil Yanko came in. The dinner jacket made him look more angular and more cadaverous than ever; but his handshake was less limp, and he smiled without apparent effort. I paid him a compliment on his house and he acknowledged it with a hint of irony. "Surprised, Mr. Desmond?"

"Fascinated, Mr. Yanko."

"Collecting can be a mania. The true art of enjoyment is in selection . . . Which, of course, involves trial and error, and rejection, until one arrives at a stable relationship. Are you interested in pictures, Mr. Desmond?"

I was interested in anything that would get me through the overture and into the opera, so I told him of my fondness for handcraft and gold-work and the mystique of colored stones. He was a good listener, and more courteous than I would ever have believed possible, though, when his attention was caught, his questions still had a crisp, peremptory tone. At dinner, he ate sparingly and drank only one glass of wine; but he was proud of his cook, and meticulous about the service. He talked then about politics:

". . . There is a dream abroad, Mr. Desmond, that we can go back to the cracker-barrel and the parish-pump: small, self-sufficient nuclear communities. A beautiful illusion; but there is now no way to make it a reality. We are, perforce, one world, mutually dependent upon complex trade patterns and the distribution of diminishing resources. So we have to rationalize and control a multitude of variables. The computer can do it. Man, unaided, cannot . . ."

Which led us, by shifts and subtleties, to the coffee and the question at issue, which he stated very simply:

". . . I made a mistake, Mr. Desmond. I chose the wrong target. I used the wrong means. The input was erroneous, the errors compounded themselves. So we erase the series and start again—which is the intention of this discussion . . . More coffee?"

"No, thank you."

"A brandy?"

"No . . ."

"Well, then . . . Karl Kruger has suggested a framework within which we could negotiate. Let me say, frankly, that I would not quarrel over minor financial details. A computation of losses and costs is a simple affair. The nub of the question for me is what you can deliver by way of immunities for the future. Would you say that was a fair statement of our position?"

"I think it needs to be amplified, Mr. Yanko. You are asking for immunity against what?"

"Prosecution."

"For what?"

"Fraud and conspiracy to murder. That's the case you're trying to build now—although I understand you're having certain difficulties."

The cool effrontery of the man left me, for a moment, speechless.

He shook his head, sadly. "Mr. Desmond, we are alone—no witnesses, no surveillance. Here I can admit to everything, and I do. You're shocked, of course. How can I, a respectable businessman, conspire and consent to murder? Mr. Desmond, the taxpayers of this country financed a vast, unnecessary holocaust in Vietnam. Some protested. Many approved, still do and still would. Calley went to jail. The Generals are still free. I have no respect for people, Mr. Desmond. They live, they die. Sometimes, to make the social equation work, they have to be removed. You and I could debate that until crack of doom. You wouldn't convince me. I wouldn't convince you. So we agree to differ and get back to the question: what can you deliver?"

"We can agree not to prosecute you or your employees for fraud and conspiracy to defraud. On the question of murder, we cannot negotiate. The matter is out of our hands. The FBI already have the documents."

"Which are damaging but not conclusive."

"But which remain in open file; since there is no statute of limitation on murder."

"Quite. But let's take the situations in order. Valerie Hallstrom—well, that's a political hot potato and no one will want to handle it."

"Ella Deane?"

"Closed. No problem."

"And Frank Lemnitz?"

"British jurisdiction and unlikely to get very far . . . Which, you see, leaves only the question of Madame Harlequin, who died in Mexico. Now, let us examine that one and see where we might agree. My attorneys have seen, though I have not, a confession by Pedro Galvez which incriminates me. On that document you could try me; but you would not get a conviction. I'd bleed, but I'd recover. Mr. Harlequin would be in no better case than he is now—with a huge financial burden and a market gone shy on him. Alternatively, if you refrain from action, publication and further investigation, you get all the things in your package with no quarrel about details . . . Can you deliver, Mr. Desmond?"

"Harlequin could. I couldn't."

"Why not?"

"He can withdraw my power of attorney at the stroke of a pen."

"So . . . ?"

"I can and will try to persuade him. However, even Harlequin's consent doesn't give you immunity from the police and the FBI . . ."

"Mr. Desmond!" He was patient and kind to my ignorance. "If there is one thing I do understand, it is what the Press is pleased to call 'the conscience of America.' I can commit myself to it quite safely."

"Which brings me to another item in the package, Mr. Yanko."

That took some of the veneer off him. His smile vanished. He jerked his head up like a startled lizard. "I believe we have covered all the items mentioned by Karl Kruger."

"We have. This one, I thought you'd prefer to hear privately. On a document emanating from your data bank, George Harlequin and I are listed as prospective targets for terrorist attack."

"The document in question, Mr. Desmond, is a private intelligence summary prepared by experts and circulated to restricted subscribers."

"But like every such summary, it contains speculation which is designed to provoke action, which, when it happens, you claim to have prophesied. In simple terms, Mr. Yanko, you say that the newest terrorist targets are Paul Desmond and George Harlequin. The PFLP and the Rengo Sekigun have never heard of us. They then say, 'who dat?'—and there we are, all wrapped up ready for delivery . . . So you see, Mr. Yanko, we, too, need an immunity clause in the contract. Can you deliver one?"

"I could convey a request to the executive of the PFLP—through friends, of course."

"And you'd get a reply?"

"Normally, yes."

"How long would it take?"

"About three days."

"Then let's exchange answers in three days' time."

"Excellent! And if, meantime, there are points to clarify, please call me at my office or at this number. If I am at home, I will answer personally."

He crossed to the desk, scribbled a number on a card and handed it to me.

I stood up to take my leave. "Mr. Yanko, thank you for an excellent dinner and an instructive evening."

"A pleasure, Mr. Desmond. My chauffeur will take you home. Don't be offended if he doesn't talk to you. The poor fellow is a mute. We're cooperating in employment programs for the handicapped. Good night, Mr. Desmond."

. . . And there it was: a beautiful, fresh olive branch, wrapped in Cellophane, tied with pink ribbon, delivered by cooing doves. If we didn't accept it, he'd drive it like a stake through our gizzards and plant us six feet deep under the asphalt of Wall Street. God rest you merry gentlemen—and keep you safe through the dark hours!

I didn't go home. I had the chauffeur drop me off at the Regency, where Suzanne was having supper with Karl Kruger. His English rose had proved so thorny that he had packed her back to London with a diamond bracelet and was now sighing after Hilde. He was happy that a deal was possible: he was very unhappy when I told him, for the first time, how we had been set up as targets for terror. He had consented to a personal diplomacy; he had not bargained for embroilment in a political situation, which touched his own country so deeply. He, too, saw merit in Harlequin's resolve to eliminate Yanko. He suggested, quite soberly that, perhaps, Aaron Bogdanovich would be willing to assassinate him. I was sure Bogdanovich wouldn't risk his organization by an attack on a prominent American industrialist.

Suzanne listened for a while in shocked silence. Then, she attacked us both, savagely. "Enough! I won't listen to another word! You talk like assassins yourselves! If the bargain can be made, make it! Otherwise, there will be no end to the insanity."

Karl Kruger mumbled an apology. "I know! . . . I know! It won't happen, *liebchen*. But it's a bone in the throat that a man like Yanko can sit there and dictate to decent people. Now we have to ask what happens if Harlequin refuses the deal?"

"What time is it now, Karl?"

"One o'clock. Time we were thinking of bed . . ."

"In London it's six in the morning. Paul, call George and let's get this over!"

"Suzy, lover, he'll need time to think about it."

"Then the more time he has the better. Go on, call him."

A few moments later I was through to London and George Harlequin was on the line. He sounded as though he had just wakened. I apologized for disturbing him so early. Then, he said:

"Have they been in touch with you, too, Paul?"

"George, I don't know what you're talking about. It's one in the morning here. I've just been to dinner with Basil Yanko. I'm having supper with Suzanne and Karl Kruger . . ."

"Oh, then you haven't heard . . ."

"Nothing . . . George, what's the matter?"

"Baby Paul and the nurse . . . They've been kidnapped."

Before I had time to say a word, Milo Frohm was on the line. "Mr. Desmond . . . listen very carefully. Do exactly as I say. The news isn't out yet. We don't know what it means, though we can guess. We're waiting to hear what demands will be made. Go back to your apartment. Call our New York bureau and ask for Philip Lyndon. He'll instruct you. When we know more, we'll call you at home. Now, will you please hang up? We need to keep the line open."

We did exactly as we were told. An hour later, we were sitting in my apartment with Mr. Philip Lyndon transcribing on tape an account of Karl Kruger's intervention and my dinner conversation with Basil Yanko.

Lyndon's own account of the kidnapping was brief, because there was little to tell. At three in the afternoon, the nurse had taken the child for a walk by the lakeside park in Geneva. As usual a detective accompanied them. During the walk, two women and a man had accosted them, disarmed the detective and forced the nurse and the child at gunpoint into a waiting car. At midnight, a caller in London had informed Harlequin that the child and the nurse were in the hands of the Popular Front for the Liberation of Palestine. He should wait in London for further messages. Police intervention would be useless and dangerous to the child and the woman. It was simple, formal and menacing as a naked blade.

What could we do? Nothing, said Mr. Lyndon, firmly; nothing except wait and be silent and do as we were told. I thought I should call Yanko and tell him the news. Mr. Lyndon debated that for a while and then suggested I leave the call until seven, by which time he would have a technician set up a unit to record the conversation. At four in the morning, he offered to drive Karl Kruger back to his hotel and Suzanne and I were left alone to watch the dawn of a hopeless day. At six, Mr. Philip Lyndon returned with his technician. At seven, I was on the line to Basil Yanko.

He was surprised to hear from me so early. "You're very prompt, Mr. Desmond. Have you spoken to Mr. Harlequin?"

"Yes."

"How did he react to my suggestions?"

"I couldn't convey them."

"Any special reason?"

"Yes. Mr. Harlequin's child and his nurse were kidnapped last evening in Geneva."

The gasp was genuine. No actor in the world could have faked the shock or the fervor of the obscenity. "Oh, shit!"

"The kidnappers identify themselves as P.F.L.P. Harlequin is ordered to stay in London for further contact. That's all I know."

"Please pass my sympathy to Mr. Harlequin and add that I stand ready to help in any way I can. You know where to find me . . ."

"In view of our talk last night, I thought . . ."

"As I remember it, Mr. Desmond, we discussed business, not the politics of terror."

". . . I thought that with your knowledge of the Arab world, you might suggest an approach to this tragic problem."

"I shall certainly give it urgent consideration. However, I must point out that I do business only with lawfully constituted governments and companies. I shall willingly seek counsel from my friends."

"That's what I hoped, Mr. Yanko."

"Thank you for calling. I'll be in touch later."

Mr. Philip Lyndon gave a sour grin of admiration. "Not a mark on him! He's like stainless steel."

"You think he organized it?"

"No. I think he set up a situation for future use and the PFLP preempted it. Now it's out of Yanko's control. He'll help if it suits him. If not, he'll sit back and do nothing."

"What about my testimony and Karl Kruger's?"

"Karl Kruger talked only business compromise. You corroborate that. The stuff about murder and terror rests on your word only."

"Same old story!"

"You should do my job for a while, Mr. Desmond. If there's no God and no last judgment, I'm going to be a very disappointed man. If you hear anything from London, call me. I'll reciprocate . . . Leave the recorder connected to the phone. I'll put in a new tape now . . . Why don't you two get some rest?"

There was one more thing I had to do before I could rest. I went out to a pay phone, called Aaron Bogdanovich and told him the whole story.

He was mildly surprised and quite unmoved. "London and Geneva. Interesting."

"Is that all?"

"For the moment, yes. If you need more, try Dial-a-Prayer. Some people find it helpful."

"That's not amusing."

"Then try this. Old Chinese proverb: When expecting a visit from the imperial executioner, it is advisable to drink large quantities of rice wine ... Relax, Mr. Desmond, this kind of thing always takes time."

We waited all day, drowsing sometimes, watching television, waiting for the telephone to ring. Nothing. We called Philip Lyndon half a dozen times. Still nothing; and he begged us not to tie up his line. At six, Karl Kruger came round for a drink and stayed for Takeshi's dinner, elaborate as a funeral feast. At ten—news of the hour on the hour!—we saw it on television: a fifth floor apartment near Geneva airport, with the nurse holding baby Paul at the window, and, beside her, a young Arab with a machine gun. The commentary was a recitative, in the thrusting, emphatic style of American newscasters:

"In Geneva today, three-year-old Paul Harlequin and his nurse, thirty-year-old Hélène Huguet, are being held hostage by two men of the People's Front for the Liberation of Palestine and a Japanese couple, members of Rengo Sekigun, a Japanese terrorist organization. The terrorists are demanding the release of two Arab prisoners, one in England, the other in Italy, convicted recently on charges of hijacking, illegal possession of arms and other offenses. The terrorists' demands were spelt out this afternoon: a plane to fly them to a friendly Arab state, a sum of two million dollars, and immunity from attack or arrest. They have set a deadline of forty-eight hours. If the demands are not met, they will first kill the nurse and, twenty-four hours later, the child. Paul Harlequin is the infant son of banker, George Harlequin, who has figured recently in . . ."

Karl Kruger reached out and switched off the set. "So! Now we know. The money is easy. Governments are not so easy. The English are stiff-necked. The Italians have to drive five hundred miles to find a man to sign a piece of paper. Loving God! What a world!" Suzanne was weeping quietly. He folded her in a great bear hug and scolded her. "*Liebchen, liebchen!* They will not kill a child! They are too clever for that! They need sympathy, too. The baby is the joker in the pack. If they harm him, the crowd will tear them to pieces."

He was still crooning over her when the telephone rang. I switched on the recorder and answered it. Basil Yanko was on the line. "Mr. Desmond. I have got my bankers out of bed. I have called UPI, who will relay the news. There will be two million dollars at disposal in the Union Bank, Geneva, tomorrow morning. A gift—a free gift. I am using all efforts in diplomatic quarters to avert this tragedy . . ."

While I was still trying to decide whether to damn him or thank him, he hung up.

Karl Kruger flung his great bulk about the room

and raged, "The son of a whore! He fixed it! He un-
fixes it! He makes himself a hero!"

Suzanne cried out against him. "I don't care! It
doesn't matter! At least he's doing something. We're
just sitting here . . ."

Again the telephone rang and Milo Frohm was
talking from London. He was dog-weary, but ur-
bane as ever. "Sorry, I haven't been in touch. We've
been busy, as you may imagine. It's three in the morning here. Harlequin's in Geneva. His London manager and I have been negotiating all day with the
Home Secretary. We think he'll bend; but, Jesus, it's
rough going. The Italians will play—we hope . . ."

I told him about Yanko's offer. His laughter
sounded like a death rattle. ". . . Holy Moses! What
an artist! I can't wait to pin a medal on him. One
piece of good news. Alex Duggan's friend is beginning to crack. His wife's pregnant. She's afraid for
Harlequin's child. Keep praying and keep your
mouth shut."

"Mr. Frohm, you've had the report on my dinner party?"

"Yes. I've had it."

"What's the word?"

"Keep the deal open—and try to keep Mr.
Kruger in New York."

"How's George?"

"Not bad. All things considered."

"Would you like me to come, or send Suzanne?"

"Hell, no! Stay where you are, both of you. The
rougher it is, the longer Harlequin will last. I just
hope I can. Do you know what happened tonight?
The Under-Secretary asked me to have dinner at his

club—best saddle of lamb in London. Jesus Christ! Saddle of lamb! Well, as the Bible says, we're laboring in the vineyard. Good night or good morning as the case may be!"

At least he could laugh, and I tried to translate his humor to Suzanne and Karl. It wasn't a good translation, but at least a raised a ghostly smile from Suzanne and a grumble from Karl.

"Saddle of lamb! And our best club claret, sir! How I remember. Why does he want me to stay in New York?"

"He didn't say, Karl. It's up to you."

"I'll have to get Hilde over. Two nights alone in bed and I get nightmares. I'll phone Munich now."

"Karl! In Munich it's four in the morning."

"What matter? If she's alone, she'll be glad to hear from me. If she's not, she doesn't deserve to sleep. Here, give me the phone!"

Suzanne burst into helpless laughter. "You can't, Karl! It's all being recorded!"

"In German, it will sound beautiful . . . That's an idea! Why don't you talk to her first? Tell her you are in bed with me and . . ."

It was a silly game; but we played it with hysterical fervor and when it was over, we replayed it over supper, until the last taste was out of it, and Karl collapsed on the bed in the guest room, and Suzy and I folded ourselves together in a merciful forgetting.

The kidnap drama has become a stock piece of political theater. You can, if you are a cynic, dictate the sequence in an hour. What you cannot know—

unless you are personally involved—is the intolerable anguish of the victim and the relatives, and the heart-stopping tensions of both the kidnappers and the negotiators.

The kidnappers are the commandos of a political group, totally committed, carefully briefed, fully aware of the personal risks. If they fail, they can expect no mercy. They will be torn to pieces by a mob, gunned down by police, or imprisoned for a lifetime. The sanction under which they live, like the threat they impose, is absolute. If their demands are refused, they will kill, because the killing is then inconsequent to them, but enormously consequent to the movement which they represent. The problem is that the act of execution must always be performed in cold blood; and the tension which precedes it may become unbearable . . . Which is why the presence of Japanese assassins is a sinister phenomenon. They have a tangled philosophy of life, but a very clear, traditional philosophy of death.

The negotiators are always at a disadvantage since they are not, and cannot be, either single-minded or wholly resolute. All are agreed that the victim or victims must be saved. Money is a minor consideration. But the dilemmas involved are legion: a government must not bow to political gangsters; it dare not risk the slaughter of the innocent. If the guilty are escorted out of the country like diplomats, the law is an object of derision; and more invasions will be made. If you tie the hands of the police, you destroy their loyalty and in the end, corrupt them. If you make martyrs, you sow dragon's teeth. If you defend the rights of oppressed minorities, you cannot appear to stifle by brute force, the expression of their grievances.

For the victims themselves, there is no recourse. Their captors may be courteous. They are also implacable. Their rescuers seem impotent. Their salvation rests upon a decency which they have seen to be abdicated. Aaron Bogdanovich was not joking when he said you could either dial-a-prayer or get drunk. He was being merciful when he ignored the last choice: sit quiet and hope that the executioner has a steady hand.

We were four thousand miles removed from it, but Suzanne and I lived every line of the drama. The television was switched on all day and half the night. We bought all the papers and read every line in German, French, English and Italian. One of us was always in the flat. When Suzanne went out, Takeshi went with her. Philip Lyndon called four times a day with a summary of his telex reports. Karl Kruger came and went at will. Hilde would arrive within a few days. Milo Frohm was busy and out of contact. All we heard from George Harlequin were the words he spoke to television interviewers and newsmen. He looked like a walking ghost, but he carried himself with dignity and spoke always with moderation and restraint. He offered himself as a hostage in return for the child and the nurse. The offer was refused.

As the hour of the first deadline approached, the waiting became an agony. New figures appeared on the screen, delegates from Arab embassies, Japanese diplomats, emissaries from England and Italy. They pleaded for time. They displayed the ransom money and sent it to the apartment by a man stripped down to swimming trunks, so that he could be seen to be unarmed. While he was on his way up, the Japanese hung the child from the window by his hands, threatening to drop him at the first sign of trickery.

At the last moment, the deadline was extended for another twenty-four hours. Fresh milk was delivered for the child. A Swiss air crew volunteered to fly the kidnappers to safety. The Italians brought their prisoner across the border and displayed him, smiling and triumphant, to the kidnappers. The English delayed, and the Home Secretary refused to comment. George Harlequin and his Swiss manager again offered themselves as hostages. This time, the offer was accepted. They disappeared into the building. There were hysterical scenes, when, long minutes later, the nurse and the child came out and were hurried into a police car and driven away.

Then, at long last, the ordeal was over. The kidnappers, with their hostages at gunpoint, emerged from the building and were driven to the airport. They entered the plane together. The detainees were brought to the foot of the steps. They laughed and waved and made signs of victory. Then the aircraft took off. The hostages would be returned on the homeward flight.

Suzanne broke down and wept uncontrollably for more than an hour. I called the doctor to sedate her. While she was sleeping, I went out and sat for an hour in the last pew in Saint Patrick's. I didn't pray. There seemed no point in saying I was sorry or grateful. It was just a clean place to be, in a very dirty world.

9

Ten days later, George Harlequin returned to New York. He came with an entourage: Julie's parents, a new nurse, baby Paul and three young men, all Swiss, very quiet, very watchful and quite uncommunicative. The apartment at the Salvador could not accommodate them all, so we rented the adjoining suites and had Saul Wells recruit another security team to guard the approaches and check all visitors and staff. Suzanne moved out of my apartment and installed herself next to the family. Harlequin wanted me to move, too. I told him there was no need; and, in any case, I was wedded to my independence. He asked me to report on what had happened in his absence. He listened attentively, took notes, commended me and closed the subject. It was no time to press him for decisions. When he was ready, I was at his service.

He was profoundly changed. He was graying now at the temples. The skin of his face was drawn tightly over the bones. His eyes had a monkish, contemplative look. He spoke little, and then quietly and with deliberation, like someone who had been iso-

lated a long time from his fellows. His movements
were different, too: not springy and eager, as in the
old days, but calculated, purposeful, almost stealthy.

He refused all social intercourse. In the daytime
he worked at the Salvador, requesting that people
came to him; which, of course, they did, out of respect for his recent griefs. In the evening, he dined
with Julie's parents and played with baby Paul. That
was the only time I ever saw him smile, and the smile
was tender but terribly sad, as if he were ashamed to
have brought the child into so brutal a world. The
only times I ever saw him angry were when he found
some breach in the intricate security arrangements.
Then he castigated the offender with cold, cutting
words. With Suzanne, he was considerate but formal.
With me, he could not be formal; but it was clear that
he wanted to be separate. Three days passed before
he telephoned and asked me to meet him for a talk
on what he called "personal matters." When I arrived, he begged me to hear, without comment, what
he had to say:

". . . Paul, you have done enough for me—more
than any man should ask of another. I know you
loved Julie and that you supported her at times when
she lacked support from me. I'm not jealous of that.
I'm grateful for it. I'm glad my boy has his Uncle
Paul. I'm glad I love you, too, as the friend of my
heart . . . I want to hold our friendship. As things are
now, I fear I may lose it. So I should like you to resign as director of Harlequin et Cie."

"Any time, George. Today, if you like."

"Today, then. I'll have Suzanne type the letter.
You can sign it before you leave. I'll also withdraw

your power of attorney and give you full indemnity
for the period of its exercise. You and Karl Kruger
covered me for fifteen million. I've relieved you of
that cover, and credited you with interest for the
period."

"In my case, that wasn't necessary."

"It was proper, Paul. You're also credited with
market losses on your stock in Creative Systems."

"For God's sake, George!"

"Please, Paul! You promised to hear me. I've prepared a press statement on your resignation. I'd like
you to read it, make any changes you like and I'll
issue it today. As soon as we're finished in New York,
I'm retiring Suzanne, with what I hope is a generous
endowment. She needs to be free, I think. She has decisions of her own to make . . ."

"And where does all this leave you, George?"

"Where I am—with a child to care for and a
business to rebuild."

"May I ask how you propose to do that?"

"Of course. I'm going to settle with Basil
Yanko."

"You mean, sell to him?"

"No, settle with him. You and Karl Kruger discussed basic terms. I can probably better them in a
personal negotiation. It rather depends on what success Milo Frohm has in London—and what sort of
compromise he can work out between the Administration and his agency. That part of it is out of my
hands."

He was deliberately vague: but I was in no mood
to press him. I wanted to quit anyway. He was giving me the chance to go with dignity. We could still

be friends: but the friendship would never be the same; because he had changed and I couldn't. Still, it was better to leave things tidy. I told him:

"I suppose you know I've asked Suzy to marry me?"

"No, I didn't. But I'm glad. I think it's a good idea."

"She hasn't consented yet."

"Why not?"

"She's still in love with you. Always has been."

He looked at me in faint surprise, as though I were talking about the price of tomatoes. "But I'm not in love with her."

"That's all I wanted to know. Thanks, George. I'll wait in New York until she's finished. Then I'll take her away . . . Now, let's get these documents done, shall we?"

In the days that followed, I felt strangely bereft and aimless. An era in my life had ended. I didn't know how or where to begin another. I stayed away from the market and from the Club, because I didn't want to answer questions about my own plans or join in the gossip about Harlequin. I didn't read the papers because the news was all bad, and the index was down and the less trading I did the better.

To fill the vacant hours, I made the rounds of naval architects and boat builders and talked about an old dream—a motor-sailer that could take me across the Pacific. I haunted the slipways, for forgotten or neglected beauties. In the evenings, I would call at the Salvador, have a drink with Harlequin, play a while with my godson, and then take Suzanne to Gully Gordon's and afterwards back to the apartment.

She, too, was distracted and ill-at-ease. Her work was temporary now. We could not share it. Decency demanded that I should not intrude into confidences from which I had been formally disbarred. Our relationship became strained and edgy. There were snappish exchanges. I felt she was shutting me out. She accused me of pushing her too hard, denying her the time I had promised to make a free decision. One night, after a slightly rowdy dinner with Karl Kruger and Hilde, she dissolved into tears and said she would rather not see me for a few days. I went on a round of parties with Mandy Ducaine and her friends, which left me jaded, sore-headed and lonelier than ever. I got back at three one morning to find a note thrust under my door. "Chéri, I'm sorry. Must see you. Suzy." I called her at breakfast time and we talked for half an hour and made a date to meet for dinner at home.

That same morning, for want of anything better to do, I strolled down to the flower shop on Third Avenue and asked to see Aaron Bogdanovich. This time I was invited into a cluttered back room, where the master of terror was engaged in the prosaic business of totting up accounts.

He waved me to a chair, scribbled a few figures and then leaned back and surveyed me with sardonic amusement. "Well, Mr. Desmond, how does it feel to be out of a job?"

"I'm getting used to it. You?"

"Undertakers and florists are always busy. And I'm still on the payroll of Harlequin et Cie."

"That's news to me."

"I thought it might be. Why did you leave?"

"I was asked to retire."

"Do you know why?"

"Reasons were given."

"Did they satisfy you?"

"No."

"Why are you hanging around New York?"

"I'm waiting to marry Suzanne—I hope."

"She's good for you."

"Thanks."

"Why did you come here?"

"I'd like to buy you a lunch."

"Thank you. I never eat lunch; but, so long as you're here, I'll give you some advice."

"Well . . . ?"

"I have no friends, Mr. Desmond. I can't afford them. There are few people I respect. Your friend, Harlequin, is one of them. He is the sort of man I should like to have been if circumstances had been different. On the other hand, he is not equipped to be the man I am . . ."

"Go on."

"He asked you to retire so that you would not be accused of complicity in his design."

"Which is . . . ?"

"What it always was—to kill Basil Yanko."

"I don't believe it. I can't! He told me . . ."

"That he was going to settle with Yanko. He will. Then he will kill him. Nothing else will satisfy him. Afterwards, of course, he will find that nothing is solved. He has asked me to help him. I will, because my people want Yanko removed. I can see—as I could not before—a way to do it. You will not stop it. It would be useless to try. I suggest that you might stay to pick up the pieces of George Harlequin, or at least look after his son."

"Would you have told me if I hadn't come this morning?"

"Yes . . . but I learnt only last night what he proposed."

"That's funny! That's really funny!"

"What, Mr. Desmond?"

"Harlequin absolves me; you bind me again."

"And that's what you've never wanted, Mr. Desmond! You want both ends and the middle of the sausage. You want respectability without virtue, possession without threat, pleasure without payment. You want mercenaries to do your killing and blind men to bury your dead. No way! No way in the world any more! Martyr or killer—that's the choice! Unless you want to join the chain gang shuffling from birth to death and crying for the Messiah who never comes!"

If he hadn't been so vehement, I should have missed it. If he hadn't been so positive, I should have ignored the tiny nagging doubt that I had thrust too long into the back of my mind. It was so tenuous that I had to search for the words to express it:

"I think . . . I think, Mr. Bogdanovich, you're setting us up—Harlequin and me, both."

There was no tremor of emotion on his saturnine face. His eyes were blank windows to a blank soul. "What precisely do you mean, Mr. Desmond?"

"Valerie Hallstrom . . ."

"What about her?"

"Let's go back over the sequence. You searched her apartment. You left. You saw a man go in. You saw her come home. You saw the man leave. You went back and found her dead. That's what you told me."

"I did."

"But she was your agent. While she was being killed, you waited outside . . ."

"So?"

"You knew it was happening. You let it happen."

"That's right."

"Why, Mr. Bogdanovich?"

"Valerie was used up. She was playing in Gully Gordon's bar—and she was talking too much, as she did to you, Mr. Desmond. Her cover was blown. Yanko had her killed. I let it happen, as you say. Now, I'm tidying up. Yanko will die very soon. Harlequin and I have arranged the details. It's a clean solution for all of us. I think you'll find we've earned our fees."

"I still say you're setting us up."

"You insult me, Mr. Desmond. You've forgotten our contract: if there's blood on the carpet, I clean it up afterwards; and you, for your part, are pledged to silence. If you can't stomach the play, walk out and go home. That's still your privilege."

"I'm going to talk to Harlequin."

"Do so, by all means . . . Your wife wasn't killed in Mexico City. It wasn't your child hung by his hands from a fifth-floor window in Geneva."

He wasn't angry. He wasn't even emphatic. He might have been reading from a children's primer. As

I stood up to leave, he stayed me with a gesture and an odd, patronizing irony:

"I meant what I said. The child will need you. And you may have to pick up the pieces of your friend. Stay around. It will not be as bad as you think. Death is a very banal event."

I left him tallying the costs and profits of flowers and walked an hour through the jostle of lunchtime New York. I was in no hurry. There was no one who demanded my company, no place that would be empty without me. I stared in shop windows and saw jumbles of meaningless objects. I looked into faces and saw only actors' masks. I smelled food and had no taste for it. I licked my lips and desired to drink and knew that I would gag on the first mouthful. I wanted company but I would have fled at a single word of greeting. I was not afraid. I was not ashamed. I was empty and discredited. My fragile philosophy was in tatters, my unreasoned code as full of holes as a Swiss cheese. Aaron Bogdanovich had shaken me to the soul, but I could not shift him an inch from the settled conviction that life was an inconsequence, easier ended than mended.

After a while, my head began to ache and my feet hurt; so I went home. Takeshi made me coffee. I didn't want to think any more. I pulled a book at random from the shelves and, without even looking at the title, began to read at the first page that fell open:

". . . I don't know who—or what put the question. I don't know when it was put. I don't even remember answering. But at some moment I did answer 'yes' to someone—or something—and from that hour I was certain that existence was meaningful and that therefore, my life in self-surrender . . . had a goal . . ."

I looked then for the first time at the title-page. It was *Markings,* the private jottings of that strange, involuted man, Dag Hammarskjold. I read on:

". . . From that moment I have known what it means 'not to look back' and to 'take no thought for the morrow.' Led . . . through the labyrinth of life, I came to a time and place where I realized that the Way leads to a triumph, which is a catastrophe, and to a catastrophe which is a triumph, that the price for committing one's life would be reproach and that the only possible elevation possible to man is in the depths of humiliation . . ."

I did not understand it; but it moved me strongly. I felt an urge to copy it down on the end paper of my pocket diary, where I could not fail to see it every day. I had just finished when Takeshi came in, coughed, hissed, bowed and begged a moment of my most valuable time.

"Yes, Takeshi. What is it?"

"There is something, sir, that I must tell you. It is not easy."

"Sit down then, take your time."

"No, sir, thank you. The things that have happened to you, to your friends . . ."

"The things that have happened . . . yes?"

"On the television. The day they hung the baby from the window . . ."

"Go on . . ."

"The one who held him was my nephew—the one to whom I always sent your postage stamps."

"Did you know before that he belonged to Rengo Sekigun?"

"When the FBI came and asked questions, then I knew. Before, I was not sure."

"Why didn't you tell them?"

"I have family, in California and in Hawaii. They are good people. Good Japanese, good Americans. In the war, they were put in camps as if they were enemies."

"Why didn't you tell me?"

"You were in Mexico."

"But afterwards? Those people could have come for me, for Miss Suzanne. We were warned it was possible."

"If my nephew had come here, I should have killed him."

"He would have killed you first, Takeshi."

"One knows such things, sir. One does not believe them. Now, when it is too late, I believe."

"You should have told me before this."

"I should have. I was too ashamed. If it is convenient, sir, I shall leave in the morning."

"Takeshi . . ."

"Sir?"

"Why do you want to go?"

"My nephew dishonors me; I dishonor you."

"Honor is a reed, Takeshi. It bends when you lean on it."

"What then do we lean on, sir?"

"Sit down, Takeshi, for God's sake! It makes me

tired looking up at you . . . You remember the man who sleeps in a grave . . . ?"

"Yes, sir."

"He told me today that there is no middle way to live. You must die for a truth or kill for it. Should I believe him?"

"That is what my nephew says."

"And what do you say, Takeshi?"

"You do not cut down a flower to make it bloom. And what use is the truth to a dead man . . . Are you ashamed because you, too, are not sleeping in a grave?"

"No . . . because I haven't the courage."

"During the war, when we read of the banzai charges and the kamikaze pilots, my father used to shake his head and say a wise coward was better than an idiot hero. I think he was right."

"Takeshi, do you have to leave? Do you have a better job?"

"No, sir."

"Why not stay a while and let's lean on each other?"

He would not demean himself to show pleasure but he made it a three-bow occasion and agreed. Then he asked whether I lacked faith in his cooking or his care—and, if I didn't, why was Miss Suzanne not staying here instead of in some great crowded hotel? . . . Which made the greatest good sense, if only I could persuade her to see it.

At five in the evening, Saul Wells came to visit me. He had been reporting regularly to George Harlequin. He had the impression that his services were not greatly valued any more. He wondered why I had resigned. The money was good; but a situation was developing that he didn't understand. He didn't want to be left holding the can. He hoped I could enlighten him.

I told him half the truth: Harlequin was a scarred man. He had to keep himself busy. He needed to be in total control. I didn't want our friendship to be strained by conflicts of policy. Saul accepted that, with a certain reserve. Then I asked him about Bernie Koonig. He was instantly animated:

"Koonig's a queer story. He's a small time hit man and he hires muscle to the number boys and the loan sharks. Frank Lemnitz used him—which we know. What we didn't know, and what it's taken me all this time to find out, is that he used to work in California for Basil Yanko, who was then married to his second wife—the one who blew herself up in the speedboat. Koonig was doing the same job as Lemnitz did in New York—chauffeur, bodyguard, you name it. After the accident, he left California and came east. He had money then—quite a lot—but he blew it and went to work for the mob. Since Lemnitz died, he's been running scared . . ."

"Have you talked to him?"

"No. Bogdanovich has."

"I was with him this morning. He didn't tell me."

Saul Wells gave me an odd sidelong look, unwrapped a new cigar and took a long time to pierce and light it. Finally, he said, uncomfortably:

"Look! I'm a simple Jewish boy. I send money to Israel and go to synagogue. Aaron isn't simple and he does different things. How he does 'em, why he does 'em, I never ask. And even if he told me, I'd know it was only a part of the answer. He's like a conjuror who puts a mint in your mouth and pumps lemonade out of your elbow. It's a trick. You expect to find a connection between the two events, and there isn't any. With Aaron there's always a connection. Like a girl goes to bed with a guy in Paris and a man buys an airline ticket in Lima, Peru, and four days later there's a body floating in the Delaware River . . . So Bogdanovich has talked to Bernie Koonig and he hasn't told you. Leave it at that!"

"What else can you tell me, Saul?"

"Basil Yanko's been in touch with me."

"The hell he has! What for?"

"He wants Lichtman Wells to handle security for Creative Systems. It's a big contract."

"You'd be a fool to turn it down, Saul."

"Yes, wouldn't I? He also offered me a personal fee of a hundred thousand."

"What for?"

"Copies of all my reports to Harlequin et Cie and any other documents I can lay my hands on. I told him I'd think about it. Then I talked to Aaron."

"And what did he say?"

"He thought it was a good idea—provided he cooked the documents before I gave them to Yanko."

"Does Harlequin know about this?"

"Sure. He didn't seem to mind. If Aaron advised it, he'd go along."

"So, why are you telling me, Saul?"

"Because I think we're both in the same boat, Mr. Desmond—up the same creek without a paddle.

Harlequin's taken over from you. Aaron's taken over
from me. They make a rough pair. I don't want to
get caught in the meat-grinder. When I was talking
to Aaron, he said, 'Get paid in cash, Saul. You can't
sign checks in jail, and when you're dead, the banks
stop payment.' "

"Did you ask him what he meant?"

"You're not hearing me, Mr. Desmond," said
Saul, mournfully. "With Aaron if you don't understand the words, you don't deserve to know."

I was still trying to swallow that piece of gristle
when Karl Kruger and Hilde arrived, panting from a
shopping spree on Fifth Avenue. Hilde had sore feet,
three new dresses, a diamond brooch. Karl had a
hole in his pocket-book and a raging thirst. Saul Wells
was goggle-eyed at Hilde's ample charms. When she
curled up on the settee, he sat as near as he could get
and talked twenty to the dozen, while Hilde sipped
her drink and smiled dreamily through the monologue. If she understood one word in ten, I was a two-
headed Hottentot; but Saul was a man, and Hilde
wouldn't ask any more until he did—and then he
would need every cent of his hundred thousand.

Karl Kruger spread his vast bulk in an armchair,
swallowed a pint of lager in record time, belched
happily and then demanded a whiskey to soothe his
nerves. Women, he averred, were the most splendid
of God's creatures, provided you had nothing to do
with them until after dark. Shopping was a pastime
for cretins of whom he was the least intelligent. When
I asked him how things were going between Harlequin and Basil Yanko, he grunted, irritably:

". . . And why should you have to ask me, eh? I

told George he was a fool to let you go . . . Things advance. They have both seen a draft agreement, which their lawyers are prepared to recommend. I talk to George; I talk to Yanko. All the time I keep asking myself how it is possible that the police or the FBI do not intervene. The man is a criminal."

"Not until they prove it, Karl."

"But do they want to, eh? I have never heard so much complicated law in my life. If you are rich in this country, you can almost rewrite the codex; and the authorities help you to do it."

"Only when it suits them, Karl—and in today's climate it does. How do you find George?"

He was suddenly grave and quiet. "I told you once there was a weakness in him. No more! He is hard as granite. He listens. He thinks. He decides. After that, nothing will budge him. Yanko is sorry he ever met him."

"But they will settle?"

"Oh, yes! But they must do it with decorum. Harlequin needs that if he is to restore his place in the market. It is not enough to win. He must win magnanimously. I have told him. So has Herbert Bachmann."

"Did he agree?"

"Oh, yes. He said: 'Karl, I am a very good actor. People will believe what they think they see. Everyone will be satisfied except myself.' "

Hilde slid off the settee, padded across the room in her stockinged feet, threw her arms round my neck and whispered, "Paul, for the love of God, rescue me from this *klumpen!*"

Saul Wells followed her, only to be snaffled by

Karl Kruger, who clapped a great hand on his wrist
and commanded:

"I want to talk to you, Mr. Wells! I hear you are
a very clever man on security. What's that, my friend?
Security for what against whom . . . ?"

Hilde trapped me in the corner of the bar,
clutched my hand and demanded to know:

"Paul, what are you going to do about Suzanne?
She's locked like a nun in that damned hotel. She
hammers all day at the typewriter. She looks at
George Harlequin with those big doe eyes and says,
'Yes, sir. No, sir,'" and he wouldn't know if she were
talking Sanskrit! God in heaven! Such a waste! I don't
like women; but she's one of the good ones. Listen,
schatz! We all go sour and get wrinkled! Don't waste
your good years. Don't waste hers, either!"

"Hilde, sweetheart, I've already asked her to
marry me. She says she wants time."

"Paul, you're a bigger *klumpen* than that one!
No woman wants time. Without a man, she doesn't
know what to do with it. Look at Karl there. He's
too fat, too old and one day he'll drop dead on the
way to the office—but I love him. When he goes, I'll
shrink up like a winter apple."

"Hilde, I love you; but you're drunk!"

"I love you, *schatz;* but you're too sober for your
own good. When are you seeing Suzy again?"

"Tonight—if I can clear you all out of here."

"Then tell her! Don't ask! Just say, 'Now or
never.' And if she argues, send her home and call
me. Karl! On your feet! Paul has guests. You, too,
Mr. Wells. Out . . . out . . . ! And for you, my Paul,
when it's settled, call me, give me your pocketbook

and I'll bring you back the prettiest bride you ever saw . . . God! How stupid you men are! Mr. Wells, bring me my shoes. Karl, you great oaf, we're going— now!"

They went, with a flurry of farewells, in a cloud of cigar smoke and whiskey fumes. I hurried to shave and shower and dress, while Takeshi, muttering ominously, set about airing and tidying the room. Forty minutes later, it was fresh and tranquil as a temple garden. The table was set, the cocktails were mixed, the candles were glowing, and Oistrakh was playing Beethoven, but Suzanne had still not arrived.

She was an hour later, run ragged and near to tears. She hadn't changed. Her hair was a mess. She had brought clothes and makeup in an overnight bag. She needed another hour to bathe and change. Takeshi, noble son of the Samurai, assured her that dinner could be served at midnight if she wanted. I made her two drinks and gloated secretly, while she poured out the woes of a horrible, horrible day.

The morning had been filled with bank business—Larry Oliver's severance, a long conference with Standish, cables from Geneva and the foreign branches, market reports, clients' problems, currency movements, frantic phone calls to place orders and take commissions from Europe. In the afternoon, Milo Frohm had come, hot-foot from London; which meant she had to twiddle her thumbs while George Harlequin and he were closeted for two hours. Baby Paul had developed a colic, which meant chasing a doctor and soothing a pair of French grandparents. Then at five-thirty—surely, this must be the most uncivilized country in the world!—at five-thirty there was a conference between Harlequin and Yanko, with their attorneys, and she had to wait again until the notes were ready, take them in shorthand, type in rough and retype again with half an hour's emendations . . . And at the end of it all, George had gone off without a word of thanks or apology. It was all too much. She could hardly wait until . . . until . . .

I didn't ask what would happen then. I shut her into the bedroom and left her to repair the ravages of the day, while I read a little more of Dag Hammerskjold and Takeshi sang, tunelessly, over his pots and skillets.

Dinner was easy. Eat, drink, listen to the music, make a compliment to Takeshi, whenever he stuck his head around the door. We didn't talk very much, because the words got in the way of the harmony. It was simple to smile and touch hands and look at each other and smile again and raise a glass and sip the dry wine of brief contentment. Afterwards, when Takeshi was gone, and we were curled up, comfortable as cats in the half-dark, I asked:

"Are you staying tonight?"

"I came prepared—if you don't mind."

"That's what it's about, sweetheart—not having to go home."

"I hurt you, chéri. I'm sorry."

"And I lost my head. I'm sorry, too."

"Paul, do you ever think of Julie?"

"In the daytime, no. Sometimes I have nightmares, seeing her in the alley, in the hospital, and myself tied down and not being able to get to her. Why do you ask?"

"The night we were at Francis Mendoza's, we

made love and you fell asleep. I was awake, a long time after. You talked in your sleep. You were calling her name, not mine. It haunted me ... Then, when George asked me to stay at the Salvador, I was delighted. I had all sorts of girlish fantasies: he would wake up, lonely, in the night and come to me; I would hear him, restless and muttering in the dark and go to him ... The first nights, I lay awake for hours, waiting, hoping ... Nothing happened. That was why I quarrelled with you. The next night I dreamed of him, as you must have dreamed of Julie. He was there, but I couldn't reach him. Then, I was free, but he was gone ... When I woke up, it was all over—finished, done. I came here the next night very late. You were out. I pushed the note under your door. Silly, isn't it? We dream of other people and we can't bear to be away from each other!"

"Sweetheart, we've done a lot of living—I more than you. We can't wipe it out. We shouldn't try. It's what makes us rich for ourselves and other people. Who's interested in a book full of blank pages? We all have phantom lovers. We all have golden dreams—and black ones, too—but, in the dreams, we're shades chasing shadows. When we wake up ..."

"That's what worries me, chéri. What happens when we wake up?"

"We look for the known face, the familiar smile. We touch the known body, smell it, taste it, comfort ourselves against it. The knowing is necessary to the loving. Without it, we have no certainty even that we are ourselves. We dream might-have-beens; but we come back grateful for what is, and who is. We can't mate with ghosts. There's no substance in them and no warmth at all . . . Hell! I'm talking like a penny philosopher."

"I wish you'd said it all long ago."

"I didn't know it then . . . Or perhaps I did and was too proud to say it. Suzy love, let's not wait any longer. Tell me 'yes' and let's start making a proper life together. Time's wasting and so are we."

"One question, Paul: the last, I promise. Can we stay close to George until this is over?"

"We can and we will."

"Then, yes, my love . . . Yes! . . . Oh, chéri, it feels good to be home."

It was strange: there was no drama in the moment at all. It was simple and calm and easy, like sliding under the lee of the land, out of the wind, out of the swing of the sea. We could still hear the storm; we could see the black clouds scudding over the hilltops; but we were safe in haven and able, at last, to spare a prayer for other poor sailormen.

In the morning, we went to the Salvador together and told George Harlequin. He said he was happy for both of us, grateful that Suzy would wait until his affairs in New York were settled. He asked where and when we were getting married. We told him we would wait until we were all back in Geneva, to celebrate the event together. He was dubious about that. His plans were uncertain. We should make our arrangements without reference to him. If he could be with us, he would be delighted, of course.

When I asked him when he thought to conclude with Yanko, he lapsed into vagueness: very soon, a week, perhaps a little longer. There were still questions to settle with Milo Frohm. He didn't say what they were. I didn't ask him. I decided I had the right to ask Milo Frohm myself. I called him from the lobby phone. He said he could spare me an hour before lunch and would be prepared, if not exactly happy, to meet me at my apartment. The preamble proved more awkward than I had anticipated.

". . . Mr. Frohm, I find myself in a difficult position. As you know, I have no longer any legal status in Harlequin's affairs. My personal position has changed, too. He has made it clear that he doesn't want me to be further involved. However, I'm still his friend and I'm worried about him. I'd like to talk to you, off the record. Do you have any objections?"

"None. Just so you understand that I have to reserve certain information."

"I understand that. I accept it."

"What's your problem, Mr. Desmond?"

"If I try to define it, I'll do it badly. Let's start with the fact that George has lost his wife and been through a brutal experience with his child. He's locked himself away in a kind of private hell . . ."

"And you'd like to get him out of it."

"I'm scared of what he may do while he's in it."

"Go on, Mr. Desmond."

"I know that a settlement is being arranged with Basil Yanko. It was I who set down the first terms."

"Yes?"

"Now I don't see how it's going to work. I fear it may be the prelude to a worse tragedy than any we have yet seen."

Milo Frohm lingered over the thought but did

not reject it. He began a cautious, sidling explanation:

"... Let's talk about the settlement—which is not, in fact, a settlement, but a very touchy deal ... I don't like it. I'm under pressure to make it. Harlequin doesn't like it either; but he's under bigger pressure ... Neither of us has any doubt that Yanko is behind everything that has happened. Some things we can prove, others we can't. Some we might prove; but only after long investigation and possibly abortive legal procedures. Anything and everything we do has acute political consequences ... Justice is the least of our concerns, because it is impossible to dispense. We can't bring back the dead. What, therefore, we are trying to achieve is an illusion that justice has been done by a mutual compromise outside the courts. Now, I think that's wrong. It discredits the law. It weakens public order, which, as of this moment, rests on a very frail apparatus of enforcement. However, I am a man under authority. I investigate, report and advise. I cannot determine action. In fact, I am being forced to bow to contrary opinion; which says that if you can't make a charge stick, you mustn't file it; that it's better to tolerate a criminal in a high place, than prove, publicly, that you are impotent against him. The theory is that you erode his power but don't confront it ... The consequence of that course is that you complete the divorce between politics and morals—and in the end, you pay a hell of a price for it."

"Don't you also pervert the law, Mr. Frohm?"

"That's not quite accurate, Mr. Desmond. It would be more correct to say that you use the law perversely. Example: Pedro Galvez's confession. It's an authentic document. Take it to court and the defense will, quite properly, attack its credibility. In our position, all we need say is that we think it won't stand up in court. Nothing illegal in that. Harlequin and the Republic are plaintiffs. They have free choice in the evidence they present—even in a murder case. We're not saying that Yanko is immune from prosecution now or at some further date. We're simply writing down the value of our own evidence . . ."

"Against a hefty cash settlement by Yanko. Which is bribery."

"It would be, if it were expressed as a consideration. It is, in fact, expressed as a voluntary reparation of damage . . ."

"Caused by criminal conspiracy . . ."

". . . On the part of employees, whom Mr. Harlequin generously declines to prosecute."

"And that's the end of it?"

"You know it isn't, Mr. Desmond. It depends on a whole combination of political attitudes, market pressures and legal maneuvers to make it viable. It requires a conspiracy of silence to make it stick."

"Misprision of a felony, in fact."

"Which is a hell of a thing to prove. I tried once and got torn to shreds . . . No, Mr. Desmond—if we make the deal, we have to make it stick."

"It won't. It's wide open at both ends. Yanko gets a suspension of threat, not a total immunity. And George Harlequin gets money for a dead wife. I don't believe either man can or will be satisfied."

"Yanko's under the gun. He'll accept."

"And George Harlequin will accept, too; but . . ."

"But what, Mr. Desmond?"

From this point, I was walking on eggs; and we both knew it.

I said carefully, "I am suggesting or dreaming or inventing the next step—another deal, under which Yanko is removed and George Harlequin gets immunity."

Again the thought was familiar to him. This time he stepped round it. "And that would worry you, Mr. Desmond?"

"It would destroy the man who has been my friend for twenty years."

"But, according to your invention, he would be immune."

"Never from himself, Mr. Frohm . . . Now, we're alone and off the record. In your view, is it possible the dream might come true?"

"It is."

"And you as an officer of the law, would agree to it?"

"No. I have said only that it may happen."

"If Harlequin were your friend . . ."

"He is, Mr. Desmond. We have become very close. I have the greatest admiration for him."

"Have you attempted to dissuade him from this next step?"

"I have pointed out the risks of it."

"And . . . ?"

"We have agreed on a principle. It was enunciated by one George Mason, delegate of Virginia, at the drafting of the United States Constitution: 'Shall any man be above justice? Above all, shall that man be above it who can commit the most extensive injustice . . . ?' "

"George Harlequin has talked murder."

"Not to me," said Milo Frohm evenly. "And to you—if you have properly understood him—in private and in the heat of passion . . . You've been very frank. I take that as a compliment. I'll try to return it. I'll convey your concern to George Harlequin."

"That's a very careful phrase, Mr. Frohm."

"I'm a careful man," said Milo Frohm, with a grin. "I have to be. I'm walking on the high wire. I'd like to be an instrument of justice. I'm paid as an agent of the law—which isn't the same thing at all, at all . . ."

He left me puzzling on that sinister riddle and searching vainly for clues to solve it. In New York it was midday. In California, it was nine in the morning. I called Francis Xavier Mendoza and told him the good news about Suzanne and myself. He was cheered beyond words. He would be in New York on Saturday and he would organize a dinner to celebrate our betrothal. I laughed at the old-fashioned word. He said he liked it even better in Spanish—*esponsales*—espousal. He might even be moved to make a song about it to be sung at the dinner. He would telephone his New York distributor to reserve the wines. The menu he would design, personally, and with great joy . . .

. . . And how was my friend? He had seen the whole horror of the kidnapping. He had prayed every night for a merciful solution . . . He understood my present fears. Perhaps, when he came to New York, he could meet George Harlequin. I thought it would be a fruitful idea . . . I, myself, had run out of strategy and he had no grace at all to lend or spend. Mendoza reproved me and told me I was the most blessed of men. I should stay close to Harlequin and continue to ask questions. I should hold Suzanne like a precious jewel and ask no questions at all . . . He was sure we would soon share that one precious bottle.

I wished I had a grain of his faith. I was convinced that George Harlequin was hell-bent on self-destruction.

On the Wednesday of that week, Basil Yanko issued a statement which was published, verbatim, in the financial press:

. . . The offer made by Creative Systems Incorporated to purchase Harlequin et Cie is now withdrawn. Recent newspaper comment, and a series of tragic events involving Mr. George Harlequin and his family, have created a climate unfavourable to the proposed merger and damaging to the interests of all parties. Investigations by law-enforcement agencies in various countries have revealed grave defects in the security of the computer services supplied by Creative Systems to Harlequin et Cie. These defects have now been remedied and Creative Systems have accepted liability for the loss and the damage sustained by their valued clients. An agreement to discharge this liability by a substantial cash payment will be signed by Mr. Basil Yanko and Mr. George Harlequin at the end of this week. The agreement will terminate all litigation pending between the two parties.

The statement was followed by a careful editorial comment. It praised the good sense of both men and the restraint with which they had conducted a difficult negotiation. It commended "the frankness with which mistakes had been recognized and the promptness with which legitimate claims had been settled." It stressed the value of "cooperation between law-enforcement agencies and all those concerned for the integrity of business practice." It predicted "an immediate rise in the share value of Creative Systems and a new respect for Harlequin et Cie in the field of international investment." When you wiped off the eyewash, you read it as a profound sigh of relief and a plea not to foul up a market which was already in a hell of a mess.

That evening I paid a brief visit to the Club and I was welcomed like a long-lost brother. Everyone had read the statement. Most agreed that it was a clever piece of laundering. No one was sorry to see the end of a very dirty episode. It was good to watch Basil Yanko eat humble pie for a change. It was better still if you'd bought Creative Systems on the fall and made a tidy profit on the afternoon market. Nobody wanted to talk murder or kidnapping or fraud. There was a general agreement that these days it paid to have a low profile and keep your political opinions to yourself. Harlequin had handled himself very well. Lots of class, that boy! The European touch, eh? Why didn't I bring him in for cocktails one night . . . I left after an hour, bathed in the reflected glory of a smart operator who had beaten the market.

On my way home, I called at the Salvador to pick

up Suzanne. She was still working and George Harlequin wanted to talk to me.

"Tomorrow will see the end of it, Paul. Yanko has already lodged his funds in escrow. They'll be passed to us as soon as documents are exchanged at five o'clock tomorrow. I'd be grateful if you'd come. Karl Kruger will be here and Herbert Bachmann."

"Basil Yanko?"

"Of course."

"Why the party?"

"It's not a party. It's a condition of the deal. Yanko agreed to issue the press statement. We undertook to provide photographic evidence of reconciliation. Karl Kruger represents the Europeans. Herbert represents Wall Street. You're the floating world. I've hired the photographer. I know it's a sorry concession, but it's the least Yanko would settle for, and the most I could tolerate."

"Very well. I'll be there. How much is Yanko paying?"

"In all, twenty-five million."

"How much are we in profit?"

"After recouping losses on the share dumping, about two million."

"Then, it's a closed book and we can all go home."

"Yes. I leave on Monday by ship. Julie's parents are nervous of air travel. I am, myself, now . . . Oh, by the way, your friend, Mendoza, called. He's invited me to dinner with you and Suzanne on Saturday to celebrate your engagement. I told him I'd be happy to come. I'd like to have given the dinner myself but it isn't possible now."

"But you will be able to make the wedding in Geneva?"

"Yes . . . yes, I hope so."

"George, did Milo Frohm mention my talk with him?"

"Yes, he did. I'm grateful for your concern; but there's no need to worry."

"I'm very glad to hear it, George. There's another thing that's been troubling me. Aaron Bogdanovich said . . ."

". . . We owe him more money. That's provided. You don't have to trouble yourself."

"I wasn't thinking of the money, George. He told me the pair of you had arranged to kill Basil Yanko."

"We have, Paul."

I stared at him, gape-mouthed.

He smiled, tolerantly. "You didn't think I'd forgotten, surely?"

"George, this is madness! It doesn't bring Julie back. It doesn't change anything that's happened. It just compounds a bloody insanity."

"Oh, it does more than that, much more!"

"For God's sake, listen to me! I started you on this road. I'm responsible for everything that's happened. I'll live with that knowledge until my last breath. But I'm telling you, begging you, to see that it's a horrible futility: a life for a life for a life . . . for what? George, I've admired you, loved you like a brother for twenty years. If my life would bring Julie back, I'd give it gladly. But it won't—not a hundred, not a million lives. The only payment I can make it . . ."

"I'm the creditor," said George Harlequin coldly.

"I stipulate the terms. Be here at five tomorrow. After that all debts are discharged!"

I was beaten and we both knew it. I couldn't accuse him because there were no witnesses. I couldn't stay him because he was too subtle and Aaron Bogdanovich knew his trade too well. I couldn't persuade him because he had stepped out of the human system into the anarchy of the destroyers. His own life or another's had no value to him any more. I left him standing in the middle of the room, deaf and blind, bereft of the last vestige of pity.

That night I argued for an hour with Suzanne. I could have no more part in George Harlequin. She could have none either. She must resign forthwith. She didn't need salary or pension or any other damned money with blood on it. The man was beyond compassion, beyond argument or reason. He had fulfilled his own prophecy, as he had known—and promised—from the first moment. He loved conspiracy. He was happy to join the assassins. Well then, let him go!

Suzanne fought me at every step. All right! He had sworn murder. He could unswear. He could be prevented right up until the final moment. He was too complex to dismiss so curtly as one beyond reason. She had worked with him for years. Yes, he might conspire, but had I never thought that my harsh judgment might be a factor in his design . . . Whatever he believed himself, she didn't believe he was capable of murder. Anyway, in spite of all, she would work out the last days of her contract. I had a duty to make the payment he demanded and attend the meeting. Did I think he was trying to involve me?

No, I had never said that. Then I should be there. If I wouldn't go, she could never again trust anything I promised. I said I had done everything I had promised. No, I had not. We had both sworn to walk the last step of the last mile with George, and that last step was still to be made . . . And so on and so on, until we ran out of words and we sat dumb and hostile, each waiting for the other to surrender. As usual Suzanne had the last word:

"Paul, nothing can happen at the meeting. The room will be full of witnesses. You will be one of them. When the meeting is over, you ask Yanko to wait in my room. Then you speak privately to George. You tell him that unless he gives you a solemn promise that Yanko will not be harmed, you will warn him before he leaves the hotel. Then you will have discharged your responsibility. I'll have discharged mine. Does that sound reasonable?"

"There's a flaw in the reasoning. If George is prepared to kill, he is prepared to lie."

"Then, if you have the slightest doubt, you still warn Yanko and tell George you're going to do it."

"If ever I'm in the dock, sweetheart, I hope I have you for the defense."

"Once you've got me, chéri, you've got me for always. So if you want to escape, now's the time."

We went peaceably to bed; but somewhere between midnight and dawn I woke to a new and terrifying thought. Suppose the meeting didn't take place at all. The documents were drawn, the intent was clear for the newspaper release, the money was already in escrow. If Yanko didn't arrive, if death caught up with him on the way, the settlement could, and probably would, be made by the new president of Creative Systems. In which case, the triumph would be complete: Yanko dead and his money safe in Harlequin's pocket. Aaron Bogdanovich and George Harlequin both had a taste for ironies, and this one was very tempting to their sensitive palates.

10

I arrived at the Salvador at ten minutes to five.
I spent a few moments with Suzanne and then went
in to join Harlequin, who was checking documents
with his attorneys. Punctually at five, Karl Kruger and
Herbert Bachmann arrived, and close on their heels,
a swarthy, bearded young man with a pair of cameras
hung round his neck. At five minutes past the hour,
Yanko's attorneys arrived and immediately settled
down to compare documents with their colleagues.

At ten past, Yanko had still not arrived and
George Harlequin made a tart comment about the
unpunctual habits of geniuses. When he had still not
arrived at five-fifteen, his attorneys were visibly embarrassed. One of them called Yanko's office and
was told he had already left. He muttered an apology and buried himself again in his papers.

At five-twenty, Harlequin was pacing the room,
flushed and angry. Karl Kruger was dying for a drink.
Herbert Bachmann and I were trying to make small
talk at the window. At five-twenty-five, Basil Yanko
made his entrance with an offhand apology about
crosstown traffic.

Harlequin snapped, "Our time is valuable, too, Mr. Yanko."

Basil Yanko was unperturbed. "This little visit is costing me twenty-five million dollars. Now, may I see the papers, please?"

He must have read them a dozen times before, but it pleased him to parse and analyze them for another ten minutes before he announced himself ready to sign. George Harlequin then insisted that Yanko's attorneys rehearse verbally the heads and intent of the agreement.

"Neither party commits nor in fact can commit to any condition which constitutes a breach of law . . .

"Where either party abstains from or is restrained from action, such abstention or restraint does not and cannot include misprision of felony . . .

"Neither party is immune nor holds the other immune from process by third parties . . .

"The liability admitted by Creative Systems Incorporated is limited strictly to the terms set down. The damages agreed and paid are accepted under full quit claim . . .

"Harlequin et Cie, and Mr. George Harlequin, personally, agree not to press charges for fraud or conspiracy to fraud against employees of Creative Systems Incorporated. Charges already filed will be withdrawn . . .

"Investigations set in train by Harlequin et Cie and conducted under their commission and authority will be terminated forthwith . . .

"Investigations initiated and conducted by law enforcement agencies are recognized as beyond the control of the parties and outside the scope of this agreement . . .

"Each party agrees to refrain from the publication in any shape or form of material or comment whether speculative or factual which might be considered contentious or damaging to the other . . ."

There was more and more. There was rehearsal of detail and a display of exhibits. Finally, the two men seated themselves at the table with their attorneys beside them. The photographer asked if he might pose them differently. Yanko refused irritably. It wasn't the signing that was important. It was the group, afterwards: five respectable money merchants with drinks in their hands, looking happy on his money. The signing resolved a conflict. The drinks and the smiles connoted all that the market needed: security, confidence, mutual trust, brotherly love. Harlequin shrugged agreement. Karl Kruger remarked that it was a pretty cavalier way to dispose of so much *geld*. Herbert Bachmann said, soberly, that the *geld* was much less important than the goodwill.

When the shabby little ceremony was over, Yanko's attorneys handed over a certified bank check for twenty-five million dollars. Harlequin folded it into his pocket-book as if it were no more than a parking ticket. Which moved Yanko to the sour comment that he had better not lose it; there was no more to come.

The attorneys repacked their briefcases and left together. Harlequin went with them to the elevator and returned with one of his Swiss security men, who would take the drink orders. All of us settled for

Scotch except Basil Yanko, who, maddening as ever, demanded a tomato juice, with a dash of tabasco, a squeeze of lemon, no salt and a sprig of fresh mint. The security man went out. The photographer drifted around fiddling with a light meter and looking for camera angles.

There was an embarrassed pause, and then the nurse came in with young Paul, fresh from his bath and ready for supper. Harlequin swept the child into his arms, kissed him, played a finger game, and then carried him round the company to say good night. When he came to Basil Yanko, he said:

"Have you any children, Mr. Yanko?"

"No, Mr. Harlequin. I have never been so fortunate. He's a beautiful child."

"He's very like his mother."

"I never had the pleasure of knowing Madame Harlequin."

"Nor will this child, Mr. Yanko . . . Here, nurse. Take him. Good night, little one. I'll be up later to tell you a story."

Karl Kruger muttered unhappily. Herbert Bachmann blew his nose, noisily. I turned away to hide the hate in my eyes.

Harlequin turned to the photographer. "You can start as soon as the drinks are served. How long will you need?"

"Ten minutes. If you and your friends will just ignore me and act normally, I'll shoot around you."

A few moments later, the security man came in with a tray of drinks and a plate of canapés. Harlequin told him:

"No calls, no visitors, until we've finished here."

Herbert Bachmann raised his glass in a toast. "To the end of dissension, gentlemen."

Harlequin made the second salute. "My thanks, Karl, for your efforts."

"I'll drink to that," said Basil Yanko. "And to you, Herbert. Thanks for coming here today. I appreciate it."

"I did it for George," said Herbert Bachmann, dryly. "Also I have certain obligations to my colleagues in the market."

Basil Yanko was tolerant but regretful. "My dear Herbert, I am one man in the world you cannot snub. I am ugly to look at—always have been, since I was a child. I am used to it now. For the rest, I know who I am and what I do. How many of your respectable colleagues can say the same?"

"I thought," said George Harlequin mildly, "we were supposed to look happy."

Basil Yanko looked at him with pale contempt. "I fear I'm the skeleton at your feast, Mr. Harlequin. If you'll forgive me, I'll take my leave."

The photographer protested. "Please, sir! Just a few more shots."

"I'll gladly dispense with the photographs," said George Harlequin. "They were your idea, not mine."

Basil Yanko raised his glass again. "I'll wait . . . Tell me, Mr. Desmond, how long will you be staying in New York?"

"Another week, perhaps. No more."

"I hear you're getting married."

"That's right."

"You're a lucky man," said Herbert Bachmann. "I hope you know it."

"I know it, Herbert."

"When I met him first," said Karl Kruger, "he didn't have enough sense to get out of the rain."

"And now," Basil Yanko was almost cordial, "I understand you've retired from Harlequin et Cie. I'd like to remind you that my offer is still open."

"Declined, Mr. Yanko."

George Harlequin added a tart comment. "I think you're wise, Paul. It's a dangerous job."

Yanko flushed angrily. "Those are contentious words, Mr. Harlequin. May I remind you that they constitute a breach of the agreement you have just signed?"

"I didn't hear anything contentious," said Karl Kruger. "Did you, Herbert?"

"No, Karl. I'm a trifle hard of hearing, anyway."

Basil Yanko tossed off the rest of his drink at a gulp and set down the glass. "I am too old for schoolboy games, gentlemen. I must go."

"If you move," said the photographer amiably, "you're a dead man." He was pointing the larger of his two cameras straight at Yanko's face. "This one is lethal. It fires six cyanide bullets."

George Harlequin challenged him. "What the devil is this?"

"Please!" The photographer waved an impatient hand. "All of you sit down at the table. Put your hands flat on the top of it."

"A floor full of security men," said Yanko in disgust, "and this happens! What do you want? Money?"

"Sit down!"

We sat in a half circle, palms flat on the polished

surface. The photographer sat facing us, the camera resting on the table, his finger on the trigger button. He explained himself, baldly:

"If anyone moves or cries out, he gets shot. If we're interrupted, you will deal with the situation, Mr. Harlequin. We're in conference and not to be disturbed."

"I've already given that direction."

"You may have to repeat it. Now, who am I? Mister Nobody. What am I here for?" From his inside pocket he took a folded typescript and a pen and laid them before him on the table. "I am here to wait, as you all are . . . Mr. Yanko, you have just drunk a glass of tomato juice. I regret to tell you it was poisoned."

There was a frozen moment of shock, then a gasp of horror.

Only Basil Yanko, sat contemptuous and unmoved. "I don't believe you."

"I'm not asking you to believe me," said the photographer blandly. "I'm telling you a fact. Very soon you will feel heavy and drowsy. After that you will lose muscle control. Then you will sleep. Shortly afterwards, you will die. It won't be painful. It won't take too long. You'll be unconscious in about fifteen minutes."

"You can't do it," said George Harlequin. "You can't just watch a man die."

"Correction, Mr. Harlequin. We will all watch him die."

"We will not!" Karl Kruger raised a big fist. The camera was aimed at his breast. He lowered his hand. "Why Yanko? Why not any of us?"

"This . . ." The photographer held up the folded sheet. "This is a death list. There are six names on it, and an account of how each person died. I will read you the names: Mrs. Basil Yanko, blown up in a speed boat; Miss Ella Deane, run down by a car; Miss Valerie Hallstrom, shot; Mr. Frank Lemnitz, shot; Miss Audrey Levy kidnapped in London, believed dead; Mrs. George Harlequin, shot . . . All these killings were organized and financed by Basil Yanko."

Basil Yanko sat rigid in his chair. He gave a harsh, humorless laugh and shook his head. "Oh, no! The oldest trick in the book! Did you set this up, Mr. Harlequin? You, Mr. Desmond?"

"I've never seen this man before in my life," said George Harlequin. "I have never exchanged a word with him until this night."

"That's true, Mr. Yanko. You see, Valerie Hallstrom was a colleague of mine. So was Audrey Levy, who was assigned to watch Lemnitz in London . . . You play rough politics. So do we."

"You can't prove a damn thing, and you know it."

"Only the police have to prove things. We don't. How are you feeling? A little heavy? That's normal . . . No, Mr. Yanko! If you try to get up, I'll shoot you and that will be very painful . . . So far, you're more privileged than any of the people you killed. You're dying; but you're dying quietly. No pain. No confusion . . . You're sweating, Mr. Yanko. That means you're fighting it. It doesn't help. Just relax."

"What the hell do you want from me?"

"Nothing. It was interesting about your wife.

Bernie Koonig told us. You were in New York. He put gasoline in the bilges. When she pressed the starter—boom! We wondered why you never knocked him off like Frank Lemnitz. You were probably softer in those days—or less experienced. How do you feel? Flex your fingers! The reactions are a little slow. You're coming along nicely . . ." He pushed the paper and the pen across the table. "You should read this while you can still focus . . . Funny thing about this stuff, gentlemen. We could pump him out any time within the next fifteen minutes and he'd be fine. If we don't, he's kaputt. As you see, Mr. Yanko, the document is in the form of a confession. Would you like to sign it?"

"I'll see you in hell first!"

"No, Mr. Yanko. We'll watch you go."

"For God's sake, man!" Herbert Bachmann's voice was cracked and quavery. "This is torture."

"I know, sir." The photographer was reasonable as any man could be. "But Mr. Yanko is impervious to suffering. Madame Harlequin died with a bullet in the belly. Her child was hung by his hands from a fifth floor window . . . the child you saw here tonight. Audrey Levy was probably tortured before she was killed . . . However, if Mr. Yanko would like to end the suffering for you and for himself, he has only to sign the confession. I should leave then, and you would still have time to get him a doctor."

Yanko still had fight in him. His voice was faintly slurred but the mockery came through. "You see, I told you it was a trap!"

"If you don't sign, Mr. Yanko, it's a trapdoor. You fall through it to nowhere. I don't care either way. Your speech is thickening. Also you're probably losing sensation in the extremities."

"Sign, man!" said Herbert Bachmann desperately. "It's your only chance."

"It's his life," said Karl Kruger. "Let him do what he likes with it."

George Harlequin said, without malice, "Whatever I tell him, he won't believe me."

There was a long silence and then we watched, fascinated, as Yanko tried to control his slackening muscles, grip the pen and write his name at the bottom of the paper.

"Pass it back to me, please," said the photographer.

He folded it, slowly, and put it back in his pocket. Then he said:

"Mr. Yanko, you will now claim that this paper was signed under duress. So it's not enough to save your life. Around this table are four witnesses—excluding myself, because I come and go. Answer one question with one word. Did you organize the deaths of those people? Yes or no?"

"But you said . . . you promised . . ."

"This time, I'll keep the promise. Yes or no?"

"Yes."

"Thank you, Mr. Yanko . . . No! Don't move, gentlemen! He'll be dead in about five minutes."

"But you promised . . ."

I could stand it no longer. I pushed back my chair, stood up and began to move toward Yanko. I heard the click of a loading mechanism and the voice of the photographer, sharp and frigid:

"Sit down, Mr. Desmond."

The camera was aimed at my middle. I moved slowly back to the chair and sat down. Basil Yanko was lolling over the table, muttering and gurgling like a drunken man. We watched in helpless silence until he collapsed, face forward, on the tabletop.

"For pity's sake!" said Herbert Bachmann. "You've got what you want. Now, let's get a doctor!"

The photographer grinned and shook his head. "He doesn't need a doctor. He'll sleep it off. It's just a modern variant of the old Mickey Finn . . . By the way, gentlemen, in case you're called to testify, you'd better see this."

He snapped open the camera and made us pass it from hand to hand. "As you see, it's a normal photographic instrument. Nothing lethal about it at all. You might like to tell Yanko when he wakes up."

Herbert Bachmann looked from one to the other round the table. He was shocked and angry. "Who arranged this . . . this horror?"

"I did," said the photographer. "It's not pretty to watch, is it? But it's quite a normal, if rather crude, interrogation method. They teach it in police schools and in the armed forces. You pay for it, Mr. Bachmann. You subsidize people to teach it to your allies—some of whom don't need lessons." He took the paper out of his pocket and handed it to George Harlequin. "This should go to Milo Frohm."

"Thanks. I'll have it delivered. Tell Aaron I'll be in touch."

"Who is Aaron?" asked Herbert Bachmann.

"No one you've ever heard of, sir," said the photographer. "Shalom!"

Karl Kruger picked up Basil Yanko's limp hand,

felt his pulse, then let the hand fall back with a thud on the table.

"What are you going to do with him?"

"My boys will take him downstairs. His chauffeur will get him home and to bed. I wish I could be there when he wakes. I'd like to talk to him."

Everyone else was asking questions. I felt I had the right to the last one.

"You've got his money, George. You've got a confession that won't hold up in court but will discredit him for ever. What's left to talk about?"

"He died tonight," said George Harlequin somberly. "I've always wondered how Lazarus felt when he walked out of the tomb."

"I'll tell you how he felt, George. He took one look at what people were doing to each other, and begged to go back!"

It was a cry of despair; an expression of utter desolation. Long after Herbert and Karl had left, and Yanko had been removed, the words hung in the room like the final blasphemy for which there is no forgiveness. The circle of my own damnation was complete. I had urged violence. I had cooperated in violence. I had seen life destroyed. I had ended by denying it as an obscenity.

When I looked at my watch, I expected to find that time had stopped. I was shocked to find that it was still only seven in the evening, that Suzanne was still typing, that George Harlequin was telling fairy-tales to a wide-eyed child, that people were still homing for supper. I could not bear to wait. I walked out, past the security men, and hurried blindly across town to join the other lost souls in Gully Gordon's bar.

It could have been an hour later, it might have been two, because Gully was eating his dinner, the place was almost empty and I was sitting alone and morbid in a booth, when George Harlequin came in with Suzanne. They sat, one on either side of me, so that I could not escape.

Suzanne held my slack hand in hers and said, "George wants to talk to you, chéri."

"What's to say? It's finished. Let's forget it."

"We need forgiving, too, chéri."

"We don't deserve it, woman. We're just as much murderers as Basil Yanko . . . Not you, but George and I. That's true, isn't it, George?"

"For me, yes. Not for you, Paul. You tried to restrain me. I would not be held. At the very last moment, you were still trying."

"What are you now, George—a father confessor?"

"No. I'm trying to be a penitent. It isn't as easy as it sounds."

"Did you expect it to be easy?"

"Possible, at least."

"George, I've run out of absolutions and indulgences. I haven't got one for myself."

"I have," said Suzanne, gravely. "I love you both . . . This is the last step, Paul. Make it for me."

"How much more do you want?"

"Everything, Paul. That's what loving means."

"Oh, Christ . . . ?"

George Harlequin sat a long time staring into his

glass, then, slowly, painfully, he began to piece out the confession:

"I wanted him dead . . . I wanted to see him stripped and trembling, waiting for the execution. I talked to Aaron Bogdanovich. He offered me a dozen choices. I never knew before how many simple and ingenious ways there are of killing a man: a puff of vapor blown in his face as he walks downstairs, a prick from a poisoned pin, a bomb in his car, a letter that will explode in his hands, a sniper's bullet, a virus culture in his drink . . . It gave me pleasure to study them, play out each sequence like a chess gambit . . . That's the symbol, of course: the chess game. The pieces are inanimate. They're bits of wood or metal or ivory. They have names, but no life, no soul . . . You argue their fate as an intellectual exercise. The arguments make eminent sense, and Aaron Bogdanovich exhibited them all. The law cannot redress injustice: you must work outside the law. The political system is beyond reform: you must destroy it before you can make a better one. You cannot achieve the ideal: you must content yourself with the expedient. The torturer is triumphant: you must eliminate him. The robber is laughing over the spoils: you choke him with his stolen gold. Democracy is a fraud because the people are gulled for their votes and duped by policies they do not understand. All men are traitors and all women are whores, provided the price is right . . . There is no answer to those arguments, except an act of faith, which I could no longer make . . . Strange! You, Suzy, and you, Paul, made it for me. You believed I was something better than I wanted to be. You couldn't convince me because you had been too close to me for too long. I could deceive you and deceive myself and make illusions for us all . . . But I couldn't deceive Bogdanovich and he wouldn't let me deceive myself . . . Came the day when a decision had to be made. I went to see him at the flower shop. He was playing with a tiny kitten, a stray that had wandered in from the street. He asked me to state exactly what I wanted. I told him: my money back and Yanko's life for Julie's. He didn't argue the decision. He simply broke the kitten's neck and laid it on the desk in front of me. Then he said: 'That's what it means, Mr. Harlequin. Can you do it?' . . . I knew I couldn't. I could hardly bear to touch the body . . ."

"But you could still watch a man go through the agonies of dying . . ."

"Yes. That's the shame of it. I could and I did and I believed I was seeing justice done."

"Do you still believe it?"

"No. I saw terror crushed by terror . . . Well, that's it! Nothing's changed. I thought you had the right to know."

He tried to stand up, but was trapped in the cramped booth. I caught his arm and held him back. "Stay, George! . . . I apologize. I'm not proud of myself, either. Bogdanovich passed a verdict on me, too. He said I wanted respectability without virtue, possession without threat, pleasure without payment . . . John Q. Citizen conniving at every horror in the world so long as it doesn't disturb his rest or his dinner . . . ! We make a fine pair, don't we?"

"I have news for both of you," said Suzanne soberly. "You tried to dispense with the law, and yet you sit here humbled by the verdict of an assassin. I think you need a change of company . . ."

On that sour note, we left it, because Gully Gordon was back, bowing his welcome, and begging us to name the music of our pleasure.

The next forty-eight hours were a limbo of non-events. Suzanne was busy ordering Harlequin's affairs before he left for Europe. I pottered about the apartment, getting under Takeshi's feet, picking up books, dropping them after I had read a page, confusing myself with plans, projects, timetables for a future which was now as vague as last year's weather. I read the papers and wondered why there was no news of Yanko's arrest. I played music and heard not a bar of it. I was like the boy in the fairy tale who lost his shadow and couldn't live happy until he found it.

I had lost more than a shadow. I had lost the small part of myself which was left intact after years of wandering and inconclusive battling. I had lost a friend—one of the few to whom I had ever committed myself with wholehearted trust. I had found a woman to love. I had forfeited the respect without which the love could not last a twelve-month. Now I was facing the ordeal of a dinner party given by a man whom I would not offend for the world, to celebrate a promise that I doubted could ever be fulfilled. Three times I picked up the phone to put him off. Each time I lost courage, and another fragment of respect for myself. Suzanne was loving and solicitous; but even when I responded, I felt I was playing the false lover, empty of hand and heart, too fearful to confess.

It was not only my private world which was out of joint. The world beyond my windowpane was a hostile place, too. I could never face it again, innocent and unarmed. Always I must wear the chainmail of the cynic, the dagger and pistols of the wary traveler. I must bite every coin before I took it, pin every man to his contract with a threat, trust no woman and look twice in my mirror to make sure that I was still myself. In this mood of disillusion— proper to my age, but most improper to a man attending his espousal feast—I set off with Suzanne to dine with George Harlequin and Francis Xavier Mendoza.

Our rendezvous was one of those old corners of New York still preserved from the barbarians—a basement cellar on First Avenue, lined from floor to ceiling with choice vintages, furnished with a refectory table, served by a single chef, two waiters and a wine-master, all dedicated to the proposition that eating and drinking together was a sacred rite, the first and last of our mortal pilgrimage. Harlequin was already there, making the rounds of the racks with Mendoza, reverent as any disciple with his guru.

Mendoza welcomed us like martyrs reprieved from the lions. He kissed Suzanne on both cheeks, clasped my hands, looked me up and down, and announced:

"Not bad! At least you have survived! Harlequin, here, has told me the story. I marvel that you are all in one piece. Now, let me show you what we have prepared . . . To begin, a canapé of Roquefort and walnuts, with that, my own Palomino, and some quiet talk. *Susana querida,* I know! They have talked you into the ground. Here, you and you only are the subject. Have you opened my bottle yet?"

"Not yet, Francis. They're not ready for it!"

"*Ay de mi!* And I thought they were civilized men. No matter, you and I will tame them. George, I know Paul is a Visigoth. I expected better from you."

"I'm a fool," said George Harlequin. "It takes time to unlearn the trade."

"Time and wine—we have plenty of both. Now, for the meal, we have a mousse of salmon, and with that a Pinot, very dry, a vintage of which I am very proud . . . George, have you never thought that Islam is a wise faith? Its promises are those we understand—sweet waters and flowers and wine and generous women . . . We Christians promise harps, which no one can play and a beatific vision of which no one understands the meaning."

"But we yearn for it, Francis. The simple knowing, the simple enjoying . . ."

"Ah! Now you have it, George! Simplicity—oneness! That's the secret we spend a lifetime learning."

"And fail, always, to understand."

"Suzanne, why are women simpler than men?"

"Are they, Francis?"

"Everywhere and all the time. We men are stupid, complicated. We wake at a woman's breast. We die, if we are lucky, in the same embrace. We walk a million miles to come back to the point of departure. Paul, what do you say?"

"It's a good Palomino, Francis."

"Good, the man says! There's no better until you get to Jerez de la Frontera—and even there it's hard

to find . . . Next, my friends, we have a filet de boeuf
en croute with a sauce Perigueux, and with that, my
Cabernet of sixty-five . . . a wonderful year, no frost,
the right rain, a wine maker's dream! We are drinking it now, eight and a half years later, a ripe time for
all of us. My friends, no matter what has happened,
no matter what may arrive tomorrow, we are the fortunate—fortunate to know, fortunate to enjoy, fortunate to be thankful. Will you join me in a blessing?"

We stood, hands joined, heads bowed, while he
pronounced it:

"We eat while others are hungry. We laugh while
others are sad. For what we have, we are thankful.
Grant us always to remember what others have not,
and where we can, to restore it. In the name of the
Father, Son and Holy Spirit. Amen."

He waved us to our places—Suzanne on his right,
Harlequin on his left, myself facing him—and said:

"I never know what grace to say. I have never
understood why the Almighty is so unequal in his
giving."

"Perhaps he's blind," I said flippantly.

"Or we are," said Suzanne.

"Or we're using the wrong measures," said
George Harlequin.

"More likely," said Francis Xavier Mendoza.
"Good appetite, my friends!"

We ate; we drank; we talked inconsequences,
happy for a while in the presence of a good man,
which was like the shadow of a great tree in a
parched landscape. We made silly jokes. We laughed
as we had forgotten how to laugh for a long time.
Then, too soon for me, came the time for the toasts,

which, said Francis Mendoza, must be drunk, not in the wine of a new country, but in that of the old, an Oporto, aged, soft, the color of fine rubies.

We were a small company, but he stood for the ceremony. For George Harlequin, the polyglot, he spoke first in Spanish, then in French for Suzanne, and for me in English:

"Dear friends! This is a moment of promise—a promise between Suzanne and Paul, who have learned late to love each other, between us all who need one another so much. If I could not share this wine with you, I should be the loneliest man in the world, and the wine would die, untasted, in the bottle. If you cannot share with each other the pain you have suffered and the forgiveness we all need—ay!—you, too, will live lonely and the wine of life will be soured for you for ever. I blessed you when you came. I beg that you will bless me when you go, friends together . . ."

"So be it," said Suzanne.

I had no words at all. George Harlequin sat silent for a long moment and then stood up, slowly. He, too, spoke first in Spanish and then in English:

"Francis, we have been honored at your table and blessed in your company. We thank you, all of us. I thank my friends, who stood with me in a dark time, and shared pain with me, and saw me do evil under the sun, and still managed to hold fast to me and forgive me. With your permission, I should like to give a gift to Paul and Suzanne. I offer it with the motto of my ancestor who was a buffoon: 'If you laugh, I eat. If you cry, God help us all!' "

He took an envelope out of his pocket and held

it out to me across the table. I took it in my hand, weighed it, prayed it would not be what it felt like; a deed of gift, an endowment. If he tried to buy me now, I should hate him to eternity.

"Open it, Paul!"

Francis Mendoza passed me the cheese knife. I slit the envelope and handed it to Suzanne. She looked at it for a moment and then tipped the contents on to her plate—a second envelope filled with scraps of paper, torn and shredded to confetti. We stared at Harlequin. For the first time in an age, we saw the old crooked quizzical smile. Someone had to put the question. That someone had to be Paul Desmond.

"What is it, George?"

"Can't you guess?"

"I can," said Suzanne.

I told you I was a dumb ox. I had forgotten that he was a clown and an illusionist. I didn't see the joke until Suzanne piled the shreds of paper in a dish and Francis Xavier Mendoza poured his best brandy over them and burnt Basil Yanko's confession to ashes.